Enjoy!

When Roger Odem Booth first mentioned he and Carl Jesse James becoming confidence men, Carl asked, "Do you really think we can make a living by conning old fogies out of their money?"

Roger smiled and said, "Yes, we can."

Carl matched his smile and made a bad pun; 'Don't you mean, 'yes, we <u>con</u>?'"

And so the "Yes, we con" trilogy begins.

Also by Karl Boyd

Signs of Our Times

Coming Soon

"Yes, we con" trilogy

The Cyrus Caper
The Texas Two Card Hold 'Em Heist

From China with Love

Nearly

The ^ Perfect Plan

The Nearly Perfect Plan is a work of fiction. Names, characters, places, and incidents are the products of the author's imagination or are used fictitiously. Any resemblance to actual events, locales, or persons, living or dead, is entirely coincidental.

ISBN 978-0-557-03498-7

Nearly

The ∧ Perfect Plan

Chapter 1

On Larson Street in Arlington, Texas, not far from the Texas Rangers' Major League Ballpark, sits a dimly lit and nearly deserted watering hole aptly named "Third Base", ("the last stop before home"). Behind the bar, on a tall leather barstool, the bartender, Beverly Darlington, a pert breasted, twenty-six-year-old brunette divorcee with grey streaks showing through her latest attempt to appear younger, sat watching the five p.m. local news on TV. Her best friend, Barbara "Barb" Clinton was seated on the opposite side of the bar, sipping a rum and coke.

While Bev's companion was a pretty, twenty-seven-year-old blonde with blue eyes, sexy lips and an outstanding figure, she was the epitome of, and often referred to as a "dumb blonde", possessing about as many brains as a yellow-bellied, red-headed sapsucker.

Barb was currently enthralled by the story and trial of Roger Booth, Carl James and their associates, which the media reported would be the "In" event of the year.

Everyone who was anyone, (and those who weren't – including Barb), had attempted to obtain a seat in Courtroom Four. They soon found such a space was difficult to come by. The bailiff was rumored to be making some big tips, but who could blame him?

Beverly wondered if Barb had offered her body in exchange for a reserved seat. As hot as she was to see these two guys up close and personal, Bev wouldn't put it past her.

When it came to making small talk, Barb wasn't very

talented. It was rumored when she ran out of things to say to a man, she started taking off her clothes. Small wonder she was a three time loser in the matrimony category.

During a commercial, while the headlines scrolled across the bottom of the TV screen in bold black letters, proclaiming "BRINKS BANDITS PLEAD NOT GUILTY", Beverly asked, "What do you think, Barb, are they guilty or not?"

Instead of answering with "I don't know and I don't care", Barb used her own private code, "I. d. k. and I. d. c." to say the same thing. Then she added, "Even if they did the crimes, Bev, I wouldn't mind getting next to either of them. They're both hunks. I'll bet they'd know how to treat a lady like me."

While thinking, "Yeah, as if they'd give you a tumble," Bev held up her hand for silence and said, "Wait a minute, Barb, the commercial is over and the news is back on."

Photographs of the two purported gang leaders flashed onto half the screen, while on the other side, Chet Holmes, the suave, handsome anchor of FYI Channel Four evening newscast, smiled into the camera,

"Imagine if you can folks, two men smart enough to dream up, and brazen enough to execute a plan to hijack not one, but three armored trucks in broad daylight and make them disappear in a matter of minutes. It's an amazing story.

"According to authorities, the Brinks vehicles were hijacked and vanished from an open highway, along with the drivers, guards and payloads totaling more than thirty-four million dollars."

Another camera zoomed in for a close-up of the good-looking, brunette co-anchor, Carmen Valdez, making sure they centered on her ample cleavage. Viewers who sang praises of her attributes claimed Carmen possessed sixteen pounds of boobies. If the ditties about her titties were accurate, tonight fourteen were on public display.

She bubbled, "It sounds impossible, but a grand jury must believe it. Yesterday, they returned an indictment against the supposed ring leaders and their team of twenty-three ex-Army buddies.

"According to sources close to the investigation, if it weren't for fate, none of the thieves would have been caught and they'd all be millionaires."

The producer switched back to Chet, who preened for the audience by pushing a stray strand of black hair back into place before saying, "But who knows, perhaps they still may. Rumor has it a book deal is in the making and Hollywood is courting Roger and Carl to write a screen play of their adventures."

Then back to cutie Carmen, leaning forward to give the camera and the audience an even better view while adding, "Everyone is asking; if it's true, how did they do it?"

Ignoring Bev's plea for silence, Barb said, "That's what I want to know. I read a report in the 'Hollywood Express' saying, 'Heads will soon roll in the hallways of the FBI'."

Shaking her head, while glaring at Barb at the same time Bev said, "Shush, I want to hear what they have to say."

The camera was back to clever Chet.

"We take you now to our reporter, Virginia Fields at the courthouse. What's happening there, Virginia?"

A grainy, windblown live picture of a willowy blonde wearing a yellow dress and standing in front of the Fort Worth Federal Courthouse appeared.

"Good evening, Chet and Carmen. As you noted, Roger Odem Booth and Carl Jesse James are being charged with several crimes, the most heinous of which is kidnapping. Other lesser accusations are assault, robbery and transporting stolen property across state lines.

"Their associates have been charged with similar crimes, but rumor has it those will be reduced in a plea bargaining arrangement.

"Except for some pre-trial motions, there wasn't much action here today, and the proceedings have been adjourned until tomorrow. Tonight, I thought I'd give you my perspective as a woman.

"I've noticed how ladies in the courtroom look at the defendants, and after speaking with a few, I believe the majority question the validity of the charges."

Referring to her notes, Virginia said, "One woman remarked; 'Even if Roger and Carl did the crimes, I wouldn't mind at all. At least these two stand-up dudes were brave and smart enough to reach out and take what they wanted'."

In the background, Chet asked, "What about the men?"

As she brushed back a lock of golden hair from her blue eyes, Virginia replied, "I think it's about fifty-fifty. But no matter how they feel about guilt or innocence, everyone is amazed at their audacity and admires the way they performed the 'Nearly Perfect Plan'. As anything new occurs, I'll keep you informed. This is Virginia Fields, in the field, at the Federal courthouse. Now back to you, Chet."

Chet smiled and said, "Thank you, Virginia. We'll take a short break and be back with news of an attempted carjacking and surprising results. Stay with us."

After reaching up and turning off the TV set, Bev said, "I didn't know they interviewed you, Barb."

Barb tittered like a school girl, "It wasn't me, silly. But you see what I mean. No woman in her right mind would want these two guys locked away for the rest of their lives."

In Courtroom Four; just as Barb proclaimed, Carl was a hunk – tall, thin and robust. Picture a lithe young man of twenty-nine, with deep blue eyes and a ready smile. As a holdover from Army days, he wore his blond hair in a flattop.

Likewise, Roger, the same age, stood six feet tall and was slim. Women described him as ruggedly handsome and loved his coal-black eyes. Neatly combed, long black hair hung over his collar, while a sly smile displayed matching dimples, giving Roger a devil-may-care look, and added to his mystique.

Both men were darkly tanned from working outdoors, with muscular bodies well-defined by a self-disciplined regimen of exercise and healthy diet. The looks they received from the opposite sex made it apparent they were ladies men. If somehow they beat this rap, there would be no shortage of women willing to share their ill-gotten riches, (and beds).

Their high-priced lawyer, Gerard Bannister, leaned over to confer with his clients and whispered, "Don't worry, most charges will be dismissed or reduced. The state has no witnesses."

Carl nodded, and Roger said, "We believe you."

As it was, everyone knew it would be difficult for the prosecutor, Gene Heath, to compile enough evidence to convict the supposed perpetrators.

Speaking with his supervisor, District Attorney Brad Perry, Gene said, "What worries me is the lack of witnesses. Even the drivers and guards who were held incognito somewhere couldn't identify one of their captors."

A short, grey-haired, almond eyed gentleman in his late sixties, Gene was a highly decorated veteran who enlisted as a Marine in time to see duty on the snow covered battlefields of Korea.

Sitting near the center of the courtroom was Robert Barrington, a loudmouthed fool and someone very unknowledgeable when it came to Gene. Robert opened his big mouth and said, "I think old Gene's got a soft spot in his heart for these Army vets he's prosecuting,"

Seated in front of Robert was a well-known and highly-respected newspaper columnist, Rodney Cromwell, who turned, looked Robert in the eyes and although he didn't know the guy, said, "You're full of shit. Regardless of his war service, Gene will do his best to convict anyone he believes is guilty of the crime with which they're charged."

Not wanting to back down, Robert said, "Everyone's entitled to their own opinion."

Rodney smiled unkindly and then sneered, "Yeah, even dumb assholes like you. If you said something like that to Gene, he'd kick your ass. Keep your comments to yourself, or I may tell him, just to be a witness on his behalf at your trial on slander charges."

The next day, Virginia's comments were picked up by the media and the nickname of the Nearly Perfect Plan Gang stuck. Ideal or not, the Nearly Perfect Plan was all everyone was talking about.

Maybe the strategy was still almost flawless. Brinks Corporation reported several millions of dollars were unaccounted for. It seems there was a large disparity between the amount stolen, (thirty-four million and change), and what money was recovered at the time of the gang's arrest. No one knew the reason for the discrepancy, and Roger and Carl weren't talking to anyone but their lawyer.

The remaining twenty-three defendants were closed-mouthed as well. The lead defense lawyer, Bill Brace, said. "Don't sweat it, guys. Without witnesses, the charges will either be dropped or plea-bargained down to the lowly accusation of possession of stolen property."

One of those charged, always a wiseacre, no matter what, said, "Yeah, after all, when the cops arrested us, we were in possession of most of the loot, more than twenty-five million dollars."

Twenty-eight men would have been on trial, but during a victory party, an unforeseeable accident killed three gang members. As Carmen noted, fate played a big part in their capture. With a little luck thrown in for good measure, it also saved the remainder from dying.

While the accused recovered, the trial was delayed for several weeks. To assure their clients received the best representation money could buy, their attorneys also asked for and were granted several delays.

At a news conference two days before the trail began, Gene told the assembled reporters, "We'll try all twenty-five defendants in one case to save taxpayers the tremendous cost of separate court proceedings."

Rodney raised his hand and when Gene acknowledged him, he asked, "What's this crap I hear about there being some resistance to allowing the three deceased members to be buried in Arlington National Cemetery, due to their possible participation in these crimes?"

Gene frowned and replied, "I hadn't heard of any problem, but I'll look into it. Those veterans served their country bravely in Kuwait and Iraq, and deserve to be buried in hallowed ground. If what you say is true, I won't stand by silently."

When the trial finally began, several interested and interesting people were in daily attendance. One individual in the first category was an aging FBI Agent, Jake Polk, the man partially responsible for the capture of the Nearly Perfect Plan

Gang. Jake was serving out his last days with the agency, but before hanging it up, wanted to see the end to his most baffling case.

Seated alongside Jake was a rookie cop from the Roswell, New Mexico Police Department, Officer Lynn Griffith, known as "Griff" to his friends. If anyone was to blame for ruining the Perfect Plan, it was he. As a result, Jake and Griff planned to split a one hundred thousand dollar reward Brinks offered for capturing the perpetrators of these brazen robberies.

Stretching his back after being seated on the hard bench all morning, Jake said, "This should be intriguing. I waited a long time to catch these guys. Now let's see what the law will do."

Griff wiped his sweaty palms on his pants.

"I hope I'm not nervous on the witness stand."

"Just relax and tell the truth."

Two persons in the second category were very interesting indeed. Although seats in the crowded courtroom were at a premium, a pair was reserved on a permanent basis for these lovely young women.

Jake nodded in their direction.

"Check out the two lookers."

Griff did and said, "They've been here every moment."

Not knowing how wrong he was, Jake shrugged and whispered, "They're probably a pair of groupies looking for romance."

Those with underworld connections knew the looker with the great body, coal black hair and eyes to match was named Maria, only daughter of Giacomo Remualdi. Don Giacomo was rumored to head the Fort Worth/Dallas Mafia family.

The other lady was a stunning blonde with deep blue eyes and a shape most women would give their four-year molars for. Her name was Julie Frasier, and she was as much in love with Carl as Maria was with Roger.

After Don Giacomo "arranged" for the seats to allow the ladies to follow the trial, he said, "This gift comes with a warning. You must keep your feelings hidden and not jeopardize your lovers by having my name connected to their supposed crimes."

Only the Don, his partners, the defendants, and Maria and Julie knew he supplied Roger and Carl with the money to back their bold ventures.

When Maria started to protest, the Don held up his hand.

"My private attorney, Gerard Bannister, will be assigned as defense attorney for Roger and Carl. If anyone can do the job, Gerard can."

Tall, dark and "cute" in a sensual way, Gerard assumed a persona of the boy next door. His brown hair was usually mussed a little, not too unruly, but as if he was too occupied with saving his clients to notice.

After spending long hours practicing before a mirror, Gerard could change his expression from one with steely eyes and a determined chiseled chin when he was cross-examining a tough witness, to one with caring, compassionate eyes and a hangdog look, as he commiserated with a person seeing things his way.

Jake leaned over and whispered in Griff's ear, "This guy is slick. I wonder where Roger and Carl found him."

Griff shook his head and replied, "I don't know, but he's making the prosecutor look bad."

After studying other renowned barristers, Gerard developed a way of speaking and mannerisms that had a way with juries. Always dressing conservatively and avoiding flashiness like the plague, he displayed courtesy and politeness to his witnesses, as well as those of the prosecution.

When he was forced to grill a person on the stand, Gerard always took time to apologize to the witness for the necessity of his forceful words.

"I'm sorry if I was rough on you, but you must understand, my clients have the right to be defended."

One of Gerard's major traits was using everyday language people in the jury box and courtroom could understand.

Women jurors loved his style, dress and manners. He appeared to be such a loving, caring boy, that the ladies wanted to take him home to raise him. He looked them in the eyes, and no matter their age, addressed them as "Miss".

From the way Gerard spoke to them, with courtesy and tact, gentlemen on the jury felt Gerard was one of them, a common man and worthy of their trust, almost like a son. As a result, it was no small wonder so far Gerard had never lost a case.

Although he never boasted about or broadcasted the fact, and at times appeared to be a country bumpkin with the barest qualifications to be a lawyer, Gerard was a graduate of Harvard Law School.

As son of a close friend of Don Giacomo; from the time he entered elementary school, Gerard was groomed to become the "Consigliore" to the Don in later life. So far, he fulfilled all the dreams his father and old friend had for his future.

From all indications, the judge, the Honorable Horst Becker, seemed sympathetic to the plight of the defendants, particularly Roger and Carl. The real reason could be His Honor was secretly addicted to gambling and deeply in debt to Don Giacomo's organization.

One of the Don's minions met with Horst and said, "You're job is to either find them not guilty or make sure they receive the lightest possible sentence. Do a good job and your gambling debts will be forgotten."

It was amazing what power the Don wielded behind the scene.

Today was the fourth day of the proceedings. The first three were taken up by Gene's opening statement and Gerard's passionate plea for a not guilty verdict when trial was completed.

Gene scored some points with the fact the defendants were found with the armored trucks and stolen money in their possession. On the minus side, much of his case was built on circumstantial evidence and lacked anything to tie the accused to the actual crimes.

As he rebutted all of Gene's statements, Gerard was brilliant in his presentation, and the jury waited to see what he'd do next.

While Roger sat at the table and conferred with Gerard, Carl leaned back, rested his shoulders against the gallery railing and reflected over the past year. It was amazing what they'd accomplished, and all because of a trip they took twelve months ago to Albuquerque, New Mexico. Carl shook his head in wonder and thought, "Who would have guessed?"

Chapter Two

(Fifteen months earlier)

Gazing out over the city of Houston, Richard Murdock, owner and CEO of Murdock Oil Incorporated, heard the buzzer on his intercom. After pushing down the correct lever, Richard asked, "Yes, Mary; what is it?"

"Reception called to say a Mister Darrin Winters is in the lobby. He claims to have an appointment, but I can't find his name in my book. Did I goof somehow, Sir?"

Richard shook his head at his own incompetence.

"No, Mary, I made this appointment last night on my personal phone and forgot to tell you. I apologize. Please have Mister Winters escorted to my office."

"Very well, Sir."

Sitting back in his chair, he thought, "She sounds relieved. After seven years as my secretary, I should have remembered to tell her about Winters. Mary's probably fretted since she got the call from reception."

While waiting for his guest, Richard stood up from his black leather chair, walked closer to a wide window overlooking the city and again gazed out over the skyline of Houston from his lofty, fourteenth floor penthouse suite.

Sixty years old, and six feet tall with a full head of snow-white hair, Richard looked and dressed like the successful businessman he was. There wasn't a pound of excess weight on his body, and even without knowing of his wealth, most women thought he was a handsome old codger.

Absently rubbing slight stubble on his chin, he thought, "Now we'll see how clever these two con men are. If I'm right, Roger Wilson and Carl Baxter are not their real names. Damn, I feel like a fool, allowing them to take me like they did, but every experience is a learning one, just as my father taught me.

"Little do they know the fifty thousand they stole is peanuts to what I have in mind. I hope this guy, Winters, is all he claims to be. We'll soon see."

Seven minutes later, there was a polite knock on the door.

"Come in, Mary."

Mary walked in, followed by a tall, handsome brown-haired man in his late twenties or early thirties.

She said, "Sir, may I introduce Mister Winters?"

Winters' suit was immaculate, his shirt fresh and starched, and he wore a bolo tie featuring a small oil derrick as the slide.

Glancing down at Winters' shoes, Richard noted they were spotlessly clean, well shined and showed no wear along the soles or heels.

Duly impressed, he thought, "Years ago I discovered a man who takes good care of his shoes is usually one of integrity. Score one for Winters."

He stood up behind his desk to greet his visitor. "Yes, thank you, Mary. That will be all."

As she left and closed the door quietly behind her, Richard extended his hand across the desk.

"It's a pleasure to make your acquaintance."

Winters walked quickly to the desk, reached across it and grasped Richard's hand firmly.

"Thank you for calling. How may I help you?"

("Right down to business – I like it. Two points for you, Winters.")

"May I call you Darrin?"

"Certainly, Sir."

"Well, Darrin to begin with, I recently dealt with two young con men, and these enterprising crooks took me for fifty thousand dollars."

Not waiting until Richard finished speaking, Darrin asked,

"And you want them found, right?"

Richard shook his head slightly.

("Someone should have told you I don't like to be interrupted, but yes, you're partially right, so I won't take away any points, Darrin.")

"Please allow me to finish."

Darrin's face flushed, "I'm sorry, Sir. Please continue."

("Watch your mouth, idiot. I have a feeling this is a big case.")

Richard smiled to ease his guest's discomfort.

"As I was saying, these men were very wise, had their act down to a fault and took this old codger to the cleaners.

"It's not the money that matters. What I lost was a very small part of my fortune. What disturbs me most is the embarrassment of being made a fool. Now to answer your question; yes, I'd like you to find these two, but not for the reason you believe.

"I admired their integrity and cunning. I guess you could say they reminded me of myself at a younger age. What I want you to do, besides locating them, is tail them over the next few months and keep me advised of their activities.

"Under no circumstance are you to approach any law officers with anything you might discover. No matter what crimes these men commit, they are no concern of yours.

"As you might have guessed, I'd like these two to take on a certain job for me in the near future. The 'caper', as I'll call it, is very complicated, and I want to know if these two have the balls to pull it off and get away.

"My question to you is; are you willing to take on this assignment or not?"

"It sounds quite intriguing," Darrin said. "Yes, Sir, I'd like to work for you."

"Without asking the fee I'll pay?"

"I understand you're a fair man. One who pays well for services rendered."

Richard smiled again while thinking, "Well spoken, Darrin and it isn't bullshit for my ears. You and I both know this job will make your day and probably your year. So far, you have three marks in your credit column and none in your debit."

"Thank you," he said. "I was thinking along the line of ten thousand dollars per month, plus expenses. If you perform this operation without being seen and furnish me timely and accurate information over the next few months, I'm sure there'll be a healthy bonus at the conclusion. Is my proposition satisfactory?"

Darrin thought, "Hell yes," and silently said, "Jesus, Joseph and Mary, for the first time in my life I've stepped into something wonderful."

A large smile beamed on his face and he replied, "Yes, Sir."

Pleased at his reaction, Richard said, "Then you're hired, Darrin. Sit down and I'll tell you everything I know about these men."

As Richard and Darrin sat talking, the two small-time thieves and con men Richard spoke of; Carl James and Roger Booth were headed to Albuquerque, New Mexico for a gambling vacation.

Roger drove his tan, gold-trimmed Oldsmobile Silhouette, (considered the Cadillac of vans), while endless sand, rocks and more sand were getting to Carl, and he was bored.

To pass time, he sat in the passenger's seat, counted road kill and continued to keep Roger informed.

"That's the sixth crushed armadillo we've run across," he said and laughed at his pun.

Roger shook his head, either in disgust or resignation.

"Whatever."

Early yesterday, when they left the balmy, tree-shaded climes of Austin, Texas, the sky was filled with small, white puffy clouds. They reminded Roger of cotton boles, ripe for picking, swaying in hot air in a west Texas field. Blowing out of the north, a cool breeze held a promise of rain in the sweet-smelling air.

At the beginning of their trip, they drove west on Route 290, through winding valleys and small peaks of the famed Texas Hill Country. The scenery was beautiful. Occasionally, they spotted a herd of fat, long-horned cattle or a flock of calico colored goats munching fresh, green grass. Cool streams meandered through rocky glens, where deer and antelope drank during evening hours.

Admiring the view, Roger said, "I love this state."

Ever a comic, Carl said, "Yeah." Then he sang, "Give me land, lots of land underneath the western sky..."

In spite of his determination not to encourage Carl in his nonsense, Roger smiled and said, "Don't give up your day job."

This afternoon was a different matter. As they moved further west, lush forests turned into small pine trees scattered among granite boulders, rocks and sandy bluffs. The wind changed and now blew hot off a broiling desert, as fickle clouds swept on to a cooler place, leaving the sky to fend on its own.

Periodically, they saw a scrawny cow searching for substance among cacti. Like Gypsies, the cattle wandered from who knew where to some distant, unknown point. Empty washes with dried, cracked mud bottoms slowly turned to dust in the heat, waiting for the next gully washer to awaken them and cause the desert flowers to blossom once again.

Carl commented on the change in scenery by saying, "I can see why so many people think Texas is a wasteland."

"Let them keep that notion in their minds," Roger said. "We have too many people from up north trying to run the state now."

As the sun reflected from the rearview mirror like liquid fire, heat waves bounced off the asphalt like flames from an inferno. Swaying upward, they threatened to melt the fragile windshield.

Attempting to defeat the sun, Roger tilted the rearview mirror toward the ceiling, but the sly orange orb still shone in his eyes from two side view mirrors. At noon, when the sun finally reached its zenith and was no longer in view, Roger's bloodshot eyeballs contained as many black spots as the body of a Dalmatian.

Although set on maximum, the air conditioner continued to struggle to repel an invasion of hot air. Up ahead, one after another, dark lake water mirages appeared on the road.

Roger pointed at one which seemed to glisten with moisture in the distance and said, "Those mirages remind me of double-blank dominoes playing leap frog."

A few minutes later, without warning, Roger passed gas.

While holding his nose, Carl exclaimed, "Phew, what was that?"

"A Winny Poo bird."

"What the hell is a Winny Poo bird?"

"It's a large black bird with a four-foot wing span, which flies in ever decreasing, concentric circles; until with the greatest of ease and dexterity, it flies up its own ass crying, 'Winny Poo'."

Carl shook his head and chuckled.

"Now I've heard everything."

Although Roger Odem Booth's initials spelled ROB, Roger wasn't always a thief, but learned the trade early. His first theft occurred the day he stole the heart of a gangly, freckled faced, nine-year-old redhead named Amy Wilson. Amy caught his eye the first day of second grade and never let go until two years later, when her family moved away.

As all young boys do, Roger wanted to impress her, but he was born into a poor family. His father, Henry, pinched every penny until Abraham Lincoln cried "Enough already", so there was no way he would part with a whole dollar to buy the doll Amy treasured.

Solving his problem in a drastic manner; Roger stole the doll. After stuffing the toy down his shirt, he hurried out the door with hands trembling in fear like a drunk on a six day binge. When he wasn't apprehended, Roger learned a new way of life. From then on, until the day he was apprehended, he stole what he needed.

A few days before his eighteenth birthday, bad and good luck caught up with Roger at the same time and changed his life.

An aging widow, Elizabeth Grimes, lived on the next block over. Now and then, she hired Roger to do odd jobs. One day, while working in her kitchen, Roger noticed a cracked cup in a cupboard filled with spare change.

Feeling lucky, he thought, "The old lady won't miss a few coins." He stole three quarters and two half-dollars.

But she did notice and called him on it.

"Roger, I know you took some of my change. Why didn't you ask if you needed money? I would have loaned it to you. If there's anything people hate, it's a thief."

Truly ashamed, he returned the money with a promise never to steal again.

Although Roger didn't know, Elizabeth was impressed with his innate and God-given abilities. When she gave him instructions, Roger never had to be told twice and most times came up with a better way to do things than his boss lady asked.

Early on, Elizabeth realized Roger was a planner and leader. Although she caught him pilfering her coins, she thought, "One little mistake doesn't make a person a criminal. Roger has more good attributes than bad. With the right incentive and a gentle push in the right direction, he could go far."

Finally making up her mind, she asked, "Have you thought about college, Roger?"

He shrugged and replied, "No, not really. My family can't afford it, and I'm not sure I could work and study at the same time. My grades would suffer and I'd be wasting my time."

Shaking her finger under his nose, she said firmly, "Education is a serious thing, not a waste of time. I've watched you work, Roger, and see a different side of you. You're smart, have great potential and shouldn't waste your life."

Then she asked again, "How would you like to go to the University of Texas?"

Wondering if she was growing senile and repeating herself; he said, "I'd love to, but, as I said, I can't afford to."

He soon discovered Elizabeth was serious.

"A few years ago, Mister Grimes – George, my husband, passed away and left me very well off. He was a professor at UT and always tried to help his students, so if I assisted you, I'm sure George would approve.

"I'll make you a proposition, Roger. If you study hard and make me proud, I'll pay your tuition and board at UT for four years."

As she made her sudden and startling announcement, Roger was taking a large swig of soda, and it almost floored him. He gulped, foam spurted from his nose, and he turned red with embarrassment.

After handing him a napkin, Elizabeth waited until he wiped his face. Then he said, "Yes, I would. Thank you, Mrs. Grimes.

I'll make you proud."

Smiling knowingly, she said, "You're welcome. Just stay on the straight and narrow path, Roger. That's all I ask."

Carl's father, Harry Carver James, was a con man extraordinaire with a checkered past, but no one seemed to hold it against him. Harry taught his young son all his secrets, so as a small lad, Carl helped his father on many a job.

Although offering no tangible proof to substantiate his claim, Harry swore he was directly related to the famous outlaw, Jesse James. Even if he wasn't, Jesse would have applauded Harry's efforts and tenacity, because it took those attributes and more to make a great confidence man.

When Harry came to her hometown of Saint Louis, Carl's mother-to-be, Connie Adams, was working as a teller at the First National Bank. She met handsome Harry when he walked in one Tuesday morning about ten a. m.

Dressed in a grey, pinstriped suit, (which surely cost more than five hundred dollars), and with a snap-brimmed Homburg on his head, Harry looked like Daddy Warbucks. A sparkling white shirt and blue tie with a diamond stickpin completed his ensemble. The shine on his shoes would have made a drill sergeant proud.

Following a short visit with the bank manager, Chester Clifford, Harry deposited fifty thousand dollars in cash. Most customers didn't do such a thing, not even in the bustling and thriving city of Saint Louis. It impressed Chester, who was a typical banker, broad-beamed and narrow-minded, with as much personality as a bucket of wallpaper paste.

After introducing himself as a stockbroker, Harry also claimed he dealt mainly in real estate. Chester bought it and waddled along with Harry to the teller's cage, where Connie sat with a smile on her face. Chester's stomach arrived five seconds before the rest of his body.

Connie was also impressed, but not with the money alone. She liked Harry's good looks, dress and manners. Before she knew what was happening, his coal black eyes, matching hair and bright smile won her heart.

A confirmed bachelor and loner, Harry was struck dumb when beholding this beautiful creature. The pale-blue frock Connie wore was buttoned to the neck, but didn't hide a curvaceous body contained therein. Her blue eyes, blonde hair and winning smile told him he had finally found his soul mate.

Connie was a well put together package, ripe for picking.

The same could be said for the bank where she was employed.

When Chester introduced her as Miss Adams, Harry's eyes lit up.

"I plan to do a lot of business here, Miss Adams. Perhaps you could be my personal teller."

She smiled pleasantly and replied, "I'll be here most days, but I'm free Saturday after lunch and all day Sunday."

Returning her smile, he gave her a sly wink.

"I'm a newcomer. I hear Saint Louis is a fabulous, growing city. Could you show me the Gateway to the West on Sunday?"

Acting coy as a southern bell at her first cotillion, she asked, "Why Mister James, are you asking for a date?"

"If you wish, call it a date. I'd like to know you better."

Batting her eyes seductively she said, "I believe I'm free Sunday."

Two or three times a week, Harry took Connie out for a candlelit dinner and dancing, but his love for her didn't interfere with his plans.

At least twice a week for the next two months, Harry visited the bank, while establishing a nice working relationship and social friendship with portly Chester at the same time.

As luck would have it, Harry was a smooth talker and Chester a good listener. During each visit, Harry checked the balance of his account. With an occasional withdrawal or deposit, (to make things look good), the amount on hand remained at or above fifty thousand dollars.

Then came the day to make or break Harry or the bank.

During his bi-weekly visit, Harry said, "Chester, I have a small problem only you can help me with."

Sticking his thumbs through suspenders already stretched to their limit trying to hold all of Chester in, the banker asked,

"What's your problem, Harry?"

Harry appeared both anxious and forlorn when he said, "I bought some property today and to close the deal, I wrote a check in the amount of thirty-five thousand dollars."

Not understanding how this could be bothering his friend, Chester asked, "How is that a dilemma? You have more than fifty thousand dollars in your account."

Harry lied convincingly, "I know, but the land owner, Mister Dobbins, is a very busy, eccentric old man. He can't bear to wait in line. If he can't cash my check immediately, he may cancel the deal. I can't afford to lose this land, Chester."

Chester smiled and let go of his suspenders. As they snapped back in place across the wide expanse of his stomach, he said, "No problem at all. I'll have thirty-five thousand dollars on hand in one of the tellers' cages. Your client won't have to wait for his money."

Harry nodded and then thought for a moment before saying, "That's fine, but what if Mister Dobbins goes to the wrong teller? The bank has eight windows. How will he know which one to choose?"

Chester grinned with satisfaction.

"Again, you underestimate my resourcefulness. I'll make sure each teller has the same amount in large bills. Mister Dobbins can pick any window and receive his money quickly. Do you have any idea when he'll arrive?"

Harry shrugged.

"He didn't say, but I expect sometime early tomorrow. I don't know how to thank you, Chester. You're a lifesaver. I'll make a bundle from this deal and it will all be thanks to you."

"What are friends for?"

They shook hands, and Harry walked out of the bank smiling.

The next morning, business at the bank was brisk. Between the hours of nine-fifteen and nine-thirty, eight separate checks for thirty-five thousand dollars were presented for payment, one at every window.

Eight different Mister Dobbins smiled pleasantly while the

teller counted out one-hundred-dollar bills. Then with a tip of his hat, each walked out of the bank, never to be seen again.

Down the block in a supercharged getaway van, Harry and Connie awaited their accomplices. Over wine and candle light, the evening before, Harry informed her of his true nature.

At first, Connie was surprised and upset, but when he presented her with a diamond engagement ring, (which she later discovered was a Zirconium), she agreed to run away with her true love.

After a ten thousand dollar payoff to each Mister Dobbins, (and his initial fifty thousand dollar loss), Harry still made a bundle, just as he promised Chester.

Ten months, seven days and sixteen hours later, Connie delivered their son. In honor of his distant relative, she named him Carl Jesse James.

Although fully intending to stay on a straight and narrow path, Roger found the road contained a few bumps and curves. But he navigated those quite easily without a guilty conscience.

Not caring what others thought; Roger didn't consider it stealing if he took his fellow students' money in poker games. His unspoken motto was, "If you can't stand the heat, don't go near the fire."

Likewise, he didn't count the profit from a beer franchise he operated as highway robbery.

"If people stood in line to pay you for something they wanted, what should you do?"

When Roger enrolled as a freshman at UT, Junior ROTC was popular. It was explained if he stayed in the program until he graduated, his efforts would win him a chance to serve as an Army officer.

("Knowing I have to go into the Army, and the pay and position of an officer is much better than the billet of an enlisted man, it's no contest.")

So he joined.

The day after graduating with a degree in business accounting, Roger was sworn into the Army Reserve as a First Lieutenant. A year later, his battalion was called up to serve in the Kuwaiti War.

The path to the same Army unit was decidedly different for Carl. A few days after his twenty-second birthday, he and Harry were busted by undercover cops in the old "Pigeon Drop" scheme.

Harry caught a five-year stretch in Joliet. Because of his young age, the judge took pity on Carl, offering him a chance to enlist in the Army instead of going to jail for three years. Again, there was no contest. Two days later, he took the oath of enlistment as a Buck Private.

Six months after basic training, Carl was promoted to Corporal and assigned as a gunner on Roger's tank. Despite their different backgrounds, two modern warriors formed an immediate bond to last for the rest of their lives.

It really wasn't Roger's fault he reverted back to a life of crime. Fate, time and location were the deciding factors. On the killing fields of Death's Highway leading to Baghdad, it was forced upon him.

Thousands of Iraqi soldiers stole everything not nailed down and a hell of a lot that was, including several kitchen sinks. If it could be torn out, pulled down and carried or driven away, it was. By foot, bicycle, motorcycle, car, truck or van, the Iraqis attempted to take their loot back to Baghdad.

And they didn't steal just one or two items. The thieves disguised as soldiers purloined everything of value from Kuwaiti homes, businesses, museums, mosques etcetera. You name it; it was gone.

The desert highway was littered with a tremendous number of valuable items. Many times Roger's tank ran over and crushed a piece of abandoned stolen merchandise worth a small fortune. Most Iraqi prisoners of war were found with their pockets crammed with jewels, gold coins and/or bank notes.

Over the noise of his tank, Carl shouted, "Look at this, Roger. This guy has seven Rolex watches on one arm and three diamond bracelets on the other."

Staring down at a mangled arm Carl held in his right hand,

Roger asked, "Are you sure both are his?"

Carl shrugged and replied, "I guess it belongs to the rag head. He's the only dead sucker with a missing limb."

To be fair, a lot of loot disappeared into the pockets, field jackets, packs, tanks and trucks of the liberators. Like Robin Hood, spoils of the rich went to the poor fighting men, who often thought, "When your ass is on the line every day, who could blame you for putting something away for your retirement?"

Then, like the fabled Lost Dutchman's Mine, they discovered the mother lode. One of Roger's warriors, an electronics warfare specialist named Alan Yoder was checking an abandoned missile silo and stumbled upon a huge cache containing gold bars and sacks of gold coins.

After appropriating several bags for himself, Alan reported his find to Roger, who surprised him by asking, "Did you check other silos for more loot?"

"No; I thought you'd want to report my find to higher headquarters."

"This is as high up the chain of command as you go with this story," Roger said. "I'll take care of the gold. Check the other bunkers. If you find more, keep your mouth shut and report back to me."

When they discovered three more complexes containing smaller amounts of glowing gold bars, but a larger amount of coin sacks, Roger was heard to say, "There's so much gold, it's too much gold," and wondered, "What should I do?"

The answer appeared out of a raging sandstorm, in the form of a black supply specialist, Sergeant A. J. Rose, who delivered truckloads of ammo and other gear to Roger's tanks on a daily basis.

After knocking sand from his fatigue cap, A. J. said, "Man, I didn't know if I'd find you in this shit. It's been a bitch getting here. What have you got to go back to the port?"

"It's interesting you should ask, A. J. How would you like to make a few extra bucks?"

"What do I have to do?"

"Take some special cargo back to the harbor and see it gets sent to Fort Hood."

A. J. looked at Roger through grit on his sunglasses and asked, "What kind of cargo, and what's in it for me?"

As quickly as the storm began, it suddenly abated. The last grains of sand settled to the desert floor, while the sun broke through, beating down with its usual body-draining heat.

After walking to a nearby pile, Roger said, "Help me dump the sand off this tarp."

Working together, they turned up an edge to reveal a pile of small wooden boxes. One box top was pried off, and inside lay four, shiny yellow metal bars. The hot desert sun reflected wickedly from gleaming gold.

A. J. blinked, shaded his eyes for a closer look and asked, "Is that gold?"

Grinning at his reaction, Roger said, "Yeah, all of it. We have seventy-seven boxes weighing fifty pounds apiece, and one hundred and seventy-four bags of gold coins weighing twenty-five pounds each."

A. J. swiped at some sand flies with his hat.

"That's a lot of gold. Where the hell did it come from?"

"Good old Saddam and his cronies."

"Do you think it's traceable?"

Roger shrugged.

"I doubt it, but who cares? Once we get the gold to the states, whoever buys it won't ask questions."

Continuing to stare at the gold, A. J. asked, "How do you want to handle this?"

His new partner in crime pointed toward some nearby shot up tanks.

"We'll pack the gold inside ammo storage lockers of our salvageable tanks. Then our welders will seal the doors shut. You haul ass back to the port and 'arrange' for the captain of a ship to take them aboard."

With a wide grin on his face, A. J. said, "No sweat. I'll get a couple friends to help me. Then I'll prepare shipping documents stating the wrecks are bound for rehab at Fort Hood."

Roger slapped A. J.'s back and said, "For a supply sergeant, you're pretty smart."

"Thanks, but you didn't answer my second question; what's

in it for me?"

"You get an equal share. There are one hundred and thirty-five men in our outfit. Everyone shares and shares alike. You're number one hundred and thirty-six."

Sticking out his hand, A. J. said, "Okay, I'll take care of it. But I need some bribe money. Can you spare a couple bags of coins? They should do the trick."

Roger shook his hand to seal the unwritten contract among warriors.

"Sure, but be careful where you spend them. It looks like this frigging war is about over. When we get back to Fort Hood and meet the tanks, I'll find a buyer for the gold."

Absentmindedly slapping at another biting fly on his elbow, A. J. said, "I'll back up my truck and you can start loading. It's been a pleasure doing business with you, Roger."

A Blue Norther with icy winds was making its presence known in Texas. Carl and Roger shivered in their light desert cammies as they walked to the orderly room to be separated from the service.

Grey clouds hid the sun, and particles of light snow blew through the air around them, as Roger said, "Going back to being a civilian will be tough, Carl. What are your plans for the future?"

Carl shivered and replied, "I hadn't thought much about what I'll do. I guess I'll take life easy. I can live comfortably for a few years from the profit we made on the gold. Do you have any suggestions?"

Roger gave him one of his evil smiles.

"I think we should form our own partnership. If we play our cards right, we could make millions. You said your father taught you his skills. Why don't we play some suckers for all they're worth? It would provide more of a challenge than sitting around, wondering how long our money will last."

Carl asked, "You had to mention the word 'challenge' didn't you? Do you really think we can make a living by conning old fogies out of their money?"

Roger smiled and said, "Yes, we can."

Carl matched his smile and made a bad pun; 'Don't you mean, 'yes, we <u>con</u>?''

When Roger laughed, Carl added, "Okay, partner, you talked me into it. Let's pick up our freedom papers. Then we'll have a drink to our new partnership."

Chapter 3

Although the devious entrepreneurship was now ten years old and so far failed to deliver the millions Roger envisioned, still, they did all right. In Texas alone, thousands of suckers were willing to throw their hard-earned money away on a get-rich-quick scheme. The fools waited like sheep about to be sheared, while Roger and Carl provided the scissors.

Roger planned their escapades and Carl worked as a "gofer". Their carefully chosen victims were wealthy, often senile older men or women who could easily afford to lose a small portion of their sometimes questionably accumulated wealth.

When the marks discovered they had been swindled, they usually were too embarrassed to attempt any retribution involving the law. Shaking their heads in wonder at their stupidity, the victims wrote their follies off as an expensive learning experience.

Four days ago, the team of Roger and Carl, plus two ex-Army comrades took a very rich old coot for fifty thousand dollars. After paying off their fellow thieves, Carl and Roger were on their way to Sandia Casino in Albuquerque. With luck, they would turn the remaining thirty thousand into sixty.

Their latest victim, Richard Murdock, was head of his own oil company, Murdock Oil Incorporated in Houston. The fifty thousand they stole from Richard was like pennies to such a wealthy man, but Roger was worried about his reaction.

The day after completing their sting, Roger said, "With

tentacles as far reaching as Mister Murdock has, I think we should disappear for a few days."

Always one to suggest gambling, Carl said, "Let's go to Sandia Casino in Albuquerque."

Although knowing most times the fools they took were so ashamed they usually wouldn't notify the police, there were times when the richer ones could afford to take action on their own and did, with sometimes devastating results.

In his mind, Roger hoped Richard Murdock was not the type and this was not one of those times.

After a pit stop in Brownfield, they headed west on Route 380. Carl drove while Roger rested his bloodshot eyes. Between Brownfield, Texas and their intermediate stop, Roswell, New Mexico, there was only a lonely two-lane blacktop road, seeming to stretch to infinity.

The scenery was vast, but desolate, filled with nothing but sand, cacti and occasional sagebrush. Making their lonely way across the dry, gritty soil, the round clusters of weeds rolled merrily along, headed for who knew where.

Staring at the seemingly unending highway, Carl asked, "Does this road have an end?"

"Two of them," Roger said and laughed. "By the way, how did Julie take the news that we were off on another gambling trip?"

Julie was Carl's latest flame in a long line of burned out promises and ashes left behind from failed romances. So far it appeared she was lighting Carl's fire more than any of the past embers slowly dying in his memory bank.

They met by accident three months ago, when they had a fender bender in a parking lot. Julie was to blame, but after one look into her bright blue eyes, the sight of her blonde hair, five feet four inch marvelously put together body and dazzling smile, Carl forgot about who was at fault.

All he wanted was her name, address, phone number and a chance to get to know her.

Julie was equally impressed with Carl's good looks, tact and courtesy after the wreck. It was her first accident, and she was shook up, but Carl was a gentleman and calmed her fears.

Their mutual admiration resulted in a first date and many more thereafter. Eventually they became lovers a few days before Carl and Roger left for Houston to con Richard Murdock out of his money.

Carl smiled at the recollection.

"She wasn't too happy, especially not after I was gone to Houston for two weeks. When we get back, I'll have to make it up to her somehow."

Roger nodded.

It appears Julie's here to stay for a while."

"Yeah, I think she might be the one to make me settle down some day."

"What happens when she finds out you aren't a day trader, but a common crook?"

"Whoever said you and I were common?"

"Answer my question," Roger said.

"We'll cross that bridge before I actually ask her to marry. Let's wait and see what this trip brings. Who knows, I may play the slots and make a million."

The van cruised through two decaying towns; Plains, Texas and Tatum, New Mexico. Both small burgs were a few blocks wide and fewer deep, filled with abandoned buildings. Vacant remains lining both sides of the street displayed missing windows and sagging doors. Alkali dust had painted the worn-out shells chalk white, and blackened, weather-beaten studs of crumbling adobe walls now resembled bleached bones of some ancient beast.

The next morning was bright and clear with no hope for rain to cool things down. The weather report promised another hot, boring day. Neither Carl nor Roger was looking forward to the miles remaining until they reached their final destination.

As he adjusted his sunglasses on his nose, Carl said, "It's going to be another scorcher."

Knowing their next destination, Cline's Corner, was a long, boring one hundred and twenty-two miles of sun scorched desert away, Roger nodded and said, "Pray for rain."

Following breakfast at a greasy spoon on the edge of Roswell, Roger drove north on Highway 285.The trip was already tedious, and Roger's rancid fumes only added more discomfort.

After rolling down his window to let out some of the aroma, Carl asked, "What did you eat for dinner last night? That was powerful."

"I had a bowl of chili with extra beans."

"Heaven help us."

Outside, a few hundred telephone poles and at least one dead skunk flew by Carl's window. Finally he broke a long period of silence by asking, "We did pretty well on this last job, didn't we?"

Roger agreed.

"Yeah, but I'm tired of these Mickey Mouse jobs requiring too much time and effort that don't make enough profit. I'd love to discover one big score for millions. Then I'd retire gracefully to a Fort Worth mansion."

Carl grinned.

"So would I, but to score that big, we'd have to knock over Fort Knox or rob an armored truck."

Pointing to a heavily armored Brinks vehicle a few hundred yards to their front, Roger asked, "You mean like the one up ahead?"

"Yeah, or one just like it. I wonder how much money they have on board."

Roger shook his head.

"We'll never know, but we can dream, can't we?"

Carl shrugged and silence filled the van again as he resumed counting road kill. When they passed the Brinks truck, he waved to the driver.

Wearing the grey, hotter-than-hell Ike Jacket uniform of Brinks Security, two men were inside the armored vehicle. The driver, Jim Young, was a sandy-haired man in his late fifties. Fourteen months ago, the guard, twenty-two-year-old Larry Grey, became an underpaid Brinks employee.

In direct violation of company policy, Larry sat in the cab with Jim, when he should be in the rear compartment guarding a seven million dollar payload.

Larry was a good talker and Jim went along with his stubbornness. The rationale for Larry's failing to live up to company standards was simple. Since the rear compartment was not air conditioned, his duty station was hotter than hell.

He gestured with his thumb toward the rear compartment while thinking, "Why should I sweat my ass off back there to please those jerks in Roswell? If the bad guys decide to rob us, what difference would it make where I was?"

Neither was overly concerned about being alone on the barren and lonely highway. Since service from Roswell to Albuquerque was established fifteen years ago, there had been no attempted robberies.

A tan van passed in the second lane, and Jim nodded to a waving passenger, as Larry contemplated his current employment's pros and cons.

("When we get done with this run, I'll check on a new line of work. At ten dollars and fifty-seven cents an hour, it's not worth the effort.

"Let's say the bad guys do hit us. What happens then? If I was in the back and wouldn't open the door, what would they do? One; they'd drive the truck down some deep arroyo and let me sit in the hot sun until my ass was fried. Or two; they'd use their superior firepower and armor piercing bullets to turn the truck, (and me), into Swiss cheese.

"Look what Brinks issued me to repel boarders; a stinking .38 caliber, six shot revolver. I had to buy my own ammo and quick loads. How cheap can they be? Now I've got twenty-four bullets against crooks armed with semi-automatic rifles, a bazooka or a Rocket Propelled Grenade (RPG). Hell, one of those weapons would make short work of the door and blow my ass away at the same time.

"If bad guys hit us, I'll do all I can, but when the going gets tough, I'll get going. They can have the damn money.")

Jim had driven these vehicles for twelve years. During his tenure with Brinks, he never experienced any trouble, but wasn't lulled into a feeling of complacency. He was one of the old breed, dedicated to his job, staying alert for any possibility.

Glancing at Larry, Jim tried to read his mind while thinking, "I often wondered what the hell I would do if the truck was hijacked. Larry told me how he feels and I can understand his attitude.

"If something happens, I'll give it my best shot and try to protect the money, but I'm no dummy. If someone stops this truck and has the means to take Larry and me out, then to hell with it. When push comes to shove, I'll give up it just as fast as Larry."

Four miles up the highway, Roger saw a sign, "Road Work Ahead" and the speed limit dropped from seventy to forty-five. An orange and white sign warned violators: "If workers are present, traffic fines will double."

After slowing the van, Roger glanced into the rearview mirror and noticed the only vehicle behind theirs was the Brinks truck. The driver apparently missed the warning sign, because the heavy truck sped on and was nearly on top of the van before Jim woke up and hit the brakes.

Roger stared at the driver in the rearview mirror.

"Way to go, Bozo. One minute more and you'd have been parked in my back seat."

Carl was busy checking out a bloody carcass of a deer which had recently been splattered and scattered over several hundred feet of pavement. He missed the excitement and asked, "What's up?"

Poking his thumb over his shoulder to indicate the armored vehicle while staring darts at Jim's reflection in the rearview mirror, Roger said, "They must hire stupid old farts to drive those trucks. The idiot almost ran into the back of us."

Glancing ahead of the van, Carl saw a traffic flagger a few hundred feet ahead and shouted, "Watch out!"

In a stiff breeze blowing across the highway, long blonde hair stood out from under her cap, telling Roger the worker was a female.

Holding a red and white pole in her left hand that displayed a stop sign in large, bold red letters, she stood in the middle of the road. Seemingly frozen in place by panic, she held up her right hand as if to fend off the van.

Roger stomped on the brakes and watched his rearview mirror in horror as the Brinks truck rapidly closed the gap between the two vehicles.

Thankfully, Jim wasn't as stupid as Roger claimed. He slammed on his brakes, the tires burned black rubber strips into the asphalt and the truck slid to a halt five feet behind the van. Grey smoke wrapped around the wheels of the Brinks truck like wispy ribbons.

Larry's white-knuckled hands were pressed against the dashboard, as he exclaimed, "Damn; that was close."

Although Roger stopped several feet short of her position, at the last moment, the frightened flagger, Jenny Jones, finally recovered her senses and jumped sideways.

Glaring at Roger over a red muffler wrapped around her face, she shouted, "Didn't you see the signs?"

He rolled down his window, smiled and said, "I'm sorry. Are you okay?"

Jenny continued to glare for a few moments, but then finally got over her mad.

"Yeah, I'm fine. Watch it next time. Inattention is how people get killed."

Roger put the gearshift in park, set the emergency brake, stepped from the van, stretched his weary back and looked at the Brinks truck.

Jim displayed a sheepish smile and waved a limp hand.

Carl joined Roger at the side of the van. It appeared there would be a considerable wait until they could proceed. He bent over, stretched his tired body and glanced sideways at Roger, who seemed lost in thought.

Turning to look at the armored truck over his shoulder, Carl said, "That was close. I think I've got brown stains in my shorts."

Roger didn't reply. He was busy checking his watch and then looking at the Brinks truck and the empty highway to their rear. The hot sun continued to beat down, and glare from the empty roadway was blinding. Since Roger seemed non-communicative, Carl left him to fend for himself and climbed back into the air conditioned van to wait.

Ten minutes later, Jenny called out, "You better get back in your van. The guide car will be here in a minute. Wait for my signal and drive slow."

Roger tipped his hat to her and said, "I apologize again. If we weren't in a hurry, I'd stick around and take you to dinner."

In spite of herself, Jenny blushed. She liked Roger's good looks, (even if the fool wasn't a very good driver), and thought, "We all make mistakes and the big guy is one I'd like to make."

Roger checked his side view mirror a final time. For more than eight minutes, his van and the Brinks truck were the only vehicles stopped by Jenny. Then at one minute intervals, two other cars arrived.

Carl saw the old gleam in Roger's eyes and knew it was when he came up with some of his best plans. Knowing the wheels were turning in Roger's head, Carl kept his silence lest he interrupt some good planning. Whatever Roger had in mind, he'd let him know when the time was right.

Two minutes later, a guide truck arrived from the north and a long line of fifteen cars, trucks and vans passed. The pilot turned his truck around, and Roger pulled in behind his vehicle.

"What did you say about knocking over a Brinks armored truck, Carl?"

"I said it would be nice, but there's no way in hell we could."

After glancing into his rearview mirror one last time, Roger said, "Maybe there is. I have an idea. Let me bounce some thoughts off you."

For the next two hours, they talked over Roger's plan while Carl played Devil's advocate, attempting to find fault with every facet. In the end, he admitted Roger might be onto something.

"We need a lot more information. This is a job for our computer expert, Alan. I'll call and see what he's doing. Knowing him, he's probably online, checking out the internet or playing games."

"Tell him I have a better pastime for him," Roger said.

A report on a friend he heard before they left Austin came to Carl's mind.

"Since we're talking about old teammates, did you hear

what happened to A. J.?

"No; what?"

"He caught Flo in bed with some corn-rowed asshole."

Roger asked, "No shit?"

"Yeah, and by the time A. J. was done with the poor bastard, he beat the sucker half to death."

Worried now, Roger asked, "Is A. J. in the slammer?"

"No; the cops didn't charge him with anything. They said he was within his rights."

"What's he doing now?"

"He's living at the 'Y'. I hear he's having a hard time making ends meet."

"Let's see what we can do to help him," Roger said. "Thanks for letting me know."

Chapter 4

When he answered the phone, Alan said, "It's your quarter."

"Hey Alan, how's it hanging?" Carl asked.

"High, dry and shriveled up. What's up, Carl?"

"Roger came up with a plan and we need your help. How busy are you?"

"Never too occupied to help you guys out," Alan said. "What kind of info do you need?"

"Anything you can find about Brinks Corporation and their armored trucks."

"Are you looking for anything in particular?"

"We're interested in how large their trucks are and what kind of communications or safety features they have," Carl said. "Basically, we need everything you can lay your hands on."

"That shouldn't be difficult. How soon do you need the info?"

"We're headed for Albuquerque right now, but we'll be back in three days."

Alan yawned.

"That gives me plenty of time. Stop by when you return to see what I come up with."

"Hold on a minute, Alan. Roger wants to ask you something."

Carl handed Roger his cell phone, and he said, "Howdy, Alan, do you know anyone who could provide us with some front money?"

"I might. What amount are you talking about?"

"We'll probably need two million for this job."

Roger heard his sharp intake of a breath.

"Wow, two million? You're talking about some heavy bread. I'll ask around."

"If we get the financing, we'll need to buy a ranch in New Mexico. Do me a favor; get on the internet to see what's available between Roswell and Albuquerque. I'd prefer some property on Highway 285 North. You can find it on a map."

"No sweat," Alan said. "Is there anything else on your mind?"

"No, you've got it. We'll see you in a few days."

Roger gave the phone to Carl. From the silence in his ear, Carl knew Alan decided the conversation was over and hung up without saying goodbye. He shrugged and punched the "end" button.

When they began this trip, Roger itched to get to the blackjack table. Now as they neared their destination, Carl saw other thoughts were distracting him. At the entrance to the casino, they stopped at a valet parking sign, and Carl asked, "How long do you want to stay?"

"I originally thought we'd stay two days. Now I think we should try our luck tonight and leave for Austin tomorrow morning. Let's set a limit on how much we can lose. What about two thousand dollars each? We need money for this new venture, so there's no sense in blowing away everything we have."

Carl nodded in agreement.

"I can see the wheels turning already. You're really getting into this, aren't you?"

"It's strange how my mind works. Until I saw the Brinks truck, I didn't have a thought of robbing one. Now, as I try to figure all the angles, it's driving me crazy. My mind won't be on the cards tonight."

A valet opened the van door and asked, "Are you checking in?"

"Yes," Roger said. "Our bags are in back."

The valet held the door open wide and said, "Go on inside. I'll take care of your luggage and park your vehicle."

Glancing at the valet's name tag, Roger said, "Okay, Jimmy, we'll see you in the lobby."

They entered the opulent hotel adjoining the new Indian-oriented Casino, where pink granite statues of Sitting Bull, Geronimo and Chief Joseph line one wall. Mirrors, bright lights and marble are everywhere. Acres of subdued, multicolored, braided Indian carpet cushion a red tiled floor.

Wearing a black skirt, maroon jacket and starched white blouse open at the collar, a cute blonde named Laura, according to her name tag, met them at the reception desk. At the center of her blouse, a black lace brassiere peeked out suggestively as it strained to hold back mounds of smooth velvety skin.

Smiling a toothy, but insincere grin, Laura checked them into the hotel in a matter of minutes, while Carl stared at her like a love sick, wide-eyed puppy. When she looked up, she blushed when realizing his eyes were focused on the contents of her bra. Then she attempted to avoid his eyes, but failed.

Still trying to ignore Carl's stare, she handed a room key to Roger.

"Thank you, Mister Booth."

Carl gave her his best smile and asked, "What time do you get off, Laura?"

With a straight face and a partial frown, she replied, "Just in time for my husband to pick me up out front."

Roger grabbed Carl by his elbow.

"Shot down in flames again, Carl. Come on; here's Jimmy with our bags."

After dropping their luggage in a well-appointed two-bedroom suite, Roger adjourned to a five dollar minimum blackjack table, where a lovely redhead with deep-blue eyes named Sue was dealing.

Three other players were at the table; one aging woman and two middle-aged men sporting hand-tooled cowboy boots while wearing matching dark blue Levis and tan corduroy shirts. Roger wasn't sure, but he thought they might be an item.

The woman was a frizzy peroxide blonde, wearing a hideous flowered dress with a short hem revealing a pair of flabby wrinkled knees badly in need of ironing. From neck to fingers, she was loaded down with thirty pounds of cheap costume jewelry.

This flower of the desert was drinking Pink Dive Bombers – "A sure to make your stomach bubble and boil witches' brew", containing pink grapefruit juice, eye of newt, virgin rum, snake oil and grenadine. Guarding and shading the frozen potion was a poorly-perceived, plastic replica of silver wings of an aviator attached to a thin, red paper straw.

After taking a sip, she looked up at Roger, flashed a half-smile, half-sneer and asked, "Feeling lucky?"

Although he wasn't sure if this sagging refugee from an old folk's home was talking about gambling or something else, Roger said, "Yeah, don't we all feel like winners when we first arrive?"

She shrugged as if she didn't give a damn, took another belt, swirled it around in her ample mouth and swallowed hard.

Roger swore he heard the liquor hit bottom.

Then after wiping her mouth with the back of her hand, she looked down at her cards and with a half-hearted voice said, "Hit me."

As Roger thought, "I'd love to"; Sue deftly slid a card from a box and flipped it over.

It was a King of Hearts, and the foul-mouthed floozy said, "Shit, busted again," flipped over her cards and shoved them in the general direction of Sue.

After pulling five one-hundred-dollar bills from his billfold, Roger laid them on the table and said, "Nickels."

Sue spread the money out so a pit boss could check her count, and called out, "Changing five hundred."

When the bored supervisor waved his hand in agreement, she counted out one hundred five-dollar-chips and pushed the stacked ovals across the table. With a smile on her lips, she met Roger's eyes with her own and said, "Good luck."

As he placed two chips on his bet spot, he said, "I hope so," and watched as Sue dealt the cards face down.

After checking his hand, he smiled and put his chips on top of his cards, signifying he was standing pat.

Knowing if he judged correctly, he would find his "lucky" table, Carl walked around the casino, mentally measuring the noise level from each crowded crap table. Then making his final decision, he walked up to the end of a long, green-felted, high-sided table.

An obliging stranger, wearing a loud yellow jacket over his bulging stomach, which made him look like a pregnant lemon, made room for Carl. Pushing his chips to one side, the yellow-coated gambler said, "Come on in; the water's fine."

Carl pointed to Yellow Coat's stack of chips and said, "Thanks; it looks like you've done okay."

Yellow jacket grinned.

"Yeah, this table's hot. My name's Willy. Good luck."

Willy stuck out his limp, meaty hand. Carl shook it and thought it was like shaking hands with five pounds of raw hamburger, but returned Willy's smile.

"Pleased to meet you. I'm Carl."

After trading in his cash for five hundred dollars in five dollar chips, Carl bet the Pass and Come lines and got odds on both bets.

Willy threw the dice, rolled a "seven", and as the dealer paid off all their wagers, bragged, "See, I told you so."

Another player nearby beat his hands on a side of the table and yelled, "Keep those dice hot,"

After making the same bets, Carl bought his lucky number – four.

Willy rolled the dice again.

Two hours later, Roger had seen enough of blackjack. Earlier in the evening, the two cowboys called it a night, so now Sue was left with only him and the old broad to beat, which she did regularly.

After quickly auditing his chips, Roger discovered six hundred and fifty-five dollars in the stack. If his math was right, he made a grand total of seventy-seven dollars and fifty cents an hour.

Under his breath, he said, "Not bad, but it's not a million dollars.

His tablemate heard his remark, belched loudly and responded with a keen observation.

"That'll be the day, when anyone makes a million dollars in this joint."

An hour ago, while Sue was reshuffling four decks of cards, Roger's companion offered him her wrinkled hand with chipped, bright-red fingernails and introduced herself as Gloria.

As Gloria continued to throw down buzz bombs at the rate of one every fifteen minutes, Roger knew she was doing exactly what the house wanted; get bombed and go bust. The casino would soon get its wish. As the evening wore on, Gloria's stack of ten dollar chips steadily diminished like Pompeii being swallowed by Mount Vesuvius.

Father Time's Mickey Mouse watch raced on and a carpet-bombing fleet of scarlet B-52s made jowl-sagging Gloria a pink, spot splattered wreck, until she looked like a hapless victim of a Kamikaze attack.

It was time to move on, so after tipping Sue two chips, Roger tipped his Stetson to her and Gloria, while saying, "Enough is enough. Thanks for a nice time, ladies."

Sue smiled as if she really hated to see him go and said, "Thanks."

With one gulp, shell-shocked Gloria shot down another high flyer and commented dryly, "Try to keep it hanging high and dry, Sport."

When Roger walked up to the crap table where Carl and Willy stood, a large, noisy and jubilant crowd was gathered there. It took Roger a minute or two to reach Carl's side. Then he asked, "What's going on?"

Willie pointed to a pretty brown-eyed brunette in a low-cut green gown, who was shaking the dice in one hand, while her heavy boobs kept time in a thin, almost transparent bra, and said, "I can't believe it. The little filly just rolled her seventeenth number in a row."

Carl chimed in and added, "Yeah, Roger, we've all been riding her coat tails. I'm over five thousand ahead."

Roger patted Carl's back in encouragement.

"I'm headed for the restaurant and some supper. Why don't you quit a winner for a change and join me?"

Breaking into their conversation, Willie said, "Hell, the little gal is just getting warmed up. Don't quit now and jinx me, Carl."

Carl shook his head.

"You go ahead, Roger. I'll stay here and turn this five grand into ten before your order is delivered."

"Don't blame me if you lose it all."

Willie frowned and said, "Send this yahoo away."

Taking his subtle hint, Roger said, "I'll be in the restaurant."

Fifteen minutes later, as he was using a piece of toast to sop up yellow yolk from his steak and eggs over easy, Roger looked up to see a crestfallen Carl making his way to the table. Roger noted his buddy looked like a Labrador retriever that had lost a downed duck in a soggy swamp. Knowing the answer already, still he asked, "Where's the money, Carl."

"What money? You were right. I lost it all."

Roger smiled and waved him into a seat.

"You look like hell, Carl. Lighten up, it's only money. If things go well in the next few months, you won't have to worry about cash for a long time."

When his intercom buzzed, Mary said, "Mister Murdock, Mister Winters is on line five."

"Thank you, Mary."

He punched the correct lever and said, "Hello Darrin. It's good to hear from you. How's your investigation going?"

"I traced the license number you gave me to a Mister Roger Booth, who lives in Austin. His roommate is Carl James. As you thought, they used their real first names, but Wilson and Baxter are not their last."

"Good, it's always nice to know who you're dealing with. I take it you've compiled a dossier on each. Is there anything interesting?"

Not knowing how he would take it, Darrin said, "They took a trip to Albuquerque to gamble away some of the money they stole from you."

"Since I'm paying for their vacation, I hope they enjoy the

trip."

Relaxing at Richard's response, Darrin said, "I'll send the information to you this afternoon by courier. These two have long records, which make interesting reading. When they return from Albuquerque, I'll continue to tail them."

"Keep up the good work, Darrin. I'll be waiting for your next report."

Chapter 5

On the return trip to Austin, the sky was clear and bright, the highway wide and seemingly endless. The sun continued to try to blister Roger and Carl through the windshield and side windows.

Finally, after two days of near record heat and a night of tossing and turning in a motel room with a squeaky, under-powered window air conditioning unit, they returned to the shady, tree lined streets of their home town.

When he was able to reach Alan with his cell phone, Carl said, "Howdy, Alan, we're back a day early. How are things going?"

"Pretty good; welcome home. Did you win?"

"Not me, but what Roger won almost made up for my losses. It was a fun trip and we came up with a new job."

"Yeah, I figured. Your request for info on Brinks told me. What's the score on this one?"

"You have to find that for us, Alan. We'll drop by in an hour to tell you all about the job."

Alan stretched to loosen his sore back and said, "You'd better include me in this new adventure. I could use a big payoff to buy the latest high tech stuff. The way the internet is growing, I need more staying power."

Chuckling at his unintended sexual innuendo, Carl asked, "Don't we all? See you shortly."

An hour later, they knocked on Alan's door and heard his voice boom down the hall, "Come in. The door's unlocked."

They entered a long entranceway and heard him pounding

away on his keyboard. Following the sound, they found Alan in a mussed bedroom sitting at a console table and staring at figures on a monitor. Behind him, daylight struggled valiantly to make its way through a dirty window with a torn screen. More post-it notes than Roger ever hoped to see were stuck here and there to walls, door jambs and a cracked mirror with silver peeling from one corner.

Alan wore old, cut-off blue jeans and a large, dirty orange tank top exposing his meaty shoulders. On bare feet he wore an old pair of decrepit flip-flops. A strong odor of unwashed body wafted from a chair where he sat with one ham-sized leg twisted under the other.

Disheveled, dirty blond hair hung over his bloodshot eyes, as he peered through thick, wire-rimmed glasses which must have been cleaned at least once last week, but still were clouded.

It was several months since Roger last saw Alan. Although he was once neat, Alan was now a slob.

Pointing to two battered, brown metal chairs nearby, Alan said, "Come in and have a seat."

Roger stretched and said, "We've sat for hours, so we'll stand."

Alan handed Carl a manila envelope.

"Whatever. Here's the info you wanted."

After turning the package upside down, Carl dumped the contents onto a nearby wobbly, used-to-be-white coffee table, which was now ringed with aged stain spots, while thinking, "If the terrible table could talk, it would brag it was home to stains from seven different soft drinks, four brands of coffee, three tea blends, (two iced and one hot), and all thirty-one flavors of Baskin & Robbins ice cream."

Shaking his head in disbelief, Carl said silently; "It would take a year and a gallon of penicillin to kill the microscopic germs and accumulated crud it contains."

Roger joined Carl at the table, viewed the documents of Alan's envelope, noted there were colored photographs of several different-sized Brinks trucks with a specification list clipped to each and said, "I didn't know they made so many types of armored vehicles. Where did you find all this information, Alan?"

Basking in his praise, Alan said, "It was easy. They'll never know I was in their files, but I hacked into Brinks' system and downloaded everything. Then I went on line, found the manufacturer of the vehicles and got more info, including the location of their security systems and transponders."

It was the first time Carl had heard the word, so he asked, "Transponders, what are they?"

Pointing to a photo of the item in question, Alan said, "It's an old fashioned way to keep track of the trucks. The device sends out a constant signal, allowing Brinks to track every stop the truck makes, its location etcetera. What really surprises me is that they haven't updated their tracking system. What they have now is practically archaic."

Roger patted Alan on the back while saying, "You're something else, Alan. You never fail to amaze me."

"There's even more. The drivers continue to use a two-way radio system to communicate. They haven't switched to cell phones."

"Why is that?" Carl asked.

"I think the main reason is heavy armor-plating. A cell phone signal probably can't penetrate the thick layer of metal."

After studying the photographs for a few moments, Carl pointed to an antenna on top of a truck and said, "We'll have to disable the radio."

Alan shrugged.

"It's easy. You take along a bolt cutter and whack off the antennas located on the roof over the driver's seat."

"It's simple, but very effective," Roger said. "I like it."

Changing the subject, Carl asked, "What about a money man?"

Alan picked up a pad of paper and handed him the top sheet.

"I phoned around and got a lead. Do you remember our supply sergeant in Kuwait, Frank Franzone? His nickname was 'Tiny'."

Looking down at the phone number, Carl replied, "Yeah, what about him?"

"Tiny runs a nightclub on Sixth Street called 'the Night

Life'. That's his number. I hear he's connected to the Mafia. It's rumored he has friends in high places."

"Good work, buddy," Roger said. "If we go through with this job, we need a lot of specialized equipment. I'll count on you to find it for us."

Leaning back in his chair, Alan pointed at his computer monitor.

"No problem. Bring it on. My friend here and I can find anything in the world."

Indicating the photos and documents, Roger asked, "How much do we owe you, Alan?"

"The only payment I want is a job on the inside. I don't know all your plans, but I do know this'll be a big caper, so I want in."

Roger pointed to Alan's bulging stomach and said, "If we let you join us on this job, you'll have to get into shape. I hate to say this, Alan, but you look like hell."

"The old 'shape up or ship out' crap, right?"

"You're right."

Suddenly Carl had a stroke of genius.

"Hey Roger, remember A. J.? Maybe we can take care of two problems at once."

Roger thought for a moment and then asked, "How would you like a bunk mate, Alan?"

"If she's blonde, five feet, four inches tall and built like a preverbal outhouse, I wouldn't mind at all."

"It's not a 'she'. I want A. J. Rose to 'baby-sit' you and help with your exercises."

"Not A. J." Alan exclaimed. "In Kuwait he drove us nuts. All he did was lift weights and do aerobics. The man will kill me in a week."

Carl was persistent.

"Do you have any other complaints about A. J., or could the two of you live side by side here? He and Flo split up and he needs a place to stay."

After sighing in resignation, Alan said, "No, I don't have anything against him, but I still think he'll kill me in the first week. I guess if I can make it through the next seven days, I can last forever."

Standing up to tell Carl that he was ready to leave, Roger said, "Good; I'll call A. J. and let him know what's up. He should be able to move in later today. The sooner you get the extra lard off your bones, the better.

"As for a place on our team, right now we're in a preliminary planning stage, so nothing has been decided. We may find we can't do the job. Anything we do now would be premature."

Alan stuck out his hand and said, "Okay, it's a deal. I understand, but don't forget me. I could use the money."

Roger shook his hand and laughed.

"We all could use a million or two. Keep up the good work."

When Roger and Carl returned to their home on Bucknell Drive in Northeast Austin, the record heat was still stalled over Austin. The air conditioner struggled to overcome the hot air trapped in the vacant home during their absence.

While waiting for the house to cool down, they sat by the pool discussing their plans.

Carl said, "Maybe I should be the one to talk to Tiny. If I remember right, he wasn't fond of officers, but I think an ex-NCO could talk to him on his level."

Looking skyward, Roger said, "Frank's six feet, nine inches tall. Even if you call him 'Tiny', you can't talk to him on that level."

Later the next morning, Carl tried to reach Frank, but an answering machine picked up, so he left a short message.

A few minutes after one p.m., Frank returned his call and said, "Whatever you want; it'll cost you."

Although Frank couldn't see it, Carl smiled.

"Still the same old supply sergeant, aren't you, Frank? I remember the deals you pulled in Kuwait. Do you still own those Ferraris you bought for a song?"

Frank laughed at the recollection and said, "I sold all but two I kept for myself and my wife. It's funny you should remember them."

"It isn't every sergeant who can buy a dozen foreign sports

cars in Kuwait, then ship them to Texas and doesn't have to pay import taxes. It must be nice to have friends in high places."

Frank laughed again.

"I'm not saying I do or I don't. But yeah, it would be, wouldn't it? I'm looking forward to seeing you again, buddy. It's been a long time. Meet me tonight at nine at my place on Sixth Street. I'll leave your name with the doorman."

"Thanks, Frank. I'll see you tonight."

"Bring lots of money."

Decked out in Western wear, including a Stetson and boots, Carl drove downtown to Sixth Street, where a diverse crowd of young men and women and a few older celebrants were strolling the streets and alleys. Meandering along like cut ants on vacation, they drank beer from long-neck bottles and listened to various styles of music blasting from garish nightclubs and honky-tonk bars.

After finding an empty space in a "pay as you park" lot, Carl stuffed a five dollar bill into the numbered slot corresponding with his parking place. Then he tried to avoid crowds of noisy students and flunker-outers littering the sidewalk like zombies on parade in a graveyard. It was often necessary to step over debris-clogged gutters and into broken-beer-bottle, glass-speckled streets to get by.

He found Frank's place; a typical Western bar and dancehall, decorated with torn, graffiti smeared autographed racing posters, worn cowboy gear and too many flashing neon beer signs. The joint was jumping.

Along one wall, a line of young men and women was formed waiting impatiently to gain entry. Lured by intoxicating double digit decibel music blaring from speakers high overhead, they looked like lemmings being led to the sea by a pied piper high on acid.

At the entrance, Carl walked to the front of the line, where several younger men frowned. Avoiding their stares, he approached a large, menacing looking moron checking IDs. The guard's arms bulged with muscles, reminding Carl of the comic strip hero, Popeye. His face featured a twice broken nose and a bad case of acne.

When Carl told Popeye he had an appointment with Mister Franzone at nine p.m., his brow wrinkled up like a five-day-old prune. Carl could tell the effort to associate Mister Franzone with Tiny probably caused his brain to overload. Then the connection finally made its way through his thick skull, and Popeye announced proudly, "Oh, you mean Frank."

Apparently, Popeye could read beyond the third grade level, so after checking a list and finally finding Carl's name in black and white, he removed the red rope blocking the entrance.

Then with a wave of a ham-sized fist, Popeye allowed him to pass. Several young ladies in line smiled Carl an invitation to join him.

Returning their smiles, he shook his head and said, "It's strictly a business meeting, ladies. I'm sorry."

Feigning disappointment, the girls formed their lips into a pout and returned to their gossiping.

The bar was packed with patrons preening and panting with suppressed passion, while hoping to make a connection with a willing member of the opposite sex. It was standing room only.

Young perspiring couples in the throes of some obscure, obscene mating dance crammed a postage-sized dance floor. Carl watched as the young ladies' low-cut blouses revealed an abundance of smooth, powdered silky breasts. Bouncing and quivering seductively, they threatened to fall out of their restraints.

Attempting to augment their imagined masculinity, the guys wore tight-fitting Levi jeans, snug colorful western shirts, name-brand cowboy hats and of course, boots.

The live country-western swing band advertised on a brightly-lit billboard outside must have been on a piss break. A long-haired, corn-rowed, raspy-voiced, black disc jockey was spinning CDs sounding like acid rock, with the volume set just below eardrum bursting level.

As he made his way to a brass-railed, marble-topped bar, a heady mixture of perfume and perspiration attacked Carl's nostrils.

("It reminds me of Friday night fights at Joe's place in

Hoboken, New Jersey.")

Six bartenders were behind the bar. Three were very attractive females, (one each redhead, blonde and brunette), wearing matching, low-cut western cowgirl blouses. It took Carl nearly five minutes to corral one of the fillies and order a J. D. and coke. Another two minutes were required to lasso the right brand and mix a weak drink. Then she delivered it with a flourish worthy of a red caped matador.

After handing the cute brunette a ten dollar bill, he received four wrinkled one dollar bills and a matching number of quarters in change.

He tipped her two dollars and stuffed the remainder into his front pocket. The neon bar light reflected off the barmaid's eyes, reminding him of a flickering candle at midnight. She gave him a brief appreciative smile and then turned her fleeting attention to another admirer/customer.

As Carl took a small sip, a huge hand descended from above and landed with a loud "smack" on his shoulder. Startled, he spilled a portion of his expensive, watered-down drink. Then he turned and stared at the chest of a huge man while thinking, "It has to be Tiny."

Slowly raising his eyes, Carl saw Frank looming over him, his smiling face outlined by a black Stetson.

Frank didn't know his own strength and Carl doubted anyone ever complained. When he slapped you on the shoulder, it was the equivalent of being hit by a Blivot, (ten pounds of shit in a one pound sack).

Taking a large sip of his pee water to steady his nerves and after finally recovering his wits, he said, "Hey, Frank."

"Hey, yourself; long time no see. What do you think of my place?"

"It's crowded. Business must be good."

Frank spread his huge hands wide, almost taking off the hats of two cowboys standing nearby.

"Sixth Street is a goldmine. These college kids love to drink, dance and chase the opposite sex, not necessarily in that order."

Realizing they were shouting to be heard over the din, Carl yelled, "Is there someplace we can go where we don't have to talk so loud?"

Frank nodded.

"Yeah, pal. Follow me upstairs. I put a ton of insulation in my office. A little country music goes a long way. Then I have to take a break."

His host turned from the bar, and as if by magic, an aisle through the ocean of humanity parted to allow him passage. Carl knew no one wanted to get in Frank's way. Quickly he jumped in behind Man Mountain Frank. After they passed, the sea of customers filled the void as if it never existed.

Frank opened a door in a far wall which appeared too small for his bulk. Carl waited as Tiny slipped through the tiny opening and held the door open. Then they entered a narrow hallway, where probably in violation of some obscure fire law, cases of Coors and Shiner beer were stacked high along one wall.

At the end of the hallway, a rickety flight of stairs with paint missing from the middle of the treads climbed to a second floor. As Frank led him up the stairway, risers creaked in protest at each step. After saying a silent prayer, Carl followed Tiny up the complaining staircase, through another small doorway and into a wide foyer.

There, Frank pulled a key chain from his pocket and opened a large, heavy oak door set into a brick wall. They entered a room spacious even in Texas standards. A high, coffered ceiling stretched across the entire width of the building, and the dark oak floor was highly polished.

In the front wall, four tall, wide windows overlooked a gaggle of people crowding the sidewalks below. Each opening was topped by heavy brown drapes mounted on a dark wooden pole.

A huge oak desk took up a large portion of the available space, with an oversized antique chair on brass rollers behind it. To the front were two straight-backed wooden chairs with black cushioned seats.

Along one wall a black leather couch accompanied a slim, gleaming, ebony coffee table. In one corner a massive safe stood like a silent sentinel. Two large bevel-edged mirrors reflected lighting from overhead recessed casings and neon lights from outside.

Pointing to the main feature of the room, Carl said, "That's a hell of a desk, Frank."

"It came from the Governor's mansion. That baby cost me five grand, and it's worth every penny."

Indicating the windows, he added, "I had to take out and replace those two to have the desk installed."

Then he motioned Carl into a straight-back chair and changed the subject.

"Enough talk about my office. Have a seat. What's on your mind?"

After sitting down, Carl said, "I know your time is valuable, so I'll come right to the point. We need a money man to finance a big score and we're willing to pay a premium fee."

"How much are we talking about?"

"We need two million dollars."

Frank's eyes lit up, his eyebrows lifted and he said, "It must be a big score. Do you need any help?"

Carl shook his head.

"Other than the money, we're okay. This job's out of state, at least six months off and involves robbing a Brinks armored truck. That's all I can tell you."

Frank appeared lost in thought. Carl kept his mouth shut and waited for Tiny to make the next move.

In time with a muffled drumbeat from below, Frank tapped his fingers on the top of his desk. Then finally he said, "I know someone with that type of money, but I won't mention his name. He operates out of Dallas, so I'll have to front this proposition for you. If I get his okay for a meet, you'll have to go to Dallas. He hates politicians and won't visit Austin for any reason."

"If you can get us the money we need, we'll travel anywhere, anytime. Tell your friend this is a very well planned job, with a payoff in the millions and something so bold no one else in the world has tried before."

Frank rocked forward in his chair, nodded and said, "You have my attention, so let me talk to my contact. I can't promise you anything, but I'll try. In the end, it'll be up to you to convince him to loan you the money. If I'm lucky, he'll give me a piece of the action for referring you.

"Just remember, if anything goes wrong and you can't repay the money on time and with interest, you'll be dead men walking."

Acknowledging the threat with a nod, Carl said, "We know, Frank."

Tiny picked his heavy frame out of his chair, stood up and said, "That being said, let's go downstairs and have a drink to our mutual success. Give me your number, and I'll let you know what happens."

Carl handed Tiny his card and replied, "Fine."

After putting the card in his shirt pocket, Frank waved Carl out the door, turned around, locked the door and led the way down protesting stairs.

They reentered the bar to find the music volume deafening. While they were upstairs, the band had resumed their noisy gig. Tall electronic speakers with red flashing lights inside pulsated wildly like blood through a ruptured vein. Carl felt powerful sound waves vibrate against his body like rolling surf waves breaking on a distant, windswept beach.

Frank flowed through a milling crowd like a coal steamer on Lake Erie, with Carl following in his swirling wake. The blonde bartender hurried to take Frank's order, as he motioned with his thumb for two young cowboys standing next to him to make room for Carl. With typical tact, Frank barked, "Move it."

They did.

Stepping up to the polished damp bar, Carl received a large glass of Jack Daniels and Coke. He raised the faux crystal glass, took a sip and discovered this drink was definitely not watered down. It was pure alcohol and burned his throat.

As they clicked their glasses together, Frank shouted above the noise, "To our mutual interests."

They took small sips of their drinks. Then Frank slapped Carl on the shoulder again and said, "I have to go. I'll be in touch."

Without another word, Tiny set his drink down and walked away. The sea of people parted again, as the Mississippi steamboat named Frank plowed through.

Too late to follow in his wake, Carl sat his unfinished drink on the bar and headed for the front door, slowly elbowing his way through a heavy, unyielding crowd.

Like cattle being led to a slaughter house, an even longer line of young preppies was leaning against a dirty brick wall. The young men pawed the sidewalk with their boots while waiting to gain entrance to the crowded watering hole.

After finding his parking lot, Carl checked his vehicle for any damage, found none, climbed in and drove away. The evening had turned cool and a smell of rain was in the air. Although the night air remained humid, Carl turned off the air conditioning, and rolled down the windows to let a brisk breeze blow through the car.

The wayward wind slowly cleansed the smell of the bar from Carl's clothes and cobwebs from his mind.

Chapter 6

Three days later, Frank phoned to say, "I got approval for you to see the money man I mentioned. His name is Mister Giacomo Remualdi. He's high up in the local Mafia in Dallas. As a result, people who have shit for brains refer to him as 'Don Giacomo'. If you want his approval, keep that in mind. Engage your brain before opening your mouth."

"We'll remember," Carl promised.

"Your appointment is Friday evening; eight p.m., at Number Three, Sycamore Drive, in Dallas. I suggest you go up a day early to check out the place. When you arrive, phone his secretary at 555-2843 and give her your phone number. If there's a change in your appointment, she'll call. You got it?"

"Yeah, Frank. Thanks."

Frank wasn't done yet; he offered more advice. "Treat Mister Remualdi with proper respect. He doesn't cuss and doesn't like those who do. Watch your mouth. If he likes you, he's a powerful friend. Piss him off, and you've got a dangerous enemy.

"One other thing, have your act together and come off as winners. Your actions reflect on me and my ability to spot quality people. Remember, it's not just your balls on the line, mine are too for recommending you."

Swallowing hard, Carl said, "We will, Frank. Thanks again for your help. Let us know what your fee is."

Frank laughed.

"We'll wait until you get back from Dallas to discuss that."

Later that afternoon, when Roger drove to Alan's home, he found a note on the front door: "Come on in."

After peeling the stick-um note from the door, Roger crinkled it into a ball and put it in his pocket. The door was unlocked, so he let himself in, locked the door behind him, searched for Alan and found him in front of his computer screen.

As he walked in, Roger asked, "How's it going, Alan? Where's A. J.?"

"He's out shopping for groceries. Most of your info is ready. This sounds like a complicated job. When are you going to fill me in?"

Roger pulled out a chair, sat down and said, "From the notes you gave us last time; I know you made some good guesses."

Alan yawned and stretched.

"I put two and two together. From the material you requested I know it has something to do with a road crew. Can you tell me the entire plan?"

"I'll give you the nuts and bolts. I'd like your opinion."

Over the next thirty minutes, Roger laid out his plan, while Alan sat on the couch, resting his feet on the shaky coffee table.

After listening attentively, he said, "No wonder Carl calls you a genius. I've seen those trucks on the road many times, but never have thought of something like this."

"Do you have any comments?"

"The basics are masterful. The only problem I see is that after you pull this job, Brinks will be aware of a flaw in their system. You could never do the same type of robbery again. It's too bad you couldn't pull off two or three heists before they wise up."

Roger's brow wrinkled as he thought about Alan's statement. Then he said, "It's funny, but Carl said the same thing."

Pausing again for a moment, he appeared to be lost in thought. Having seen Roger in action before, Alan wasn't surprised.

Then Roger smiled.

"You know, Alan, you're a genius yourself. Why not pull the

same job two or three times? If we can do it once, we can do it again."

Alan shook his head.

"I just told you they'll catch on after the first and you agreed. Weren't you listening?"

Roger's smile grew larger.

"Yeah, I was. But what if after the first robbery Brinks doesn't realize what's happening because there's no one to tell them? Suppose they were missing a truck, the driver and the guard?"

"What happens to them?"

Now Roger was grinning.

"We keep them for a while."

Alan looked shocked.

"Isn't that kidnapping?"

Roger grew serious again.

"In a sense of the word; yes. We'll have to consider the point, but you gave me a good idea."

Changing the subject abruptly, Roger said, "Right now I have more work for you, Alan. Can you hack into Brinks' computer and find out how much money each truck carries at any given time?"

Alan shrugged.

"Probably, but it will be a lot of data to download. Are you talking U.S.A. wide, or do you want to narrow the list down to a few states?"

Roger ticked off his choices on his fingers.

"Check Texas, New Mexico, Arizona, Nevada and Utah. Those are the states with wide open spaces.

"One place I want you to look at closely is Roswell, New Mexico. On Highway 285 heading north, we saw one Brinks truck, so there may be others. Even if there aren't, if the one we saw carries enough money to make it worthwhile, it's the truck I want to hit first."

Looking up from where he was making notes on his computer, Alan asked, "Anything else?"

"Yeah; we need to know how many guards are assigned to each truck and if there's a pattern to the assignments. Do larger payloads have more than one guard etcetera? You get the picture. Anything you discover will help."

When Roger returned home, he found Carl watching TV and said, "You have an admirer, Carl."

"Who is it?"

"It's your buddy, Alan. You two geniuses think alike."

"What do you mean?"

"He also thinks we should do more than one job."

"Where'd he get an idea like that?"

"You did say it was a shame we couldn't do more than one, didn't you?"

Carl nodded.

"Yeah, and you said after one robbery, Brinks would catch on. What changed your mind?"

"Let me explain."

Richard's intercom buzzed, and Mary said, "Mister Winters is on line four."

"Thank you."

He picked up the instrument and asked, "What's up, Darrin?"

"I've been tailing Roger and Carl for the past few days and there have been some interesting developments."

"Go ahead; I'm listening."

"One night last week, Carl met with an unsavory character named Frank Franzone in a bar in downtown Austin. They talked over a proposition requiring a large amount of money.

"I used my long distance microphone and heard the city of Dallas mentioned, so I believe our two friends will be headed there shortly to talk to someone about a loan to finance their next venture."

"So they've found a new job," Richard said. Then he asked, "Any idea what it is?"

"No, but I'll follow them to Dallas to find out. On another subject, while Roger seems to be a confirmed bachelor and plays the field, Carl has fallen in love with a lovely young woman who ran into his new convertible a few months ago. They've become an item and he spends several of his nights at her place."

"Good for him," Richard said. "Man can't live by thievery alone. Perhaps she'll steal his heart."

"You sound like a romantic."

"Love knows no boundaries, Darrin. Keep a sharp eye on our two felons. I'm very interested in what they're up to."

Chapter 7

As they sat watching news on FYI, Carl said, "I have a date with Julie tonight. I'll tell her we'll be out of town on business for a few days."

During the past few days, Carl spent several evenings with Julie renewing their love for each other after his long absence. If the old clichéd saying, "absence makes the heart grow fonder" was to be put to the test, they both would have received high marks.

The more time they spent together, the closer they became. Carl's plans of a possible marriage proposal were growing more serious each day. But with the new development of the Brinks trucks, he was still reluctant to tell Julie the truth about his chosen profession.

Tonight, they were eating at the Hong Kong restaurant on Sixth Street, enjoying a delicious Chinese dinner of marinated grilled shrimp, sweet and sour pork and sesame chicken served on steaming hot platters. Tempting aromas wafted around their heads and caressed their nostrils as Carl said, "I could eat a Panda if they cooked it right."

Julie laughed.

"I don't think it's on the menu."

Afterward, they spent a few quiet moments drinking hot tea, listening to Chinese music playing in the background and watching other customers.

Breaking the silence, Carl said, "I'll be out of town again for a few days. Roger and I have to meet some investors in Dallas on

Friday. We leave early tomorrow morning."

Julie frowned and said, "I'll miss you."

While walking back to the car, they found the evening had turned cooler. Carl gave her his jacket and Julie snuggled close.

At her apartment door, she kissed him and asked, "Can you stay the night?"

Carl grinned.

"Only if you'll let me leave about four a.m. – Roger wants to get on the road early."

After leading him into her apartment, she closed the door behind them and said, "Roger and your business in Dallas can wait until I'm through with you."

When Carl pulled into the driveway at five-thirty the next morning, he saw lights were on in the living room and kitchen. Already packed and ready to leave, Roger was waiting and said, "I have the information in my briefcase. The only item missing is the amount the trucks carry. Alan promised to have the figures tomorrow. We'll call him from Dallas."

As the day dawned clear and cool, they made their way toward I-35 through the daily, maddening Austin commuter crush. Finally the van crawled through bumper-to-bumper traffic onto crowded lanes leading north to Big D. When they reached Georgetown, traffic thinned and Carl set the cruise control at seventy.

As he drove, Carl listened to Roger practice his speech, found no fault in his presentation and said, "Stop worrying, Roger. You'll do fine. What's the worst thing Mister Remualdi can say; no? If he says yes, we're on a roll and can plan this job in earnest."

Roger decided to get back at Carl for his lousy puns by saying, "That's funny, I thought we were going to do the robberies in New Mexico, not Earnest, Colorado."

Carl shook his head, but Roger saw a smile flicker around the edge of his mouth.

After arriving at the hotel as planned, a valet took their keys while two bellboys unloaded the bags. They checked in and found their two-bedroom suite on the twelfth floor. Roger called the number Frank provided and talked to a secretary named Maria. She confirmed the meeting was still on with Mister Remualdi at eight p.m. Friday.

"Please arrive fifteen minutes early for screening. Give me your cell phone numbers and if there's a change in your schedule, I'll let you know. Feel free to enjoy the sights and sounds of Dallas. You don't have to remain cooped up in your hotel room."

"We will," Roger said. "I like your voice."

"Thank you," she said and disconnected.

He hung up while thinking, "So much for mixing romance with business."

When they tried to reach Alan, his answering machine picked up, so Roger left their number and told Alan to call ASAP.

Early the next morning the phone rang and Roger answered with a sleepy "Hello".

With a happy sounding voice, Alan said, "It's seven-thirty. Don't tell me you're still in bed. A. J. has me up every morning at six."

"Good morning, Alan. Good for you and A.J. What's up?"

"I have your information. I hope you appreciate my efforts."

"We do and hope the figures are favorable."

Without waiting for an answer, Alan asked, "You got a pen handy? Here goes. Two trucks depart weekly from Roswell carrying loads in the four to seven million range.

"There are several trucks in Las Vegas and most payloads exceed ten million. The problem is they don't travel long distances. But don't let that deter you. There's one great target traveling every Monday from Laughlin to Las Vegas with a load usually exceeding fifteen million."

"Good news, Alan. What about the other states?"

"I'm working on them, but it takes time to hack into their data base. Give me a couple more days."

Looking up, he saw Carl standing in his doorway and said, "Good enough," handed him the figures, and Carl whistled appreciatively.

Turning his attention back to Alan, Roger said, "I'm sharing your information with Carl. Thanks again for your speedy reply. When we get back I hope to have good news."

The next morning, after sleeping in until eight a.m., they ate a room service breakfast of steak and eggs, washed down with freshly brewed black coffee and orange juice.

During the night, a cold front blew in with severe thunderstorms, dropping large amounts of rain in some parts of the Metroplex and causing minor flooding.

The thunder woke Carl, but Roger slept through the deluge. As they ate, they watched the Weather Channel. After seeing reports of flooding, they were glad they arrived in Dallas a day early. On the Interstate, traffic was backed up for miles.

"Later this morning, if the streets are clear, we should locate the address Frank gave us," Roger said.

Carl nodded as he buttered another piece of toast. "It's a good way to spend part of the day. If we just sit around this room, I'll go bonkers."

In the lobby, a jovial, pot-bellied porter named John provided a Dallas map and marked the easiest route to Sycamore Drive while saying, "That's the ritzy district of Dallas. Only high rollers live there."

When they arrived at the small elite subdivision, where a large brick sign at the entrance designated the area as Rockwood Creek, they discovered John's prediction was correct.

Although there was no way to tell how many rooms each edifice contained, all were large and stately. Most featured tall, white columns, long, wide manicured lawns and broad-leafed trees to provide shade for sparkling blue pools.

Complete with canvas covered, stainless steel barbeque pits, brick, tiled or concrete patios dotted the surrounding landscape. Each house was separated from its neighbors by high, stout brick walls or ringed with tall, wrought-iron fences.

Sitting on a private cul-de-sac, dwarfing its nearest competitor, at number Three Sycamore Drive, they found the home of Mister Remualdi. It was a three-storied brick dwelling with arched windows and a portico featuring six white brick columns.

Looking around and mentally measuring other mansions, Carl said, "He has the biggest home in the neighborhood."

Roger smiled and remarked, "Crime must pay."

The mansion was surrounded by a closely clipped, immaculate lawn. Large oak trees stood like silent sentinels and sparkling white rocks outlined smaller shrubs and flower beds.

With eight-foot high spikes sticking up forebodingly every six inches, a wrought-iron fence enclosed the house and its acreage. At twenty-foot intervals, the wall was broken by thick, red brick columns.

Two matching massive columns supporting an impressive heavy gate comprised a front entrance. When it was closed, as now, an overlapping R was displayed in the center.

A security camera scanned the driveway and any visitors. Outside the gate, at one side of the driveway, a two-way radio console was supported on an aluminum pole.

Carl nodded in its direction.

"Apparently he doesn't like unannounced visitors."

Behind the fence, two large Doberman Pinschers ran free while two burly men in black sweaters playfully threw sticks to retrieve.

Carl watched saliva drip from the animals' mouths and remarked, "I wouldn't want to be the guy climbing over the fence in the middle of the night."

Roger agreed and added his astute observation, "At least we know where we're going. Check to see how long it takes to get back to the hotel."

By Carl's watch, it took thirty-seven minutes.

He said, "We'll leave at seven p.m."

A light rain and drizzle fell on and off during the remainder of the day. After the rain washed away most of the smog in the city, the night air was cool and refreshing. As they made their second trip to Mister Remualdi's home, there were still a few puddles in the streets, but they encountered no flooding.

When they arrived at the gate, Roger pushed the call button and announced, "Mister Booth and Mister James to see Mister Remualdi."

A husky male voice sounding like Ironsides on TV

answered, "Wait for the gate to open and stop completely. Then proceed to the top of the driveway and park. Turn off your ignition, but do not exit your vehicle. You will be met and given further instructions. Do you understand?"

After glancing at Carl to be sure he heard the message, Roger said, "Yes, we do."

"Thank you. The gate is opening."

With a soft click and a low hum, the entrance swung open. It took less than a minute, but seemed longer.

After the gate shuddered to a stop, Roger released the brake and eased the van to the top of the driveway, where he stopped and shut off the engine as instructed. They sat motionless as two heavily muscled men in dark suits approached the vehicle, one from each side.

Carl whispered, "The guards look like they could bend steel bars with their eyebrows."

A third man stood nearby with a Doberman pinscher straining against its leash.

Ironsides said, "Good evening, gentlemen. Please step slowly from the vehicle and keep your hands in sight at all times."

They stepped out as ordered and heard a low growl.

"Thank you," Ironsides said. "Please place your hands on top of the vehicle and spread your legs. Do not make any sudden moves."

After they complied with his request, the two frisked them professionally as the dog handler moved a few steps closer.

Roger thought, "Whoever Mister Remualdi is, he doesn't take any chances with visitors. These guys are pros."

When he was satisfied their visitors were clean, Ironsides said, "Move away from the van so we can search your vehicle."

After completing the search, including Roger's briefcase, the other guard gave an okay signal and handed it to Ironsides.

Their guide gestured toward the mansion.

"Please accompany us to the house. Your vehicle will be parked. We'll walk the remainder of the way."

As they fell into step with Ironsides and his assistant, Carl noted the dog handler and his canine companion were walking a few paces to one side and said, "Your security is commendable."

"Thank you. We do our best for our employer."

Approximately one hundred feet from the front steps, Ironsides said, "Don't be startled by the lights."

Suddenly the entire area was bathed in an explosion of brightness as hidden spotlights in the ground lit up the exterior of the home. Roger was half-blinded and Carl threw up an arm to shade his eyes. Behind them, they heard the dog growl again.

Glancing at their guards, Roger saw they had silently donned dark glasses.

Ironsides shrugged as if they should have known and said, "Motion detectors."

As they approached the house, it was obviously larger than they thought. Two massive, dark stained wooden doors were set into a grey bricked façade. Ten wide, green marble steps led to the spacious entranceway.

After mounting the steps two at a time and opening the door on the right, Ironsides said, "Please follow me, gentlemen."

They entered a large, round foyer tiled in yellow and red Italian marble, featuring a concentric pattern of hand laid squares.

Leading upward to the second floor were two matching curved stairways carpeted in a rich red color similar to the one in Tara. The entire foyer was open from the ground to the third floor ceiling, and lit by a shining crystal chandelier at least eight feet in diameter.

In the center of the foyer was an antique, handmade wooden table with a circular marble top, featuring four sculpted legs curving upwards and forming a cage in which a carved ball was held captive. Atop the table was a briefcase.

Flanking each stairway was a large, antique half-circle table with matching marble top. Hanging above these tables were identical tall, bevel-edged mirrors. On the surface of each table was a large, fluted antique vase filled with an assortment of freshly cut flowers.

Beams from the chandelier reflected into the mirrors and back again, like lightning on a cold winter night.

After placing Roger's briefcase alongside the other on the

center table, Ironsides opened both, removed all documents from the original and placed them in the duplicate.

Pointing to the replacement, he said, "Your briefcase will be returned to your vehicle. Your new one holds a supply of paper, pens and a calculator. When your business is completed, you may keep it as a gift from Mister Remualdi."

Ironsides handed Roger the replacement briefcase, and then led them up the right hand staircase. A long hallway lined with dark oak doors was at the top. He turned to the right, and they followed to an open door at the end, where he ushered them into a large den, tiled with light brown marble flecked with gold streaks.

In the background, light classical music was playing softly through hidden speakers. Bookcases lined two walls with shelves containing leather bound books and a collection of Italian crystal. Overhead recessed lighting reflected brightly from the glass.

Three oils of peasants working in fields hung from a third, while a large portrait of a seascape dominated the fourth.

Below the largest painting sat an ornately carved wooden desk with curved legs, and a brown leather chair on rollers. In front were two chairs with comfortable-looking seats and upholstered arms.

After leading them to a matching couch and long, low coffee table near one bookcase, Ironsides said, "Please be seated, gentlemen. Mister Remualdi will be with you shortly."

Without another word, with his footsteps cushioned by a soft oriental rug, Ironsides walked silently from the room and closed the door behind him.

Knowing their actions were probably being monitored, Roger and Carl sat in silence for a few minutes. Then the door opened and Ironsides re-entered, followed by a man resembling a motion picture Mafia leader. They knew instinctively this man was their host.

Ironsides waved them to their feet.

"Gentlemen, Mister Remualdi."

Approximately five feet, eight inches tall, their host was heavy in stature with a full head of grey hair. His suntanned face was rugged and he wore a neatly trimmed, wide moustache beneath an aristocratic nose. Under his tailor-made dark grey suit he wore a light grey shirt and a blue paisley tie.

Walking toward Roger with his hand extended, he said, "Ah, Mister Booth, I'm pleased to meet you."

His handshake was firm.

Turning to Carl, he said, "And you're Mister James. Welcome to my home."

He shook Carl's hand with the same masculine grip, as Roger said, "Thank you for seeing us. We know you're a busy man."

"True; but never too busy to see such enterprising young men. Your latest con in Houston was masterful, well planned and executed."

Noting their shocked looks, he chuckled and said, "Don't be surprised. I know you two well. It's always wise to know your friends and much wiser to know your enemies even better. Rest assured, Gentlemen, I consider you in the first category."

"Thank you again, Sir," Roger said.

"Please be seated. Frank gave me a glowing report and said you have a job requiring capital. Would you tell me about it?"

"Certainly, sir," Roger said. He sat down on a chair next to the desk while Carl sat stiffly on the edge of the other.

Roger began his presentation by saying, "Let me show you some figures and explain our plan in detail."

Their host leaned back in his brown leather chair, folded his hands together as if in prayer and said, "Proceed."

For the next twenty minutes, after handing their host a copy of their proposal with Alan's figures penciled in, Roger outlined the plan for the first robbery and subsequent robberies, (providing the first was successful).

Mister Remualdi listened attentively, and although there was a pad of paper and pen nearby, made no notes.

When Roger completed his briefing, Mister Remualdi said, "Your plan is ingenious. I don't know why someone hasn't come up with the idea before. It's simple enough, but are you sure your figures are correct?"

"Yes, Sir. Our computer expert has never failed us in the past, and we believe his estimates for this job."

"And you think you can successfully perform more than one robbery?"

"Yes, Sir, we do. If we detain the drivers and guards, they can't report how they were robbed. After two or three trucks disappear, the drivers won't stop for anything."

Mister Remualdi continued to nod in agreement.

"I assume you have the manpower, but not the money. Am I correct?"

"Yes, Sir," Roger repeated. "We need at least two million dollars to purchase the ranch, vehicles and other equipment."

While rubbing his moustache with a knuckle of his left hand, Mister Remualdi stared Roger in the eyes and said, "That's a hefty amount. If we choose to make such a loan, our organization would require a significant amount of interest. Have you taken this into consideration?"

"Yes, we have."

Their host nodded again and asked, "Could you afford an interest payment of thirty-five percent? This amount is in addition to the normal six percent we charge for a loan through our bank."

Roger nodded to indicate he understood the intricacies of the deal and said, "Yes, Sir."

Referring to Roger's proposal, Mister Remualdi said, "You're a very perceptive young man. I'm glad to see you also have business sense. If we agree to your proposal, we will require payment of the entire investment in full, including interest within seven days of your first job. Frank assures me he told you the consequences should you fail to repay the loan."

"After the first robbery, the loan will be repaid in full," Roger said. "The same basic equipment will be used for all the jobs, so I don't see any additional expenses."

Mister Remualdi leaned forward, placed his hands on his desk and stared intently as he said, "If things go wrong on your first attempt, there won't be any way for you to repay us."

Carl spoke for the first time.

"We'll make sure the job goes off without a hitch."

Mister Remualdi held Carl's eyes with his as he said, "Be sure you do."

Now that the well had been primed, Carl added, "There's one more consideration. You'll have the ranch plus all the equipment as collateral."

"True, but the price of the ranch would not equal the loan amount, nor would we make any interest. My associates and I will consider all of this. Besides the money, do you require anything else?"

Wondering if this was the proper place to bring it up, and then deciding it was, Roger said, "If we receive the loan, we'll need to acquire a rocket propelled grenade and launcher."

Mister Remualdi raised his eyebrows as if he was surprised by Roger's request; however, he didn't hesitate in answering, "My representative will give you the name of a contact. Is that all?"

"Yes, Sir, we can acquire all other material and equipment on our own. Thank you for your time and assistance."

When their host stood up and said, "Thank you, Gentlemen," it was apparent the interview was over.

After shaking hands with the Don, as if by magic, the door opened. Ironsides stood there waiting to escort them from the mansion. He waited patiently until Roger stuffed his paperwork into the new briefcase and closed it. Then he said, "Right this way, gentlemen."

When they walked out the front door, Roger and Carl found their van waiting with motor idling. Roger turned to thank their guide and discovered they were alone. Without another word, Ironsides had disappeared behind a now closed front door.

As the van topped a small rise, the front gate opened. While waiting, Roger turned to Carl and placed his finger in front of his mouth. Then he made another silent motion with his hand like a bug crawling across the dash.

When they returned to their hotel and parked, Roger carried both briefcases to the rear, raised the hatch and placed them on the carpeted floor. As Carl watched silently, he removed a heavy Mexican rug from a plastic bag and covered both cases.

After entering their room, Roger immediately clicked on the TV, turned the volume up high and signaled Carl to follow him to a desk, where he picked up a pen and wrote, "Take off your suit and put it in a garment bag."

They changed, left their room and walked down a hallway to the elevators. Then Roger dialed a number on his cell phone from memory.

When Alan answered, Roger said, "I have more work for you."

Alan didn't sound too surprised.

"What now?"

"Do you know someone in Dallas or Fort Worth who could locate electronic bugs?"

"Let me check my files," Alan said, and laid down the phone.

In the background Roger heard a computer hum. Then Alan came back on the line, "One of our guys, Roscoe Hynes, owns an electronic surveillance business in Dallas. He knows me, so mention my name. His number is 555-1475. What's up?"

"It's probably nothing," Roger said. "But I'll feel better knowing if we were bugged or not. Thanks, Alan. I'll get back to you."

When Roger dialed the number and got a recording, after the beep, he mentioned Alan's name, gave Roscoe a brief resume, left his cell phone number and asked Roscoe to call ASAP.

"Let's go eat," Roger said, leading the way to the elevator.

They ordered their meals in a small restaurant off the lobby, and Roger was about to say something, when he felt his cell phone vibrate. He answered, and a hoarse voice asked, "Is this Roger Booth?"

"Yes, it is."

"I'm Roscoe Hynes. I got your message. Are you a friend of Alan's?"

"Yes, I am. You come highly recommended."

Roscoe coughed again before he asked, "Were you in our old Army unit? Your name sounds familiar."

"I drove a tank in Kuwait."

"I thought so," Roscoe said. "What do you need?"

"We had an interview tonight with a very important man. I

have a feeling he wants to learn more about our business. I would like you to check our van, two briefcases and our suits for listening devices. I may be wrong and there might not be any bugs. Either way, I'll pay the freight."

"Okay," Roscoe said. "How soon do you want this done?"

"Tomorrow morning will be fine," Roger said. "We check out of the hotel at nine. Can we meet you on the way out of town?"

Roger heard him cough again. Then he said, "Sure; I don't like the night air anyway. You got a pen and paper? My address is 2575 Highland Lane, in south Dallas. Look for I-35 East, get off at McCart exit and take a right. Highland Lane is the second left."

"We'll be there tomorrow morning between nine and ten."

The next morning, it was still cool, but the weatherman on Channel Seven forecasted no rain for the immediate future. After checking out and loading their luggage aboard the van, Roger drove carefully through rush hour traffic. Carl kept the radio volume on high and sang along with any songs he knew.

Following Roscoe's directions, they found 2575 Highland Lane. It was a large yellow colonial-style house setting a short distance from the busy street. A withered brown lawn was a foot tall and the long thin lot was filled with poorly maintained flowering bushes.

A worn out, badly dented, blue Dodge pickup with three flat tires and one empty rim sat in front of one stall of a two-car garage. A late model, white Ford panel truck was parked a few feet from the other paint-scarred door.

Roger pulled the van up to the nose of the newer vehicle, and they climbed out. They turned to walk down the sidewalk and were startled when an older, short, bald man stepped from behind the van. He was wearing grease-stained overalls with "Roscoe" stitched in red over one pocket. Holding his index finger in front of his mouth, he indicated they should continue on to the house.

As they reached the door, they turned to watch Roscoe circle their van while holding a small antenna in his right hand and monitoring an electronic device with his left.

Nodding an answer to his own silent question, he walked to the rear of the van and quietly opened the hatch. He waved the antenna over the briefcases and suit bags, nodded again, left the rear hatch open and walked toward them.

When Roscoe reached the door, he opened it, waved them into the interior and followed quietly. After closing the door, he turned to face them and said, "Yep, you've got a shit load of bugs aboard your van; at least three or four."

Without waiting for a comment from either, he asked, "Do you want me to pinpoint the bugs and disable them, or leave them operating? If they're turned off, whoever is listening will know. If you don't, you'll never be able to talk without being overheard. It's your choice."

"Can you tell how powerful the bugs are?" Carl asked.

Roscoe shook his head.

"Not unless I examine them up close and personal, but I'll bet they can broadcast for a mile or two. The signal's pretty strong."

Roger asked, "Can you pinpoint where the bugs are without alerting the guys who put them there?"

"Yeah, I can scan your suits, van and briefcases without disturbing them. Then I'll know where they're located."

"Go ahead," Roger said. "I want to know how many and where they are."

"What do these fellows want to know?" Roscoe asked.

"It's none of your business, Roscoe, but I like your style. In the near future, we may need someone with your knowledge and experience. Are you open to a spur-of-the-moment invitation that could bring some big bucks your way?"

"Anytime, just give me a call."

"Let's go out to the van," Roger said. "You stay here, Carl. The less noise the better."

Pointing toward the kitchen, Roscoe said, "There's coffee on the stove. Help yourself. There's also soda pop and beer in the refrigerator."

Although it was early, the thought of a cold beer made Carl's mouth water. He found the refrigerator and was halfway through a bottle of Coors' Light, when Roger and Roscoe returned.

Roger's face was grim with worry when he said, "Roscoe found five bugs. One's located in the arm rest of your seat, Carl; and there are two in our suits and one in each briefcase. These guys were thorough; so we'll have to watch what we say."

Surprising Roger, Carl said, "To hell with them."

"What do you mean?"

Carl was on his high horse. His face grew stern and he said, "I'm tired of this Mickey Mouse shit and I'm not going to have to watch my step for the next two hundred miles. These guys can kiss my ass. Why should we keep the bugs in place and let them listen? I've got a better idea."

Roger thought for a moment and then said, "Maybe you're right. What's your plan?"

"I say we ditch the bugs so they'll know we're on to them and at the same time, send them a message."

Wondering what Carl had in mind, Roger said, "Okay, you lead and I'll follow. How much do we owe you, Roscoe?"

"One hundred dollars will do nicely. Then keep me in mind for this job you mentioned. I make a pretty good living here, but I'd like to get away. The pollution's killing me."

After handing Roscoe the money, Roger said, "Will do. Thanks for your help. We better get back on the road. I'm anxious to see what Carl has in mind."

"Turn in here," Carl said

As they drove down the freeway, Carl found an electronic device in the arm rest, carefully removed it and held it in his hand. Following his instructions, Roger turned into a Burger Barn drive-in and pulled up to a large plastic covered menu board, where they heard a metallic voice boom out, "May I help you?"

From across the seat, Carl said, "Yeah, we'll have two cups of coffee, black."

The clerk's voice changed. Now it bubbled out as if he was deep inside a wash bucket full of soap.

"Yes, Sir. Will that be all?"

Reaching across Roger, Carl placed the listening device on the side of the call-in box and said, "Yeah, how much do we owe you?"

Static screeched like a hoot owl searching for a mate, as the barely understandable heavy-metal rocker said, "The total will be two dollars and seventy-seven cents. Please drive to the second window."

Roger pulled up to the window, paid for the drinks, picked up two leaky, cardboard coffee cups, handed one to Carl and drove off.

Ten minutes later, as they drove along an access road to I-35, Carl said, "Stop here for a minute. I need to take a leak."

Following his instructions, Roger pulled up in front of a music store where an outside speaker was blasting out loud hard-rock music.

With music vibrating in his ears, Carl opened the rear hatch, took out their garment bags, searched their suits and located both bugs. If he made any noise, he didn't give a damn. Six feet from the largest speaker, he selected a tall telephone pole studded with nails from one too many advertisements, and attached the two bugs to it.

After climbing back into the van, he said, "I feel a lot better."

The briefcases took a moment of thought, but Carl was up to the challenge. Leaning over, he whispered, "How attached to the briefcase are you?"

Motioning him closer, Roger said, "Save the documents. Shit-can both cases."

"Got ya."

A museum of railroad memorabilia is located forty miles south of Dallas on I-35 East, where thousands of train and railroad related items are displayed inside the main brick building. Outside, steel train tracks filled with various aging to modern rail cars are spiked to creosoted railroad ties.

Steam engines dating back to the eighteen hundreds are on display, but the museum is best known for its steam whistle collection. From nine a.m. until six p.m., every hour on the hour, a variety of steam whistles and bells plays a very loud rendition of "I've Been Working on the Railroad".

When Roger stopped the van in a parking lot, Carl stepped out carrying both empty briefcases. Fourteen feet from the biggest whistle, he found a red, wide-wheeled baggage cart with several old tattered suitcases and valises on its platform.

After wedging the lids of the briefcases open with folded napkins, he added them to the pile, returned to the van, got in and said; "Now we can talk about anything. Let's go home."

Chapter 8

Beginning his latest report to Mister Murdock, Darrin said, "Two days ago, I tailed Roger and Carl to Dallas, where they stayed in a hotel.

"The evening of the second day, they drove to see a Mister Giacomo Remualdi, who lives in a swanky part of north Dallas.

"I checked around and discovered he is purported to be the leader of the main Mafia family in town. I find it very interesting Mister Remualdi held an hour-long talk with Roger and Carl in his private home."

"Your news is fascinating," Richard said. "Is there anything else?"

"Yes, Sir; this morning your two con men stopped off at the home and business address of a Mister Roscoe Hynes. From Mister Hynes actions, I take it he's an electronics expert. He checked over their van for possible bugs."

"Did he find any eavesdropping devices?"

"I believe so," Darrin said. "On the way back to Austin, Roger and Carl made stops at three different locations.

"The last place was a museum of railroad memorabilia, where I saw Carl leave two briefcases atop a railroad baggage cart. After they left, I checked the items and found two small but very powerful listening devices, one in each briefcase."

"You left them in place, didn't you?"

"Of course, Sir."

"Where are my friends now?"

Darrin smiled.

"I believe they're headed back to Austin. I'll pick them up at their home, keep them under surveillance and report to you again when I have more information."

"Keep up the good work, Darrin," Richard said and disconnected.

As they continued on their way to Austin, the sun broke through a thin line of clouds and seemed to smile down on their recent endeavors. Carl's success in disposing of the listening devices left him in a good mood, and he searched for more country music. As Roger drove, he maintained an upbeat attitude concerning their chances for the loan and began making plans for the future.

When they rang Alan's bell, A. J. opened the door. Wearing a zippered, light blue jogging outfit with black and white running shoes, he looked fit and healthy. When A. J. saw them, his black face lit up with a bright smile.

"Come on in guys. Alan's on the treadmill and still has ten minutes to go. We have time for a cup of coffee."

They shook hands with A. J., followed him into the kitchen and noted it was cleaned recently. Roger could see the presence of A. J. in the transformation.

When they passed the computer room, the terrible table was missing, and Roger said, "I see you got rid of the pile of crap Alan called a coffee table."

A. J. nodded.

"Believe me, it was the first thing to go."

Carl laughed.

"I don't think the garbage men will take it."

Still chuckling, A. J. walked to the counter, took three cups from a cabinet and said, "Sit down and relax guys."

The coffee pot perked merrily and an aroma of freshly brewed coffee filled their nostrils. A. J. put the cups on the table and reached for the coffee pot.

"So, how did the trip pan out?"

"We don't know yet," Roger said. "Mister Remualdi was very interesting and has an outstanding organization. Their security is the best I've ever seen."

Changing the subject, Carl asked, "How many pounds has Alan lost so far?"

"Six," A. J. said. "He's done remarkably well and hasn't cheated on his diet. When he wants to, Alan can put away some groceries."

Motioning toward the doorway, Roger said, "Speak of the devil."

Alan stood leaning heavily against the door jamb in a grey running suit soaked with perspiration. His face was red and he appeared winded.

"What's up, buddy?" Roger asked.

Alan took a few gulps of air before speaking.

"There they sit; my jailers and torturer, drinking coffee in my kitchen while I run my ass off. It figures."

Stumbling over to the remaining chair, he sat down heavily. An aroma of perspiration filtered from his damp clothing. When he placed his arms on the table, sweat ran off his forearms and formed into small pools.

Alan tried to joke.

"Man, I'd kill for a doughnut."

A. J. got up from his chair, poured Alan a large glass of ice water, handed it to him and said, "Drink this. Then cool down for a few more minutes and go take a shower. By the time you get back, sausage and eggs will be ready."

Tilting the glass up, Alan emptied it down his parched throat and smacked his lips. Then he turned to Roger and Carl and asked, "To what do I owe the pleasure of your company?"

"We wanted to know how you're doing on your diet and ask about the Brinks payloads," Roger said. "Did you find anything interesting?"

"There are a couple of items. Every week a truck from Laughlin hauls a lot of money and they don't use a big armored vehicle."

"How much money is 'a lot'?" Carl asked.

"The most they carried was twenty-two million. An average load can be anywhere from fifteen to seventeen million."

"And they don't use a heavily armored truck to transport such a large amount?" Roger asked. "I wonder why."

Alan yawned and said, "I think it's because Laughlin sits on the Colorado River and there's only one road heading north which has steep inclines and sharp winding turns. A larger vehicle would have a hell of a time climbing those hills and might overheat."

"A smaller truck will make our job easier," Carl said. "It means less weight for the eighteen-wheeler. How often does this truck make its run?"

"It leaves very early every Monday morning. The earliest dispatch was 0600 hours and the latest 0800. They must like to beat the heat."

"How many employees are on the truck?" Carl asked.

"One driver and one guard."

"That's good news, Alan," Roger said. "What's the other interesting item?"

"I double-checked the Roswell schedule and discovered I missed a truck. This is a large one, the same type you saw on the way to Albuquerque. It makes the run between Roswell and Albuquerque once a month carrying an average of ten million dollars. Again, there's one driver and one guard assigned."

"Is this truck in addition to the one we saw?" Roger asked.

"Yeah, the one you saw travels the same road and averages between five to seven million."

"The first one still makes a tempting target," Carl said. "How many guards are in this truck?"

"The same; one driver and one guard. Why pay for an extra guard when you got by with one for so many years?"

"Brinks is in for a surprise," Roger said. "I agree with Carl. We could get our feet wet on a fairly easy job and still make enough to pay off Mister Remualdi."

A. J. had listened attentively, but remained silent. Now he asked, "What kind of job do you have in mind for me?"

Holding up his arms as if showing his muscles, Roger said, "You'll be our training NCO, A. J. This will be a military operation, so everyone has to be in top shape. Making sure they are will be your responsibility, plus you'll have a place on the team."

"If you're willing to talk about the job in front of me, I

thought I must be in. That's cool; I could use a large piece of change. Flo keeps asking for more child support. If I make enough, maybe I can buy the bitch off."

Sensing that A. J.'s blood was beginning to boil, Alan interceded, "How did it go in Dallas? What are your chances?"

"It was a very interesting meeting," Roger said.

With Carl's help, Roger told them about the visit with Mister Remualdi.

When they heard how Carl disposed of the bugs, Alan said, "Damn, Carl, your idea was cute."

A. J. agreed.

"After a few hours of listening to crap, I think they'll catch on."

"And so," Roger concluded, "we think our chances are good."

A.J. said, "It's time for you to hit the shower, Alan. Can you guys stay for breakfast?"

"Why not? Thanks for the invite."

When he returned from his shower, Alan wore a light green shirt and a pair of tan Dockers. Roger noted he had moved his belt in one notch. The old, badly bruised hole stood out on the leather.

Alan held a file of papers in his hands. After sitting down and beginning to eat, he got down to business.

"I checked the multiple listings and there are five ranches for sale along Highway 285 between Roswell and I-40. From the descriptions they look promising, but the owners are asking more then one million. The lowest price I found is one million, two hundred and fifty thousand."

Roger shrugged.

"If and when he calls, Mister Remualdi and I'll have to talk about the difference."

"Think positive, buddy," Carl said. "It'll be when."

Three days later, A. J. brought Roger and Carl a list of other possible targets. After reviewing them, they still chose the three trucks discussed earlier.

Each passing day without a call from Mister Remualdi made them worry more about their chances. To keep their minds occupied, they reviewed the details of the first robbery. Everything added up to a successful job. Now it was up to the Don.

Seven days after their meeting, Mister Remualdi finally phoned. His first words echoed those of Alan.

"Your estimate of one million dollars for a ranch in New Mexico is a bit low. You may need as much as two million."

Roger apologized for his error.

"I agree, Sir. Several realtors told me the same thing."

"Think nothing of it, Mister Booth. My association will lend you up to two million dollars. The interest rates I quoted are still in effect."

"Thank you, Sir. We appreciate your confidence in us."

"My associates and I believe your job is a good investment. The additional funds you require will be distributed on an as needed basis. Your expenses should be minimal, not to exceed another one million dollars."

"That amount will serve our purposes nicely," Roger said. "Thank you again."

"The loan is subject to one restriction," Mister Remualdi warned.

Roger feared there might be a catch, but kept his cool and asked, "Yes, Sir. What is that?"

"One of our people will join you to keep track of your expenditures."

Breathing a sigh of relief, Roger said, "Of course. Your man will be welcomed here."

The Don corrected Roger's erroneous assumption, "My representative is not a man. She is my daughter, Maria, who served for many years as my secretary and assistant. Maria is very knowledgeable in financial matters. I believe her services will be indispensable in assisting you and keeping your expenses to a minimum."

Roger found the addition of a woman to the equation intriguing, so asked, "When will she arrive?"

"Maria will leave for Austin tomorrow morning, contact you and present the loan documents for your signature. Until she can arrange permanent accommodations, she'll stay with relatives in Austin. Remember, I trust Maria with my money and life. Treat her with the same respect you would offer me."

"We will, Sir."

"Thank you. Do a good job and make us all proud. Goodbye for now."

Carl had been listening on the speaker phone. After Roger hung up, he could hardly contain his happiness at the good news. He stood up and slapped Roger on the back.

"Congratulations Buddy. In the next few months we have our work cut out. Maria is something else to think about. How are you going to handle her?"

Spreading his hands wide, Roger said, "Just the way I told the Don. Hell, she already knows our plans. We'll treat her as one of the guys."

"If she's a good-looking woman, it might be hard to do."

Carl's words echoed Roger's thoughts, but he didn't reply.

Two days later, Maria called. Roger recognized her voice as the secretary he spoke with in Dallas.

"I apologize for not phoning sooner, but I arrived late last night and didn't want to disturb you. I have the paperwork for the loan. When and where would you like to meet?"

"What about noon today? Why don't you stop by here first? We can sign the papers and then go to lunch. Do you like Tex-Mex food, Miss Remualdi?"

"If we're going to work together, Roger, let's use our first names. Please call me Maria. Yes, I love Mexican food. I have your address. I'll drop by at eleven-thirty."

"We look forward to meeting you in person."

A few minutes before noon, a black Jaguar convertible pulled to the curb across the street. The top was down and the driver was a female; a young woman in her late twenties with long, raven black hair hanging halfway down her back.

After taking a small brush from her handbag, she ran it through wind-tousled hair. Roger saw she was very pretty and her eyes were dark. From this distance he couldn't tell if they were black or deep blue. She wore very little makeup, allowing her natural beauty to shine through. Her face and arms were tanned and a subdued shade of red lipstick outlined a full, sensual mouth.

The car door opened, she stepped out, and Roger caught a fleeting glimpse of long, slender, well-tanned legs. Her waist was thin, she was well endowed and her jet-black dress matched her hair. It took little to improve on perfection, but a single strand of black pearls hung around her neck.

Reaching into the rear seat of the convertible, Maria retrieved a briefcase similar to the one Roger received from her father several days ago. Then she turned and walked toward the front door.

"Our guest has arrived, Carl," Roger said. "She's a very pretty woman. Behave yourself."

"Don't worry about me. I'm already spoken for."

The door bells chimed, Carl opened the door and Maria shook his hand while saying, "Good morning, Mister James. Or should I call you Carl?"

("How the hell does she know who I am? I'd remember if I met her. She's a knockout.")

"Good morning, Maria. Please call me Carl."

Giving her hand to Roger, she said, "And you're Roger. At last we meet."

Roger clasped her small manicured hand in his. "Welcome to Austin."

Maria smiled as she looked into his eyes and said, "You're probably wondering how I knew which was which. I watched your presentation to my father several times, so I'm well aware of whom you both are."

Carl sounded shocked as he asked, "We were video-taped?"

"Naturally," Maria said. "As you know by now, my father leaves very little to chance."

Before they could respond, she held up her hand and said, "Before we go any further, let me make a few things clear. First, I'm not here to interfere with your plans. You run the show, Roger. If you ask me to do something I don't agree with, I'll let you know. Then we can settle our differences as equals.

"Second, I'm not here to spy. My father has a business

arrangement with you and I'm his representative. I'm here to protect his interests and control the way you spend his money. Do we understand each other?"

They both nodded, and Roger said, "Yes."

"Very well; let's get the paperwork out of the way and after lunch I'll fax it to my father's office. You're free to pursue any land you think will serve your purpose, but the cost shouldn't exceed two million dollars."

"Fine," Roger said. "As soon as the paperwork's completed, we'll leave for New Mexico. We have leads on several properties for sale. I hope to find and buy a ranch within a week."

Maria continued to smile.

"While you're gone, I'll find a place to live and buy some furniture. By the time you return, I should be settled in, ready to go to work."

"We may extend our trip for another week to travel to Laughlin," Roger said. "Our computer expert discovered another interesting target there."

Maria nodded.

"When the phone is installed in my new apartment, I'll leave the number on your answering machine. If you need to reach me, my cell phone number is 555-3970."

As she laid out the paperwork, Maria explained everything thoroughly while Roger thought, "For the next few months, it's going to be interesting, working with this beautiful woman."

Looking up, she caught him staring at her and blushed momentarily, but in a moment was all business again. Maria avoided looking directly at Roger until she finished explaining the documents.

As long as it took to get approval, it seemed strange to Roger that it required only a few minutes to sign their lives away.

Afterward, Maria gathered up the finished product, placed the papers in her briefcase and said, "Here are your copies, Roger."

Their fingers touched and he felt a tingle.

Maria felt it too and wondered, "God, what's going on here?"

Regaining her composure she said, "I'll follow you. After

lunch I have to find an apartment."

"We'll be using Roger's tan Oldsmobile van," Carl said. "My car is in the shop for an oil change."

"While we're talking about his vehicle, have Carl tell you about his accident," Roger said. "I think he's in love with the woman who hit his car."

As usual, lunch at Tres Amigos was delicious. Roger and Maria ate enchiladas with green chilies and Carl opted for a large serving of chicken fajitas.

Maria enjoyed Carl's explanation of "the Day of the Accident" and was intrigued that he and Julie were now an "item".

After lunch, they accompanied Maria to her car, where she said, "Call me when you get back. As soon as we receive the contract, the loan will be approved."

Then she changed the subject abruptly by saying, "By the way, my father wishes to congratulate you on the ease in which you discovered the listening devices. There are very few of his associates who realize he can monitor their conversations."

Sensing they were speechless, she laughed, "I see my announcement surprises you. Don't worry. The bugs were more of a test of your intelligence than an information gathering device. My father knew you discovered the microphones the first day and was pleased with your ability to spot trouble."

Roger was first to regain his composure and said, "Your father is full of surprises."

"I'll tell him you said so."

After Maria departed, Roger said, "Okay, we have the money approved, so we need to get to work. Pack your gear and let's get on the road."

Bright and early the next morning they departed for Roswell under clear blue skies. After crossing the Texas state line, they traveled the same desolate highways, but now things looked a little brighter. The possibility of a big score led them on like a shining beacon.

Roger said, "I have some thoughts about our electronic

gizmos. The most important item is the message board like the one we saw in Houston at the comedy club."

"Yeah," Carl said. "I remember when the comedian held it up to his ear. The words he programmed into it scrolled out like they were coming out of his mind and onto the board. He was cool and the gag got a lot of laughs."

Roger chuckled at the recollection.

"Although Alan could probably find one on the internet, I think we'd be better off letting Roscoe Hynes take on the responsibility. What did you think of the old codger? Do you believe he'd be willing to join our team?"

Carl nodded in agreement.

"He knew his business. I've been thinking about the transponders and how we need someone who can disable them. Maybe Roscoe is our man."

"There's also the possibility the guard or driver might have a cell phone," Roger said. "We can't let them make a call."

"I may have the answer to that," Carl said. "I read about a device several movie theaters and restaurants have installed to block signals from incoming and outgoing cell phones. If we have something like that, we'll be able to prevent any calls. Roscoe should know about it."

"We also need to deal with the transponder and be able to remove it in a matter of minutes," Roger said. "If we can get rid of the signaling device without interrupting the signal, I have an idea to prevent the trucks being missed for several hours."

"I'm with you. It's right up Roscoe's alley. He did say he was willing to take on a good paying job, didn't he?"

"Yeah," Roger said, "Roscoe's our man."

As they drove through the hot New Mexico desert, Carl's thoughts were of Julie. He missed her already. She took the news of their unexpected trip well, but when he told her they might move to New Mexico to run a ranch, she asked, "When did all this happen? You never mentioned it before."

Holding her hand, he said, "We've thought about something like this for quite a while and believe the cattle feeding station will be a profit maker. I've told you how we talked about owning our own business, now we want to try.

"We'll be in New Mexico approximately six to eight months to get the operation up and running. Then we'll leave it in the hands of a foreman and be absentee landlords."

"How long will you be gone this time?"

"At least two weeks. After we buy a ranch, Roger wants to spend a couple of days gambling in Laughlin. When we get back I'll make it up to you."

Julie withdrew her hand from his and said, "I don't have any strings on you, Carl. This is all a surprise."

He reached out and took her in his arms while saying, "I know, but you know I love you. Trust me and it will work out."

She smiled up at him, "I love you too and will miss you, but we still have tonight. How late can you stay?"

Breaking into Carl's thoughts, Roger asked, "What's on your mind, buddy?"

"Julie was surprised at our sudden desire to own a ranch."

"I thought she might be. I'm sorry our plans are messing up your love life."

"We'll work it out, Roger."

"After the jobs, we'll find a buyer for the ranch and move back to Austin," Roger said. "You can always tell her we went 'bust'."

"If things work out, we can let the members of the team run the place. It'll keep them busy while we wait for the money to cool down."

"Your idea makes more sense."

On a clear, hot day, they arrived in Roswell and contacted a local realtor named Julia Jones, who promised to show them several ranches along Highway 285 the next day.

When Julia picked them up at nine a.m., the morning sun was already blazing low on the horizon. The outside temperature gauge on her 2004 Buick Riviera registered ninety degrees. Small puffy white clouds dotted a clear blue sky, but there was no chance of rain in the local forecast.

After leaving the city limits, traffic thinned, and there was little to see except an occasional herd of elk or small deer roaming the desert, grazing along the four-lane highway with their heads down. Seldom bothering to glance up at the intruders, the animals displayed no fear of the automobile.

Roger made mental notes of curves, gullies and small hills along the highway and saw several places where they could possibly stage a successful robbery.

("Later, Carl and I will check them out.")

Although most houses weren't visible from the highway, along the way were crooked wind-blown signs and weathered gates to mark the entrances. Gravel roads filled with pot holes ran from the blacktop, over hills to who knew where.

With his dry humor Carl remarked, "It looks as if you'd wear out two wagon tongues just getting to the mail box."

Julia smiled and said, "The ranchers like privacy, that's why they built their homes away from the main road, plus they don't hear the eighteen-wheelers. There's a lot to be said for solitude."

"I guess we'll find out," Roger said. "It's a long way between neighbors out here."

At the first ranch they met Fred Wilkins, owner of a spread of nine thousand, two hundred acres of sand, cacti and sagebrush.

"Running a ranch is difficult enough," Fred said. "A feeding station requires a lot more men and work, but there's one advantage. The cattle will all be in one place instead of being scattered over thousands of acres. I never considered setting up a feeding operation, so maybe you fellows have the right idea, but you also have a lot to learn.

"I'm asking one million, four hundred and fifty thousand dollars for my place. After the sale, I'll round up my cattle and auction them off."

After walking around the property with Julia, they discovered the ranch house, main barn and several out buildings were at least sixty years old. The house was in good shape, but the barn and other sheds would require repair and a fresh coat of paint.

The equipment accompanying the sale was also disappointing. They thanked Fred for his time and answers. He knew they wouldn't be returning, but still said, "Good luck wherever you wind up. With the weather around here, it takes luck and a hell of a lot of hard work to make a go of it. You two are young, so you'll enjoy the challenge. I'm ready for a rocking chair."

Their second stop was the Crossed X Ranch, approximately seventy-five miles north of Roswell. Their host, Joe Wells, was deeply tanned and as weather-beaten as a windmill behind his house. He said, "I own eight thousand, seven hundred acres of dust and more dust, with a little grass thrown in. I want one million, two hundred and seventy-five thousand dollars for my spread."

His house had been painted recently and the barn and out buildings were newer than Fred's. They also displayed the effects of the harsh bitter winters, constant wind and blowing dust.

Although the sale included two beat-up pickups and a large manure-stained cattle truck, the ranch lacked any equipment Roger was looking for.

Joe kicked up dust with his boots and said, "When I sell my ranch, I'll also sell off the cattle. I like the idea of a feeder station. Have you talked to owners of similar operations?"

Carl admitted, "No, we haven't."

Watching as dust settled back to the ground, Joe said, "You should. On the way back to Texas, head east along I-40, where you'll find several. Stop in and speak with the owners. Then you'll have a better idea of what you're up against."

After dropping them at their motel, Julia promised to show three more ranches in the morning. Because places to eat were few and far between on the highway between Roswell and the ranches, they missed lunch and were starved.

As they headed for the restaurant and an early dinner, Carl said, "The fresh air makes me hungry."

Roger smiled and remarked, "You don't need an excuse, but yeah, it helped."

Before taking a bite of his juicy, medium-rare steak, Carl asked, "What do you think of the prospects so far?"

"I'd rate them as dismal. Joe's place did have some potential. It's further from the highway than Fred's, so no one would observe us. Several men could live in the ranch house and the bunk house could hold more, but we don't know how many employees we need. Like everyone tells us, we have a lot to learn."

Carl agreed.

"A worker at Joe's told me he only has two men who work full-time. During roundups and at branding time, he hires others part time."

Their honey-haired, gum-chewing waitress sashayed by, batted brown eyes and asked through cherry-flavored lips if they'd like more tea. They both declined. As she left Carl heard her pop a gum bubble.

Roger followed her sexy movements with his eyes, grinned and said, "Besides not knowing what the hell we're doing, the biggest obstacle I've seen is the lack of equipment. I didn't see a backhoe or any usable trucks, so we'll have to buy those on the open market. I'm glad Mister Remualdi authorized an additional one million. We may need it."

Shaking his head at their apparent stupidity, Carl chuckled and said, "First, let's find a ranch to buy."

Roger laughed.

"That would be a good beginning."

After dinner they stopped by the motel office to check if there were any messages. Carl hoped Julie had phoned and was disappointed when she hadn't.

An aging clerk sporting a mop of white hair and leather-tanned neck as thick as a tree trunk said, "There's a man waiting to see you in the bar next to the restaurant."

"Any idea what he wants?" Roger asked.

The snow-topped, senior citizen scratched his head.

"No, but the guy asked for you by name. He'll be easy to spot; he's thin as a rail and wears a beat-up, brown cowboy hat."

Carl laughed.

"There can't be more than four of five people in the bar resembling his description."

Tapping his skull as if he had a revelation, the clerk said, "I think his name is 'Slim'."

Roger grinned at his antics.

"Well, you've narrowed the search down to two or three. Come on Carl; let's see if we can find a guy named Slim wearing a brown cowboy hat."

They were wrong. Slim was the only customer in the bar and they knew instantly how he earned his nickname.

He was so thin a strong wind would blow him forty acres away in the time it took to tell the tale. Long arms hung down over longer legs, and stringy, sandy-colored hair peeked out below the brim of a sweat-stained, brown Stetson.

Slim wore well-worn blue jeans, a multicolored, long-sleeved shirt wearing thin in the elbows and a pair of old, but sturdy cowboy boots. A faded blue bandana was wrapped around his neck. First-time viewers didn't have to be told Slim was a real cowboy.

A clean-shaven, heavily tanned face displayed a hooked nose which had been broken two or three times. A few small scars bled through his tan. His blue eyes were clear, reflecting intelligence. From wrinkled furrows in his forehead, Roger estimated his age at fifty.

On the minus side, Slim had three detracting features. An eagle could nest in the hair protruding from his ears, and if ever stranded on a desert island, Slim was well prepared.

A silver earring shaped like a horse shoe and studded with six rhinestones hung from his left earlobe. It would make a good fishing lure if attached to fifty yards of fishing line he could braid from his nose hair.

A glass dark with whiskey was in his right hand and a thin, lumpy, hand-rolled, half-smoked cigarette dangled from his left. As his eyes met theirs in the mirror behind the bar, Slim turned to face them. Smoke curled around his head like a wispy halo, as he asked, "Mister James and Mister Booth?"

"You found us," Roger said. "I'm Booth and he's James. We answer to Roger and Carl." Pointing his index finger at Carl, he said, "He's Carl. What can we do for you?"

"Actually, it's what I can do for you. Joe Wells said you were looking for someone to ramrod a feeder station. If it's true, I'm your man."

After shaking Slim's hand, Roger said, "You sound

confident enough. How did you know where to find us?"

"I phoned around the local motels until I found where you were staying."

"I like your initiative," Carl said. "What do you know about feeder stations?"

Slim jerked his thumb over his shoulder and said, "I worked my share, from here to Saint Louis. They're stinking places to work and live, but the pay's good."

"How much experience do you have?" Roger asked.

Slim leaned back, grinned and then chuckled as he said, "From what I hear, I've got about thirty more years than the two of you combined."

Carl nodded his acquiescence.

"You have us there, Slim. When it comes to knowing anything about a feeder station, we're complete idiots."

He stared at them in disbelief.

"Then why in hell would you want to own one?"

"It's the money," Roger said. "Didn't you just say they paid well?"

"They do, but the hours are long and they also require a hell of a lot of hard labor. Until you get used to the stink, the smell of cow shit will drive you crazy."

"Okay," Roger said. "You've made your point. Now, if you had to pick a ranch from the five for sale around here, which one would you buy?"

Slim didn't pause a moment.

"The Crossed X Ranch. It's better suited to convert into a feeder station. You need space to put up feeding pens. The other ranches don't have a level area near the ranch house like the Crossed X does."

Carl frowned and said, "Joe claims the ranch is nothing but dust and a little grass thrown in."

Knowing by Carl's statement that he was with a couple dudes, Slim said, "You don't need much grass. Your feed is mostly hay or sacked grain. Every day you feed hundreds of cows.

"On the other end, literally, they drop a lot of crap, so you also need a place to pile up the manure. The most important thing they require is good water. Joe's place has three good wells and several tanks we can use in a drought."

"You did you homework, Slim," Carl said.

"I thought about opening my own feeder station, but I couldn't find a backer. Most people don't want anything to do with an ex-con. I might as well tell you about my record now and get it out in the open."

"Anyone can make a mistake, Slim," Roger said. "Why were you in the pen?"

"Petty larceny; I was drunk, down on my luck and thought robbing a service station was a smart idea. Then the little old lady behind the counter came up with a .357 caliber cannon to match my pocketknife. Needless to say, I gave up without a fight.

"The judge handed me two years, but with good behavior I got out in eighteen months. The robbery happened five years ago. I've never been in trouble since and don't ever intend to be. You only have my word, but it's good."

"We respect your honesty, Slim," Carl said.

Nodding in agreement, Roger said, "We've both done things we should have gone to jail for, but were lucky. We won't hold your past against you, Slim."

"Thanks, Roger. Does that mean I have a job?"

"Slim, we don't even own a ranch yet. How good are you at teaching others? If we buy Joe's place, could we count on you to train some of our friends?"

"I guess I could. Before I went to Vietnam, I taught marksmanship in the Army. My officer told me I was a natural leader. Maybe he was right. Who are these guys?"

"They're friends of ours from our own Army days," Carl said. "We inherited some money and thought we'd help out our buddies. Since they were discharged after Desert Storm, they've been down on their luck."

Slim nodded knowingly.

"At least you guys got a parade. I went from a rice paddy and a firefight on Monday, to Hawaii and hula girls on Wednesday. Then when I got to L. A., a teenybopper spat at me."

"Yeah," Carl said. "You 'Nam' vets got the shaft. So you know how we feel about our buddies."

Slim paused to spit into a paper cup before saying, "Yeah, I do. If they're willing to learn, I'll do my best to train your guys."

"Then you're our man," Roger said. "Stop by tomorrow at eight and we'll go out to talk to Joe. You can point out the good features of his ranch."

"I'll be in the restaurant. Thanks again. I'll see you at eight."

After finishing his drink in one gulp, Slim shook their hands and walked out the door. His bowlegged walk reflected the hours he'd spent riding horses.

They watched as Slim climbed into an ancient, beat-up, red Dodge pickup, and Roger said, "Maybe our luck has changed. Slim appears to be the answer to our prayers."

"I like the idea of him being an ex-con," Carl said. "When we start working on the garage and other modifications, he won't ask too many questions. As a Vietnam vet, the guys can relate to him."

"Let's go to our room," Roger said. "I'll call Julia and cancel tomorrow."

In the morning, when they arrived for breakfast, Slim was seated in the restaurant wearing Levis and a faded tan shirt. His hair was slicked back and tied into a small ponytail. On a chair next to him, a new grey Stetson stood on its crown.

While they ate, Slim told them how to set up and operate a feeder station. It required several men to handle all the details. There were many items to consider, such as ordering feed and hay, buying feeding chutes, water troughs etcetera. Slim knew his business and Roger and Carl silently thanked God for sending him their way.

When they got around to equipment, Roger held up his hand.

"As far as that's concerned, we'll leave it up to you to determine what we need. You're the expert. If we purchase the ranch, you can order whatever is required. Money's no problem. What about buying a backhoe to move the manure?"

"It's a 'must' to keep the ranch clean and the cattle healthy," Slim said. "Yeah, a backhoe with a big bucket would be great."

"When we're up and running, how many men will we

need?" Carl asked.

"A dozen should be sufficient. How many men were you planning to hire?"

"We have more than twenty men," Roger said. "The way we have it planned; there'll be enough work for all. We also need three or four good used pickups."

First Slim shook his head, but then he nodded.

"That's a lot of men, but you know what you want better than I do. You're right about the pickups. These gravel roads will tear up your van. One special item I'd like is a road grader. There's gonna be a lot of big cattle trucks coming in and going out on your gravel road. A grader would let us keep it halfway smooth."

"If you think we need one, buy it," Roger said. "Some of our guys are topnotch mechanics. They can keep anything running."

"They'll be busy," Slim said.

Roger glanced at his watch.

"We should get on the road and speak to Joe."

"I'll drive," Slim said. "Joe's road is in pretty bad shape. My old truck doesn't look like much, but I keep it repaired. It's also got a good air conditioner."

"When we get back I'll buy the gas," Roger said.

"Fair enough," Slim said, while thinking, "So far, my new bosses and I are getting along swell. I'm glad I stopped off to see Joe yesterday. Maybe this time fate rolled me a 'seven'."

When Slim drove up, Joe was seated in a rocking chair on the veranda. He stood up, walked out to meet them and said, "Howdy, I see you met Slim."

"Yeah," Carl said. "He talked us into coming back to look at your ranch. We're slowly improving. Now at least one of us knows how to work cattle."

Joe chuckled at the truth in his words.

"You couldn't ask for a better top hand. Slim had his problems in the past, but now he's straightened himself out. He's a good worker and a friend."

While Roger dickered with Joe over the price, Slim and Carl

walked around the ranch house area. Slim explained where he would install feeding pens and water stations.

A close look at the bunk house revealed eight men could live there comfortably.

Carl said, "The bathroom space is limited, but if the men take turns, it's adequate."

In one end of another large building housing a well-stocked kitchen, two stoves and ovens, a commercial refrigerator and a walk-in freezer were installed. An ice maker sat inside a larger room used to store staples, while two double sinks and shelved cabinets filled another wall.

After checking the space, Slim said, "There's room for more than one cook."

Carl agreed.

"I think the ranch house is large enough to accommodate six men, and the kitchen could be used as an auxiliary."

As he joined them and heard their last statements, Roger said, "There's also a den where Alan can set up his computers. I think Carl, A. J., Alan, Roscoe, Slim and I will live in the main ranch house."

"An additional and larger bunk house will be required, Carl, so add the extra expense to your list. If twenty or more men are going to live here, we'll need a shower/bath house."

Slim had a revelation.

"Didn't you say some of your guys were construction workers? Why couldn't they expand the existing bunk house?"

"Yes, I did," Roger replied. "That's a good idea, Slim. When the men aren't attending Cattle Handling One Oh One, it'll give them something to do."

Slim's idea started wheels turning in Carl's head. "All the men won't arrive at the same time. If we send construction workers out first, couldn't they expand the bunk house?"

"That's a good idea," Slim said. "I'd rather keep my classes small and make sure everyone understands how to handle cattle."

"Then that's what we'll do," Roger said.

Joe suggested a tour of the ranch.

"You'll find a few rough roads I scraped out over the years that lead to the four corners of the ranch and some side roads. We use them to check barbed wire fences."

"How close is your nearest neighbor?" Roger asked.

"About four miles as the crow flies, but if you drive the winding roads between here and there, it's probably closer to five or six."

Following an hour of haggling, Roger and Joe finally agreed on a price of one million, two hundred and fifty thousand for the ranch.

They shook hands to seal the deal, and Roger said, "We'll close forty-five days from today, Joe. I'll ask Julia to prepare the paperwork and bring it out for your signature and write an escrow check for ten thousand dollars. My agent will transfer the remaining funds ten days prior to the closing date."

Joe wore a large smile on his face as he said, "I'm ready to retire and let someone else do the work. Good luck to you three. I hope you become millionaires."

Roger glanced at Carl, and with a sly smile, said, "That's our dream."

Chapter 9

When they awoke the next morning and looked out the window at the sun already high in the sky, they knew it would be another hot, sweltering day. Somehow Roger and Carl didn't mind. Things were moving along nicely. Now the only big task remaining was to find a place to pull off the first robbery.

Following a good breakfast of steak and eggs washed down with black coffee, Roger drove the van north on Highway 285. There were miles to explore before they would find the perfect place.

They noted several possibilities and stopped frequently to check out good and bad aspects of each. Finally they settled on a spot fifty-seven miles north of Roswell and fifteen south of the ranch. The nearest town, Vaughn, was twenty-five miles north. The closest ranch entrance in either direction was four miles away.

After driving north for four miles, they made a U-turn, drove five miles south and found the sparse pasture land was bisected by dry washes and fenced the entire distance. There were no ranch roads on either side.

Carl said, "The location is great. No unwanted or unexpected visitors will stumble upon us in the middle of the job."

After climbing back into the van, Roger said, "That was easy."

"I don't think anyone saw you," Carl said.

"Then let's head for Laughlin."

Before they left Roswell there was one last chore to accomplish. After finding the address of the State Highway Department, Roger located the street on a map of Roswell. Carl drove the van to the location, where they found a parking lot packed with a wide variety of maintenance vehicles.

"Check it out," Carl said. "There are loops of razor wire along the top of the fence, but the gates are wide open."

No workers were present, so Roger walked in boldly and used his digital camera to photograph markings on the vehicles, including front, side and rear views. The trucks, (all GMC models), were streaked with a mix of alkali and sand. Each door was marked with the seal of New Mexico.

Richard answered his home phone.

"Good morning, Darrin. What's new with my two con men?"

"I'm in Roswell, New Mexico and something big is up. Roger and Carl came here last week and bought a large ranch about seventy-five miles north."

"Interesting," Richard said. "Where did they get the money?"

"That's what's really remarkable," Darrin said. "Last week, a young woman showed up at Roger and Carl's home. I later learned she's Maria Remualdi, the only daughter of Don Giacomo. She was carrying a large briefcase and they spent time going over papers, signing documents etcetera.

"Then they went to a local Mexican restaurant and ate dinner. By the time their meal was over, the three were very chummy. Since that time, Roger has deposited two million dollars in his business account. It appears whatever Roger and Carl are up to, Don Giacomo is backing it."

"Is Don Giacomo what they call Mister Remualdi?"

"Yes, Sir," Darrin said.

"Is there anything else?"

"I asked around and discovered they hired a man named Slim Miles to run the ranch. Rumor has it they plan to turn it into a cattle feeding station. For the time being, that's all I have to report. I'll keep an eye on our boys and advise you of any new developments."

"You've given me a lot to think about," Richard said. "Good work, Darrin. You're earning your pay."

"I try, Sir."

After putting the van in gear, Carl pulled onto the highway. The sky was blue and empty of clouds. From the looks of things, it was going to be another scorcher.

Squinting in the glare, Carl pointed upward at the blazing sun and joked.

"Maybe I'd better ask the local Indian tribe to do a rain dance to cool things off."

Roger chuckled.

"It might help. I made reservations for two nights at the Riverside Hotel. Tomorrow we can check the first fifty miles of Route 95. Once we get past the long, steep climb out of Laughlin, the remainder of the road is too flat and open for our purposes. The next day we'll check out the Nevada State highway maintenance trucks."

"And in between we gamble a little, right?" Carl asked.

"Yeah, you can get back to the crap table. I hope you win enough to pay for this trip. We have to keep up our image for the I. R. S."

Carl handed Roger an atlas and said, "I checked the Nevada map and area where we plan to work. In case we don't find a decent location on the highway, I think I found an alternative.

"About sixty miles north of Laughlin there's a side road off Route 95 leading to a small town named Nelson. Ten miles down the Nelson road there's a "T" intersection at Route 163.

"The road to the right goes to Nelson and the left leads north to Route 95. We could set up a phony detour at the intersection of Route 95 and Nelson Road. If we can direct the Brinks truck onto Nelson road, we'll have ten miles of deserted highway to work with."

"Let me take a look," Roger said and studied the map for a few moments.

"You're right, Carl. It's a good spot. We'll drive up there

tomorrow and check it out. Your idea might be better than our original plan."

After driving across the Colorado River into Laughlin, Carl turned into the Riverside Hotel and Casino. The parking lot was packed, so he paraded up and down rows looking for an empty space.

Suddenly Roger pointed to a parking lot across a dusty street and said, "Look over there. Are those what I think they are?"

"They look like Nevada highway trucks," Carl said. "I wonder where the workers are."

"I don't give a damn. Pull over by that tree and I'll take some photos. This makes my day."

After grabbing his camera from the rear seat, Roger climbed out, crossed the street and stood in the open taking a series of photographs. Moving around the trucks as he recorded the markings, he thought, "They're all GMC models. The company must give the states a big discount."

In less than five minutes he was satisfied, rejoined Carl in the van and said, "Talk about luck. I thought we might have to drive up to Las Vegas to find a maintenance yard."

After checking in, they took an elevator to the eleventh floor and discovered their two-bedroom suite overlooked the mighty Colorado River. This close to the Mexican border the once strong, powerful waterway was reduced to a gently flowing stream.

Rubbing his hands together in anticipation, Carl said, "Let's hit the buffet and then do some serious gambling."

After lunch, while Carl tried his hand at craps, just for fun, Roger decided to play a quarter poker slot. To his surprise he was dealt more winners than losers. At the end of two hours he had filled three tall cardboard cups with coins.

Carl didn't fare too well at the crap table he chose, but did manage to win two hundred dollars. When his luck turned colder than an Eskimo's igloo, he searched the casino for Roger, found him with his horde of quarters and said, "It looks like you did all right. Do you want to take a break and get a drink? For once I quit while I was ahead."

Putting his hands together in mock prayer, Roger said,

"Miracles do happen. I don't have any idea how much I'm ahead. Let's cash in."

When the coin machine stopped counting, the quarters totaled six hundred, twenty-seven dollars and fifty cents.

Roger said, "Amazing; I never have any luck with the slots."

"Maybe this is your day. Let's have a drink and rest for a while. My legs are killing me. I wish there was some way to sit down and throw those dice."

"I'm tired myself. I think I'll pack it in. If you want to gamble some more, go ahead."

"Nah," Carl said. "I've had it. Lucky day or not, it's time to hit the sack. We have a busy day ahead tomorrow."

The next morning, they woke to a seven-thirty wake-up call. By nine a.m., they had finished breakfast and were headed north on Highway 95. The days were beginning to run into one another. Everyone was the same; hot and dry, featuring miles of the same desolate, deserted, desert scenery.

After leaving the greenness of the Colorado River and Laughlin behind, the road climbed steeply for several miles. On the way, they passed a number of big rigs struggling up the inclines and around sharp curves.

At several points they stopped to check the possibilities, but the more they saw, the less likely it was their original plan would work.

As he pulled the van back onto the highway, Roger said, "The road has too much traffic and there's no place to stop the armored vehicle where it couldn't be seen by others. Let's give your idea a shot."

They found the small, weather-beaten Nelson signpost and turned right. The side road was a narrow two-lane blacktop filled with various sized cracks and crumbling, asphalt-weeping potholes, crying out to be repaved.

Driving slowly over ten miles of rutted road until they reached the intersection of Route 165, Roger never saw a vehicle in the rearview mirror and only met one car. During the fifteen minutes spent inspecting the site and talking things over, they didn't see another automobile or truck.

Carl laughed and said, "The place is so quiet you could hear a horny toad fart."

The wind whistled as it cut uneven patterns into the light dusty soil, sounding like a wail of an Apache warrior chanting his death song as he prepared for the final battle. A few strands of thin dry grass and short tasseled weeds waved bravely at the visitors.

They took time to turn around, drove back to Route 95 and then returned over the same route traveled earlier.

Roger said, "The location looks perfect. There are two small hills to each side of the actual robbery site to hide our action. With a few minor variations, we can use the original plan."

Carl agreed.

"If Alan's report is right, this will be the biggest job yet. This road has a couple of other advantages as well. We can do the robbery with fewer men in three crews; two small and one large, and won't have to worry about traffic."

As Roger turned to the left on Route 163, he said, "Let's make a loop up Route 165 to Route 95, then down to Nelson Road and return here to check the mileage."

By two p.m. their reconnoitering was complete. Two hours later they arrived back in Laughlin, ate a late lunch and drank nearly a gallon of iced tea. The hot desert air was dry and sucked the moisture from their bodies like a sponge.

Wiping his mouth on a napkin after finishing another glass of tea, Roger said, "I didn't realize how tired I was. Let's take it easy today, gamble a little tonight and leave early tomorrow morning."

"Yeah," Carl said. "I'm worn out myself."

Before leaving the next morning, when Roger phoned Maria, she answered on the third ring, and was pleased to hear his voice.

"I'm in Dallas," she said. "I'll be in Austin tomorrow. My new apartment is nearly furnished and I'm just packing some odds and ends."

Roger still got a thrill from hearing her voice. "I got lucky, won a few dollars and felt like buying you something, so I picked up a gift for you in Arizona."

"You didn't need to, but I appreciate your thoughtfulness. What is it?"

"You may be the boss lady, but you won't find out that easily. We arrive home tomorrow afternoon. I know a restaurant in north Austin that serves the best Italian food in town. You'll have to come to dinner with me to get your present."

To his surprise, she said, "Pick me up at seven. I'll be ready."

Although she couldn't see it, Roger smiled.

"It's a date. I'll tell you about the trip and you can fill me in on what you accomplished while we were gone. Then I can write dinner off as a business expense."

He thought he detected a change in the tone of her voice when she said softly, "I'm not always interested in business, Roger."

"I'm happy to hear it. I'll call you when we get in."

Chapter 10

When Roger rang Maria's bell, she met him at the door wearing a charming tan skirt and multicolored peasant blouse. Her black hair was combed into a long, curved ponytail and her eyes sparkled with happiness.

"Welcome to my humble abode. It's a long ways from being finished, but I'm working on it."

Glancing around the room, he said, "It's very nice."

The living area was furnished in European style with an antique Italian couch accented by warm, glowing wood. Taking center stage were two matching chairs covered with rich, brocaded maroon material.

A group of French paintings hung on one wall and an antique beveled mirror on another. A braided German rug covered part of a wooden parquet floor. Drapes in a red and bronze combination added to the ambiance.

"Would you care for a glass of wine?" She asked. "I have a lovely bottle of Bordeaux on ice."

"Let me do the honors."

As he poured the rich, red wine, Roger asked, "What should we drink to?"

"Let's toast to success in your venture and new friendships."

Raising his glass high, Roger said, "I'll also praise your beauty tonight, Maria. You look lovely."

"Thank you."

"I'm pleased to see that you're more than just a business associate. I'm looking forward to knowing more about you."

Maria stared into his eyes and her blush became more pronounced.

Holding her eyes with his, Roger reached for her hand, as she thought; "He doesn't know I'm already in love with him."

Feeling a flush to her cheeks, Maria said, "The feeling is mutual. Finish your wine and let's go. For some reason, I'm famished."

Dinner at Mario's, a trendy Italian restaurant in northwest Austin was marvelous. They ordered an assortment of pasta and ate by candlelight. A dark, rich wine served with the meal added to their pleasure.

After dinner they strolled to Anderson Mall and spent an enjoyable hour watching youngsters skate on the indoor ice rink.

The night ended too soon, but Roger knew his time with Maria was just beginning. He left her at her door with a tender kiss and promise of more to come.

The time came to see if Roscoe Hynes was interested in joining their team. After finding his business card, Roger dialed his number. When he answered, Roger could tell the smog must be thick. Roscoe's voice was hoarse and scratchy.

"Roscoe, this is Roger Booth from Austin. A few weeks ago, you did some work for my partner and me. Do you remember us?"

"Hell yes. You said you might have a good-paying job to take me away from this damnable smog."

"We need your electronic expertise, Roscoe. We're taking a team of men to New Mexico to work on a ranch. I think you'll like the weather out in the wide open spaces."

"What's in it for me?"

"You get an equal share of the profits. How would you like to become a millionaire?"

"You bet your ass," Roscoe said without hesitation. "How soon do I report?"

"In a week or two, but as of today you're on the payroll. For starters you get five hundred a month. Is that all right?"

Roscoe coughed and said, "That's fine. I'll wait for your call."

Referring to a list in his hand, Roger said, "I have some things I want you to purchase. If you have a pen and paper, I'll give you the items one as a time and we can discuss them as we go along."

"Fire away," Roscoe said.

As Slim walked out to the corral, the sky was cloudy and it looked like another overcast day in central New Mexico. He saw three other cowboys sitting on a top rail, watching two horses run in circles within the enclosure.

"Howdy, guys. Are you three amigos ready to teach gringos how to handle cattle?"

"Yeah," Carlos Sanchez, the spokesman for the trio said. "Bring 'em on. Do they have any idea at all what they're getting into?"

"Not a clue," Slim said and chuckled.

Another of the real cowboys, David Zavala, asked, "You think they'll know which orifice of the cow the shit comes out of?"

Carlos smiled.

"They'll find out if they go pumping on their tails to get milk."

"I don't think they're that stupid," Slim said. "But you never know, do you?"

The third of the Amigos, Jesus Martinez shrugged and concentrated on braiding the end of a rope to prevent it from fraying. Neither he nor the others were looking forward to teaching twenty-four greenhorns how to handle cattle, but that's what they'd been hired for. That and their construction experience.

David was an electrician and Carlos did framing and trim, while Jesus knew the plumbing business backward and forward. With their kind of experience, of course the Army turned them into truck drivers. They spent their time in the Middle East hauling heavy tanks on transports through the sands of Saudi Arabia on the now famous "end around" run into Iraq.

When Carl contacted them in San Antonio, they were working odd jobs after their discharge. None were married or seriously entangled with a member of the opposite sex, but they were ready for more action and adventure, so he didn't have to talk very long to have them sign on the dotted line.

After flying out to Roswell last week, the trio spent time getting acquainted with Slim and the ranch. They liked both. Slim treated them with respect, and once they got the ranch up and running, the place looked like a winner.

"When do we get into the building phase?" Jesus asked.

"After the first team of eleven men gets here," Slim said. "We'll train them in-between working on the bunk house. Every week after that, Roger will dispatch another group, and we'll teach them the basics. The first bunch of dudes arrives this afternoon, so we better get our act together.

"Here's a list of the guys we have to train and some notes I made about my thoughts on how to teach them the bare essentials. I'd like you to see if you can add anything."

Slim handed out the paperwork and they settled down to talk things over. From where they sat, it looked like a long, hot spring and summer. They'd find out this afternoon.

Tapping his copy with his fingers, Carlos said, "I know some of these guys from the Army. If they handle themselves here as well as they did in Kuwait and Iraq, they'll do fine."

Chapter 11

(Eight months later.)

Pointing in an arc to encompass the entire ranch, Carl said, "It's a good thing Joe Wells isn't around to see his old ranch. Since he headed for California, we've made a lot of changes."

Roger agreed.

"Yes, we have."

In one fenced-off pen, Slim and a team of eight men were working with a small herd of cattle, feeding and watering them. A. J. drove the back hoe and led a four man team cleaning up manure from another. Six pens were built in conjunction with the bunk house expansion and construction of the new bath facility.

Slim was no dummy. Early on he told Roger he knew something was fishy.

"You've got way too many people working for you and it's no coincidence they're all Army vets. What the hell's going on, Roger?"

Since there was no way around it, Roger told Slim their plans. Slim wasn't happy about being fooled; but when faced with a possible million dollar payoff, he agreed to join the team.

"You won't be directly involved with the robberies," Roger said. "Your main job is keeping up appearances while we're gone. If we find something else you can do, we'll let you know."

Their head carpenter and architect, Charley Wilson, was leading a crew of six men putting finishing touches on what Carl called "the jail".

Charley was thirty-nine, one of the older men on the team and following in his father's footsteps. His dad was a Seabee in World War II. During the Kuwaiti war, Charley was an NCO in the civil engineering squadron of Roger's armored division.

If it weren't for a heart murmur discovered in a routine annual physical, Charley would still be constructing buildings and tank barns in Iraq. He owned a voice like a fog horn, and they heard him bellow, "Get the lead out."

Under Charley's close supervision, a thirty by twenty foot outbuilding was being converted into a windowless holding place to house the Brinks drivers and guards.

The siding and windows were removed and replaced with solid, three-quarter-inch plywood walls, double-insulated inside and out. The only entrance was a solid steel door with a heavy bolt lock.

Four Army surplus cots and an equal number of chairs were bolted to the floor. A sink and commode provided washing and toilet facilities, and a hand-held shower head attachment could be hooked to the sink faucet. Privacy wasn't a factor. There was no shower curtain and a small drain in the floor removed the bath water.

Looking things over, Charley said, "It's primitive, but it works."

A double entryway was added and a small sliding door installed in the front wall of the interior. The food for the prisoners could be delivered without allowing a view of the surrounding area, plus it kept the captives from knowing day from night. For their comfort, an air conditioner/heater was installed in the ceiling.

From locked steel cages high in the ceiling, two sixty-watt bulbs provided light and would remain lit twenty-four hours a day.

Charley and a team of ten carpenters, plumbers, electricians and masons were the first members of the team to make the trek. As soon as they were settled, and after being trained by Slim and the three amigos, they began work on Roger's projects.

Prior to leaving Austin, Roger and Carl stopped by to see

"Doc" Marberry, a young medic in Iraq, responsible for saving the lives of many wounded warriors in Roger's unit. Both times Carl was hit by shrapnel, Doc patched him up, so Roger and Carl felt they owed him big time.

When Doc was discharged, Roger loaned him money to complete his college education and medical school. He graduated at the top of his class and set up shop in Austin, where he prospered.

Periodically, Roger and Carl called upon their old friend for advice and supplies. As a result, Doc wasn't surprised to find them on his doorstep.

"Speak of the devil, or devils. I was just talking to Wiley Jenkins about you last week. He says you're recruiting people for a new job. I'm not available, but you knew that already. What do you want this time?"

Roger shook Doc's hand and said, "Mostly information, Doc. What type of serum do you have that is easily injected, fast working and will knock out a couple of people for several hours?"

Knowing Roger wasn't asking for info alone, Doc said, "Versed or Diprivan will do the job. If you need something of that caliber, I have a small, unaccountable bottle of Versed, and can supply you with syringes and needles. There's enough serum in the container to knock out sixty people for three hours per injection."

Pausing for a moment, he asked, "Do you know how to use a syringe?" Then without waiting for a reply, he told them, "Fill the syringe with fifty-five CCs of serum and squirt out about five CCs. Inject the rest into any leg, arm or neck muscle and in five seconds the drug will take effect.

"There are two important things to remember: One – Use a different syringe for each patient to prevent the spread of disease. Two – Be careful, don't stick yourself."

Carl smiled at Doc's dissertation and asked, "Are there any serious side effects, Doc?"

"There may be some short-term memory loss, but nothing severe. Your 'patients' will wake up a little groggy, but they'll be well and healthy."

"Thanks again, Doc," Roger said. "How much do we owe you?"

"Two thousand will do nicely."

When Roger paid him with one-hundred-dollar bills, Doc grinned and added, "Make sure you destroy the bottle and bury the syringes and needles. I don't mind helping you guys out for old times' sake, but don't involve me in any of your schemes."

"Don't worry, Doc," Roger said. "We never heard of you."

"That's the way I want it. Be careful, good luck and keep the serum refrigerated."

Three weeks later, when Carl, Roger, A. J. and Alan drove up to the ranch house, they found Charley's crew had finished the bunk house addition and was presently installing the commodes, showerheads and sinks in a twelve-hundred-square-foot bathhouse.

After shaking hands all around, Charley turned toward the latest addition and bragged, "Two more days and it'll be ready for use. Then we start on the garage."

"Great, Charley," Roger said. "You've done wonders."

The garage was the most important item on Roger's list. It was a three-car structure to be built into an existing mound of dirt, five hundred yards from the ranch house. Each stall would be wide and high enough to hold the largest Brinks truck manufactured.

Upon completion of the project, the front entrances and three sides would be covered with dirt and sand. The only thing visible would be the reinforced roof. To an outsider, it resembled a concrete slab on a hill used to store manure.

During the initial construction, Slim expressed reservations about its use; "If you're going to hide those trucks under cow shit, you better install a heavy duty ventilator. After cow crap sits a while, it percolates and brews up methane gas. If it's allowed to accumulate and you're down there for any length of time, you'll be deader than a heifer frozen in a blizzard."

With the passage of time, the days were getting shorter and colder. Everyone was glad to see summer depart with its long, hot days, but now the winds from the north were something to contend with.

After the men arrived, Slim kept them busy learning how to handle cattle. When they weren't in his classes, Charley drove them hard to complete all the building tasks before winter set in.

Roger had hoped the men could mix the concrete for the garage by hand, but Charley shot down Roger's dream when he said, "Hell, it would take us a year to mix the amount we'll need, so I'll order it out of Roswell. What's the chance any truck drivers will ever come back out here?"

A month later, to cheers of the assembled workers, the last heavy concrete truck poured its load. As he shifted into double low, the driver known as "Griff" waved goodbye.

The flow of construction vehicles to the Crossed X Ranch had torn up the gravel road like a furrowed field in the spring. Even with a grader working overtime, the two mile ride to the highway was rough, and Griff didn't want to blow a tire.

With a flourish of his trowel, like Houdini and his cape after one of his escapes, Charley finished the roof of the garage, waved to Roger and Carl and said, "Thank God it's done. Man, it's hot. I'm ready for a cold one."

Charley was so talented at working with concrete, it made the team punster, Wiley Jenkins, remark, "Charley's so good he has no 'piers'. He's the only guy I know who can make wet concrete 'set up' and beg for a trowel."

After the garage doors were installed and reinforced by steel bars placed every two feet, A. J. and Slim used the backhoe and grader to move dirt and sand to form a slanted ramp and fill in around the other three walls.

When he saw the finished product, Roger said, "It looks just like I thought it would. Good work guys."

Driving slowly up the rutted driveway in his dirty, mud-splattered van, Roscoe was the last to arrive. He parked in front of the ranch house next to one of five recently repainted GMC pickups.

Off to one side, Roscoe saw a large, four-wheeled, rusty metal trailer hooked behind a heavy-duty, low-sided dump truck. Its ramps were down in anticipation of loading the back hoe aboard.

The next day, while proudly displaying the electronic gizmos and gadgets he brought along, including the components for a message board, Roscoe said, "I bought the pieces individually, and your computer expert can help me build it. If I purchased one of those rarely used items on the open market, it'd leave a trail a mile wide and three miles long."

Holding up a cell phone masking device, he said, "I brought along two of these, just in case one goes bad."

"The Army taught us all about redundancy," Roger said. "Good work, Roscoe."

After helping unload his treasures, Roger took Roscoe aside and asked, "Roscoe, how do the transponders work? Do they get their power from a separate source, or are they connected to the truck battery?"

Roscoe spit between his feet and said, "It's the last one. The unit has a built-in antenna that allows Brinks to trace the movement of the vehicle. If a truck gets hijacked and the transponder ain't disconnected, they can follow its signal right to the robbers."

"Could you substitute another power source before you remove the transponder?"

Roscoe caught on fast.

"I get it. You want the thing to keep sending out signals, don't you?"

"Yes; could we hook the unit to a portable battery without interrupting its signal and then cut the wires to the truck?"

"Sure; what do you have in mind?"

"Here's what I want you to do," Roger said.

As Roscoe watched, Roger drew a diagram on a blackboard. When he realized what his boss had in mind, Roscoe grinned and said, "That's a smart idea. Brinks won't know their truck's missing for hours. No wonder Carl says you're brilliant."

"Flattery will get you everywhere, Roscoe. I thought it best we give Brinks something else to confuse them."

Pointing to the diagram, Roscoe said, "I can hook up a battery and have the transponder off the truck in a couple minutes. I'll buy the battery from a junk yard, so no one can trace it to us."

The last few items on Roger's list were slowly but surely being completed. As Carl watched Roscoe install the final electronic surveillance items in the walls and ceiling of the jail, Roscoe said, "I ran the wires into the den, so we can monitor everything from there."

While Alan tried to find and secure all the items Roger wanted, he spent a good part of each day on the computer. He also put several thousand miles on the pickups, driving from town to town, buying a few items here and a few there, always paying cash.

"You keep running all over New Mexico and you'll wear the tires off our trucks," Slim said.

After downloading the photographs from Roger's camera, Alan focused on the markings and sent detailed e-mails to a friend specializing in decals. Within three weeks he received fifteen sets for each state.

Roger inspected them and said, "You'd never know they weren't the real thing."

When another contact furnished the same number of out-of-date license plates and Roger saw the tags, he asked, "What about dates, Alan?"

Sounding a little miffed at his work being questioned, Alan asked in return, "When you see construction trucks with mud on their license plates, do you think anything about it?"

"I get your drift. Good job."

Alan spent days searching the internet for vehicles to fit the requirements Roger laid on him. He finally found and purchased a used eighteen-wheeler tractor with two trailers.

When they were delivered, Roger and the lead mechanic, Phil Snyder, looked them over. Roger said, "These are the items that can't go bad."

Phil patted the hood of the tractor and said, "They won't. I guarantee it. I'll have my guys go over them and make repairs where necessary. For safety's sake, we'll install new brakes, rebuild the radiator and replace all the tires."

Just as twenty-nine-year-old Phil was NCOIC of the

maintenance section for Roger's tanks in Iraq, he was now in charge of three other mechanics on the team. If not for his expertise and common sense approach, backed up with the re-supply prowess of A. J. in Iraq, Roger's tankers would have been up a dry wadi with no way out.

When Phil came home to find his job taken by a long-haired hippy, who hadn't washed the grease out of his locks in months, he decided, "To hell with it," and opened his own small shop.

He was doing all right, but being single, Phil still longed for adventure. When Carl called, Phil hung a "Closed" sign on his door and reported for duty.

Out of several candidates for the job, a redneck from Alabama, Herb Pitzer, was selected as the driver of the eighteen-wheeler. He had a southern accent so thick you felt his words should be covered in syrup.

Herb was a gentle giant carrying two hundred and forty-five pounds around on a six foot, five inch frame. Not an ounce was fat. He had muscles in places others didn't even know existed, but was mild as a lamb unless riled. Then his eyes got a steely look and you thought twice about messing with Herb.

When Herb was called to active duty, he was driving big rigs for a transport company in Peoria, Illinois. While he was overseas, someone else took his place. Herb returned to find his services no longer required.

When Carl called, all he said was, "I'll be there in two days."

Thin as a rail and lacking a little in the "smart department", Sam, "Skinny", Gibson, was Herb's partner and an aspiring novice truck driver who yearned to follow in Herb's footsteps.

Since he was the youngest of the thieves, everyone treated Skinny as if he was their brother or son. His father, Master Sergeant Bradley, "Big Bad and Ugly", Gibson, was killed in action in Kuwait.

When Skinny heard his dad bought the farm, he dropped out of high school at the ripe old age of seventeen to join the Army.

Skinny asked for and was granted permission to join Big Bad and Ugly's old unit. When he arrived in Roger's tank brigade; he was immediately taken under the wings of the veterans. After his discharge, along with the rest of the older men, Skinny remained a member of the team.

The day after Mister Remualdi sent Roger a name of a contact for the RPG, they discussed the need for more than one.

Roger said, "It's simple, if we use an RPG on any job, the game is over and we won't be able to pull another, so we only need one."

As he scratched his head, A. J. said, "Yeah, I see what you mean. Let's hope we take the weapon along and never use it."

Carl nodded and added, "Amen."

Three days later, Carl and A. J. went to Albuquerque and met a gun dealer. For five thousand dollars cash they received an armor piercing RPG launcher and four M-16 rifles.

When they discussed the need for other weapons, Roger said, "Besides the rifles, there's no reason. Either the driver and guard give up willingly or we use the RPG."

For an additional three hundred dollars, the dealer provided four handcuffs with keys, a package of wire-reinforced, plastic restraining straps and a large, oversized camouflaged tarp. If the RPG was used, hopefully the tarp would hide the wreckage.

Following Roger's instructions and pictures provided by Alan, Charley's crew manufactured and painted the required construction warning signs. After they stored them with the other equipment in the barn, Roger saw them, frowned and said, "They look better than the real thing. Now take them outside, kick them around and muddy them up. I've never seen a road crew with new equipment."

Shaking his head in wonder at the street smarts of his leader, Charley admitted, "I never thought of that. Come on guys; set up the signs and let's play 'King of the Hill'."

When work on the jail was finished, Roger gave the men a task of making alterations to the cattle trailer. Explaining his concept to Charley, he said, "We'll need a welder to reinforce two ramps to accommodate the weight of the larger Brinks armored trucks."

Roger handed him a drawing and said, "Here's another item that will come in handy. It's a special cage to install at the rear of the cattle trailer."

After he explained the reason for the addition, Charley said, "That's pretty smart, Roger. I'll get right on it."

Shortly before the garage was finished, all the changes were completed. After viewing the result, Slim told Roscoe, "Roger's one smart cookie. I don't know exactly what he's got in mind for this cage, but knowing him, it's something special."

Yesterday, Roger helped Alan unload two hundred orange traffic cones and store them under a hay pile in the barn. As he took a semi-white handkerchief from his pocket and wiped perspiration from his brow, Alan said, "Those are the last items on our list. I'm glad we're done."

"So am I. We begin training tomorrow. A. J. and Carl are out in the back forty laying out the grid."

In an arroyo a half mile from the ranch, Darrin Winters sat back on his haunches and wiped perspiration from his brow. Although late summer was disappearing fast, there were still days in the high nineties out in the desert of New Mexico.

It wasn't as if he wasn't used to hot weather. After two tours in Afghanistan, Darrin thought he'd never be cool again in his lifetime. The deserts of Southwestern America were nothing in comparison, but out in the noonday sun he still perspired like a hog in heat.

Following his discharge from Special Forces due to a severe wound leaving one arm a little shorter than the other, Darrin tried several occupations, but eventually found detective work was right up his alley.

He'd always been good at figuring out mysteries, so four years ago he became a private eye. Although he enjoyed working for himself, trying to make a living tracking down wandering wives or husbands got old after a while.

Until he got the call from Mister Murdock, Darrin was eking out enough to get by on and making a name in the PI world. Now he was in the big time and loving every minute of this adventure.

The past eight months were interesting, very interesting indeed. He kept his employer, Richard Murdock, well informed of the men who came to visit Roger and Carl in Austin, and also showed up here, working on their ranch in New Mexico.

So far, Darrin identified seventeen of the twenty-some-odd men living and working on the ranch. He discovered they were all ex-Army members who fought with Roger and Carl in Kuwait and Iraq.

Darrin just returned from tailing A. J. and Carl to Albuquerque, where to his amazement they purchased an RPG and a launcher, plus several weapons and other equipment.

Now he was out in the desert, sweating his ass off, watching the same two guys lay out some kind of grid or practice field while thinking, "What the hell are these guys up to? I know they aren't terrorists. Hell, they fought and many were wounded fighting terrorism. And what the hell is the three car garage for? Why did they bury it after it took so long to build?

"Listen to me. The sun is driving me batty. It's time to report to Mister Murdock. Maybe he can make heads or tails of this."

Maria and Julie took their separation from the men they loved stoically. Although Julie wasn't happy with the idea, she believed the cattle feeding service was a path to her future with Carl. In the past six months, Carl managed to sneak away from the ranch for three weekends and spent them with her in Austin.

Roger longed to be with Maria, but knew he must stay where he was to see the tasks completed to his satisfaction. Maria saw his absence as just one more bump in the road caused by the life she chose. Before he left for New Mexico, they dated several times, but so far she had failed to get Roger into her bed.

As customers clamored for the services provided by the new feeding station, Slim's wishes came true. Within days of posting the "Grand Opening" notices, business boomed.

During the building phase, Slim kept busy ordering hay, alfalfa and sacked grain to fatten up the cattle. He also supervised the work as water lines were installed to fill the troughs. The day after they buried the garage, the first cattle truck arrived, loaded with twenty-six heifers to be fattened up for the slaughter house.

As Slim and a group of supposed cowboys watched the

driver back into the chute area, he said, "Here's where I find out if you remember what I taught you."

Although Slim trained them well, there were still some small mistakes. When several cows from the first truck escaped, the new cowboys used two pickups to round them up.

Slim grinned as he remembered the day.

"It was a Chinese fire drill, Carlos. Imagine a bunch of Hollywood dudes in two pickups trying to corral some mean-spirited heifers. Talk about your Keystone Cops – it was lucky as hell they got the cows back into the pen. I would have bet on the cattle."

As Slim and the three amigos encouraged them, the men soon became proficient. There were no other incidents, and Slim said, "They still have a hell of a lot to learn, but sometimes they surprise me."

Each morning at six a.m., (except for Slim and Roscoe, who were considered old duffers), everyone performed daily calisthenics. As the men grew accustomed to the heat, A. J. added a three-mile evening run. Combined with hard work, the exercise and running routine had the desired effect. The men became lean and mean.

In the kitchen, Wes "Cookie" Hardy supervised two other men in preparing the evening meal. The epitome of a "mess sergeant", Wes was short and stout, with a bass voice you could hear across a battlefield when mortar shells were landing.

One day Wes winked and said, "If you kill a cow by accident, Slim, we'll have steaks for supper tonight."

Slim glared at him and said, "The way these guys work, I wouldn't call any dead heifer 'an accident'. I'll be watching you, Wes."

Except for not having a lit cigarette with two inches of ash hanging out of his mouth, Wes resembled the original Cookie from the Beetle Bailey comic strip.

Instead, to make sure no one ever found ashes of tobacco flakes in his food, his trade mark was an unlit cigar tucked into one corner of an ample jaw.

As he ambled through the kitchen, Roscoe said, "I hope you've got peach cobbler for desert tonight, Wes."

"No such luck, buddy. All I had was cherries."

Looking disappointed, Roscoe said, "I guess I can suffer through two or three pieces."

In Kuwait, Wes kept the men supplied with the best food available when other messes went without. He and A. J. worked as a team to insure Roger's tankers were well fed and supplied with the latest equipment. As a result, Wes and his staff shared in the gold payoff.

When Carl called, he was working in a barbecue shack in downtown Llano, Texas. He didn't hesitate a minute in joining. Now here in the desert southwest, his culinary accomplishments, combined with lack of fat or carbohydrates in their diet, aided in the men's transformation.

Looking up from his stove, Wes said, "It's going to be another hot son of a bitch today. You better mix up a big batch of iced tea for supper, Mike."

To everyone's surprise and delight, Alan stayed on his diet. At the last weigh-in, he had lost twenty pounds.

Roger said, "Not much more to go, Alan. Keep after it."

When Roscoe and Alan completed building the electronic message board, Floyd Jensen, a twenty-four-year-old gunner on a tank in Kuwait and a would-be electronics nut, watched them test the device.

When the screen came to life and messages scrolled by, Floyd exclaimed, "Way too cool. If I was the driver or guard, I'd either crap my pants or grow wings and fly out of the truck."

After shutting the device down, Alan said, "We hope they're as smart as you are, Jensen."

The computer age caught Floyd unaware, but after the gold payoff, he laid plans to catch up and open his own business. Though not his fault, the business went bust. When Carl called, Floyd was working at a car wash for minimum wage and tips. After hearing the proposition, it didn't take five seconds for him to throw down his rag, give the boss man the finger and walk out the door.

When they decided to use Slim's truck as a substitute for the armored vehicle, and Wiley and Clete came by to get the vehicle,

Slim said, "You yahoos take care of my pickup. It don't look like much, but it's all I have."

"Keep your britches out of the crack of your ass," Wiley said. "We won't damage your vehicle."

Carl watched and timed the men, and then reported, "We have to get it down to ten minutes for the robbery. I estimate it'll take twelve minutes to clean up afterward."

Roger made a notation in his log and said, "Keep after them until they get it right. I don't want any wasted motion out there on the highway."

Four days before the actual robbery, Roger declared they were ready.

"According to Alan's estimate, twelve to fifteen vehicles on each side of the road will see our highway department trucks and crews at work. It's not many witnesses to a crime they don't know is taking place."

"No one will pay any attention to us," Carl said. "The delayed drivers will be anxious to make up lost time. We'll just be shadows in the morning."

After checking his log book, Alan said, "We clocked the time, and from their last stop in Roswell, it takes between fifty-five minutes to one hour for the truck to reach the first site."

Roger stretched his weary back and said, "We're as ready as we can be. Tell the men to knock off and get some rest."

The next night, the entire team assembled in the bunkhouse for Roger's final briefing.

"Everything looks good. Does everyone understand exactly how this goes down?"

They answered with a chorus of, "Yes, Sir."

"Are there any questions?"

No one said anything. It was silent as the Tomb of the Unknown Soldier at midnight.

Roger smiled at their professionalism and said, "Okay. Our first target arrives in two days and the big one gets here three days later. Alan will find the departure times and notify the team leaders, who will make sure each team is set up well in advance."

Carl added, "The men who stay behind have to keep

everything running smoothly. If a truck arrives with cattle, off-load them ASAP and send the driver on his way. If there's a truck here when we get back, the driver won't see anything except for another big rig and our pickups. The dump truck and backhoe will look like they're returning from work somewhere on the ranch."

"During the next two days, nobody goes to town. Continue to practice your parts in your minds. The plan is simple, so should run like clockwork. Everyone knows what to do if things go south and we have to use the RPG."

"Yeah," A. J. said. "The other two jobs are blown out of the water and there goes our profit. We finish up as practiced, take the money and leave the wreck behind. Most of the loot from the first robbery goes to pay off Mister Remualdi, so it doesn't leave much for us."

Roger nodded and added, "Let's all do our jobs and prevent anything like that from happening."

Chapter 12

The next night, Alan hacked into Brinks computer system and discovered their target would make its last pick-up in Roswell at 0800 hours. There was no way to know the exact amount on board, but he said, "From past records, the take should be between six and seven million."

Carl tried to hold back a grin, failed badly and said, "I hope you're right."

After checking his watch again, Alan said, "We watched them load the money at the last bank and it usually takes four to five minutes. At 0805, the rush hour traffic will still be fairly heavy, so I added an extra ten minutes for the truck to reach the outskirts. From there, it should take about an hour to reach the first check point between 0855 and 0900."

Roger stood up to get another cup of coffee.

"Okay, at 0700, we depart for the checkpoints. By 0815, everyone should be set up and have their signs and cones in place."

Carl nervously bit his thumbnail and added, "Now comes the hardest part of the job – waiting."

After spending a restless night, everyone woke to an alarm clock's jingle at 0500 hours.

Harry Charles, the weather man on FYI Channel Seven told his viewing audience, "It looks like a cool day today, with a north wind at five to ten miles per hour, but no rain is forecast."

Cookie and his assistants had been up since three a.m.,

preparing a hearty breakfast. Floyd was first in the dining room. When Roger walked in, Floyd said, "Go get 'em. I'll be watching for you to roll over the hill with the armored truck."

Roger smiled and said, "Keep the home fires burning, Floyd."

A few minutes later, Slim walked in, poured a cup of coffee, carried it to Roger's table and announced, "I'm ready to roll."

"Take it easy, Slim, and drive slowly," Roger said. "All we want you to do is let us know when the armored truck gets close to checkpoint one."

Thirty minutes after the teams departed as scheduled for their assigned sites, Slim left the ranch in his old truck, drove slowly toward Roswell for twenty miles, then made a U-turn and headed north again at a snail's pace.

Team one drove the greatest distance, south toward Roswell over two miles of hills and dips in the road past the actual robbery site. There the driver made a U-turn and pulled the pickup onto the shoulder.

Speaking over his shoulder to the men in the rear, he said, "Get with it. Set out the signs first and then the line of cones."

Following his instructions and their preset time schedule, the men of team one began erecting traffic signs informing drivers of road construction ahead. Then they laid out a line of orange traffic cones beginning at the edge of the road and slanting in toward the center of the two-lane highway, until they eventually blocked the first lane.

Where the cones ended, Bill Casey, a young man of twenty-three stood holding a flagger pole. Bill wore blue jeans and a bulky, down-filled green jacket with the lower portion of his face covered by a faded orange scarf.

Throughout his combat tour, Bill was with Roger and Carl as an ammunition loader. When Carl called asking him if he'd like to make a few extra "unaccountable" bucks, Bill was down on his luck and jobless.

While helping them on their last con job in Houston, Bill enjoyed the challenge of the "game" and was looking forward to the big payoff promised after this Brinks caper. Lately though, he found he liked the solitude of the ranch and working with cattle.

To his credit, Bill had already signed up to stay on afterward and keep the place running.

Team two completed the same operation two miles north of the actual robbery site, on the opposite side of the road. When they finished putting their cones in place, Alan took his place as a flagger, wearing an orange reflecting vest and a blue scarf over his mouth.

In a gloved hand, he held a slow/stop sign on a red and white striped pole. While displaying the slow sign to southbound traffic, Alan allowed all oncoming vehicles to proceed.

The largest team, number three, set up camp a mile north of team one, on the same side of the roadway, at the actual robbery site. On the way to their position, they added to the line of cones from team one, spacing them out over a one mile course blocking the first lane.

At the end of the line of cones, Roger took the flagger position, wearing gloves, dark sunglasses, a long-haired black wig, a phony moustache and a cap pulled low over his eyes. He also allowed northbound traffic to pass without stopping.

After listening to reports from each team, Roger waved to Carl and called out, "Everyone's on time and the checkpoints are manned."

Carl waved to acknowledge his statement while thinking; "Now we wait for Slim's call."

After checking the electronic message board and its power source hidden in a large cooler next to the flagger pole, Roger watched as the backhoe was unloaded and the disconnected trailer was parked on the shoulder.

One of Herb's favorite country songs, "Old Flames", was playing on the radio as he drove the eighteen-wheeler with the large enclosed trailer south toward Roswell. When he reached a turn-around just past checkpoint three, Herb made a U-turn and drove north until he reached a point where two high ridges and a dip in the highway separated the big rig from the robbery site.

After parking the rig on the shoulder with the engine idling, he and Skinny jumped from the cab. Working quickly, Skinny set out four small, red warning cones behind the truck and then returned to the cab to keep warm. Herb raised the hood and remained partially hidden, supposedly working on the "disabled" motor.

A latecomer to the team, Will Stone, drove the backhoe to the edge of the road and parked the machine a few feet beyond the last cone. Will served in Kuwait in the infantry and was a good buddy of Phil Snyder, who recommended his name to Carl.

So far, Will had done more than his share while working with the cattle and never complained. This was his first foray into the crime scene, but the thought didn't upset him.

As he often said, "After my time in the killing fields of Iraq, nothing bothers me and probably never will."

During a lull in traffic, Hiram Clements pulled the dump truck across the highway and drove south down the median. Then he made a U-turn. The truck tires threw up twin plumes of dust, which settled quickly in the dry desert air. With the engine idling, Hiram parked in the median alongside the northbound lane, one hundred feet from the end of the cones.

As a former National Guard First Lieutenant, Hiram was the only other ex-Army officer on the team besides Roger. Since he was also an older troop, thirty-eight and prematurely balding, some enlisted men thought it was a hoot he liked to drive the backhoe and pile up manure. But Hiram saw the job as a real challenge and didn't mind the smell.

Although Hiram took his share of ribbing, the men respected his ability as an excellent tactician and hard worker.

Wearing ski masks and thin cotton gloves while hidden from view, Roscoe and Charley sat inside the payload compartment of the dump truck on top of the camouflaged tarp.

Glancing at his buddy, Charley saw Roscoe was holding a long handled bolt cutter and appeared nervous.

Charley slapped him on the back and said, "Calm down, buddy. Before this day is over, we two old farts will show these young whippersnappers a thing or two."

Roscoe coughed and said, "Just be ready with the masking device when I ask for it."

Wearing a set of cammies, leather gloves and a red and white full-face ski mask, Carl stood on the shoulder beside a pickup, with the RPG and launcher hidden behind him and covered by a small tarp.

Each flagger held a radio to his ear and listened as everyone checked in. When Roger heard the men were in place, he checked his watch and said, "It won't be long now."

Suddenly the radio crackled to life as Slim announced, "Our target is approximately one mile from checkpoint one. There are no other vehicles in sight behind it."

At checkpoint one, as the Brinks truck approached, Casey displayed the slow sign and motioned to the driver to reduce his speed.

The Brinks driver, Jim, slowed his heavy vehicle to less than forty-five miles per hour. Casey waved him on and spoke into his microphone, "Check point one, the target has passed us."

Casey watched as the armored truck crested the first hill beyond site one. Then he turned his sign to stop and stood in the middle of the second lane. The next vehicle to arrive was Slim in his old red truck. Slim stopped with his pickup blocking the second lane and winked.

According to Alan's watch, when he heard Slim's announcement, the last vehicle headed south passed by two minutes ago. He turned his flagger pole to stop just as a big rig loaded with port-a-potties came into view. After braking to a halt, the driver looked either bored or pissed off at the delay, but when Alan waved, he returned the greeting.

When he received the word, Will pulled the backhoe onto the blacktop and lowered the bucket to the ground, blocking the second lane. At the same time, Hiram put the dump truck into double-low gear and let the vehicle roll forward slowly toward the backhoe.

Carl uncovered the RPG, hid it behind his leg and stood ready to fire.

Just before the armored vehicle arrived at his checkpoint, Roger removed the message board from the cooler, placed it behind his legs and displayed the stop sign to oncoming traffic.

When he saw the signal, the dump truck moving and the backhoe blocking the second lane, Jim stopped his vehicle just short of Roger's position and said, "Shit, this is all we need. Now we'll probably be late getting into Albuquerque."

As Hiram pulled the dump truck forward and stopped alongside the driver's door of the armored truck, Roscoe seemed to have overcome his initial fright. Moving with agile ability considering his age, he vaulted over the side of the truck bed with a bolt cutter in his right hand.

Thanks to a good pair of tennis shoes, he landed softly atop the target. With one snip, he removed the radio antenna. Then turning quickly, Roscoe reached down and took a masking device with a magnet attached to the bottom from Charley's hands and placed it on top of the cab.

Jim stared intently as Roger pulled the message board into view, punched a button and the first command scrolled across the screen: LOOK TO YOUR RIGHT.

Following the strange instructions, Jim turned his head and saw Carl holding the RPG. Confused and frightened, he glanced back at Roger, who punched the command button again.

After reading the next message: THAT'S AN ARMOR PIERCING MISSLE AIMED AT YOUR CAB. OBEY THE FOLLOWING COMMANDS AND YOU WON'T BE HURT. WAVE YOUR HAND IF YOU UNDERSTAND, Jim waved both hands in the air and said, "Oh, shit!"

With his hands raised and face pale, Larry looked like he had already obeyed Jim's command.

("I knew it – and they've got an RPG, just like I said they would.")

Roger punched the command button and the instructions continued: PUT THE GEAR SHIFT IN NEUTRAL. LEAVE THE MOTOR RUNNING AND KEYS IN THE IGNITION. EXIT THE VEHICLE IN THIRTY SECONDS OR WE'LL FIRE.

Both doors flew open.

As the Brinks employees left the vehicle, from his lofty perch, Roscoe stuck his bolt cutter between the door and the frame.

When Jim and Larry stepped from the truck with their hands raised, two masked team members approached from the rear to blindfold and handcuff the Brinks employees.

After removing the warhead from the RPG launcher, Carl

laid both pieces of the weapon in a wooden box in the bed of the pickup. Then he reached through an open window of the vehicle, removed a small black medicine bag, took out two syringes filled with knock-out serum and walked quickly to where Jim and Larry stood.

When Carl reached their side, he removed a cork protecting the end of a needle, squirted out a small amount of fluid, plunged the needle into Larry's right arm and injected the serum. Larry dropped like a stone.

Carl quickly performed the same procedure on Jim. Then he watched as the Brinks employees were carried to the pickup and strapped in an upright position in the front seat.

During this time, Roger gave a signal, and Will backed the tractor out of the way. Roscoe amazed everyone with his dexterity as he swung down into the cab of the armored truck and quickly drove away.

The stolen vehicle rolled over two hills to where Herb and Skinny waited with the doors to the trailer open and two ramps lowered to the ground. They guided Roscoe onto the shoulder, helped line up the armored truck with the ramps and watched as Roscoe drove the vehicle carefully into the interior.

After Skinny retracted the ramps, he climbed into the trailer. Herb swung the doors shut, retrieved the traffic cones, lowered the hood, climbed into the cab and drove off.

Leaving the lights on, Roscoe stepped down from the cab and smiled weakly at Skinny, who was holding a battery with two attached cables. Although it was cool outside, Roscoe's shirt was soaked with perspiration and his heart beat like the vibrations from Rosie the Riveter's favorite tool as he thought, "Damn, what a ride."

Reaching into his coat pocket, he retrieved a heavy crescent wrench and crawled under the armored truck, while Skinny held a flashlight so Roscoe could see what he was doing.

As the big rig pulled onto the highway, Roscoe quickly located the transponder. After carefully removing the device, he noted there were two thin, red and black wires attached to battery connections.

He hooked the replacement battery to the transponder and

then used a small electrical probe to insure current was flowing to the device from his replacement. When he was sure it was working properly, Roscoe cut the original wires, double-checked the signal again and said into his microphone, "It's working perfectly."

He winked at Skinny, and while holding the transponder and battery in shaking hands, took a deep breath to steady his nerves and walked to a side door.

At the robbery site, team three retrieved the cones and signs, while Will and Hiram drove their vehicles to the trailer and hooked it up. Then Will drove the backhoe aboard and they chained down the machine. When he received the go ahead signal, Hiram pulled onto the highway and drove toward the ranch.

At checkpoints one and two, Alan and Bill turned their signs to slow and allowed the delayed vehicles to pass. From the south, in addition to Slim's truck, eight assorted vehicles were lined up. Behind the Port-a-Potty carrier were a total of eleven cars, vans and trucks in the southbound lanes.

When Roger received word the armored truck was safely loaded, he checked his watch. The entire process had taken ten minutes and seventeen seconds. Shaking his head in amazement, he said, "Way to go, guys."

After team one cleaned up their site and reported all signs and cones were on board, Roger said, "You're cleared to depart."

Two minutes later, team two reported in.

"One of our damned cones blew off the road, and it took an extra minute to retrieve."

Roger smiled at the small SNAFU and ordered, "Head for the shed."

After picking up and loading their cones and signs, the members of team three drove to the site where the eighteen-wheeler had been parked and took time to erase all tire tracks. They returned to their vehicle and Carl said, "I counted cars. While you were working, seven vehicles passed by."

After glancing around for one last site check, Roger said, "We're done here. Let's head for the ranch."

As soon as Casey gave Slim the go-ahead signal, he continued north in the first lane at a slow pace, allowing the other delayed vehicles to pass by. When one driver gave him the finger for driving below the speed limit, Slim smiled and tipped his hat while thinking, "Race on fool, hell ain't half-full."

At the turn-in for the Crossed X Ranch, Slim saw Roscoe standing by the side of the road, holding a car battery in his right hand and the transponder tucked under his left elbow.

The only trace of Herb and the big rig was a patch of dust settling back to earth. Herb was making tracks down the gravel road, and to hell with worrying about tires.

Roscoe hurried to the pickup as Slim leaned over the seat to open the door, and Roscoe said, "Thanks."

His shirt was so wet with sweat, Slim said, "Damn, Roscoe, you look like you were the last one out of the swimming hole, buddy."

"It was hot in that frigging truck."

They drove north through Vaughn and Encino. When they arrived at the large truck stop at Cline's Corner; Slim pulled off the highway into the parking lot and parked close to a group of big rigs with their motors idling.

He kept watch as Roscoe stepped from the truck with the transponder in one hand and the battery dangling from the other, and walked nonchalantly toward an empty cattle trailer.

After checking, he found the cab empty and thought, "Apparently the driver's in the restaurant having coffee."

Roscoe walked to the side of the trailer, reached in through the slats and laid his load on manure-matted hay. To hide them from view, he used his gloved hands to pile dung-caked hay around the devices.

Slim gave him the all clear sign, and Roscoe walked back to the truck, removed his gloves and threw them into the truck bed. Glancing down at his hands, he said, "Damn, I got cow shit all over myself. You got any paper towels, Slim?"

"No, you'll have to clean up inside. You should know better than to play around with cow shit, Roscoe."

"You ain't funny, asshole."

Still laughing, Slim moved the truck to the parking lot,

climbed out and asked, "Walk behind me, will you, Roscoe? I don't want anyone to know I'm with you."

"Order some coffee for me and quit braying like a jackass. I told you, it ain't funny."

While Roscoe washed his hands, Slim ordered black coffee for Roscoe and a glass of milk and Danish for his own breakfast.

A few minutes later, they watched as the cattle truck pulled back on the highway, headed west.

After completing the job, everyone at the Crossed X Ranch was running on adrenaline. When they returned, the stay-behinds told them there were no customers during their absence.

First things came first; Jim and Larry were quickly transferred to the jail, where their handcuffs and blindfolds were removed and they were placed on individual cots. Watches were stripped from their wrists. Shoe strings, belts and all personal items were removed.

Watching the proceedings on closed circuit TV, Carl turned to the monitor, twenty-eight-year-old Fred Smith, and said, "It should be another hour before they wake up. Let me know when they do."

Fred was an old hand at watching prisoners. While serving as an Army MP, he spent several weeks in Iraq and never cared to leave the United States again. It made him sick to see the poor starving conscripts Saddam asked to face the power of America. As a result, he'd make sure these guys were taken care of.

Carl slapped his leader on the back and said, "Congratulations, Roger. Everything ran like clockwork. This one will go down in history."

Roger smiled and said, "In three more days, we hit them again, same time, same place. By that time, Brinks may have recovered their transponder, but it won't lead to us. As far as they know, after the driver and guard stopped at Cline's Corner for coffee, they kept on truckin', so the vehicle won't be missed until later today."

The equipment was removed from the pickups; and all items were accounted for and hidden in the barn, while the used decals were burned in a fireplace.

An hour later, Fred reported Jim and Larry were conscious. He, Carl and Roger gathered in the den to watch the captives for a few minutes on a TV screen. Thanks to Roscoe, taped sounds of city traffic and an occasional far-off wail of an emergency vehicle echoed through speakers hidden in the walls of the jail.

"Hopefully, they'll believe they're being held in Albuquerque," Roger said while picking up a microphone. A masking device muffled his voice as he said, "Welcome, gentlemen."

His announcement startled their guests, so he paused a moment to give them time to adjust. Then he said, "We apologize for the inconvenience. You'll be with us for a few days, so relax and enjoy your vacation. Food, fresh underwear, socks and clothing will be provided daily.

"By the sink you'll find soap, toothpaste, washcloths and towels. I'm sorry, but you won't be allowed to shave. You can shower if you use the hand-held sprinkler head over the floor drain. The overhead light will remain on twenty-four hours a day."

Staring up at the camera lens with an incredulous look on his face, Jim asked, "Who are you and why do you want to keep us? You have the money. Let us go."

"You'll be released shortly. Don't worry. Nothing will happen to you. Do not attempt to escape. It's impossible and you'll only injure yourselves."

Larry gave the camera the finger and snarled, "Go to hell."

Roger shrugged and said, "Have it your way. In a few minutes breakfast will be served. When the food arrives, sit on your beds until the trays are slipped through the slot. Follow my instructions or you'll go hungry."

Jim sighed and replied, "Okay, we'll do as you say."

Larry continued to stare at the security camera with hatred in his eyes.

Roger handed the mike to Fred and said, "Keep a close eye on them."

Two hours later, Roscoe and Slim returned and reported their mission of deception was completed successfully.

Roger shook their hands and asked, "How'd it go at checkpoint one, Slim?"

Slim spat at a bug crawling through the grass as he said, "Hell, those yahoos behind me didn't notice a thing. As soon as Casey gave the go ahead, they passed me like Kamikaze pilots. By the time I arrived at site three, they were over the horizon and making tracks for the interstate."

"How'd it go at Cline's Corner?" Carl asked.

Slim grinned and a twinkle appeared in his eyes. "We planted the transponder on an empty cattle truck. Roscoe got cow shit all over my pickup, so I'll probably have to fumigate it."

Roscoe kicked a stone across the gravel driveway in apparent anger.

"You and your big mouth, Slim. Hell, if anyone is monitoring the transponder, when the truck doesn't stop in Albuquerque and keeps heading west, they'll have a heart attack."

The men changed clothes and returned to work. An hour later, when a shipment of forty cows arrived, they handled the job as if they'd been doing it for years.

As the sun sank behind blue and grey snowcapped mountains to the west, Roger dispatched a man to lock the ranch gates. When he returned, heavy machinery operators began to dig into the ramp. Within two hours, they had cleared the first stall.

Hiram used the backhoe to scrape manure from the concrete slab, while Casey washed the accumulated crap and crud from the hidden door with a high-powered hose.

Walking by carrying a crowbar, Roscoe said, "Watch where the hell you point that thing, Casey. I don't need any cow shit on my clothes."

When the door was raised and propped open with a scrap piece of one-by-four, Casey heard a motor of a ventilator hum as fresh clean air rushed in to replace the stale odors. It sounded like a toy freight train about to jump the tracks.

Charley and a team of four men made their way down the stairs, pulled pins from steel reinforcing bars and removed them. The four-by-fours blocking the entrance to the first stall were disassembled and placed to one side.

As Aleksander Kawalski wiped residue of cow manure from his gloves in a pile of sand, he said, "Damn, it's still hot this early in the morning. Chicago was never like this."

Although he was a hard worker, Alex, (as he was known by the other team members because they couldn't spell his name or pronounce it correctly), was a follower, not a leader.

Railroaded into the Army by a friendly judge when he was caught shoplifting, Alex soon found himself in Kuwait, serving as a gunner in Roger's tank brigade.

When he was never promoted above the rank of Corporal, and knowing brains weren't a prerequisite for being in the Army, Alex figured it was because no one could spell both his names.

Although he also earned a share of the Kuwaiti gold profits, when Carl called, Alex was down to less than five hundred dollars in the bank, jobless and wondering where his next meal would come from.

Needless to say, he joined, but stayed mostly to himself, reading, watching and learning. So far, the job was everything his leaders said it would be. He liked the solitude of the ranch, so thought maybe he'd stay on after the robberies.

After Herb backed the eighteen-wheeler into the cleared space, and Skinny lowered the ramps, Roger said, "Casey, you have the honor, but don't ding it. We don't have insurance."

Before Casey backed the armored truck into its final resting place, Roscoe climbed on top of the vehicle, retrieved the cell phone blocking device and said, "We can't do without you, little buddy."

A crowd of cowboy robbers watched as several men reassembled the door to stall one. Then Casey and Hiram filled and rebuilt the ramp.

When the job was completed, Carl and Roger led everyone except Fred, (who stayed behind to monitor their guests), into the interior. They gathered around the door at the rear of the truck.

Jim's key ring dangled from Roger's index finger, and he said, "Let's see what's inside." He found the right key, unlocked the door, pulled it outward and said, "Damn, its heavier than it looks."

Reaching into the truck, Roger picked a sack at random and asked, "What have we here? The tag says there's seventy-five thousand dollars inside."

As Roger stood aside for a moment, Jensen reached into the interior, hefted a heavier money sack and said, "Beautiful."

Roger took the sack gently from Jensen's hand and said, "And it all stays right where it is."

Jensen looked crestfallen and several men looked at Roger inquisitively, but he said, "Don't be upset. Later there'll be plenty of time for you to hold as many money bags as you want. Alan will stay and count the loot. When he's done, I'll let you know the total.

"We owe our backer approximately four million and it comes out of this money. As soon as we pay him off, the rest is ours free and clear. In three days, we hit the next truck, which carries almost twice as much, and it belongs to us."

For a few more moments, the men stared at the pile of money sacks. Then the crowd broke up and they walked up the stairs with pride in their steps. Roger could tell they were psyched out and yearning for more adventure.

Finally only Roger, Carl, A. J., Roscoe and Alan remained. After swinging the heavy door shut and locking it, Roger gave Alan the key.

"Pick out someone to help you count the money, but don't open any bags. Whoever you choose will spread the word. Sort out enough to pay Mister Remualdi three million, five hundred thousand."

"What's with the extra money?" Carl asked. "Our interest is only forty-one percent."

"I can do the math," Roger said. "If we pay Mister Remualdi a little extra, it'll put us in good standing with him. Remember, he has to pay Frank a finder's fee. Hell Carl, in a few days we'll have more than enough money to go around. Don't be greedy."

"I'm not and I apologize. You're the boss. If it weren't for your idea, we'd probably be robbing a casino and get killed in the process."

"Everyone else agree?" Roger asked.

Alan and A. J. nodded and Roscoe said, "Hell yes. Pay the man."

Lying on a slight rise of a sand dune, Darrin stared through his night-vision goggles. He couldn't believe what he witnessed earlier today and then tonight. It was mind boggling.

("I don't believe it. They actually knocked off a Brinks truck in broad daylight. What a pair of balls Roger and Carl have. I've seen teamwork, but this was something else. But why the hell are they keeping the guard and driver?")

"To hell with it," he whispered aloud. "I have to report to Mister Murdock. I know he said not to say anything about Roger and Carl's crimes, but this is a horse of a different color."

After punching in Richard's cell phone number, he listened to the phone ring several times before Richard's sleepy voice asked, "Yes, what is it, Darrin?"

("Shit, I forgot about the time difference.")

"You won't believe it," Darrin said.

Richard sat up in bed, now fully awake, and said, "Try me."

"They stole a Brinks armored truck in broad daylight and just now finished burying it in one of the slots in the garage."

Impressed at Roger and Carl's audacity, Richard said, "So that's why they covered the garage."

"What should I do?"

"Nothing," Richard said. "Good for them. It's the kind of initiative I like to see."

"But they kidnapped the driver and guard and are holding them in the strange building I told you about. Shouldn't I notify the authorities?"

"Hell no," Richard said. "I told you at the time I hired you. You are never, and I mean never, to report anything Roger and Carl and their band of thieves do. That was our agreement and I insist you keep your part of the bargain."

"All right, Sir; just as long as I'm never implicated in anything like kidnapping."

"Believe me," Richard said, "Roger and Carl will never harm a hair on anyone's body. You've seen the reports of their past activities. Has anyone ever been injured?"

"No, Sir," Darrin said. "I see your point."

"There must be a reason for holding the employees prisoner. Figure it out and get back to me."

"Yes, Sir," Darrin said, but was talking to a dead instrument.

Chapter 13

At twelve fifty-seven p.m., a phone rang in the Roswell Brinks Branch Office, and Clyde Rhodes answered.

"Clyde, this is Ed Reeves in Albuquerque. Did truck number 471 get off on time? He hasn't checked in, and the bank wants to know where the truck is. Did the driver report any trouble?"

"No, he didn't. According to my log, at five minutes past eight, the truck left its last stop and at eight-twelve cleared the city limits. We haven't heard from Jim since."

"Something is strange," Ed said. "Maybe the truck broke down. If it did, Jim hasn't called. Can you check the transponder signal?"

"Hold on, Ed; I have to go across the hall."

Clyde punched the hold button and walked quickly to the signal room, where a young lady named Alice Faye was making entries in a log. Although it was hot outside, the air conditioner made the office feel like Christmas time in the Antarctic, so Alice wore a long-sleeved green sweater.

Glancing up, she saw Clyde with a worried expression on his face, and asked, "What's up, Clyde?"

"Have you heard from Jim Young in truck 471?"

"Not since he cleared the city limits. What's the problem?"

"Ed Reeves is on the phone," Clyde said. "Jim hasn't checked in and didn't show up at the bank. Something is wrong."

Alice stood up; walked to a large machine filled with reels of tape and said, "Let me check the tapes."

When a Brinks truck is moving, its transponder sends out a

continual steady toned signal on a separate wavelength. If the truck stops for any reason, the signal changes to a low warbling sound. The machine Alice was checking automatically records each stop and inserts a white mark on the tape. The duration is noted and when the truck resumes its journey, the machine annotates the tape again.

She heard the tape emitting a steady tone and knew wherever the truck was, it was on the move.

Alice expected a few white marks at the beginning of the tape and they were there, indicating time the truck spent pausing at traffic lights in Roswell. After that, for a number of feet, (approximately one hour), the tape was clean.

There shouldn't have been any more white marks, but there were five, three of which were close together. The first stop lasted seven minutes. Then the truck moved a mile and a half and stopped a second time for three minutes. After that, it proceeded on for sixteen minutes before stopping for a third time for less than a minute.

Before stopping again for fifteen minutes, the truck continued on for an hour and five minutes. Then the vehicle rolled on for an hour and seven minutes, and stopped the last time for ten minutes.

From that time, the armored vehicle continued westward and was now far beyond the city limits of Albuquerque. If her computations were correct, the truck was approaching Gallup.

("It doesn't make any sense. Jim shouldn't have stopped at all. Maybe he made an unauthorized stop for coffee at Cline's corner, but these other stops don't make sense. What the devil's going on? I better double-check everything.")

Clyde stood by silently as Alice did her first computation, frowned, checked the tape and her calculations again and said, "That's impossible."

"What's wrong?" Clyde asked.

"The transponder tape tells me truck 471 is approaching Gallup and still moving west. Why would Jim and Larry be headed toward Arizona? They know where they're supposed to be."

Clyde picked up an extension phone, punched the flashing

button, held his hand over the mouthpiece and said, "Check the figures again."

Exasperated, she said, "I already did."

Clyde heard Ed talking to someone in the background and broke into his conversation.

"Ed, something strange is going on. According to the transponder, truck 471 is approaching Gallup and is still moving west."

"That's crazy. Why would Jim do something so weird? There must be a malfunction in your equipment."

Clyde motioned to Alice and asked again, "Is the tape recorder working correctly?"

Glancing up from her calculations, Alice grimaced and looked annoyed. The frown didn't leave her face when she said very distinctly, "The equipment is working perfectly. Truck 471 is right where I told you."

"Ed, I'll get back to you. It looks like something happened to truck 471. Either they ran off with the payload or were held up. I have to notify our headquarters."

"Okay," Ed said. "Should I call the state police?"

"No, I'll handle it from here. Let me talk to Albuquerque and see what they say. Hang loose. I'll get back to you."

He hung up before Ed could reply and then dialed the number of the main office from memory. When the operator answered, he didn't have time for niceties. He demanded, "Let me talk to John Grayson."

When his district supervisor answered, Clyde identified himself and said, "Truck 471 is missing, John, and I want your approval to call in the FBI."

"Hold on a minute. How long has this truck been missing?"

("Why is it whenever a truck is a few minutes late, everyone assumes it's been robbed?")

John was a conniver who always covered his own ass, no matter what. He didn't know, but his latest boss realized what a horse's ass John was and how he would slough off responsibility for anything unfavorable to a subordinate. But he was a U. S. Government civil service employee, and almost impossible to fire.

His current boss figured John's past supervisors promoted him to get rid of him. Well, as far as he was concerned, this was John's last stop. He kept a log of John's transgressions and was ready to go to the mat to get him fired.

"Ed Reeves called a few minutes ago and said truck 471 didn't arrive at the bank," Clyde said. "The truck left Roswell at eight-twelve a.m., with an ETA of twelve-fifteen p.m. When it didn't show, the bank called Ed and he checked his radio room. There have been no radio messages from truck 471 since it left Roswell."

"Are you sure the truck hasn't broken down somewhere?" John asked, while thinking, "What the hell is going on? This is something different."

"The driver hasn't radioed or called to say it did," Clyde said. "I think they've been held up."

"What makes you think that?"

("I sure as hell don't want to cry wolf and be embarrassed.")

"There's something else very weird," Clyde said. "The transponder tells us truck 471 is approaching Gallup."

Glancing at Alice, Clyde knew she heard his remarks and was fuming inside. Her face was so red it looked like a traffic light. Clyde took the hint, stopped asking her about her calculations and cut John off at the pass.

"Before you ask, John, yes, we checked the equipment and it's functioning perfectly. There's something wrong; I feel it in my bones."

"This is strange," John said and thought, "Maybe Clyde's right." Then he asked, "How well do you know the driver and guard? Could they be attempting to abscond with the money?"

("That's all we need. If it's true, the newspapers will have a ball.")

"I've known Jim Young for years. He's a dedicated family man with four kids and a wonderful wife. He'd never think of taking Brinks money."

"What about the guard?" John asked. ("Maybe he's the culprit.")

"Larry Grey's a good employee. He's single, but dependable and has been with us for over a year. If he wanted to rob a truck, he's had time to hit bigger payloads than this."

"How much money were they carrying?" John asked, and silently prayed, "Lord, don't let it be big."

"It's just over seven million."

John was quiet for a minute and his mind raced, while he tried to come up with a way to cover his ass one more time.

("Why is it always me? If I hesitate, it'll be my ass. I'd rather be wrong than have my boss chew me out for doing nothing. What the hell, I'll let Clyde call the Feds. If it's a screw-up, he'll catch the heat.")

Finally he said, "Okay, I agree. Call the FBI and tell them what you told me. If the truck crosses a state line, it falls under the jurisdiction of the FBI. Then call the state police and ask them to check the truck's route."

"I'll get right on it," Clyde said and hung up before John could reply.

("I better check with Alice one more time.")

"Alice, how positive are you of the location of the transponder?"

Putting her hands on her hips, she stared darts at Clyde. If she had a chimney, it would be blowing smoke black as night.

Although she was close to losing her temper, Alice held it inside and said very slowly, "I told you twice. I checked and double-checked. My calculations are correct. The truck, or at least the transponder, is still moving west at a steady rate and approaching the Arizona border."

When he saw the fire burning in her eyes, Clyde thought, "Alice is pissed at me. I shouldn't have questioned her ability."

Sighing and lying, he said, "Okay, I apologize. I wasn't questioning your ability. I'll alert the state police."

Alice calmed down enough to remember the unauthorized stops.

"There's something else; the tape shows the truck made five unauthorized stops. Three were between here and Vaughn. The other two were at Cline's Corner and somewhere in Albuquerque. I don't know what to make of them."

"What about road construction?" Clyde asked. "The first three stops sound like roadwork to me. Cline's Corner may have been for coffee. It's not approved, but I know some drivers stop there. I don't know what to make of the last stop in Albuquerque. Jim and Larry didn't arrive at the bank."

"I guess it makes sense," Alice said. "I thought you should know."

"New Mexico State Police, how may I help you?"

"This is Mister Rhodes from Brinks Security in Roswell. I want to report a possible robbery of one of our trucks."

Clyde heard a series of clicks. Then a man answered.

"This is Captain Tom Redland, how may I help you?"

After identifying himself, Clyde said, "One of our trucks may have been robbed, Captain."

"What gives you that idea?"

Clyde explained the details.

Although Tom felt the circumstances were peculiar, he asked, "You're sure the truck didn't break down somewhere between Roswell and Albuquerque?"

"We don't know. The driver and guard have cell phones. If their radio malfunctioned, they could have informed us."

"All right," Tom said. "I'll issue an all points bulletin for your missing truck. My troopers will check every mile of highway between Roswell and Albuquerque. If we find anything, I'll let you know."

"Thank you, Captain. I hope it's a false alarm, but just in case, I'll call the FBI and ask them to coordinate their search with you."

Before calling the FBI, Clyde walked across the hall to where Alice still sat at the tape console. She was frowning again. Glancing up, she pointed toward the monitor and said, "This gets weirder by the hour."

"Now what's wrong?" Clyde asked.

"Truck 471 should have run out of gas thirty minutes ago, but keeps on moving."

"Where would Jim be right now?"

"They're somewhere between Gallup and Holbrook, Arizona. What's going on with this truck?"

Despite cold air blowing from an overtaxed air conditioner,

Clyde's armpits were damp and dark with perspiration. He threw up his hands in frustration.

"God help me; I wish I knew."

Jake Polk, an aging and slowly balding FBI Agent, was nursing a hangover from too much Jack Daniels the night before. Jake's mouth tasted like a sewer so foul the rats had abandoned it. The veins in his bloodshot eyes resembled canals on Mars.

After hanging up the phone, Jake thought, "Finally, something big. The only frigging thing wrong is I have to get my horse's ass of a supervisor to let me to handle it. If I know Bill Mudd, he'll probably want it for himself. Damn, it's been ages since I had a chance to solve something as nice as a Brinks robbery. Well, I might as well get it over with."

Wearing his usual "piss off Bill" clothes, Jake sauntered into Bill Mudd's office without knocking first. His grey slacks were wrinkled and displayed a few drops of this morning's stale coffee. His yellowed shirt looked like he slept in it, (he had).

This morning, after too much booze with too many floozies, when Jake stood too close to his razor, his hand wasn't very steady. As a result, his face and wash cloth were so bloody it looked like he was in a machete fight without a weapon. Small patches of torn toilet paper adorned his chin in two places and his right cheek proudly displayed a third.

Jake's shirt bulged in two places, from a package of Salem cigarettes in his pocket and at his beer-bellied waist. To top off his appearance, his shoes looked like he stepped in fresh dog shit and it splattered. Jake didn't give a damn as long as it had the right effect on "good old Bill".

Bill Mudd, Jake's immediate supervisor, was seated behind his highly polished desk, leaning back in his chair reading some obscure FBI memo. As usual, Bill was trying hard to look superior and important, and failing miserably.

Today, Bill wore his "preppy" look; a three-piece blue suit with a crisply starched and sharply pressed sparkling white shirt. His perfectly knotted paisley tie was held down by a gold tie clip.

A "Look at me, I went to Harvard" button was pinned to his lapel and his shoeshine would have earned a basic trainee a three day pass to chase broads in San Diego.

The fact there was nothing on top of Bill's shiny desk told Jake what a horse's ass Bill really was. Jake's own desk was piled high with folders and files of open cases and witness interviews.

When referring to his backlog of paperwork, Jake often said, "Its more paper than forty monks could use to wipe their asses for six months."

Bill looked up and when seeing Jake in his face, shook his head in disgust at Jake's posture, bearing and dress.

Sarcastically, he said, "Don't bother knocking, Jake. Just walk in looking like a slob. What's on your mind?"

Knowing from Bill's snide remark he had the undivided attention of his boss, Jake gave him a short version of what went down.

"Brinks reported an armored truck missing between Roswell and Albuquerque. The driver and guard haven't checked in by radio or phone since they left Roswell.

"Now the signal from the transponder indicates the truck is about to cross the Arizona state border. The two employees may be attempting to make off with the money. I answered the initial call and would like to work this case."

As he looked at Jake over the rim of his square glasses, Bill took time to consider his request. Bill was half Jake's age, but was Jake's boss and knew it pissed him off. He also knew Jake's reputation.

Shortly after serving two tours of duty in Vietnam, at the age of thirty, Jake joined the FBI. At the time, he was considered old for a rookie, but immediately after reporting for duty, became involved in a triple homicide investigation.

Following a hunch and due mostly to luck, Jake apprehended two men responsible for the murders within a week; becoming the "darling" of the press and a hero for several years thereafter.

Since then, nothing much had gone Jake's way. He worked several murder cases, but most were considered "slam dunks"; crimes with sufficient evidence to arrest the culprits within a few days.

Taking his time and making Jake wait, Bill thought, "Jake has rested on his laurels for too many years. The man's a dinosaur, well past his prime. It's time for him to retire and make way for a younger, more ambitious man; one who wears a suit and has some pride.

"Jake's ways are outdated and slow. Hell, I doubt if the idiot's computer literate. The only time I've seen him use one is to play solitaire between phone calls.

"For those reasons, I resisted assigning him to anything halfway important. Now he wants to head up this Brinks investigation, and from the looks of things, it'll be another slam dunk case.

"If so, maybe even Jake could solve this one in a hurry. The best thing about giving him the job is that it'll get him out of my hair for a few days. Who knows, if Jake solves one more case, maybe the old fart will think about retiring.

"What the hell? Why not do it?"

Finally he made up his mind

"Okay, Jake. You've got the case. I'll monitor your progress and give you all the assistance I can. Keep me informed, and tell me what you need."

Jake thought, "I can't believe it." With an insincere smile, he said. "Will do, Boss."

At three-eighteen p.m., Captain Redland phoned Clyde.

"My troopers checked Highway 285 and I-40 between Roswell and Albuquerque. There's no trace of your armored truck."

"I thought so," Clyde replied. "The transponder tells us truck 471 is almost to Flagstaff."

"Have you heard from the FBI or the Arizona Highway Patrol?"

Shaking his head in resignation, Clyde said, "Not yet. You're the first to report anything."

"We'll keep looking. I told my troopers to check I-40 from Albuquerque to the Arizona state line. It appears your truck has vanished into thin air."

Not knowing what to say in response, Clyde added, "My

signal technician says the truck should have run out of gas long ago, but the transponder tells us it's still on the move."

Now it was time for Tom to shake his head as he said, "You have a real mystery on your hands."

"As if I didn't know it," Clyde thought. But he said, "Thanks for your help. Let me know if you come up with anything new."

Also mystified, Jake contacted the Arizona Highway Patrol and spoke to a Major named Floyd Atkins.

"I dispatched six patrol cars to check I-40 between the Arizona state line and Flagstaff," Floyd said. "So far, the armored vehicle hasn't been found."

"Thanks; keep looking and I'll get back to you."

With no help from Arizona, Jake decided to phone Clyde Rhodes to see if there was any news.

When Clyde came on the line, Jake identified himself and said, "The Arizona Highway Patrol couldn't locate the armored truck. Is it still on the move?"

Jake could hear the tiredness in Clyde's voice when he said, "Yeah, we estimate truck 471 is approaching Flagstaff, but the signal's getting weaker."

"Do you still think the truck's on I-40?"

"There's no other road paralleling the interstate," Clyde said. "It has to be there."

"Well, it's not. Could it be inside another vehicle? Is that why we can't see it?"

"It would have to be a very large truck," Clyde said. "I don't understand how anyone could commandeer one of our armored vehicles and load it onto an eighteen-wheeler in such a short time. There has to be some other explanation."

"The highway patrol can't locate your truck and it's still headed west," Jake said. "What other explanation could there be?"

"I don't know. Maybe you're right, but how do we find it?"

"On what frequency does the transponder operate? Could we use triangulation to pinpoint its location?"

"Nine hundred," Clyde said. "The tone is steady when the

truck's moving and warbles when it stops. We can't use triangulation if it's on the move."

"I'll check with the Arizona Highway Patrol," Jake said. "Maybe they can come up with a plan. Call me when the truck stops again."

After punching the "clear" button, Jake consulted his notes and dialed the number of the Arizona State Highway Patrol. When Major Atkins answered, Jake summarized the developments, or the lack thereof.

"Mister Rhodes, the supervisor for Brinks branch office in Roswell, says the truck's still on the move and has to be on I-40."

"If so, it's invisible," Floyd said. "My troopers have checked every mile.

"It may be hidden inside a big rig," Jake said. "The transponder's still operating, but maybe the perps didn't know how to turn it off. Do you have a way to triangulate the signal?"

"No; we don't have any vehicles equipped for that, but we do have a list of amateur radio operators willing to assist law enforcement. They can locate the direction of any signal they receive."

"I never thought about them," Jake said.

"I'll have our radio section locate several HAM operators. They'll be standing by, awaiting your call."

Chapter 14

On I-40, a trucker named Hank Turner was driving the big rig carrying the transponder. For the past week, Hank hauled cattle from several ranches in Arizona to a feed lot outside Amarillo, Texas. After seven days on the road with no female companionship, he was anxious to return to his home in Flagstaff and his young wife, Sherry.

Two years ago, after a long courtship and living together for a few months, Hank and Sherry married. Sherry, a long-limbed, well-endowed brunette, was two years younger than he.

To relieve the boredom of the open highway, Hank kept up a lively Citizen's Band Radio, (CB), banter with other drivers on both sides of the Interstate. They banded together, using the CB to keep track of "Smokey Bears".

Hank's call sign or handle was "Wagon Master," and he was talking with another trucker called "Cowpoke". Today there was an unusual amount of chatter about the number of police patrolling the highway.

"The Bears are thicker than fleas on a hound dog," Cowpoke said. "In the last fifteen minutes, I counted six. Keep your pedal off the metal."

"Ten-four, good buddy," Hank said. "Anyone out in radio land know the reason for all the bears?"

Another trucker broke in and announced, "Dog Meat here. Yeah, they're looking for a Brinks armored truck. They think the driver and guard ran off with a whole shit pot full of money."

"Can you believe it?" Hank asked. "How do they know the

truck's out here?"

Informing the listening audience and spending his fifteen minutes of fame in the limelight, Dog Meat said, "The dummies forgot to take a signaling device off the armored truck. Now the cops are following it, but can't locate the vehicle. From what I hear on my police scanner, it must be like Wonder Woman's plane – invisible."

Hank chuckled.

"I haven't seen an armored truck. Has anyone else?"

No one had, and the location of the money laden vehicle remained a mystery. Until Hank reached the outskirts of Flagstaff, the CB airways remained full of chatter about the missing truck.

After slowing to the posted speed limit, Hank turned off onto the road to his and Sherry's small farm and pulled in the drive to park next to the barn. With thoughts of what waited for him in their bedroom on his mind, Hank smiled in anticipation.

He hurried inside to kiss Sherry, take a quick shower, shave and climb into bed. The news of the missing Brinks truck was quickly forgotten. There were more important things to consider.

Out of breath and excited, Alice sprinted into Clyde's office and said, "The truck just stopped somewhere in Flagstaff."

Clyde phoned Jake with the news, and Jake contacted Floyd in Phoenix.

"I have four HAM operators standing by," Floyd said. "They'll search for the direction of the signal. If four work at the same time, maybe we'll get lucky. When we get a location, I'll let you know."

""I'm leaving in ten minutes to fly up to Flagstaff," Jake said.

"I'm headed there myself, so I'll meet you at the airport."

As two law officers, Sergeant Perry "Red" Parrish and Corporal Raymond Timmons, marked a city map with the reported coordinates, the HAM Operators found the warbling signal at the assigned frequency and determined the direction of the signal from each of their locations.

Timmons marked his map and said, "The truck's parked on the outskirts of town, Red. It should be easy to find. There aren't many houses out there, mostly small farms and woodlands."

A crusty older man of fifty-five, Red was a thirty-two year veteran of more than his share of crime filled years. After serving as a patrolman for several years and being promoted steadily upward, fourteen years ago he finally became a Sergeant and supervisor of the Flagstaff office.

Since then, Red had enjoyed the glorious scenery of the nearby Grand Canyon and watched his children grow up to have children of their own. If he counted correctly, he now had seven grandchildren. Some of the brass wanted him to take the tests to become an officer, but Red was happy where he was.

"Radio the troopers and give them the coordinates," he said.

Basking in the afterglow of their lovemaking, Hank reached over, kissed Sherry again and said, "That was wonderful."

She smiled up at him and agreed.

"It's been a while."

Hank's stomach growled and he said, "I'm hungry."

Sherry kissed him on the back of the neck and gave him a hug.

"I can't imagine why."

After rolling out of bed, Hank stretched his arms toward the ceiling as he said, "Damn it, if there's one thing I don't want to do, it's shovel cow shit out of the trailer. But I better get with it. If I don't do it now, it'll be a hell of a mess tomorrow after it sits and ferments. I'll be back in less than an hour."

Sherry jumped up from the bed, headed for the bathroom, smiled over her shoulder and said, "Go ahead. I'll start supper in forty-five minutes. After you finish, take another shower. By then dinner will be ready.

"Don't forget to wear your old boots and leave them outside. Don't track cow crap into my house."

Hank followed Sherry into the bathroom, kissed the top of her head and said, "I won't, sweetheart."

Then after giving her another squeeze, he reluctantly let go, dressed and walked out the door.

In the barn, he found a pair of coveralls, gloves and his old boots. After changing clothes, Hank grabbed a long handled rake and carrying it over his shoulder, walked to the rear of the trailer, opened the doors, hooked them in place and climbed inside.

The odor of manure was strong, and Hank wrinkled his nose in distaste. Then he walked forward to the front stalls, where he raked the manure-clotted hay and debris from each until he came to the third set. In the left stall his rake hit a heavy object.

("What the hell is that?")

Reaching down with gloved hands, Hank moved some hay and discovered the object was a car battery. Two wires ran from it to a strange, round device. His rake had pulled one loose.

Forgetting about the shit on his gloves for a moment, Hank started to scratch his head, but stopped in time.

("Who the hell put this thing on my trailer? Where did it come from and what is it?")

Picking up the transponder, he turned it over to look at the bottom. On a burnished brass plate the word, "Brinks" stood out in raised black letters.

Hank dropped the device as if it was the stolen Mona Lisa, ran to the rear of the truck, jumped down and landed heavily. His left ankle hurt, but he didn't give a damn. Limping toward his house, he called out, "Sherry, you won't believe it."

At the Brinks Branch office in Roswell, across the room, Alice called out, "We lost the signal."

"Great," Clyde said. "Now what do we do?"

In Flagstaff, Officer Timmons picked up the phone, listened to the caller and shouted, "Red, the HAM operators lost the signal. The transponder quit broadcasting."

Red held his two fingers about an inch apart and remarked, "Damn and we were this close. Let the troopers know. Tell them to keep up the search. The truck has to be out there somewhere. If they have to, they can go door to door."

"Yes, Sir," Timmons said.

The phone rang again and Timmons took the call. After a moment, he motioned for Red to get on the extension.

Timmons was smiling as he said, "Sergeant Parrish is on the line. Please repeat what you told me."

"Sure; my name's Hank Turner and I drive an eighteen-wheeler. I heard other truckers talking about a missing Brinks truck. Tonight I found something in the back of my rig I think is connected to the armored truck."

"Describe it," Red said.

"Its round and had wires attached to a car battery, but I accidentally knocked one loose."

"What makes you think this is connected to the missing Brinks truck?"

"It says Brinks on a small brass plate," Hank said. "The damn thing has to be from the truck."

Timmons cupped his hand over the receiver and said, "It sounds like the transponder."

Red nodded and then asked, "Where are you now, Hank?"

"I live at 442 Oak Creek Drive, on the east side of Flagstaff, just off I-40. Take the Willow Street exit and turn left under the overpass. Oak Creek is the second left. My rig's parked next to the barn."

"Don't touch anything," Red said. "A patrol car will be there shortly."

"I picked it up, but was wearing gloves. As soon as I saw the name on the bottom, I dropped it, and it's still there."

"Thanks for your call, Hank. I'll be talking to you soon."

"I'm happy to be of help," Hank said and disconnected.

As he headed for the door, over his shoulder Red said, "Get on the radio, Ray, and let the patrol cars know where the truck is. I'm going out there myself. If anyone calls, relay their messages to me on channel twelve."

"Yes, Sir."

A block from Hank's farm, Red knew this had to be the place. The darkness of the night was shattered as red, white and blue strobe lights streaked the sky with multicolored rays like a giant gumball machine gone awry.

("Damn. It looks like a Chinese fire drill down there.")

He pulled into the driveway and slammed on the brakes to avoid hitting one of five police vehicles spread over the driveway and adjacent lawn with their lights flashing. While blinking at the glare, he said aloud, "It looks like a damned carnival midway."

Disgusted, he climbed wearily from his cruiser and said aloud, "Jesus, Joseph and Mary," while thinking, "I'll bet by now those bozos have compromised the entire crime scene. Where the hell do they find such dumb assholes?"

After making his way past and around the vehicles, Red walked to the rear of a stinking, feces-smeared trailer attached to a dirty, rain-streaked tractor. The trailer doors hung open and three of Red's troopers stood in the back of the truck talking to a young man dressed in overalls and grimy boots.

Red put his hands on his hips and shouted, "Get the hell out of the truck, you dumb sons of bitches."

Startled by Red's command, the three policemen hurried to comply with his orders. Limping badly, the civilian jumped from the truck and ran toward a nearby house. Alerted by Red's outburst, two other troopers suddenly appeared in the rear of the truck.

Thinking, "Damn it; they've been all over the place," Red shouted again, "Get your asses out of the trailer. What the hell's wrong with you men? You know better than to compromise a crime scene."

After jumping down, the two troopers joined the others. All five looked sheepishly at Red, who stared at them for what seemed like an eternity before speaking. His nostrils flared and it wasn't from the smell of the cow shit as he said distinctly, "I'll talk to you jerks later. Who the hell was the first officer on the scene?"

A Corporal raised his hand, stepped forward and replied sheepishly, "I was, Sergeant Parrish."

Red looked at the trooper's name tag and asked, "Then why the hell didn't you seal off the area, Officer Tibedoux? Why did you let these assholes mess up my crime scene?"

Tibedoux came to a rigid attention and said, "No excuse, sir. We were all excited. We thought we found a clue to the missing armored truck. I goofed."

Red continued to chew ass.

"You're not in the Army, Officer Tibedoux. 'No excuse'

isn't going to cut the mustard this time. You're relieved of all duty."

Pointing toward a patrolman making his way through the gaggle of patrol cars parked willy-nilly on the tire tracked lawn, Red said, "I see Sergeant Phillips coming up the driveway, Tibedoux. Give him your log book and then return to headquarters. Consider yourself under barracks arrest."

Turning to the other troopers, raw fury showed on Red's face as he said, "You four are relieved of anything to do with this investigation. Return to headquarters, but don't take any calls pertaining to this case. Refer them to me on channel twelve. Do you understand me?"

Five crimson and shamed faces stared back at him, and they replied as one, "Yes, Sir."

"I'll talk to you in the morning. Be at my desk at 0800 hours sharp. If I'm not done here, wait until I get there. Got it?"

"Yes, Sir," the troopers repeated.

"Then get the hell out of my sight and let me get on with the investigation."

Turning to Sergeant Phillips, who was holding Officer Tibedoux's log book, Red asked, "What entries did Tibedoux make?"

"Hell, Red, there's not one entry pertaining to this job."

Red sighed.

"I figured as much. Man, I am pissed off."

Phillips grinned.

"I couldn't tell."

Red's shoulders shook slightly as if he felt a sudden chill, but he shrugged it off and said, "Let's try and salvage something from this screw up. Call out four other troopers for traffic control. Keep everybody, including the press away from this property.

"Bring up some floodlights and get the photographer out here to document the area before we attempt entry. Have the fingerprint expert come out to dust the evidence. Log yourself in as sergeant in charge and I'll take second billing as investigating officer."

"Should I note the five bozos' entry into the crime scene?" Phillips asked.

"Definitely; put it all down for the Captain to see. If there's any left after I get done with them, he can chew some more asses."

Shortly after the transponder was found, Major Atkins arrived in Flagstaff and received a preliminary report by radio from an old friend of many years, Sergeant Red Parrish.

Red was waiting at the crime scene for the photographer and fingerprint expert to arrive. When the technicians were done, he would evaluate the evidence and give Floyd a more detailed report.

Then Floyd phoned the airport to confirm the Estimated Time of Arrival, (ETA), of Agent Polk. When an air traffic controller said the plane was five minutes out, Floyd decided to wait until it landed to give the bad news to the FBI.

When Floyd told him, Jake was exasperated.

"What do you mean, they didn't find the truck?"

"There was no truck," Floyd said. "The transponder was removed somewhere, somehow and placed aboard this cattle trailer. We've been following a false lead."

Jake shook his head in anger.

"Damn, where can this lousy truck be? What about the driver and guard? Have they been located?"

"Not to my knowledge. They, along with the truck, seem to have vanished into thin air."

Shaking his head again, Jake said, "No they didn't. There has to be a logical explanation."

"If there is, it's beyond me."

"Take me to where the transponder was found," Jake said.

Floyd led Jake to his cruiser and waited for him to buckle his seat belt before putting the car in gear.

"The cattle trailer's on a farm on the east side of town about fifteen minutes from the airport. Do you want me to use the siren?"

"No, just get us there in a hurry. Don't attract any more attention than you have to. I don't want the press to get wind of this robbery."

On the way to Oak Creek Drive, there was little

conversation between the law officers. Jake was lost in thought, and Floyd was mystified.

As they pulled into Hank's driveway, the officer on duty recognized Floyd's vehicle and waved him through the roadblock.

On the opposite side of the road from Hank's place, a small crowd of people from the surrounding neighborhood stared, pointed to the additional police car and wondered, "What the hell's going on over there?"

Red and Sergeant Phillips had secured the trailer and Red was directing the police photographer recording the crime scene.

A fingerprint expert stood next to the trailer, waiting patiently for the okay from Sergeant Phillips to enter the area.

Both sergeants saluted Major Atkins, but the photographer pretended not to notice a superior officer, and the civilian print taker just smiled.

Floyd returned their salutes as he said, "Good evening. This is Agent Polk from the FBI. He has jurisdiction here."

Red shook Jake's hand and said, "I'm Red and this is Harvey."

"Just call me Jake. I'm sorry, but I didn't have time to bring any lab people with me. It looks like you're doing a good job. For the time being, I'll be an observer. You can continue to process the crime scene."

Red handed Jake the preliminary report while commenting, "The trailer was compromised by five of my officers, and I accept responsibility for their actions. The first trooper to arrive didn't secure the crime scene in accordance with standard procedures. He's been relieved of duty and placed under barracks arrest. The remaining four are on restricted duty. I'll deal with them later."

Floyd shook his head in disgust and said, "That's a hell of a note. What were they thinking?"

"They got carried away with the chase," Red said. "By the time I arrived, two troopers had viewed the transponder, and the other three were standing in the rear of the trailer. I hope they didn't touch anything. I'll find out tomorrow when we discuss their lack of procedures."

Letting Red off the hook, Jake said, "I doubt much harm was done. As smart as these crooks are, sending us on this wild goose chase, I'm betting there won't be any evidence."

"You're probably right, but it doesn't excuse the actions of my men. They know better."

Floyd was still frowning.

"Take what action you deem appropriate with those five, Red, and I'll back you up."

The photographer, Clarence Thomas, broke in and said, "I'm done here. Can I photograph the stall?"

"Go ahead," Harvey said. "Let us know when you're done."

As he reloaded his camera with a new roll of film, Clarence thanked his lucky stars. When he heard the location of the transponder he was smart enough to wear a pair of boots. Now his foresight was about to pay off.

There was no polite way to describe Clarence – he was a mess; thirty-eight and looking fifty. The clothes he wore appeared to have come from the bottom of a bin in a Goodwill store.

One of his co-workers once said, "Clarence has a laugh like a hyena. It can shatter glass."

Another remarked, "Clarence's eyebrows are so bushy you'd need a weed whacker to trim them."

The oil on his slicked down hair could fuel a fleet of destroyers for a week.

The vest Clarence wore contained so many pouches he looked like a traveling salesman with all his wares on display. But his co-workers were also aware Clarence knew his business.

His boss, Phillip Spears, commented, "If crime scene photographs had a category for an award, Clarence's would have earned at least an honorable mention."

Trying to avoid stepping in the cow shit, Clarence walked carefully to the third stall on the left where the transponder and battery lay on the floor.

("God, talk about crappy details to draw. Watch out for that manure, Clarence. Man, it stinks like shit back here.")

He laughed at his unintentional pun and thought he heard glass break.

After ten minutes work, and taking a roll of photographs from every conceivable angle, Clarence signaled he was through and climbed down from the trailer.

Using a set of stairs they found in the barn to board the trailer, Jake, Red, Harvey and Floyd followed Clarence's footprints, outlined by hay which oozed soft, slimy residue, and walked toward the front of the trailer.

"Damn," Jake said. "The cow shit is ripe. If you have a handkerchief, you better use it."

Red waved his hand in front of his nose while saying, "Whew; what a place to begin an investigation. Now I'm glad I gave this job to you, Harvey."

Outside the third stall on the left was a large pile of matted hay mixed with manure. The transponder was lying where Hank dropped it.

"Is it okay if I look at the transponder?" Jake asked.

Harvey nodded and said, "Sure."

Using a wooden pencil from his shirt pocket, Jake carefully turned the device over. By the light of Harvey's flashlight, he read "Brinks" on the brass plate and said, "There's no doubt this is the transponder. They cut the wires, removed it and hooked cables to this battery to power it on its journey. I have to hand it to our crooks, they're damn smart."

Floyd nodded in agreement.

"Now we have to figure out where they put the device on the trailer and how they did it without being seen."

"Has anyone interviewed the driver?" Jake asked.

"We waited until we could view the evidence and make sure it was what we were looking for," Red said. "The driver, Hank Turner, is waiting inside. He's a little shook up. I don't blame him."

To indicate his thinking, Jake shook his head and said, "I don't believe Hank has anything to do with this. The robbers probably picked his truck at random. Let's leave the crime scene to the fingerprint expert and go talk to Hank."

When they reached the back door, Floyd held up his hands. "Before we go inside, take off your shoes. I'm sure Mrs. Turner will appreciate it."

After removing their footwear, they wiped their grimy hands in the grass. Then Jake knocked on the front door. Hank answered and invited them in.

"I'm Agent Polk from the FBI," Jake said. "This is Major Atkins of the Arizona Highway Patrol. I believe you know Sergeants Parrish and Phillips."

Hank offered his hand and said, "I'm Hank Turner."

Jake displayed his dirty palms and said, "We better not shake until we wash our hands."

Hank laughed and then called to someone in the kitchen, "Bring them some wet wash rags and an old towel, Honey."

A minute later, Sherry walked into the living room and Hank said, "This is my wife, Sherry."

Without commenting, she handed out damp wash cloths and held a towel for them to use. When they finished, she wrapped the wash cloths inside the towel and tucked it under her arm. Then she nodded toward their stocking feet and said, "Thanks for removing your shoes. Can I offer you gentlemen some coffee?"

The other officers declined, but Jake said, "I could use a cup; black, please."

As Sherry returned to the kitchen, Jake got down to the business at hand by asking, "Do you have any idea how the device got onto your truck, Hank?"

"Not a clue. Last night I slept in my rig alongside the road on the western side of Tucumcari. This morning about eight a.m., I topped off with diesel at a service station and headed for home.

"After that, I only stopped my rig twice today; once, about ten-thirty for breakfast at Cline's Corner and again about one p.m. at a truck stop on the western side of Albuquerque."

Jake added the information to his notes as he commented, "Then the transponder was placed aboard your truck at one of those two places. At five minutes after eight, the Brinks truck left Roswell and would have arrived at Cline's Corner about the time you stopped for breakfast. Did you see the driver and guard? They would have been wearing Brinks uniforms."

Hank shook his head.

"No; I didn't see the truck or the two men you described."

Sherry returned with Jake's coffee. He thanked her, and she

walked quietly back into the kitchen while looking worried.

"What's the name of the truck stop in Albuquerque?" Harvey asked.

"Ridley's," Hank said. "It's at exit 154."

"Where did you park at both locations?" Red asked.

"At Cline's Corner, I parked in back of the restaurant. I could see my rig and didn't notice anything suspicious. But I was busy eating and talking with other drivers, so I suppose someone could have stuck the thing on my trailer when I wasn't looking."

"What about Ridley's?" Jake asked.

"I parked behind the service station and was only gone a few minutes, but couldn't see the rig."

After jotting down the names of the truck stops, Jake said, "We'll check both places. I'll phone Captain Redland and his men can interview the employees at each truck stop."

Sherry looked through the kitchen doorway, and Jake raised his empty cup in a salute.

"Great coffee, Sherry. Thank you."

She managed a weak smile, but didn't respond.

"At least we have a lead, although it's mighty thin," Floyd said. "Whoever planned this job knew what he was doing."

"Yeah," Jake said. "But like all crooks, he'll make a mistake soon, and I'll be there to catch him. I like a good challenge."

"Well," Red said, "you should love this one."

The day dawned bright and clear, but there was a chill in the air. Early in the morning, Roger called a meeting in front of the ranch house.

When the men were in place and settled down, he said, "After today, we have only two more jobs to go. So far the Feds don't have a clue as to what's going on. Since everything worked out so well yesterday, we'll use the same place for the second robbery."

Casey threw up his hands in mock disgust and said, "Hell, if I'd have known that, I would have left the cones by the side of the road instead of picking them up."

Roger smiled, but ignored the interruption.

"The FBI and the highway patrol must be busy as bees in

New Mexico and Arizona. I hope the cattle truck carrying the transponder rolls on to California. It'll make it easier to pull the second job and get away successfully.

"Alan finished counting the money from the first truck. The final figure is just over seven million, four hundred thousand dollars. I spoke with Mister Remualdi last night. He's sending a courier by plane today to pick up the Don's money. I'll go into Roswell to meet him. Whoever shows up will rent a car to drive back to Dallas, so no one will look in his bags on a return flight."

"The Don covers all bases, doesn't he?" Carl asked.

"He's smart and a good business man," Roger said. "I went over the expenses so far and it adds up to a little over two million, four hundred thousand.

"Mister Remualdi gets three million, five hundred thousand, which covers our loan and interest of forty-one percent, with a bonus of one hundred and sixteen thousand.

"Carl and I discussed the overpayment and we believe it's a smart move on our part. The Don took a big risk by loaning us the money on only our word. The bonus I mentioned is less than forty-five hundred dollars per team member. Does anyone have any objection?"

"If we pull off all three jobs, how much do you think our final cut will be?" Jensen asked.

"Each man will walk away with at least one million," Roger said. "If we only do two jobs, the payoff will be half as much."

"Again, does anyone have any objections?" Carl asked.

No one raised his hand, so Roger said, "Fine. I'll meet whoever comes for the money. Then we own this ranch free and clear. Two days later we'll be rolling in money. Think positive."

During the evening it rained heavily in Flagstaff. The next morning Jake waded through water to get to the door of Red's headquarters on Fallow Road. Outside, he found a damp newspaper in a plastic sleeve, so picked it up and carried it inside.

Red, Harvey and Floyd were waiting in Red's office, and Red asked, "How's it going, Jake?"

While wiping his hair with a damp towel Red handed him,

Jake said, "About like the weather. Everything about this case is all wet. Here's your newspaper."

"I read it at home," Red said. "Be my guest."

Jake helped himself to a cup of coffee from a brown stained glass beaker sitting on a hot plate and pulled the paper from its wrapper. He unfolded it, read the headlines and said in disgust, "Damn, the newspapers are having a field day."

He threw the Flagstaff Beacon on top of a desk, where it slid off onto the floor. The headlines glared up from the scuffed, grey-tiled, badly-in-need-of-mopping floor: "Brinks Truck Missing – Police Haven't a Clue".

Red kicked the offending rag under a desk while saying, "Just keep saying 'No Comment'."

"What did your lab technicians come up with last night?" Jake asked.

"Not a thing," Floyd said. "You were right, there were no fingerprints, and the car battery and cables are dead ends. They could have been purchased anywhere. The crime lab says they used a common wire cutter on the original wires of the transponder. There are millions of those on the market. The only thing we could positively identify on the side of the truck was cow manure."

"This whole case is a big load of cow shit," Jake said. "Has the New Mexico Highway Patrol come up with any leads at the truck stops?"

Red shook his head.

"No one saw anything. It's another dead end."

Thinking out loud, Jake said, "Hank says he had his truck under surveillance at Cline's Corner, so I'll bet the transponder was loaded aboard at Ridley's. I don't know how it got there, but it's a place to start. For the next few days, the FBI will interview every trucker who stops there. Maybe someone saw something."

Red nodded and said, "Yeah, but the truck, driver and guard are still missing. Their disappearance has created a feeding frenzy for the press."

Another thought came to Jake's mind, "Has anyone contacted the employees' next of kin?"

Red spoke up.

"I talked with Clyde Rhodes late last night. He and the driver, Jim Young, are good friends, and he notified Jim's wife."

Checking his notebook, he added, "The guard, Larry Grey, is single and doesn't have any family in Roswell, but Clyde said Grey has a sister in Texas, and he'll notify her."

Turning to Jake, Red asked, "What are your plans for the rest of the day?"

"I have to phone in my report. Then I'll spend today here in case you come up with anything new. Tomorrow I'll fly to Albuquerque, rent a car to go out I-40 to speak with the workers at Ridley's Truck Stop. After I interview them, I'll drive to Cline's Corner to do the same. The next morning I'll head for Roswell."

Floyd stood up and said, "Although I don't think anything will show up, we'll keep looking for clues on the cattle truck. The actual crime was committed in New Mexico. The only thing entering Arizona illegally was the transponder."

"I believe I can make a case for FBI jurisdiction to continue," Jake said. "We consider the driver and guard as kidnap victims, so it falls under our jurisdiction."

Red got up from his seat, stuck out his hand and said, "Good luck, Jake. Keep in touch. Let us know what you find."

Joining the standing ovation for having accomplished very little, Jake said, "I need a ride to the crime scene. I want to poke around some more"

"I'll drive you there," Floyd said. "What do you have planned, Red?"

"I have some men waiting to hear their fate. If I don't see you before you leave tomorrow, Jake, it's been a pleasure meeting you. I'm just sorry we couldn't solve your problem."

Every day when Albert Jacob Rose, (A. J.), woke up in New Mexico, he wanted to pinch himself to make sure he wasn't dreaming. When he was positive his current life was real, A.J. would smile into the mirror and say, "Thanks guys," to God and Roger. It seemed either of them, or both, were always there to help when he ran into trouble.

A. J. was born into a poor family, but his God-fearing

mother kept him on the straight and narrow. The family scraped together enough money to get him through high school and then into college, but in order to make ends meet, he joined the Army Reserves. In his sophomore year, his unit was called up to go to Kuwait and kick Saddam's ass.

There he met Roger, Carl and their buddies, and earned his share of the Kuwaiti gold caper. With the proceeds, he bought his mother a new house and helped his siblings, but never returned to school to finish college. Education didn't seem important anymore. He received his fair share in Kuwait.

One brilliant thing A. J. did was keep the gold a secret from his bitch of a wife, Flo. She was cheating on him since the day he left for duty, with some corn-rowed asshole named Charles. When he came home and caught the two of them in bed, he kicked Charlie's ass and walked out on Flo.

Flo filed for divorce and was after all she could get in child support and alimony. When Roger called asking him to set up housekeeping with Alan, A. J. was down on his luck. He jumped at the chance to get out of the "Y" and have some privacy.

Then the "Brinks Job" came along and here he was, on his way to becoming a millionaire.

"Get shaved and your ass to work," he said aloud to his reflection. His image smiled back as if he knew a secret and wasn't talking.

Roaring like a lion over the phone, Bill Mudd asked, "What the hell is going on in Flagstaff, Jake? I thought you'd have this case cleaned up by now. Did you see the headlines today? Where are the armored truck and the employees?"

("I knew I shouldn't have given this job to Jake.")

Although Bill couldn't see it; Jake gave him the finger and said, "No one knows. The crooks took the transponder from the armored truck and put it aboard a cattle trailer. We found it last night, but there was no trace of the truck, the driver or guard."

("Rave on, asshole.")

Bill's anger slowly abated and he remarked, "So it was an inside job after all. You have to find those two and the money. What are your plans?"

("Maybe Jake can still pull his nuts out of the vise.")

Jake ran his hand through thinning hair and noticed three strands had hooked around his pinkie. "I'll finish up here today and tomorrow morning. Then I'll fly into Albuquerque, rent a car and check out the two truck stops. Maybe I can get lucky."

Bill snarled into the telephone.

"Luck has nothing to do with it. Use your head and put your training to work. These two guys can't be far away. Keep me posted."

("Damn Jake, anyway.")

When Bill hung up before Jake could reply; Jake looked at the phone, slammed the receiver down and thought, "Screw you, Mister Mudd."

Chapter 15

At noon, Roger left the ranch and drove the van into Roswell to meet the courier. He had no way of knowing who the man was, but Maria assured him whoever showed up would recognize him and make his name known.

The van hadn't been driven in two weeks, so the motor ran a little ragged. On the gravel road, the tires threw up pebbles, which rattled merrily through the wheel wells. Then they rejoined their comrades at the side of the road, waiting to ambush someone else.

Roger nursed the van up to cruising speed, and the motor smoothed out. The day was cool, but the sun was shining brightly, and he enjoyed the desolate, beautiful landscape. Yellow-flowered cacti stood like statues along the highway, looking like representatives from the local Chamber of Commerce waving hello.

The cold wind whipped up small dirt devils, which raced across sparse, dusty fields, swirled like miniature tornadoes and then died in the lonely dust.

("Believe it or not, I'm beginning to like New Mexico almost as much as Texas, but I still yearn for the cold, clear water of Barton Springs on a warm summer afternoon.")

According to his watch, when he arrived at the small airport in the southern part of the city, it would be fifteen minutes before the plane from Albuquerque arrived. To pass the time, he bought a newspaper and sat down to read the news. He figured Mister Remualdi's man could find him.

Becoming engrossed in a story of a man lost at sea for several days, Roger didn't hear the arrival announcement. When someone touched him on the shoulder, he was startled. He turned and was surprised to see Maria wearing a crisp white dress with small black flowers embroidered in a scattered pattern, highlighting her raven-black hair.

She gave him a dazzling smile and said, "You could have met me at the gate."

Roger intended to give her a small hug, so he stood up and put his arms around her. Instead, she kissed him on the lips. Her tongue searched for his and found it. The intimate kiss lasted a full minute.

Two cowboys wearing creased Stetsons and sharp-pointed boots stood nearby, whistling and applauding their efforts.

Finally they broke apart. Maria blew the two a kiss, and they laughed, but one actually blushed.

Roger said, "Wow; I knew I was glad to see you. From your reaction, the feeling must be mutual."

Maria reached up, caressed his cheek and said, "You might say that. I missed you."

Taking her hand in his, he felt her shiver and knew it wasn't from the air conditioning. He kissed her palm and said, "I could tell. How long can you stay?"

"I have to leave early tomorrow morning, so we only have the rest of the day and this evening to spend together. Let's find my luggage. Then you can show me the big town of Roswell."

"There isn't a lot to see except for the Alien Museum. In the fifties, a flying saucer supposedly landed near here. Why Roswell? I haven't a clue."

Maria found her bag on the carousel. Roger carried it and her small carry-on to the Swifty Car Rental booth, where she rented a Lexus for a one-way trip to Dallas.

Still carrying her luggage, Roger followed the attendant and Maria to the rental car parking lot, where she took the keys from the admiring young man. If drool were water, he could have flooded forty acres.

She motioned toward the rear seat and said, "Throw the suitcases in back and I'll drive you to your van. I didn't make a reservation, so you'll have to lead me to the best motel in town."

"I choose the Western Sun. It sets away from the highway so you don't hear the big rigs drive through your room."

"I wouldn't like that. I want peace and quiet. The Western Sun it is. You lead and I'll follow."

Maria dropped Roger at his van, where he opened the rear hatch and transferred four heavy money boxes into the trunk of the Lexus. During the night, unknown to the others, Roger packed an additional two and a half million dollars for Mister Remualdi to invest. If things went South on the second job, Roger wanted the team to have some money to fall back on.

At the motel, Roger unloaded Maria's luggage and left the money in the trunk.

He whispered in her ear.

"It's as safe there as anywhere. It would look strange if I lug in four big boxes and haul them back out tomorrow. Besides, no one knows the money is there. The parking lot is well lit and the motel has excellent security personnel. They patrol all night."

After registering for a room with a king-sized bed, Maria received the key to Room 101 and motioned Roger to follow her. Walking behind her with her bags in his hands like a well-tipped bellhop, Roger enjoyed every minute of the spectacular view ahead.

Maria opened the door and held it so he could enter first with her luggage

"Just set them anywhere."

He put them in the small nook that served as a closet and asked, "Now what do we do?"

Maria moved into his arms, smiled up at him and kissed him hungrily. When their lips parted, she looked deep into his eyes and said, "That's up to you."

Surprised at the turn of events, Roger asked, "Do you mean what I think?"

If anything, her smile grew in size.

"If you think I want to spend the afternoon and maybe the evening here with you, you're reading my mind. Do I shock you?"

"No, I hoped you felt something for me, because I feel a

love for you deep in my heart. I've loved you since I first heard your voice on the phone so long ago in Dallas."

She kissed him again and replied, "You're a romantic. It's what I love the most."

They spent the afternoon making love and exploring each other's bodies. When the sun went down and the room was as dark as Maria's eyes, Roger decided to come up for air and refreshment of a different type.

"I'm starved. Let's go eat."

"I wonder why? It must be the fresh air because I'm hungry too. Where do you recommend?"

"There's a nice family restaurant a few blocks away that serves the best steak in New Mexico."

"Ah," she said, "lots of red meat for my man. Get dressed and let's go."

They ate steaks, medium well with rich pink centers, and drank a bottle of delicious, New Mexico Chablis. After dinner they held hands across the table like young high school sweethearts and talked for an hour.

Staring into her eyes, Roger said, "I wish you didn't have to go home tomorrow."

She kissed his knuckles and said, "Me too, but my father is all business. He wants his money and trusts his courier to deliver. We still have the rest of tonight, but I need to be fresh tomorrow morning, so I'll have to be in bed early."

"I think I can arrange that."

In the middle of the night, heat lightning caused loud thunder. The sounds awakened Roger and Maria, but the rain held off for another day. During the few hours of sleep between lovemaking, Maria slipped off his arm and curled against his back.

Now she turned, put her head on his bare shoulder and snuggled close.

"I love thunder. When I was young, my mother told me it was the sound of angels in heaven bowling. I believed her and always wondered if they removed their wings while they were rolling balls down the alley. I know it's not true, but I still like to think they're up there having fun."

The next morning Roger awakened alone in bed and heard water splashing as Maria showered. Lying there, he watched her slide her sexy body into silk panties and a lacy bra, apply a light tint to already glowing cheeks and lip liner to a perfect mouth.

She smiled at him in the mirror, and for his amusement, did a reverse striptease, shaking her small derriere, while dressing slowly and seductively.

Reaching out to slap her rear end lightly, he said, "Keep doing your dance and you won't get away as early as you planned."

"I wish I didn't have to go, but my father will be anxious for me to arrive. I'll drive straight through and be there late this evening."

Roger rolled over so he could reach her and caressed her hair as he said, "I'll call to make sure you arrive safely."

Maria sat on the edge of the bed, held his hand and stared into his eyes.

"I have to go. Yesterday and last night were wonderful. When you get done with the jobs, I'll be waiting."

"The second job is on for tomorrow morning. Somehow, I have to explain why I was forced to stay overnight. Drive carefully and tell your father thanks from all of us. You can also tell him when I get back to Texas I'm going to marry his daughter."

"I will. My father thinks very highly of you. I believe it's the reason he sent me to Austin. Maybe he wanted us to meet."

"I hope so. I'd hate to have a father-in-law as powerful as he is who doesn't like me."

Taking his head in her hands, she kissed him tenderly and said, "Until next time."

Roger watched her walk out the door with her bags. When he heard Maria drive off; he got out of bed, took his shower, dressed and headed for the ranch.

As he finished a very long and tiring day, Jake was speaking with the owner of Cline's Corner and his employees. From where they stood in a sandblasted parking lot, the hot New Mexico sun bore down heavily on his bare head. The desert heated wind felt like a hair dryer set on high.

They told the same story heard at Ridley's Truck Stop; none of the employees could remember Hank Turner's truck or anything suspicious from two days before. As far as they were concerned, it was business as usual.

The owner, Terrance Worley, said, "One thing I know for sure is the Brinks truck never stopped here. I'd remember if they did. They're not supposed to leave their vehicle unattended, but sometimes the driver sends in the guard for coffee to go."

Jake handed his card to Terrance and said, "If you think of anything else, please give me a call. Thank you for your time."

Then he stretched, yawned and felt sand in his throat.

"I'm bushed and can't drive all the way to Roswell tonight. Is there a motel nearby?"

"There's one a few miles east on I-40," Terrance said. "The closest one south is in Vaughn, about forty-five miles away."

Jake blew out a breath of tired air. The hot wind sucked it up and spat it out.

"I couldn't stay awake long enough to drive that far. I'll settle for the accommodations on I-40. Thanks again for your help."

At a family restaurant adjoining the motel, Jake ate a platter of chicken large enough to stuff a moose. At midnight, he left a wake-up call for eight a.m. and finally poured his bloated, worn-out body into a squeaky bed, with a mattress thinner and lumpier than a blueberry pancake.

The spinning wheels in Jake's mind slowly ground to a halt. He was asleep before the sheep arrived, so he never got a chance to count them.

Roger, (the Hood), and his band of merry men were up early the next morning. Although it thundered in the east and they saw lightning strikes until late in the night, there was no rain in their vicinity. The road would be dry, so there would be no reason for anyone to question a highway work crew doing its thing.

As the sun poked its orange globe over the horizon and chased the dark clouds away, Alan carried an apple and cup of black coffee on a plate and joined Roger and Carl at their table. At weigh-in time yesterday, Alan had lost the last pound of his goal.

"Celebrating with some carbs?" Carl asked.

Alan bit into the apple and smacked his lips.

"Do you know how long I dreamed of eating fruit again?"

"Good for you, Alan," Roger said. "I'm proud of you. We all are."

He took another bite, and juice ran down his chin. "Last night I hacked into Brinks' computer system. Our target is scheduled to depart at 0815 hours and should arrive at the robbery point around 0920.

"They still use just one guard. Brinks must be so shook up over the robbery they can't think straight. The Feds and state police are running all over Arizona, trying to locate the truck."

Reaching across the table for the coffee pot, Carl said, "The authorities will have a heart attack when a second truck comes up missing today."

"Let's not get overconfident," Roger said.

"I'm only thinking positive, as you asked."

After eating a hearty breakfast, they waited for their departure time. Everything went according to the plan. By 0845 all check points were established, with traffic signs and cones in place. The same flaggers held their poles, ready to stop the armored truck and any other traffic.

Slim did his "slow driver" routine again and reported over the radio, "There's a Ford Windstar van in the second lane a quarter of a mile behind the target. Both are about a mile from checkpoint one."

As the vehicles approached the construction area, the driver of the van saw the signs, sped up and passed the armored truck. Casey gave him the signal to proceed.

Then as the armored truck approached, Casey moved his hands up and down, signaling the driver to slow down.

The driver of the armored truck, Tony Perino, slowed his vehicle, as the white van ignored the reduced speed limit, raced on, flew past checkpoint three and disappeared over the next rise.

Two minutes later, the armored truck came into view, and

Roger turned his sign to stop. The drivers of the backhoe and dump truck made their prearranged moves, blocking the second lane and median while Tony obeyed Roger's signal.

With one exception, the second robbery was carried out with nearly the same efficiency as the first. Before Tony finally gave up, Roger was forced to use his final message: IT'S NOT YOUR MONEY. IT BELONGS TO BRINKS. THEY ARE INSURED. DO NOT DIE FOR BRINKS.

By the time Tony finally made up his mind, the guard, Robert Watson, was already out the door.

As Roscoe drove off in the armored truck, Tony and Robert were sedated and carried to a pickup. With the assistance of Herb and Skinny, Roscoe loaded the heavy vehicle into the trailer.

At the mark of ten minutes and twelve seconds, the doors slammed shut.

Putting his hands together, Roger stared up at a light grey cloud drifting by and prayed.

"We're getting better at this. Thank you, Lord."

After the flaggers allowed the backed up traffic to proceed, the teams cleaned up their check points and returned to the ranch. Slim picked up Roscoe with the battery powered transponder and they drove to the first truck stop east of Cline's Corner on I-40.

Roger was not using the same location twice.

"A little variety is good for the Feds."

"Roger's pretty damn smart," Slim said.

Roscoe agreed.

"You got that right. Man, these two jobs went off slicker than snot."

Slim laughed and remarked, "I'd like to be a fly on the wall of the Brinks office in Roswell when they get the news they lost another truck."

Following a restless night, due to thunder and flashes of heat lightning during the early morning, Jake was out of sorts until he ate breakfast. Then with clear blue skies overhead, his mood changed to one of hope. Maybe things would get better in the near future and he would solve this latest crime spree.

As he drove south on Highway 285, Jake came upon a road

construction site and slowed his vehicle to join a line of cars and trucks in the second lane, waiting for a flagger wearing an orange vest to move his sign from stop to slow.

As Jake approached the line of vehicles, the worker did just that. The cars and trucks moved around him and drove on.

Jake congratulated himself.

"I timed that just right."

His FBI trained mind subconsciously noted two men wearing orange vests on the opposite side, raking and shoveling. Nearby, three other men were seated in a highway maintenance pickup.

A mile down the road, Jake saw two more workers on the opposite side. They were busy loading a backhoe aboard a trailer attached to a large yellow dump truck. Two other men were throwing more signs and cones onto a New Mexico State maintenance pickup. He didn't note anything else being accomplished, so Jake thought, "Whatever they're doing; it must have been a quick fix."

Further south, Jake saw a third construction crew on the opposite side doing much of the same thing.

("I hope there isn't any more construction between here and Roswell. I want to see what the latest developments are. I hope they found the truck, but I doubt it. I can hear Bill Mudd giving me grief already.")

After setting the cruise control to seventy-two, Jake allowed the vehicle to take over the driving. Studying his mental notes of this mystery, he wondered, "What else can go wrong with this investigation?"

As the loud speakers were activated, Larry and Jim heard a click. Since they made up their minds to try to pinpoint where they were, they had become acutely aware of such sounds. The noise of nearby traffic and an occasional wail of an emergency vehicle siren told them they must be in a large city.

Larry hated the loudspeakers, and after being penned up for so long, was in a bad mood. "What the hell do they want now?"

The familiar voice of their keeper echoed through the speakers, "Sit on your bunks and don't make a sound."

Larry was getting more upset as each moment passed.

"What's going on? I'm getting tired of this loudspeaker bullshit."

Jim was also tired of the same thing – Larry's crap.

"Do as they say. Maybe if we cooperate, we'll get out of here sooner."

Larry moved slowly to his bunk, sat down, shot the bird at the camera again and said, "Yeah, in a pig's ass."

The door opened and they watched in dismay as four masked men wearing overalls and gloves carried Robert and Tony into the jail and placed the newcomers on the two empty cots. The newest prisoners wore overalls and sneakers, the same clothes issued to Larry and Jim on a daily basis. Not a word was spoken until the team members departed. Then Jim yelled, "Who are these men?"

The monitor, Leslie Carson, spoke into the mike, "They'll tell you when they wake up and you can explain the routine to them. They'll be with you for a few more days."

Jumping up from his bed, Larry waved his fist in the air and demanded, "What do you mean by 'a few more days'? You bastards said we'd be released soon."

Leslie refused to answer any more questions and turned the microphone off.

Roger looked on and said, "They look confused."

Leslie laughed and said, "Wait until the new guys tell them they're also Brinks employees."

"Keep your eyes on them twenty-four hours a day. Ten more days and they'll be released. Don't let your guard down for a minute."

"Not with a cool one million bucks waiting," Leslie said. "Don't worry; they'll be here when you return from Laughlin."

After Roger left, Leslie kept a close eye on his "pupils", as he liked to call the prisoners. Leslie was an ex-schoolteacher who joined the National Guard to pick up a few spare dollars. The pay of an educator was not enough to keep his wife, Kimberly, in the manner in which she was raised.

But Leslie didn't have to worry about her now. Four months after his unit was called up to serve in Kuwait, she filed for divorce, citing irreconcilable differences, (whatever the hell that meant). Leslie figured her rich old man, Howard the II, was to blame. Howard was upset enough while they dated, let alone when they married.

Leslie returned to the states, and like many others, found his job was gone. When Carl called, Leslie was barely surviving on welfare and aid of food stamps.

"Hell yes, I'll go along. What do I have to lose that they haven't already taken? Sign me up and tell me when to report."

Because of Skinny's burning desire to be a big rig driver, Herb had a problem. Herb was teaching Skinny the tricks of the trade, but knew his pupil wasn't quite up to snuff yet. He wasn't about to let Skinny drive the semi out on the open highway. Skinny didn't have his trucker's license yet. If Herb screwed up now, Roger would have his ass.

Patting Skinny on the back, he said, "Wait until we get back from Laughlin, Skinny. The only way to learn is to watch me handle the rig with the cattle trailer on the way there and back. I hate to say it, but you're not ready for the open road.

"This truck and trailer are the most important pieces of the Laughlin plan and we can't afford to have them screwed up. Do your part and help with the ramps."

Skinny wasn't all that smart at times, but did understand logic when he heard it.

"Okay, but promise you'll let me drive the rig on the ranch when we get back."

Swinging the big rig in a half-circle, Herb said, "It's a deal. Hang on; I have to park behind the mound again. When you make a turn like this, remember to swing wide. If you don't, you'll run over curbs and blow a tire. It's the first mistake a rookie makes."

When Jake arrived in Roswell, it was still hotter than a wiener roast turning into a forest fire. He hoped the town might have received some rain during the night to cool things down, but it didn't happen. The small burg was as dry as the Gobi Desert and nearly as hot. Jake thought as late in the summer as it was, it would be cooler here than in Albuquerque, but was wrong.

Walking into the local Brinks branch office, he found they kept the air conditioning as cold as he liked it – nearly freezing.

Jake thought he saw his breath when he met Clyde, who shook his hand and then asked, "Have you eaten lunch yet, Agent Polk? Why don't we run down to Danny's? We can talk there."

"Just call me Jake, Clyde. Danny's is fine."

After Clyde introduced him to Alice, she asked, "How was the trip from Albuquerque?"

Jake slapped his pants to rid them of alkali dust. "Long and dusty. Thank goodness there wasn't much traffic or road construction."

She nodded knowingly.

"A couple years ago the county enlarged the highway from two lanes to four. It's a wonderful road now."

The trio rode in Clyde's car to the café. Jake's investigative eye told him the vehicle was a five-year-old Toyota with more dents than its years.

While drinking mint flavored iced tea and eating Caesar's salads, they discussed the missing truck.

Clyde said, "No one knows where the vehicle, driver or guard is. They seem to have vanished into thin air."

Pausing with his fork halfway to his mouth, Jake said, "A couple days ago, an Arizona state trooper made the same observation. The signaling device is at the FBI lab in Phoenix and they're checking for any leads. I thought I might talk to you, Alice, about how the transponder works."

Setting down her glass of tea, she said, "I thought you might want to see the tape. I have it spooled up so I can show you the entire route and the stops the truck made. Maybe you can make sense of it."

Their young brunette waitress, who was wearing steel braces on her teeth, stopped by and smiled as she asked if they'd like refills. Jake accepted, and she was pouring his glass full, when suddenly Clyde's cell phone rang.

"Sorry about the interruption," he said.

From the startled look on Clyde's face, Jake knew

something was wrong. He watched silently as Clyde listened for several moments without replying. Then Clyde's face turned scarlet, either from embarrassment or anger as he said, "You've got to be kidding me. Don't do anything until I get there. I'm ten minutes from the office."

After slamming the phone closed, he bit his lower lip and said quietly, "We lost another truck."

The startled waitress looked on as Clyde threw some bills on the table and said, "Come on; we have to get back to the office. Truck 749 didn't make it to Albuquerque."

The waitress checked the amount left behind, smiled at her tip and said, "Thanks", but Clyde didn't hear her. He was already out the door.

Alice hurried after him saying, "This is unbelievable."

Jake was right on their heels and asked, "Are you sure it isn't a prank call, Clyde?"

After climbing into his battered Toyota, Clyde waited until Jake and Alice joined him. Then he said, "No, I don't think so. My assistant, Brad Little, says Ed Reeves was on the phone. The truck didn't report in when it reached the city limits and didn't make the delivery to the bank. What the hell's going on? I'm sorry about the language, Alice."

"I've heard worse. Don't worry about it. I know you're upset. I am too. For goodness sake, two trucks in three days. It's impossible."

Jake sat wearily in the rear seat, trying to find an elusive seat belt and said, "No, it isn't. These guys are good. I bet the transponder shows the truck is moving west toward Gallup, just like yesterday."

"We'll soon know," Alice said. "When we reach the office, I'll check the tape.

On the way, Clyde broke most of the Roswell speed limits.

("If I get stopped for speeding; Jake's FBI badge will save me from getting a ticket.")

Immediately upon arriving, Clyde phoned Ed Reeves and John Grayson in Albuquerque.

While Clyde made his calls, Jake followed Alice into the signal room, where she checked the tapes.

"Well, you were wrong, Jake. The truck isn't headed for Gallup. It's moving east and is almost to Tucumcari."

Jake pursed his lips together in disgust. "They're smart, very smart. We know we're only chasing the transponder, but now the crooks send us in the opposite direction, so we waste time trying to find the device. While we do what they want, the thieves hide the truck, driver and guard somewhere. I almost admire the guy who planned these jobs. He won't be easy to catch."

Alice checked the tape of the second truck to see if it stopped anywhere along the route and noticed a similarity between it and the first one. She spooled the tapes up, side-by-side, so she could compare the white marks and said aloud, "Something's strange."

Jake looked at the tapes, then her, and asked, "What is it?"

"Oh, I'm sorry, Jake. I was talking to myself. I noticed the stops the first truck made, and those of the second truck are almost exactly the same. The only exception is the stop at Cline's Corner. The second truck stopped for fifteen minutes approximately twenty miles to the east before it moved on. Since then, it hasn't stopped."

Jake sat down on a hard wooden chair and wiped a brow suddenly wet with sweat, even in the cool of the office.

"Let me see the tapes and tell me where you get all your information."

Alice spent the next half hour explaining the signals of the transponder to Jake. As she finished, she said, "I think the first truck probably stopped for road construction. The three short stops are consistent with the traffic pattern at a road work area. Clyde thinks the one at Cline's Corner was an unauthorized coffee break or to use the bathroom."

Jake frowned and shook his head.

"The owner of Clines' Corner was very sure the first truck didn't stop there, and I believe him. As for road construction, I passed some on the way here. As I remember, most work was on the opposite side of the highway, and there were three different zones. They would coincide with the marks registered on the tapes."

Pausing for a moment, he thought about what he had seen.

Then he said, "Just before I arrived, the second truck must have passed through the same work area. Funny, but I didn't see it. With the robbery on my mind, I think I would have remembered."

"Maybe you just missed it," Alice said. "But how could anyone steal one of our trucks while it's moving? Talk about impossible."

Clyde entered the room and caught the last of their conversation

"Well, it's not and someone did. Ed confirms the truck hasn't reported in since it left Roswell, just like truck 471."

"How much did they get this time?" Jake asked.

Clyde shook his head in disbelief at the audacity of the robbers."Eleven million dollars. God, my boss will have a heart attack. An eighteen million dollar loss in four days. What's next?"

"How many trucks a week do you dispatch from Roswell?" Jake asked.

"One a week, and a special monthly shipment – the one today. It's always dispatched at the end of the month and has the biggest payload. I wonder if the robbers knew."

"You can bet they did," Jake said. "The job three days ago was just a warm up, and the crooks may have more robberies planned. In the future, you should ask Captain Redland to assign patrol cars to guard your trucks."

Clyde frowned and began pacing nervously as he said, "I wish we thought of it before today. I'm liable to lose my job."

Trying to calm him, Alice said, "No one could see it coming. How can anyone blame you?"

Clyde walked away to call Captain Redland. The armpits of his shirt were dark with perspiration.

"I hope you're right, Alice."

Chapter 16

As they ate lunch, Roger and his men sat at tables in the large dining room, congratulating each other. Wes had prepared a large platter of hamburgers and the food was disappearing fast.

No cattle trucks were scheduled for delivery until three p.m., so they were on a well-deserved break. Those working in the feeding pens rotated with others, sharing the meal and labor. When they were finished eating, Roger tapped his spoon against his glass to get their attention.

Then Carl said, "Okay, we're done with New Mexico. Those not scheduled to work today will spend time getting rid of everything according to plan. Make sure to double-check each item and don't leave anything to chance."

Charley stood up and said, "We'll keep the best fifty traffic cones. The others, together with the outdated New Mexico license plates will be dropped down an abandoned well. That's your job, Jensen. Take Whitey along. Fill the pit with rocks and sand, and transplant some cacti to hide the site."

Jensen frowned and asked, "Why do I get all the crappy jobs?"

"Everyone loves a hard worker, especially one who doesn't bitch all the time," Whitey said.

After the excess traffic signs were torn apart and burned, Slim added the surplus vests and decals to the bonfire. Jensen collected the ashes in garbage cans and dumped it down the well with the other items.

Charley set up shop to repaint the remaining signs to reflect the new information for Nevada. When they were dry and scuffed sufficiently, he added them to the other equipment hidden in the barn.

Fewer personnel would be involved in the third robbery, so lots were drawn to determine who would participate. Those whose names weren't drawn would stay behind to guard the prisoners and run the feeding station.

When he drew a short straw and was eliminated from going on the last job, Pete Crawford exclaimed, "Shit". He was more upset when his twin brother, Clete, drew a long straw and was assigned as a pickup driver. But he hid it well and said, "Have fun, brother."

Still maintaining his record for the shortest sentences ever uttered in eight months, Clete said, "I'll try."

Roger, Carl, Alan and Roscoe were considered essential, so were exempted from the lottery. A. J. and Slim would stay behind in charge of the men at the ranch.

Late in the evening after the gate was locked, and although there was a threat of rain, the second stall was uncovered. It was a moonless night and the work area was lit by headlights from ranch pickups.

Dark shadows and an occasional lightning strike off in the distance gave a surreal atmosphere to the surroundings.

Charley yelled, "Come on guys, we have to beat the rain."

They did, and the assembled men watched Herb back the eighteen-wheeler around the mound into position for offloading its precious cargo. As cheers and jeers rang out, Clete was selected to unload the vehicle.

The second truck was parked in its reserved spot and the four-by-four barrier and steel bars replaced. Then Tom "Ghost" Clark manned the backhoe. Ghost was a twenty-six-year-old ex-Army Ranger and recon man with a steel pin in his left arm from damage caused by mortar fire.

Tom earned the nickname of Ghost for his uncanny ability to snoop and poop in the enemy's front or back yard without them knowing. He owed his life to Roger's fast response to the mortar fire, when their tanks beat off a company of bad guys, killing over thirty. When Carl called, Tom didn't think twice. The money would be nice, but he wanted to repay a greater debt, one of honor.

Casey drove the grader to rebuild and fill the ramp. At three a.m. the job was completed and everyone headed for the garage to view their loot.

Roger opened the rear door of the second armored vehicle, and the men cheered when they saw a stack of money bags.

"Alan says there's at least eleven million here. He and Roscoe will count it while the rest of you guys get some sleep. We load the trucks tomorrow and leave the next day for Nevada.

"Until we get back, there'll be no trips to town, no drinking and no women. After we complete this last robbery and return safely, we'll have the mother of all parties."

"Pay attention," Carl said. "Everyone has their orders. Your motel or hotel rooms have been reserved and your team leader will give you your room assignments. We'll hand out the cell phones just before we leave. Remember, they're for communicating with other teams only. No personal calls will be made.

"It's just like your Army days. You all know the date and time of the job. Take the routes indicated on your maps and arrive at your hotel on time. Pay everything with cash and stay in your rooms as much as possible.

"Watch TV or take a dip in the pool, but keep to yourself. Again I know it's tempting, but no phone calls back home to the sweethearts. There'll be plenty of time for talking trash later.

"If you see other team members, don't acknowledge them, and don't draw attention to yourself or your trucks. The light bars, phony decals, vests and poles for the flaggers are behind the seats of the vehicles. The remainder of the equipment will be in the cattle trailer. When we arrive at the assembly site Monday morning, we'll unload it.

"Be there according to schedule and transfer everything to your vehicles. After you load the barricades and signs, remember to wear your vests and helmets. Are there any questions?"

When no one raised his hand, so Carl said, "The briefing's over. Good luck."

As he and Casey walked up the stairway to the fresh night

air, Jensen said, "Watch your head and anything that drips on you. It's unbelievable how bad cow shit smells."

"Yeah," Casey said. "But the crap covers up some valuable real estate. I'll put up with the stink for a million dollars."

"I'm with you."

Ghost Clark stood in the evening breeze and shivered, but it wasn't from the wind, as he thought, "There it is again. A feeling as if death's icy fingers were playing chopsticks on my spine."

Someone was watching. Several times during his days as a Ranger and recon man, Tom felt this eerie tingle. Each time, Ghost discovered later his mind wasn't playing tricks. He and his men had been scoped by the enemy. They weren't by themselves then, and Roger's men weren't alone now.

Roger climbed out of the stinking garage to find Ghost sniffing the air like a hound dog on a possum hunt, and asked, "What's up, Ghost?"

Ghost nodded toward the sand dunes, a half-mile or so away and said, "I don't know. I have this feeling someone's out there, watching us. Over there, I think. Don't look in his direction."

"I won't. What do you want to do about it?"

"I'll do a little recon later in the morning. I don't like thinking someone is scoping out our action without knowing who or why."

"Good enough," Roger said. "Let me know what you find."

The next morning, Alan reported, "The tally was eleven million, two hundred thirty-seven thousand, eight hundred and fifty dollars. The total for the two robberies was just over eighteen million, six hundred thousand dollars."

Regardless of what happened in Laughlin, each man would be assured of at least five hundred thousand dollars. The good news spread throughout the camp like wildfire on an open prairie, setting the tone for the remainder of the day.

On I-40, west of Tucumcari on a cool fall day, the transponder and battery from the second Brinks truck were resting in the open bed of a blue Dodge pickup chained down on an orange and white trailer. It was hooked behind a matching U-haul truck displaying a huge painting of a jumping fish and the words, "Rockport, Texas".

Inside the larger vehicle, blissfully unaware of the device, were Gene Deacon and his wife, Jealene. They were moving from their house in Albuquerque to a new job and home in Waverly, Ohio.

Gene was a biochemist, who had been recently promoted to the position of chemical engineer at the General Electric plant near Waverly. Jealene was four months pregnant with their first child and extremely nervous about towing the trailer.

A few minutes before noon, they stopped to eat lunch at a truck stop outside of Santa Rosa. A half-hour later, Slim and Roscoe arrived on their second mission of deception.

When he noticed the pickup chained down on the trailer, Roscoe said, "There's a perfect place to hide the transponder. Pull in close to the side of the trailer. I'll put it and the battery in the bed of the pickup."

After checking to see if anyone was watching, Roscoe opened the door and stood on the running board. With a grunt, he lifted the heavy battery and placed it and the transponder in the bed of Gene's pickup.

Ten minutes later, Gene and Jealene returned to their vehicle and climbed into the cab. From the restaurant, Slim and Roscoe watched them pull back onto I-40 and head east. Then they casually finished their meal of catfish, fries and hush puppies, walked out, climbed into Slim's old, beat-up pickup and headed for the ranch.

Slim picked his teeth and hummed a chorus of "Oh, Susannah", as miles of telephone poles flashed by his window. Roscoe fell asleep halfway home. With every bump in the road, his head bobbed up and down like a bobble-head doll with the seven-year itch. When Slim shook him awake, Roscoe had a sore neck.

When Richard Murdock answered the phone with another sleepy "Hello, Darrin," his caller was ready.

"Sorry to awaken you, Sir, but I believe I know what Roger

and Carl are up to."

Slightly irritated, Richard asked, "What is it?"

"They intend to rob three Brinks armored trucks," Darrin said and waited for Richard's reply.

Richard's mood changed for the better with the news.

"They do? How did you come up with the answer to my query?"

"It was easy," Darrin said. "Roger, Carl and their gang robbed the second armored truck today. They just finished burying it, and locked up the Brinks employees again. There's still one more space left, so what else could the answer be?"

Amazed, Richard asked, "They robbed another one? Was there any trouble this time?"

"No, Sir, if possible, this job went even smoother than the first. These guys are pros."

"You're beginning to sound like me," Richard said. "Do you have any idea how much money this truck had on board?"

"No, Sir, but I'm sure the FBI will let us know tomorrow morning."

"Good work, Darrin. Keep me advised."

"Goodnight, Sir," Darrin said.

When he heard nothing in reply, he knew his boss was going back to bed and thought; "It's where I'm headed, just as soon as I can crawl to my truck."

The next morning, there was light fog hanging over the far-off mountains when Roger walked up to where Tom stood by the barn with a toothpick hanging from one side of his mouth.

"Well, Ghost," Roger asked, "What did you find?"

Tom removed the mangled toothpick remains from his teeth and threw it into the air. It drifted off on a light northern breeze.

"Not much; there were a couple sets of tracks, and someone lay down near the top of a small sand dune. Whoever it was knows some Special Forces tricks. Around the spot where he did his scoping, he poured out a bottle of human piss to scare off any snakes or wild animals."

"I never heard of that before," Roger said.

"Yeah, this guy is a pro. I lost his trail in a rocky canyon.

You think it's anything important?"

"I don't know," Roger said. "Keep your eyes and nose open, Ghost. Let me know if you get a whiff of this jaybird again."

Work continued on the ranch as usual. The prisoners were fed, well and often. Monitors maintained their surveillance of the four men and listened in as they talked in hushed tones.

Knowing no one had ever attempted such a feat before, the captives were amazed at the audacity of their captors.

Robert asked, "Why are they holding us for so long? They have two trucks loaded with money. Isn't that enough?"

"I wondered the same thing," Jim said. "Now I know the answer. They intend to rob at least three trucks. There's no other reason to hold us captive."

"What makes you think that?" Larry asked.

"Reason it out. If they turn us loose, we'll tell the authorities how they stopped our trucks. They can't let us go until they complete at least one more big robbery."

"By now Brinks knows our trucks are missing," Tony said. "How will they pull off another successful hijacking?"

"I don't know, but look at us. They stopped us and here we are. Whoever planned this knows what he's doing. We have to get out of here."

Larry waved his hand in a circle to encompass the entire jail and said, "I don't think it's possible. How would we escape? Look at the steel door. There aren't any windows, and the walls and ceiling are solid wood."

Pointing to the cameras in the ceiling, Tony agreed.

"They monitor us twenty-four hours a day. I'm with Larry. It's impossible."

Robert nodded in agreement.

"So far, they've treated us well, but I don't think they would respond kindly to a revolt, although I doubt we could start one. I say we stick it out and wait for our release. Hell, Brinks is insured for any losses, and I won't get killed for their money."

Jim surrendered to the majority.

"I suppose you're right. Does anyone have any idea where we are?"

Pointing at the walls, Larry said, "The traffic noises sound like a big city and there are sirens at all hours. I think we're in Albuquerque or some other large city. I don't know how long we were knocked out, and they took our watches, so we don't have any concept of time."

"My guess is Albuquerque," Robert said. "They fixed this place up like it was Fort Knox."

"I go along with you on the city," Tony said. "There's too much traffic for Roswell."

"I agree," Larry said. "Let's listen to the sounds and maybe we can pinpoint something to tell the authorities."

As he sat, watched and listened to the captives on closed circuit television, Carl turned to Fred and said, "I believe we have them fooled. Keep playing the recordings. I hope none of our guests realize there are only two."

"I don't think they'll notice. The traffic noise makes them drowsy and they sleep a lot."

"If I were in their shoes, I'd sleep my life away," Carl said. "They have no radio, TV, or sense of night or day. It would put me to sleep in a hurry."

"They don't know how nice it is. The trash on TV isn't worth watching."

Carl laughed and said, "Call me if they get any ideas of trying to escape. I think they've talked themselves out of it, but you never know."

"I'll keep a close eye on them and pass the word along to my replacement."

"What the hell was that?" Gerald "Whitey" Whitestone asked. He and Mike Darling were stacking hay in the barn, and Whitey saw something slither out of sight behind the pile they were working.

Mike hadn't seen anything and asked, "What did you see?"

Whitey pointed toward the rear of the pile and said, "Something moved behind that bale. It looked like a snake."

"A frigging snake?" Mike asked. He dropped the bale he was holding and jumped back. "Shit, I hate snakes."

Both Whitey and Mike were ex-Army National Guard

Corporals, who served as spotters for Roger's tanks in Kuwait. When he got a call from Roger to report for duty, Whitey was a roofer, finishing up a series of small houses in Round Rock, Texas.

Mike was working as a mechanic in a Ford dealership in nearby Georgetown, doing minor repairs and marking time until something more worthwhile came along. He figured the chance to be a millionaire was what he was waiting for, so here he was.

The two friends bowled together in Austin on Wednesday nights and were always competitive, but as far as Mike was concerned snakes were a completely different matter. Whitey could have Mike's share and whatever glory came with them.

"Let me get a rake," Whitey said.

"Let me get the hell out of here," Mike said. "Then you can play around with any old snake you find."

"What are you, chicken shit? To hear you tell it, I thought you were Mister Macho personified. Wait until the girls back home hear you ran away from a snake."

"They'll probably give me points for brains. It's obvious you don't have any."

Mike watched from a truck bed where he climbed to see Whitey make a fool of his self, and if he wasn't careful, get snake bit too.

After pulling a rake from the bed of a pickup, Whitey moved toward where he saw the serpent. Using the tines, Whitey pulled a bale away from the wall. Behind it was a large rattlesnake, coiled to strike. Its rattles made a "whirring" noise, something Whitey would never forget as long as he lived.

Jumping back in fear, he yelled, "Shit."

"You damn fool," Mike said. "I told you not to mess with him. Now you've got him pissed. Listen to those rattles."

Whitey clambered into the truck bed, stared back at the rattler and said, "The damn thing must be six feet long."

Pointing in the direction of the corral, Mike said, "Go get Slim. I'll keep an eye on your buddy for you."

When Whitey returned with Slim and several other team members, Mike wordlessly pointed to the snake, still coiled and rattling away.

Slim frowned, shook his head and said, "That's all we need, a damned rattler."

The Crawford twins, Clete and Pete, were in attendance, looking at the snake as if they had plans to use it for one of their well-known pranks.

When he noticed the twin's interest, Slim said, "You two yahoos keep back and leave the damn thing alone. If it's anything we don't need, it's you jerks messing with a rattler."

Roger walked up with a shotgun and handed it to Slim.

"Do the honors, Slim, and try not to mess up the skin. I can make Whitey a good belt from the hide."

"Not me," Whitey said. "I don't need anything to remind me of that monster."

After getting as close as he dared, Slim blew off the snake's head with one blast from the weapon. The headless serpent continued to thrash around in circles for several minutes afterward. When the body finally came to a quivering rest, Pete picked it up, held it out to Whitey and said, "It's all yours."

"Go to hell, Pete," Whitey said.

"Not so macho now, are you?" Mike asked. "Let's get back to work."

"I hope she didn't have any babies," Slim said and winked at Mike.

Whitey turned a little whiter and asked "You mean the snake was a female?"

Slim smiled knowingly.

"Yep, they usually have up to twelve babies at a time. Better watch your step, Whitey. Come on guys, the show's over. Let's get back to work."

Slim winked at Mike again, and the gang returned to their chores.

Roger took the snake from Pete, just in case he and Clete had any plans. They both looked forlorn.

Whitey's face turned the color of chalk as they left him with forty more bales of hay to move. It took him all afternoon, as he handled each one with the rake from an arm's length away, while Mike looked on, grinning.

Bill Mudd wasn't an Indian, but was on the war path. He shouted over the telephone, "What the hell's going on, Jake? I gave you a simple job to do and you can't even find your ass with both hands. Now another truck is missing."

("Damn you Jake. How am I going to explain this to my boss? It'll look like hell on my performance report.")

"These guys are smart," Jake said. "You thought the driver and guard ran off with the first truck. Well, they didn't. How was I supposed to know there would be two robberies in four days? Am I a mind reader?"

"No, you aren't, but you're not making any progress either. If we can't find those trucks, the FBI will be a laughing stock. I'll give you another week to solve these robberies. If you don't make any headway, I'll replace you.

"You have a clear signal from the transponder. Follow it and find those trucks. Get the drivers and guards back to their families."

Bill hung up without another word.

Jake counted very slowly to ten before gently placing the phone back in its cradle.

"I'm not falling for the same old trick twice," he said. "Where's the truck right now, Alice?"

"It's almost to the Texas state line,"

Thinking aloud, Jake said, "I'll call the Texas State Police. They can sit in one spot and watch for an armored truck in the eastbound traffic on I-40. They won't see one, but I need to verify it."

As Clyde walked in carrying a cup of coffee and a sugar doughnut, Jake noted he had a half pound of powered sweetness sprinkled on his shirt.

("If Clyde puts on any more weight he can audition for the job as the Michelin tire man.")

Clyde hadn't heard their entire conversation, so he asked, "What about the transponder?"

"We'll wait until some citizen calls to report a strange-looking device in their truck or car," Jake said. "We're not wasting time and manpower chasing a ghost. I know there won't be any fingerprints on this one either. The mastermind behind these jobs is too smart and clever."

While wiping a pint of sugar off his shirt with a napkin, Clyde asked, "Then where do we start?"

Jake was ready with a plan.

"Alice, I want you to review both tapes again and pinpoint the three locations where the two trucks stopped on Highway 285. I'll take the information to your state highway department and check with the road crews who were working there during the last three days. They may have seen something we didn't."

After gathering up her paperwork, Alice said, "I'll have a transcript in an hour."

"I'll phone the highway department and set up an appointment for this afternoon," Jake said. "Where's your telephone directory?"

Alice retrieved the phone book from her desk and gave it to him. Jake searched through the pages, located the number, walked to the phone on her desk and dialed.

"New Mexico Highway Maintenance Department, how may I help you?"

"This is Agent Polk of the FBI. Please connect me with the supervisor in charge of road construction."

"Certainly, Sir," the operator said. "That would be Mister Cranston."

The phone rang three times before Cranston answered.

"This is Agent Polk with the FBI," Jake repeated. "We're investigating a missing Brinks armored truck, and I need some information."

"How may I help you?" Cranston asked.

"I need to talk to the workers on a road construction crew who were working on Highway 285 today, approximately fifty-five miles north of Roswell."

"Let me check. Can you hold?"

"Sure," Jake said.

The twang of guitars and country music filled his ears as Jimmy Buffet sang "Margaritaville".

While Jake waited, he looked around the room and a bulletin board caught his eye. Thumb tacked to the board was a pair of glasses with thick lens. Under the eyewear was a neatly printed sign in black, block letters asking, "Did you lose these?"

Beneath the question was a partial answer, scribbled as if the person writing had problems with his penmanship or eyesight. It read: "I can't really tell. You see, I lost my glasses. . ."

Jake chuckled at the wit of the unknown author.

Three minutes later, as Jimmy was crooning the last of his ballad, Cranston returned to the phone and asked, "Where on Highway 285 did you say?"

"I'd say fifty to sixty miles north of Roswell. Early this morning, I encountered one crew in the southbound lanes and saw at least two others in the northbound lanes."

"I'm sorry Agent Polk, but we have no crews assigned to work on Highway 285 this week."

"They were there," Jake said. "I saw them with my own eyes. There were three or four state highway pickups, and I saw a large dump truck with a trailer and backhoe attached. Please check again."

Cranston sounded offended when he said, "It won't do any good. I assign all work on Highway 285 from Roswell to Cline's Corner. There have been no requests for work to be completed anywhere on the road during the past two weeks."

"Can you check with other districts?" Jake asked. "It's very important. Whoever was working might know something about the disappearance of two Brinks trucks."

In disbelief, Cranston asked, "What do you mean by two of them? When did the second one disappear?"

"This morning," Jake said while thinking, "Damn, why did I slip up and open my big mouth?"

"It was almost a carbon copy of the robbery three days ago, but I'd appreciate it if you didn't tell anyone else about this until it's announced officially."

Still sounding as if he was offended, Cranston said, "Of course I won't."

("Sure you won't, old buddy. Hell, in five minutes the story will be all over your office. Within the next half-hour it'll be all over town. Damn, Jake, sometimes you are a dumb ass.")

"Thank you for your assistance," Jake said. "I'm working with Clyde Rhodes at the Brinks office. If I'm not here, please leave a message."

Puzzled by Cranston's statement, Jake remarked to Alice, "Something is strange. The district supervisor for Highway 285 swears there was no road construction on the highway today or two days ago."

Suddenly Jake slapped his head with his open palm.

At the sound, Alice jumped and asked, "What's wrong, Jake?"

Jake was incredulous as he said, "I'll be damned. Of course there wasn't any work being done. The only job they did was to rob the trucks, and I was almost a witness to the second robbery. I got there right after the crooks took the truck somewhere. That's why I didn't see it.

"All I saw were several crews taking down signs and cleaning up the robbery site. It looked the same as any other road construction, and I fell for it just like the two drivers must have."

"If it's true, these crooks are really brilliant," Clyde said.

Alice thought, "I can't believe what I'm hearing," and asked, "Where are the trucks?"

Jake shook his head to indicate he didn't have a clue.

"That's the eighteen million dollar question."

"At least you can let everyone know what happened," Clyde said. "My men will spread the word so our drivers can be wary of any road construction."

Jake paused and thought for a moment.

"No, not yet, Clyde. We have to keep this information to ourselves. If we let the crooks know we're on to them, they may call off any future robbery.

"Over the next few days we'll set up road blocks on Highway 285 and man them during the same time of day the robberies were committed. Everyone who uses the highway on a regular basis will be stopped and interviewed.

"I'll inform the highway patrol and they can follow two miles behind each of your trucks. If your drivers run into trouble, or if they're stopped by phony road construction, they can radio the patrol cars and they'll arrive within two minutes.

"This way we'll thwart any future robbery and catch them in the act. It's the only way we'll get your money back."

"I don't care about the money," Clyde said. "Well I do, but I'm concerned more about the drivers and guards. I know them all and don't want anything to happen to them."

"They're being held somewhere so they can't tell how they were stopped," Jake said. "It's the only logical reason for their disappearance. After the perps rob enough trucks, they'll release the men."

"Okay," Clyde said. "I'll go along with your idea. Just don't put any of my men in jeopardy. Remember, neither of the trucks radioed a report of the robbery, nor did they use their cell phones. I know for certain Jim owned one and carried it with him at all times."

Jake nodded absently.

"Those are other mysteries I have to solve, but let's take them one at a time. I'll call Captain Redland and speak with him about trailing your trucks and the roadblocks."

After listening to Jake's theory of how the two Brinks trucks were stolen somewhere on Highway 285, Captain Redland said, "We can spare the men and vehicles to follow the trucks. I agree that interviewing daily drivers on the highway is a good way to find witnesses, but I'm sorry I won't be able to help you until 0800 hours, the day after tomorrow.

"Albuquerque is hosting a Western Governor's Conference and the rest of my troopers will be providing security. As soon as the dignitaries leave town, my men will assist you."

"I understand," Jake said. "I plan to explore on my own to see if I can find any clues. When your men become available, have them contact me at the Brinks office in Roswell."

Temporarily stymied, Jake was still exuberant at the information he now possessed. As he walked to his car he whistled a few lines of "On the Road Again".

The next day Roger, Carl and Roscoe were on the road again, driving a ranch pickup south toward Roswell. On the radio, Willie Nelson strummed his guitar and sang a song with the same title. Carl was feeling good and sang along with the words he knew.

Roscoe was in a foul mood. His neck still hurt.

"I hope I'm not going to have to listen to you wail all the way to Nevada."

Carl gave Roscoe a one finger salute and kept singing.

Roger said, "Don't give up your day job, Carl."

As they passed the site where the two robberies took place, they smiled at their success while thinking, "Goodbye, New Mexico. Hello, Nevada."

Three teams totaling fifteen men were on their way to Laughlin and other nearby towns. The original plan called for only thirteen, but superstitious Carl didn't like the number.

Shaking his head in resignation, Roger said, "As a precaution and to satisfy your illogical mind, we'll take along two extra men."

("Maybe Carl's right. I don't want any bad luck on this job. So far, fate has smiled on us, and I hope she continues to do so. In a few days we'll find out".)

Over the next two days, the teams left at one hour intervals. Team one, consisting of two trucks, each carrying three men, and team two, three men in another pickup, would travel the northern route to Laughlin.

A truck from team one was headed for a motel in Bullhead City, while the occupants of the second vehicle had reservations at a hotel in Laughlin. The men from team two would stay in a local motel in Kingman. Prior to their departure, all magnetic signs signifying ownership by the Crossed X Ranch were removed from the vehicles.

Team three left the ranch an hour apart, taking the southern route through Roswell and on to I-10 near Las Cruces. It consisted of Carl, Roger and Roscoe in a pickup and Herb, Skinny and Alan in the eighteen-wheeler.

All the vehicles and the big rig in particular were inspected thoroughly. Afterward, the head mechanic, Phil Snyder, said, "The trucks are in great shape. They won't have any problems making the round trip. I know you're worried about the big rig making the steep climb out of Laughlin, Roger, but don't sweat it. On the outside it may look old, but the motor runs like new.

"We installed a new radiator and water pump and put in five

gallons of fresh coolant, so the motor won't overheat. Knock 'em dead. I wish I was going with you."

Roger shook his hand and said, "It's the luck of the draw, Phil. Keep your eyes on the prisoners. If things go well, we should be back in a week. If not, you can read about us in the newspapers."

Thinking positively, Phil said, "You will be back in a week."

Before the eighteen-wheeler was dispatched, it was inspected by Roger and Carl. They tested the special cage to be sure it would work as planned and made some special adjustments to a wooden barrier at the rear of the cage.

Fourteen cattle stalls, seven to a side, as well as most of the middle compartment, were packed with bales of hay. The equipment for the job was hidden behind the front row. The sides of the trailer were stained with manure, and the aroma of accumulated cow shit was almost overpowering.

With the special cage retracted and doors shut, there was nothing to distinguish this trailer from any other big rig on the highway.

As Roger drove south on Highway 285, he wasn't aware Jake passed them on the opposite side headed north.

Alice provided Jake with a transcript of the two transponder tapes, both of which estimated the first stop was fifty-seven miles from the city limits. Jake intended to go over the entire area searching for clues.

("If you know where to look, there are always clues.")

After a good breakfast, Jake left his motel at nine a. m. On the advice of Alice, he asked his waitress for two ham sandwiches to go. At a local convenience store Jake purchased a small Styrofoam cooler, a medium sized bag of ice, two cans of soda and four bottles of spring water.

Last night there was a late evening thunderstorm, so today the morning was cool, but dark clouds still dotted the horizon. Although Jake liked the pleasant change, he didn't want to drive in a rainstorm.

Jake pulled out of the Fast Stop parking lot, and Herb and his passengers drove by, but Jake took no notice of another stinking cattle truck in a cattle town. An hour later, a pickup with a male driver and two passengers dressed like cowboys passed him on the opposite side.

There was nothing interesting about a truckload of cowpokes on their way to town to raise hell. There were more important things on Jake's mind.

("When I solve this robbery spree, I'll earn a well-deserved promotion and pay raise. If I get enough money, I'll buy the boat I want. There's no doubt I'll solve this case. It's only a matter of time. I hope old horse's ass, Bill Mudd will get off my back long enough to let me do my job.")

Over the next three days the weather remained unseasonably cool. The sun shone each day and there were small clouds in the sky, but nothing foreboding. Roger contacted the other teams by cell phone and they reported the traffic was light on the interstate. There were no delays by accidents or flat tires.

When Herb called in, he said, "The rig's running like new."

"Great, Herb. So far, everything's going according to plan."

At the end of a long uneventful trip, Roger and his passengers were tired and thirsty. They pulled into a convenience store parking lot in the thriving metropolis of Bullhead City for a short break.

Before continuing on, Roger phoned Herb and discovered the big rig was fifteen miles behind their vehicle. They waited in place until Herb passed by. Then Carl pulled out and followed him into Laughlin.

"Everything's fine," Herb reported. "The truck continues to run like new and the temperature gauge is pegged on the cool mark."

Roger and his two companions pulled off onto the shoulder and watched as the big rig rolled out of the city and began the long climb up the steep grades of Highway 95.

Thirty minutes later Alan phoned.

"The hard part's over and we're at the top. The truck ran as smoothly as Phil said it would. I'll call you when we get in."

At the Starlight Motel in Boulder City, Herb parked his

vehicle at the rear of the last building. When Roger made reservations, he asked for a room with two queen sized beds as far away from the highway as possible. As a result, there were very few vehicles parked in their area.

As soon as they unloaded their luggage, Alan connected his laptop to a phone jack and hacked into Brinks' schedule. Their target was still listed for an early morning departure, leaving Laughlin at seven forty-five a.m. Alan phoned Roger with the good news.

After a filling meal in a nearby diner, they returned to the motel, uncovered the equipment and moved it to the rear of the trailer. Then they caught a few hours of shut eye.

Chapter 17

At 0400 hours, everyone arrived at the assembly site. There was no moon and the night was so dark you could have carved it up and served it as chocolate pie.

Leaving Laughlin behind, Roger and his passengers drove truck four northward on Highway 95. A few miles up the road they pulled onto the shoulder of the dark, deserted highway.

By the light of a flashlight, Carl peeled the backing from the Arizona highway decals, while Roscoe pressed them in place. Then they replaced the New Mexico license plates with mud-splattered, outdated Arizona tags.

Roscoe installed a yellow and white light bar on top of the cab and plugged it into the cigarette lighter. When they tested the lights, the beams cut through the darkness like gamma rays.

The three trucks of teams one and two drove south on Highway 95 and turned left onto Nelson Road. At a predetermined spot, the driver of truck one, Hiram Clements, pulled onto the dirt shoulder, cut the lights and kept the motor running.

The driver of truck two, Will Stone, continued on a short distance, made a U-turn and drove until he was directly across from truck one. He parked there with the lights out and the engine idling.

Truck three continued on to the intersection of Nelson Road and Route 165. After pulling to shoulder, the driver, Clete, waited for Herb to arrive. As soon as they were in place, all three drivers switched plates, while their helpers applied the decals and installed the light bars.

Herb drove down Highway 95 from Boulder City and turned left on Route 165. When he saw truck three, he turned right. When the big rig passed him, Clete pulled his vehicle lengthwise across the road, blocking the intersection and turned on the flashing light.

Clete climbed down from the cab, took a collapsible flagger's pole from behind the seat, quickly assembled it and stood at the side of the truck. He wore a reflective orange vest with a white helmet pulled low over his eyes and a scarf hiding most of his face. He looked like something or someone out of a Darth Vader movie.

Herb drove to where trucks one and two waited, stopped, and he and his passengers jumped down from the cab. Skinny opened the rear doors of the trailer and climbed aboard. Herb and Alan helped him swing the cage out and back, toward the right side of the trailer.

Two men from truck two joined Skinny and helped hand down traffic cones, barricades and signs. As each item was unloaded, Roscoe checked it off his list, while each driver assured his cargo included the correct signs.

When his vehicle was properly loaded, Hiram sped off to the intersection of Nelson Road and Route 165, where he and his helpers unloaded a set of barricades, erected them across both lanes and attached a sign: Road Closed – Detour via Route 165. An arrow pointed to the right.

Two men from truck three joined Hiram and his men, but Clete and his truck remained in position as Hiram sped off toward Nelson. The tires threw up a trail of gravel, which splattered down around Clete like hail from a thunderstorm. A mile down Nelson Road, Hiram made a U-turn.

At one-quarter mile intervals, he and his team placed three signs along Nelson road. The first: Slow — Road Repairs Ahead. The second: Detour Ahead. The third: Flagger Ahead — Be Prepared to Stop.

Then Hiram and his crew returned to the intersection, turned right, drove a mile down Route 165 and made a U-turn. On the return trip to the intersection, the team stopped three times and erected similar warning signs.

After turning right on the shoulder at the intersection and passing Clete with a wave of his hand, Hiram returned to the assembly point, leaving Clete standing alone at the lonely crossroad. A cold wind blew the scarf around his face.

As Hiram and his teammates approached the tractor trailer, they saw bales of hay were being unloaded and piled haphazardly alongside the trailer. They looked like giant Shredded Wheat cereal.

Truck one slid to a stop and Hiram allowed the two extra passengers to jump out to assist in the unloading. Then he sped off again, headed for the intersection of Highway 95 and Nelson Road, where Roger and his passengers waited with their flashing light bar illuminated. The quivering white beams cut into the dark like lightning against a black rain cloud.

Carl and Roscoe remained seated in truck four; both dressed in sand colored fatigues.

Wearing rust colored overhauls, tan work boots, a long-sleeved red shirt, an orange reflective vest and a black face mask, Roger stood at the side of the truck holding a red and white flagger's pole with the stop sign displayed to prevent anyone from turning onto Nelson Road.

The gradually sloped, straight-as-an-arrow Highway 95 was virtually deserted. Since their arrival, Roger hadn't seen a car headed north, and only two vehicles passed his position going south.

The first was a van containing three sleeping passengers and a bored, chain-smoking driver. The second was a small, high-powered silver Porsche. Sprawled across the passenger's seat, cuddled up against a young excited driver was an equally high-powered, well-stacked, long-haired blonde in a sequined gown displaying enough cleavage to rival the Grand Cooley dam.

Both vehicles traveled well in excess of the speed limit and took little notice of Roger or his vehicle.

Two minutes later truck one slid to a halt. As the dust slowly settled, Hiram and two other occupants jumped out and ran to remove their equipment from the truck bed.

Two sets of barricades were quickly assembled and placed

to block both lanes of Nelson Road. A sign was hung from two nails: Road Closed for Resurfacing – Detour to Nelson via Route 165. An arrow pointed north.

While Alan moved truck four to the shoulder, Roger took his place in front of the barricade as a flagger. In the distance he saw a vehicle approaching from the south.

Hiram and his men climbed into the cab of truck one and burned rubber as they sped off toward Boulder City, drove a mile and made a U-turn. At quarter-mile intervals they erected three warning signs. Then Hiram drove truck one past Roger to a point two miles south and made another U-turn.

The truck stopped four times. Hiram and his team placed a warning sign at each site. After the work was completed, Hiram returned to where Roger waited.

During the elapsed time, several vehicles from both directions passed by, but none appeared interested in what was taking place.

With the flashing light illuminated, Hiram parked truck one on the shoulder. A passenger from his vehicle, Wiley, took over for Roger at the flagger position.

Roger climbed into truck four, drove to the assembly point and stopped at the rear of the trailer. Carl and Roscoe stepped out to collect their equipment, while Roger drove down the road a short distance, made a U-turn and returned to the assembly point.

As Alan and another team member climbed into the bed of truck four, Carl walked up carrying the heavy RPG launcher in one hand and projectile in the other. With sand colored camouflaged fatigues and a baseball cap cocked to the side of his head, he looked like a desert rat from World War II. After handing the weapon to two men in the truck bed, Carl rejoined Roger in the cab.

Roscoe carried the message board and power source to truck four and laid the device on the seat between them. Before he turned and climbed into the passenger seat of truck two, Roscoe said, "Good luck. Let's hope we bury the RPG. I'll see ya later."

After driving toward Highway 95 until he rolled over a sandy ridge, Roger glanced into his rearview mirror to make sure he couldn't see any of the teams' vehicles. Then he drove on another half-mile, made another U-turn and stopped.

He and his helpers set out two warning signs a hundred yards apart. Fifty feet from the last sign they laid out a line of orange traffic cones. For another one hundred yards the cones angled in until they blocked the right lane.

At the end, Roger parked truck four lengthwise across the road to block the armored vehicle. Alan climbed out dressed in dirty blue jeans and a ragged, grey sweatshirt. Scuffed, black Brogans were on his feet and a red scarf was tied around his chin.

Alan stood a few feet from truck four holding a red and white flagger's pole. The flashing light reflected off his vest and safety taped helmet, making him look like a tired, hard-working road construction crew member longing for a coffee break.

Roger spoke into his microphone, "Go truck two."

As Will drove around truck four, he waved his hand in the "Hook-'Em" sign as if attending the Cotton Bowl. Upon reaching the intersection of Highway 95 and Nelson Road, he drove on the shoulder, around the barricade and past Hiram in truck one.

After illuminating his flashing light, he turned left, drove five miles south, made a U-turn and parked on the shoulder.

Roscoe remained seated as Will walked to the rear and removed a large sign with two legs. With a grunt like King Kong, he lifted it and placed the legs in slots at the end of the truck bed.

With a loud 'thud', which resounded through the lonely desert and echoed off the mountains, the heavy wooden sign dropped into place. It read: Road Work Ahead – No Passing Zone.

Will returned to his seat and spoke into his microphone, "Truck two is in place."

Then Will and Roscoe sat watching the side view mirrors, awaiting the arrival of the armored truck. Roscoe held a bolt cutter in sweaty hands. His heart pounded, sweat dripped from his brow and he had an urge to piss.

"Check in by the numbers," Roger announced, and one by one, each man responded.

When Roger finished checking off each team member, he turned to find Ghost Clark standing nearby. He arrived so silently, Roger wasn't aware he was there and it startled him, but he recovered quickly and asked, "What's up, Ghost?"

"I've got that feeling again. Someone is spying on us."

As if he was checking his men, Roger looked around casually and asked, "Where do you think this intruder is?"

"No idea. You want me to take a look?"

"No, Ghost," Roger said. "We don't have time and I can't spare you. Let's see what happens. In case someone is trying to horn in on the action, let the guys with the M-16s know."

"Will do, Boss."

When Roger turned to say "Thanks", Ghost was already gone. Shaking his head, Roger thought, "The man certainly lives up to his name."

Chapter 18

The New Mexico State Police finally responded to Jake's request, so he and two officers were now interviewing every driver headed north on Highway 285. So far, it appeared everyone was either blind or deaf. No one saw a thing.

"How much longer are we going to stay out here?" Officer Leroy Tibbets asked. Leroy was a tall, lanky black man, twenty-seven-years-old, who ate his fair share of doughnuts every morning. Accordingly, his shirt buttons were straining to hold his gut in place.

"We've been at this crap for three days," he said. "Enough is enough."

Officer Robert, "Bob", Black blew on his hands. He was white, but could have passed for Leroy's twin as far as his stomach was concerned. It was obvious he hadn't met a meal he didn't like.

"Yeah, I know what you mean. This Agent Polk is a pain in the ass. We haven't talked to one person who saw a thing."

Across the highway, Jake sat in his rental car, wondering when he would catch a break and talking to himself.

"So far we've questioned two hundred people and not one lead. Yeah, some saw the perps acting like construction workers, but nobody noticed anything out of the ordinary. The guy I just talked to said he was pissed because they held him up for ten minutes and he was late to work. He was a real help. He couldn't remember if the workers were white, black, Asian or Chinese coolies.

"Three days of freezing my ass off and nothing to show. I'm no closer to catching the crooks than I was last week. Why am I here?"

On the northbound side, Officer Black was interviewing a Spanish-American, Mister Juan Gonzales from Roswell. Juan was tall and lean and wore his long brown hair tied back in a ponytail. His swarthy face was pock marked and there was the mandatory thin moustache under his nose.

As he and Bob spoke, Juan displayed a mouth full of rotten, tobacco-stained teeth.

"I saw several work crews both days, but there was nothing about them to make me suspicious. They were just construction workers, the same as you see all the time."

"So you didn't see a thing," Bob said while thinking, "This guy's breath would take varnish off the wall. Send him on his way. Hopefully the FBI asshole will let us go home early for a change."

After blowing his nose into a stained handkerchief, Juan said, "Not at the construction site. But up the road a few miles, I saw something strange."

"What was it?" Bob asked. ("Probably some guy with a flat tire. I'm colder than road kill. Get on with it, you old buzzard.")

"I saw a guy dressed like a cowboy standing alongside the road waiting for someone. He was holding something in his hands – a black box. He also had a shiny object under his left arm. It's unusual to see anyone alone out here so far from civilization, so it stuck in my mind."

Bob made a notation in his log book and then asked, "Is that all?"

His feet hurt, he was cold, tired and hungry, and he thought, "There was a cowboy waiting alongside the road for someone. Hell, he was waiting for another one so they could go to town, drink and raise hell."

"Nothing other than an eighteen-wheeler that appeared to be broken down about a mile from here," Juan said.

Too concerned with his rumbling stomach and keeping his hands warm, Bob didn't pick up on the new item.

"Okay, Mister Gonzales. I'll make a note of it. I have your

phone number. If the FBI thinks this guy is important they may call you later. You're free to go. Thanks for your time."

Juan smiled and his teeth looked like hell as he said, "I'm always happy to help the police."

Looking up from his notes, Bob saw Agent Polk cross the highway and heard him say, "Okay, we're done here. Let's head for the barn."

Bob thought, "It's about time. I can taste the coffee already."

After handing his notes to Agent Polk, Bob left the office. On the way home he stopped for coffee and a sugar-coated confection at a local Polish bakery on Beall Street. Following a lively ten minute conversation with the fat, bald proprietor and his equally wide, jolly wife, Bob drove home.

Bob's wife, Brenda, was starting supper, so he grabbed a cold bottle of beer from the refrigerator and turned on the TV. He leaned back in his favorite worn, but still serviceable recliner; the phone rang and Brenda answered it.

Brenda's hair was brushed back and a loose lock hung over one eye, as she copied a sexy move Ida Lupino made on Humphrey Bogart in an old movie on channel nine. She slinked seductively into the room, but it went right over Bob's head.

She purred, "It's for you, Bob," and held the pose for a few seconds longer.

Bob was clueless. Pausing to take a swig of his beer, he eventually picked up the cordless phone and said, "Bob Black. Go ahead. It's your nickel."

"This is Agent Polk. Why didn't you mention the man alongside the road?"

"I didn't think it was relevant to the investigation," Bob said. "He was quite a way up the highway from the phony road construction."

"I decide what's important and what isn't," Jake shouted. "The black box could be the battery we found and the 'shiny thing' was probably the transponder. Did your interviewee say anything else about the man?"

"No, just what I wrote in my report."

Bob sat his beer down on a nearby table and thought,

"Agent Polk sounds pissed. What the hell did I miss?"

"Did Mister Gonzales say if he saw the man get picked up?" Jake asked.

"He didn't say."

"He didn't say, or you didn't ask?"

Bob knew he had screwed up and said, "Both."

Now Jake was livid as he shouted, "Officer Black, get your sorry ass back to the office. You and I will take a ride out to visit Mister Gonzales. I want you to see how to conduct a real interview."

"Yes, Sir; I'll be there in fifteen minutes."

"Make it ten. Use your siren."

"Yes, Sir," Bob said to a dead instrument. Without a word to Brenda, he hung up and raced to his police car.

Brenda shook her head and thought, "I just can't catch Bob in the mood anymore." After flipping her hair back in place, she reached for a cold bottle of beer.

Darkness slipped quietly away like a lover in the middle of the night. Will noticed the sun was rising slowly. Then he saw truck lights approaching in his side view mirror.

The Brinks truck passed by, and Will started to pull out behind the heavy vehicle, but stopped short. A small black Chevy coupe was tailgating the armored truck.

"Damn, I almost hit the jerk;" he thought as he tromped on the gas and caught up with the coupe. The truck headlights revealed two occupants. A woman was driving and a man appeared to be asleep in the passenger's seat.

Will spoke into his mike.

"The target is four miles from the intersection. There's a car right behind him and two people are inside."

"We'll take care of it," Roger said. "Get ready, everyone."

After slowing his vehicle to thirty-five, Will dropped back. Behind him he saw lights from two vehicles. The flashing beacon on his pickup helped illuminate the No Passing sign, and he prayed, "Obey the sign, you two jerks and stay behind me."

Three men at the intersection sprang into action. Two moved the barricade from the right lane of Nelson Road to the northbound lane of Route 95 and turned the sign over. The reverse read: Highway 95 Temporarily Closed for Repairs – Detour via Nelson Road to Route 165. An arrow pointed to the right.

Wiley stood in front of the barricade with the slow sign displayed to oncoming traffic.

As they approached the intersection, the Brinks truck and Chevy coupe slowed. Wiley signaled them both to turn right. They complied and he waved them onward. To the south a short line of vehicles led by truck two was slowly approaching.

As the armored truck and coupe disappeared over a slight rise in the road, Wiley turned his sign to stop and stood in front of the barricade with his hand raised, palm outward.

Will and the four vehicles lined up behind his truck came to a halt. Wiley walked around truck two and approached the next vehicle on the driver's side.

Two men began to return the barricade to Nelson Road.

The first vehicle was a large Ford SUV powerful enough to tow fourteen rail cars round the world at a hundred miles an hour. The driver rolled down his window, and a cloud of cigar smoke rolled out to blow away in the wind.

He asked, "What's the problem?"

Wiley held his smile and said, "You're in luck, Sir. Highway 95 has been closed for repairs, but we just received word they're re-opening the road. Please wait until my men move the barricades and it'll save you a twenty mile detour."

The smoker chomped down hard on his cigar; spittle ran down his chin, and he said, "Thanks."

Attempting to look bored, Wiley asked, "Have any luck in Laughlin?"

The beer-bellied driver shrugged and spoke around his cigar butt, "Not much. Win a little, lose a little."

Wiley continued to smile.

"Maybe your luck will change when you get to Vegas."

After taking a deep drag and exhaling enough smoke to hide a destroyer at sea for two days, the driver said, "I hope so."

Will moved truck two to the shoulder, blocking the view of the barricade long enough for one of the men to turn the sign over.

Nelson Road was closed again.

Bowing like an actor taking a curtain call, Wiley said, "You're free to go, Sir."

He moved his sign to slow and waved the line of cars onward. Two drivers tapped their horns and waved. Wiley smiled to himself and walked to the edge of the road.

("Good luck, assholes. We're the ones who are going to break the bank.")

Still clutching his trusty bolt cutters, Roscoe climbed from the cab and into the bed of truck two. Two men from the barricades joined him.

Roscoe banged his knee on the tailgate and cursed under his breath, "Shit, breaking a leg is all I need."

In a hurry to catch up with the armored vehicle, Will spun the tires in the gravel, the truck skidded sideways, and Roscoe was nearly thrown out. It was doubtful Will heard him, but Roscoe shouted into the wind, "Damn you, Will, take it easy."

Wiley remained in place to insure no vehicles drove around the barricade, dodged the flying pebbles and coughed in the dust.

The two men accompanying Roscoe reached down in the truck bed and pulled M-16 rifles with banana clips from an open wooden box. Like large snowflakes on a cold winter night, white Styrofoam packing peanuts flew through the bed. Then the wind caught the nodules and they swirled off to become road litter.

Roscoe watched the white pellets scatter along the roadway as he clung to the roof with one hand. In the other he clutched the bolt cutters as if his life depended on them.

The Brinks driver, Jerry Pribble, was upset at the detour and said, "Damn, this is a lousy road."

The guard, Joe Rivers, nodded, "Yeah, it is. Why didn't the road crew fix this one first?"

"It beats the shit out of me. I wish the car behind us would get off our ass. There's a woman driving and I don't think she has the balls to pass."

"That's cute, real cute," Joe said.

The driver of the Chevy coupe, Barbara Ewers, was called "Barb" by her friends. She and her husband, Norman, nicknamed "Norm", were residents of Las Vegas. For the past twenty-two years Norm worked for the Human Heart Life Insurance Company. Sixteen years ago he and Barb met and married a year later.

Norm was promoted regularly for his outstanding work. As a result, he reached a plateau allowing them to live fairly well. Barb never worked, but remained a housewife, caring for four young children, one boy and three girls – ages eight to fourteen. Five years ago, Norm was promoted and assigned to the head office in Las Vegas.

This morning they were returning from a well-deserved, three day vacation in Laughlin. As far as they were concerned, the trip was fairly successful. They won approximately six hundred dollars. Although it wasn't something to shout about, it was better than going bust.

Last night they gambled until the wee hours of the morning. She played slots and he tried his hand at Blackjack. Barb lost small and Norm won a little.

By five-thirty a.m., they were tired and ready to go home. Norm yawned and said, "Babe, I'm beat. Would you mind driving? I know it's still dark, but you have better night vision than I do."

"Like hell I do", Barb thought. "Which one of us is wearing glasses? It's not you, Norm." But she said, "Sure, why not."

("I really don't mind so much, but I get tired of Norm's lousy excuses.")

Barb stared at the back of the Brinks truck and thought, "I caught up with him five miles back and couldn't get around. Now here we are on this lousy road stuck behind this monster truck. It's thrown up enough dust to cause another drought in Kansas.

"I never knew this road was here. I wonder how long this detour is. The fool behind me is driving like an idiot. Look how fast he caught up to me."

Carl stood behind the bed of truck four with the RPG

launcher hanging at his side, loaded and ready to fire. He nodded to Roger and said, "They should be here in a minute."

Twenty feet away, Roger held the electronic message board. Alan stood next to him holding the flagger pole with the stop sign turned toward the armored truck.

The Brinks truck approached, slowed and stopped. Ten feet to the rear, Barb also stopped her car and thought, "Now what?"

Glancing at Norm, who was snoring softly, she saw his legs jerk spasmodically, as if he was having a wet dream.

Barb turned her attention back to the pickup behind her, as it swung out, passed her and stopped next to the Brinks truck. She watched open mouthed, as a man in the back of the truck stepped to the side, climbed onto the Brinks truck, raised a bolt cutter and snipped off two antennas.

("I don't believe it. There's another guy, and he handed something to the first one. Now he's putting it on top of the truck. What's going on?")

In his side view mirror, Jerry watched a figure in black jump on top of his truck.

Joe heard and felt the guy land on the roof and asked, "What's going on?"

A flash of red light caught Jerry's eye and he turned his attention to the front. Another dark figure wearing a ski mask and standing next to the flagger held an oblong box covered with glass. The red light Jerry noticed came from the box.

White letters began scrolling across an amber screen. He read the first line and shouted, "Holy Cow, Joe, it's a holdup. Get on the radio and call it in."

Barb squinted through her bifocals and tried to read the message, but her concentration was interrupted when her car door was jerked open.

She turned and stared into a strange man's eyes. His face was covered by a ski mask and he was holding a rifle in his hands. She tried to scream, but nothing came out. Norm's door was yanked open and another masked man with a gun stood there. He shook Norm awake.

Wiping sleep from his eyes, Norm asked, "What the hell?" Then taking one look at the rifle, he raised his hands quickly and asked, "What do you want?"

The masked intruder pointed his weapon at Norm and said, "Shut your mouth. Sit still, behave yourselves and nothing will happen."

Joe threw the microphone down in disgust and said, "The radio won't work. They must have cut off the antenna."

Jerry was concentrating on the message board. After reading the first message, he looked to his right, where a figure was aiming an RPG at the truck.

Joe held up his cell phone and reported, "My phone's dead too."

Jerry continued to read the messages scrolling by, and his mind raced.

"Can I back up? No, the damned car is behind me. Are they in on this? There are trucks on both sides. If I try anything, we'll get our asses blown away. To hell with it. Like the message says, Brinks is insured. I'm not about to die for them."

"Get out, Joe," he ordered. "Be careful."

Jerry climbed down and a thought hit him.

"If I close the door, the keys will be locked inside. How will you get in then, you jerks?"

Before he could take any action, Roscoe stuck his bolt cutter between the door and the frame.

("Damn, they thought of everything.")

Two men stepped behind Jerry and Joe. The Brinks employees were quickly handcuffed and blindfolded. Shackled and unable to see, Jerry could still hear. Footsteps came from behind him and suddenly he felt a needle stick, a stinging sensation in his left arm and thought, "What the. . ."

Jerry never finished his silent question. As he fell, a team member caught him in his arms. Joe was already in slumber land.

As Roger and Carl walked toward the coupe, Roger ordered, "Take care of them as planned."

Behind them, the sleeping men were loaded into the bed of truck two and covered with a tarp.

Roger looked into the car and thought, "The driver's very pretty but scared out of her wits. Her companion is trying to put on a "game face" but his hands are shaking."

Leaning close to Barbara's window, he smiled and said pleasantly, "I'm sorry you stumbled upon the scene, but please don't be frightened. Nothing will happen to you. Do as my men say and you'll be fine. We'll be gone in a few minutes. Okay?"

Barb nodded, and Norm said, "Yes, Sir."

Carl held a syringe in his right hand as he walked up next to her window and said, "Please give me your arm."

Not knowing what else to do, Barb did as he said and felt a needle prick her skin. Then the day turned black and she slumped in her seat.

Norm cried out in fear.

"What did you do to my wife?"

Carl walked around the car and approached the open passenger door.

"She'll sleep for a couple of hours. So will you. Give me your arm."

Norm struggled fruitlessly as Carl clamped his arm against the door frame and injected the serum into his right forearm.

Norm slumped in his seat while Roger looked on approvingly. Then he spoke into his microphone, "Bring me the message board, Alan."

"Get on with the loading," Roger ordered. "Leave the truck for Alan and me. When you finish, Carl, bring me three money sacks."

One of the men moved truck four across the road and parked it, while Roscoe climbed into the cab of the armored vehicle and gunned the motor. It was less than half the size of the larger trucks he drove a few days ago and the shift lever was different.

As he drove down the road grinding gears, Roscoe passed the eighteen-wheeler, made a U turn and pulled up behind the big rig.

Leaving Roger and Alan behind to deal with Barb and Norm, Carl and the other men followed in truck two.

Herb and Skinny had the ramps lowered and guided Roscoe up them and into the interior. After easing the bumper against the front, Roscoe shut it down, climbed from the cab, bent his weak, weary knees and crawled underneath.

Skinny shined a flashlight beam under the truck, which cast

evil shadows in the dark stillness, while Roscoe hooked up the extra battery. After removing the transponder, he handed the two items to Skinny, who carried them to Carl at the rear of the truck.

Carl took them and placed them in a wooden box in the bed of truck two, where the two Brinks employees snored on. One was a tenor, the other a bass.

Roscoe followed, and as Carl walked off, he leaned into the bed and cushioned the delicate cargo with two old throw pillows purchased in a Roswell thrift store for forty cents apiece.

Two men removed the decals from truck two and switched the license plates back to the originals from New Mexico. Then they carried the used items to the cattle trailer, where Carl checked them off his master list.

Four more men walked up. Two carried the weapons, including the RPG, and the other two held the vests, helmets and other equipment intended to be returned to the ranch.

After making sure each item was accounted for, Carl turned to two team members who were assigned the task and said, "The only things missing are the light bars, license plates and decals from trucks one, three and four. When we arrive at the barricade, make sure you collect the equipment from truck one and four. Dispose of them in a dumpster as planned."

The younger of the two started to raise his hand to his brow, but paused midway, lowered his arm, grinned sheepishly and said, "Yes, Sir."

Carl returned the smile while thinking, "Just for a moment I thought you were going to salute, but then you remembered you weren't in the Army anymore and grinned."

"Tell the driver of truck two to wait for me," he said. "I'll be there in two minutes. Make sure the Brinks guard and driver are properly concealed. In ten minutes call in the flagger and truck three. Be sure he gives his equipment to Skinny."

"Yes, Sir," they repeated, ran to the rear of the trailer and jumped down.

After opening the rear door to the Brinks truck, Carl removed three money bags. Then he closed and locked the door. As he walked to the rear of the trailer and climbed down, he took time to read the tag on each bag, did the mental arithmetic and added up the total. It came to a little more than two hundred and twenty-five thousand dollars.

Pausing for a moment, he watched as the men formed a line and manhandled bales of hay back onto the trailer, where they piled them around the armored truck until it was concealed from view.

Ten minutes later Clete arrived in truck three. Before leaving his station, he removed the light bar and decals and changed the plates. He climbed down from the cab and gave his equipment to Skinny. Then Clete joined the labor party.

They continued to load all the hay until bales were stacked in a neat pile from floor to ceiling. Then the special cage was swung in and the doors were closed.

Pointing to Clete and his helper, Carl ordered, "Stay behind and rake out any tire tracks."

Then he walked to where Will sat in truck two, raised the tarp and checked the slumbering Brinks employees. Their chests rose and fell as they breathed in the damp evening air. Before tucking the sleeping beauties in, he glanced at the well-worn pillows in the box and grinned. ("Leave it to the old fart to find something like those.")

When Carl climbed into the vehicle, he saw Roscoe sitting beside the driver, clutching a pack of cigarettes and looking frightened. He leaned over Roscoe and said, "Take me to the robbery site, Will."

Will stopped his vehicle near truck four. His passengers got out and transferred the transponder and battery to truck four.

"You're done here, Will," Carl said. "Pick up your men. Then take the guard and driver to the motel and leave them. Don't be seen."

"Yes, Sir," Will said and drove off.

After handing the money bags to Roger, Carl said, "I counted a little over two hundred twenty-five thousand. Do you think that's enough?"

"Yeah, go ahead and get in the truck. We'll be there in a minute."

While dictating a three part message, Roger stood over Alan's shoulder as he programmed it into the computer of the message board. When the messages were loaded, Alan inserted a destruct code at the end, looked up and said, "It's a nice gesture. I hope your idea works."

"If you were in their position, what would you do?" Roger asked.

"Just as you asked. You really are something else, Roger."

Alan stood on the side of the road, waiting for Herb to arrive, while Roger completed his last task at the robbery scene.

Then Roger kissed Barb tenderly on the cheek and said, "Sweet dreams, Barbara. You'll wake up to a better day."

With a smile on his face, he turned and walked to truck four.

Before climbing into the pickup to leave, Ghost took one more look around. Whoever it was, he was still watching them. Ghost could feel it in his bones and the chill running up and down his spine.

("Whoever you are, you're good. I just hope you aren't connected with the law. Let's get out of here.")

As the men from truck three eliminated all signs at the crime scene, Herb drove slowly down Nelson Road. The big rig paused long enough to pick up Alan and then moved on.

The men from truck three finished their cleanup job. Then they and the remaining men followed the big rig to the Highway 95 intersection.

As truck four approached the barricade, Roger checked his watch. Even with the unplanned interruption of Barb and Norm, the job took only forty-six minutes. Glancing at Roscoe, Roger noted the old codger's shirt was wringing wet and his hands trembled as he tried to light a cigarette.

"I didn't know you smoked," Roger said.

"I didn't either," Roscoe said. He coughed and smoke went up his nose. Carl patted Roscoe's back. Roscoe had a hell of a time getting his breath back. Carl shook his head and suggested, "Now would be a good time to quit."

"Go to hell, Carl."

Hiram had removed the light bar and decals and replaced the license plates on his truck previously, so he handed the equipment to a passenger in truck three and said, "Truck two left ten minutes ago."

Roger addressed the assembled men.

"Okay, you all know the drill. Get in your vehicles and stick with the plan. We'll see you back at the ranch."

Two minutes later, Roger turned right and drove north toward Boulder City, while truck one turned south toward Laughlin.

After the occupants moved the barricades so Herb could turn right onto Route 95, truck three remained behind a few moments, watching as Herb drove north with his high-priced load. Then the barricades were replaced to block Nelson Road, and truck three headed south.

When making the decision to leave the barricades and signs behind, Roger said, "This is the last job and those items are untraceable. We'll leave the Feds with more problems and no solutions."

It was a beautiful morning in southern Nevada. The weather was warm and getting hotter. The sun shone brightly overhead, and high in the sky, the contrails of two jet airplanes had formed a cross.

Roscoe wondered, "Could it be an omen of good luck."

His throat still hurt.

Fate had continued to smile on Carl and his friends. While whistling an old Hank Williams' tune, Carl thought, "Thank God we brought fifteen men instead of thirteen."

Chapter 19

When Jake and Bob returned to the Brinks office in Roswell, it was still colder than a penguin's ass in Antarctica. After throwing his notebook on top of his desk, Jake sat down wearily in his chair.

Knowing his ass was in a sling, Bob stood at attention in front of Jake's desk.

Jake thought, "What a monumental waste of time our trip was." But he couldn't let Officer Black know how he felt, not after raising so much hell.

They interviewed Mister Gonzales again, but Juan couldn't provide any more information. When Jake asked him about the suspicious man, Juan replied, "I didn't see anyone pick him up. In fact, I'm not sure which of the two days it was. All I know is what I told Officer Black; this man looked like a cowboy and was holding those two items."

Since it was late and Juan was tired, he forgot to mention the broken-down eighteen-wheeler. Jake would never know an important clue.

Jake was frustrated and cursed silently, "Juan's description of this guy fits several thousand New Mexico residents. Give it up, Jake."

So, empty-handed, and feeling a little foolish, he and Officer Black returned to Roswell, where Jake looked up at Bob and said, "Relax, Bob; get on the phone and call everyone we interviewed. Ask them if they saw this cowboy character. Stay with it until you get something. I want answers."

"Yes, Sir," Bob said while thinking, "I've said the same thing all day." He took out his notebook, sat down at Alice's vacant desk and began dialing.

Jake felt as if he had missed something, so he pulled the worn and smudged transcripts of the tapes from the bottom drawer of his desk.

("I'll lay out the robbery scenario, as I see it, on a piece of paper. Maybe it'll help.")

Tuning out Bob's voice in the background, Jake began each trip as the two trucks did, in Roswell. When considering the times both trucks stopped for traffic signals, he knew, "There's nothing unusual there."

Then he focused on the length of the three stops on Highway 285. Stops of seven minutes, three and one minute for the first truck were recorded. The second truck stopped for eight and one half minutes, three and one half and one minute. They were nearly identical and he wondered, "What does it tell me?"

Recalling the phony work crews he saw, Jake's memory told him, "Approximately two miles north of the first point; there was a crew on my side of the highway. I drove over a couple hills and saw a truck on the other side with three occupants and two men with rakes and shovels. Was it an act or were they covering up something? If so, what was it?

Jake placed a question mark alongside the note and continued his musing.

"A mile or so south, I saw a dump truck with a trailer and three guys loading a backhoe. Why were they using the backhoe? Was it another act? If the equipment was used in the robbery, what part did it play?"

After adding another big question mark, he went back to his recollections.

"I saw the rest of that crew, (or was it another), taking down signs and picking up traffic cones. One was a flagger like the guy who stopped traffic on my side. Why was my side blocked off? I didn't see any work being done."

A flashbulb went off in his mind and Jake knew the answer; "They stopped everyone so there wouldn't be any witnesses. While the southbound traffic waited, the perps loaded the armored truck into another vehicle."

He paused a moment to scratch an itch on his cheek and then returned to his memories.

"There was one last crew on the other side, but by the time I saw them, they had picked up their equipment. What was their mission?

"Hell, they were there for the same reason. The flagger held up northbound traffic long enough for the perps to perform the robbery. When they got word the job was done, they let everyone proceed. No wonder no one saw anything."

Returning to his question marks, Jake thought them over again.

"What was the first crew on the opposite side doing? They were raking and shoveling. Why? The hijacking was over and they should have been making tracks like Bugs Bunny when Elmer Fudd is after him."

Suddenly he knew the answer.

"It was no act. They were covering up something to do with the robbery. Now I've got something to look for. I can find the spot and check it out."

Moving on to the second question mark, he asked his mind, "What part did the dump truck, trailer and/or backhoe play?"

A thousand-watt light bulb went off in his head. Inspired with sudden wisdom like Moses was when he came down from the mountain, suddenly Jake saw the whole picture.

"The perps let the truck pass the flagger in the northbound lanes. At the same time they stopped traffic headed south. Then they stopped all subsequent vehicles heading north. They communicated over hand-held radios, cell phones or walkie-talkies.

"At the second phony flagger in the northbound lanes, they blocked the lanes with the dump truck and backhoe. There was no place for the armored vehicle to go.

"Somehow they convinced the driver and guard to give up in a hurry. Not enough time elapsed for a long drawn-out battle and there was no evidence of a shoot out. As far as I can tell not a shot was fired in anger. What the hell happened to the truck, driver and guard?"

"Okay," Jake said aloud. "That opens up another can of worms. Why didn't the driver or guard contact their office by radio or cell phone? They knew they were about to be hijacked, so why didn't they let someone know? Could the driver and guard actually be involved? No, not with two different crews, it wouldn't be possible.

"So, the perps stop the truck. Somehow they get the guard and driver out, incapacitate them and carry them off. Where? Who knows?"

Bob looked up at Jake inquisitively and asked, "What did you say?"

Jake had completely forgotten Bob. He was embarrassed and said, "Nothing, Bob, I was just talking to myself."

Jake continued to think, "Listen to me, talking out loud like a canary with no food. Bob probably thinks I'm an old fart who's lost his marbles. This case has made a dingbat out of me."

Checking the transcripts again, Jake thought, "After the robberies, both Brinks trucks moved a half mile and then stopped. That would put them in a dip between two large hills. I'll bet it's where they loaded the trucks onto or into something. Man, it had to be a big rig; those Brinks trucks are huge and heavier than a battle ship."

When he thought about it a little longer, Jake knew it answered another question.

"Those guys with the rakes and shovels were covering up tire tracks."

"Now I have to look at all three sites," he said aloud.

Bob looked up at Jake again, but didn't say anything.

("If the old fart wants to rave on to himself; it's all right with me, just as long as he stays off my ass.")

A voice in the back of Jake's mind said, "You missed something. And he wondered, "Was it the guy along the road?"

Try as he might, he couldn't connect him with the robbery.

"The stranger wasn't it. What is it?"

Rubbing his bloodshot eyes, he leaned back in the chair and arched his aching back. Not giving a damn what Bob thought, he said aloud, "To Hell with it. I can piece it all together at the crime scene. Whatever I missed will have to wait. I'm too tired to think straight."

As Bob hung up the phone from another useless call, Jake caught his attention and asked, "Anything new?"

Bob shook his head.

Jake stretched again and said, "Let's knock off for tonight. I think I have a pretty good idea how the perps pulled these jobs. I'm sorry I jumped your ass, Bob, but you need to learn to listen and ask pertinent questions."

When he was sure everyone was gone from the robbery scene, Darrin shrugged off the light brown piece of burlap he had turned into a cover and helmet of a sort. The disguise worked, but he was worried about one tall muscular guy who kept looking his way.

He was one of the few gang members Darrin hadn't identified yet. For some reason Darrin thought he looked familiar, but whoever he was, he had the build of an ex-Ranger or Special Forces man.

Months ago, when Roger and Carl were first here, Darrin tailed them at a distance. When they turned off the main highway, he drove past Nelson Road and then went cross country in his rented Range Rover. He was sure this was the location for the third robbery. The site was something else. Roger and Carl couldn't have asked for a better place.

As scoping their action from a mile away, Darrin watched while they spoke and then tailed them at a safe distance as they made a round robin tour of the area.

Then he knew for sure, "Yeah, this has to be the place."

Knowing it was the key to the whole operation, when the teams left Roswell; Darrin followed Herb and his crew in the eighteen-wheeler. As they joined up with Herb outside of Laughlin, he caught sight of Roger, Carl and Roscoe in their pickup.

After deciding that wherever the big rig went, the rest would surely go; Darrin followed the semi to the Motel. When they stopped for the night, he rented a room where he could keep track of Herb and his passengers.

Figuring the team would leave early the next morning, he

arose at two a.m. and drove to the site. By using the four-wheel drive, he managed to move to within a mile of the area. Then he parked his vehicle behind a large sand dune and walked and crawled to a favorable hidey-hole overlooking the area where he thought the hijacking would occur.

Watching in fascination at the precision with which the robbery went off, Darrin had to hand it to these guys. They really had their act together. Even when the woman and man arrived uninvited behind the truck, Roger and Carl didn't get rattled. They took care of business.

Now the robbers were gone, and the only ones left behind were the couple in their coupe. After approaching the vehicle silently, Darrin found both occupants sleeping peacefully. Although noting the three money bags under the front seat, he left them untouched. Before departing, he wrote down the license plate for future reference and then quickly returned to his vehicle.

Picking up his cell phone from the passenger's seat, he dialed Mister Murdock's number and heard his boss say, "I'm getting a little tired of being awakened early in the morning, Darrin. What's so important it couldn't wait until the sun is up?"

"I'm about halfway between Las Vegas and Laughlin. Your two con men and their gang just hit another Brinks truck."

"No kidding?" Richard asked. "These guys are the men I've been looking for. How brazen can you be – three trucks in less than ten days? I love it."

"I thought you would be pleased," Darrin said. "This time there were some witnesses, but I believe Roger and Carl bought them off."

"How did they do it?"

"They knocked them out the same way they did the driver and guard, but left this couple three bags of money from the truck."

"Like I said, Roger and Carl are smart. What happened to the driver and guard?"

"They were loaded on a truck headed toward Las Vegas," Darrin said. "The strange thing is Roger's gang left their barricades behind. They've never done it before."

"That's because this is their last job," Richard said.

"Remember, three slots in the garage for three trucks?"

"You're right, Sir."

"Follow them and see where they go."

"I already know where that will be," Darrin said. "They're headed back to the ranch for a burial party."

Richard laughed.

"Keep me informed. "It'll be interesting to see how much money they got this time."

When Barb awoke from her slumber, she was slumped down in the front seat. The sun had been shining in her eyes and tiny trails of tears were running down her cheeks. Her head ached and her neck was stiff, so it took a minute for her to remember where they were and what happened.

Glancing across the seat where Norm was still asleep, Barb started to wake him, but then remembered the men who drugged them.

Pushing herself up in the seat, she looked out the side window, but there was no one in sight. Whoever the men were, they were long gone, and so was the Brinks armored truck.

Shaking her head to clear the cobwebs, she wondered, "Did I just imagine it? No, my sore arm says it was real. Man, what a bummer."

She reached across the seat and shook Norm. He opened his eyes, blinked in the sunshine and asked, "Are they gone?"

"Yes; I thought I was dreaming, but know it was true."

Pointing to the message board lying on the dashboard, he asked, "What's that?"

"I don't know. One of the robbers used it to send a message to the driver of the armored truck, but before I could read what it said, we had guns pointed at us. Look, there's a note attached."

She raised the piece of paper to eye level and squinted through her bifocals. "It just says, 'PUSH'."

"Go ahead," Norm said. "Maybe the crooks left us a goodbye note."

After punching the button, Barb watched as the message board turned red, and white letters began scrolling slowly across the screen: GOOD MORNING, BARBARA AND NORMAN.

WE HOPE YOU DON'T THINK TOO BADLY OF US. PLEASE LOOK UNDER YOUR SEATS. I'LL WAIT A MINUTE.

The screen remained amber, but the white letters disappeared. Although the message left her perplexed, Barb did as it said. She rummaged under her seat and found two heavy money bags.

Norm fumbled under his, found another, held it up and asked, "Where the hell did this come from?"

They were startled when the screen came to life again: THERE IS TWO HUNDRED AND TWENTY-FIVE THOUSAND DOLLARS IN THE SACKS YOU ARE HOLDING. IT IS OUR GIFT TO YOU IF YOU WILL FORGET WHAT YOU SAW HERE. TAKE A MOMENT TO THINK ABOUT IT. I CAN WAIT.

Holding the two bags in her hands, she looked at Norm and said, "Holy smoke, there's two hundred and twenty-five thousand dollars here. I never thought I would see this much money."

Norm tried to sound indignant, but his objection came off like a fart in a wedding procession.

"It's stolen, so it's not theirs to give. The money belongs to Brinks."

As if they could read his mind, more letters started scrolling across the screen again: IF YOU THINK THE MONEY BELONGS TO BRINKS, I HAVE UNDERESTIMATED YOU. BRINKS IS INSURED. THEY WILL NOT SUFFER ANY LOSS.

REMEMBER, WE KNOW WHO YOU ARE AND WHERE YOU LIVE: BARBARA AND NORMAN EWERS OF 4477 THUNDERBIRD LANE, LAS VEGAS, NEVADA.

TAKE OUR GIFT AND YOU WILL NEVER HEAR FROM US. TURN US IN TO THE POLICE AND WE WILL PAY YOU AN UNWANTED CALL.

I SUGGEST YOU WAIT TWO YEARS BEFORE YOU SPEND ANY BILLS OF LARGE DENOMINATION. THEY MAY BE TRACEABLE. THE SMALLER BILLS SHOULD NOT BE, BUT WATCH YOUR SPENDING HABITS AND

DO NOT BUY ANY BIG TICKET ITEMS.

UNLESS THE POLICE ARE SURROUNDING YOUR CAR, YOU ARE HOME FREE AND CLEAR. SO ARE WE. TAKE THE MONEY AND GO HOME.

DRIVE SAFELY. THIS TAPE WILL SELF-DESTRUCT IN FIVE SECONDS. ONE, TWO, THREE, FOUR, FIVE... BOOM!

When she read the last line, Barb actually jumped.

The message board crackled and went blank.

Norm said, "God, this is spooky. Let's get out of here."

Barb turned the key and heard the motor start with a steady purr. Norm broke the seal on one money bag and dumped the contents on the seat between them.

She smiled at him while thinking, "Yeah, Norm, go ahead and count the money. I know we'll keep it, but I'll control the purse strings. Hell, now we can afford a new car, one you'll want to drive."

She put the coupe in gear, drove until she reached the barricade at Highway 165 and waited while Norm climbed from the car, moved the bars and replaced them after she drove through.

Norm crawled back into his seat, where bundles of bills were scattered across the brown leather upholstery like dying leaves on a fall afternoon.

With a satisfied look on her face, like Garfield after a hearty meal, Barb turned left in the direction of Las Vegas and home.

The supervisor of the Las Vegas Brinks office, Timothy Wythe, was worried. The monthly truck from Laughlin was late – very late. The vehicle was due into Vegas no later than twelve noon and it was now twelve twenty-seven p.m.

Although the signal office tried to reach the driver by radio, they received no reply. Then Tim remembered the latest news from New Mexico, where two armored trucks and more than eighteen million dollars were missing.

A natural worrier, Tim was highly strung and nervous about the amount of money in his care. Whenever he was stressed out, he chewed his fingernails. Now, without noticing, jagged nail clippings flew through the air, littered the floor around his desk and stuck to his trendy white sneakers.

("Now our truck is missing and has the biggest monthly payload. I can't wait any longer.")

While dialing the Nevada State Police office, he noted the time on his desk clock. It was twelve thirty-one when Captain Harold Crookshanks took his call.

After introducing himself and explaining why he was calling, Tim said, "The truck has been a few minutes late before, but never this late. We haven't heard from the driver since he left Laughlin."

Harold referred to a state map and asked, "Does the truck travel Highway 95?"

"Yes; they pick up I-515 outside of Henderson and take the interstate to the American Bank on Valley View Boulevard. I checked and the truck hasn't arrived."

Harold's memory was sharp too, as he asked, "Aren't two Brinks trucks missing in New Mexico?"

"Yes, Sir; I hope this isn't number three."

Harold picked up his pen and said, "Give me your phone number. I'll dispatch a patrol car from this end of the highway and our Laughlin office will do the same. If the truck is broken down somewhere, we'll find it."

Pausing a moment to recall what he read in the paper, Harold asked, "Didn't I read about a signaling device your firm installs on the trucks? I know the newspapers said the Arizona State Police chased the thing all over the state. Does this truck have one?"

"Yes, it's called a transponder. I can check with our signal office. Maybe they can give us a lead."

"Do that and get back to me," Harold said.

Up to now, it was a very quiet month, but with the news from Laughlin, Harold was pumped. He was ambitious, wanted to make Lieutenant Colonel and be set for life as far as his retirement was concerned. Maybe this missing Brinks truck was the key to his future.

He got up from his desk, walked to the communications console to make the calls to his troopers and thought, "Find the armored truck, solve these crimes, Harold, and you'll be a Major by next week."

When he saw Tim walk into the signal room, the signal officer, Lucas Wren, glanced up from his work and asked, "What can I do for you, Tim?"

"I need a favor, Luke. Can you check the transponder on truck number 368? I need to know where it is."

"Sure, stand by a minute while I look at the tape."

In thirty seconds, Luke said, "The truck is stopped somewhere. The tape has been warbling for over an hour."

Tim wiped back a few strands of brown hair that had fallen across his brow and asked, "How many stops has the truck made since it left Laughlin?"

"I'll check the white marks. There shouldn't be any."

He bent over, checked the tape and said, "I was wrong, Tim. This is the second time the truck stopped. The first was a couple hours ago. It stayed there for nearly an hour and then moved on until it stopped where it is."

Tim grimaced and asked, "Can you pinpoint the location?"

"Possibly, but you'll have to authorize interrupting the tape."

Tim shrugged as if it didn't make any difference now.

"Go ahead. I have a feeling we won't find the truck there anyway. The transponder has probably been removed. That's what the crooks did in New Mexico and Arizona."

Luke glanced up at Tim in surprise and exclaimed, "You have to be kidding me. How can anyone steal two trucks in four days in New Mexico, and then turn around and steal another here in Nevada? It's impossible."

Tim shook his head.

"That's what they said when someone stole the first two, Luke. Now we know it wasn't impossible. I doubt if we'll ever find the transponder or the truck.

"What about the driver and guard?"

Tim sat down in a nearby chair, leaned on a desk and put his head in his hands.

"The first four men haven't been found, so they may be dead. We're dealing with a ruthless group. I wonder how many more robberies they have planned. If we don't stop them soon, we may have an epidemic on our hands."

After stopping at a Quick Stop convenience store on the outskirts of Las Vegas, Roger went inside and asked a clerk on duty for directions to the MGM Grand casino, while Carl dropped the battery and transponder into a Dumpster behind the store. Then they both returned to the truck and drove out of town.

At a seedy motel on the outskirts of Boulder city called the "Do Drop Inn", truck two pulled into the parking lot. The r & p in the sign were burned out, so the peeling-paint, badly in need of repair sign flashed off and on advertising: Stay at the Do D o Inn.

The Driver, Bill "Smoky" Parkinson, who took over for Will several miles back, pointed to the sign and said, "Very appropriate, wouldn't you say?"

Smoky earned his title by chain-smoking two or three packs of cigarettes every waking day. Although he knew the ramifications of smoking; cancer, emphysema etcetera, he just couldn't quit.

His fellow passengers, Will and Charley, made him stop and get out at rest areas if he wanted to puff on cancer sticks. They weren't going to put up with secondhand smoke.

While staring at him in disgust after he returned from yet another smoke break, Charley said, "After all the time in foxholes over in Iraq when you couldn't smoke, why in hell couldn't you give those fags up?"

Smoky was ready with an answer.

"Hell, it just made me want a nicotine fix more."

Will and Charley sat and waited as Smoky parked next to the office and went inside, where he met the proprietor, an over-the-hill-but-didn't-know-it, balding drunk.

On his torn yellow shirt, stained with coffee or tobacco, there was a nametag tilted almost sideways. Someone had scribbled "Willie" on it in red ink. Willie wore a soiled pair of Dockers and his fly was flying at half mast.

Sitting on a couch nearby was Willie's alcoholic girlfriend, looking as if she just crawled out of a dumpster behind a doughnut shop. Powdered sugar was sprinkled in the cleavage of her cut-too-low blouse. It and its contents had seen better days, but neither was talking.

On her lapel, a dime sized speck of something blue shone out in all its glory. Perhaps it was her tooth paste from yesterday or moldy residue of a piece of food from the day before.

The beauty queen of Joe's Bar wasn't wearing a bra, so more than half a very uninviting, freckled and unbound breast peeked out at Smoky.

He thought, "I'm not interested you old bitch," and asked Willie, "How about renting me a room for a couple hours, old timer?"

Willie displayed a mouth full of teeth rotted nearly to the gum and tried to smile. His breath reeked of cheap rotgut wine when he replied, "It'll cost you, Bub."

"I'm willing to pay. How much?"

Wino Willie pinched his lips together and it reminded Smoky of a festering wound he once saw in Vietnam.

"It'll be twenty-five dollars for two hours."

Smoky thought, "If I lit a match right now old timer, you and your girlfriend would go up in a cloud of smoke."

At the sound of money about to change hands, the ears of Willie's greasy girlfriend perked up.

Smoky leaned on the counter and beckoned Willie closer.

"Tell you what, old timer, if you've got a nice room in the back of the motel, I'll give you fifty dollars for the afternoon. What about it?"

Bad breath Willie tried to act nonchalant, but it wasn't his bag. His hands trembled as he snatched the fifty dollar bill from Smoky's hand and said, "You got a deal."

Willie's hung-over and hanging-out girlfriend staggered to her feet and grinned. Her run-down ruined tennis shoes pointed in two directions because she had them on the wrong feet.

Her breath was worse than Willie's, (if that was possible), and two front teeth were missing. In anticipation of some cheap wine, she licked her lips which had cold sores in both corners. As she stood up, her tattered, dirty skirt unwrapped from one blue-veined leg and Smoky caught an unwanted and unappreciated fleeting glimpse of badly-stained bloomers.

The boozer handed Smoky a key and said, "Room 134. Don't leave the place a mess, and bring the key back when you're done."

"Thanks, old timer," Smoky said and tipped his 'go to hell' cap to the smelly old broad.

The sweetheart of the Do D o Inn tittered, which shook her age-spotted, unfettered titties.

Smoky had seen enough. He took the offered key and walked out.

Three minutes later, as he watched in the rearview mirror, Smoky saw the slowly shuffling drunk and his lovely companion leave the office unlocked and hurry toward a liquor store down the block.

There were no other vehicles in the motel parking lot. While Smoky was checking in and checking out the boozer's sweetheart, he noticed the keys to every room were in the rack. There would be no witnesses.

After donning a clean set of white cotton gloves, Smoky motioned to Will and Charley to do the same. Then he backed the pickup as close as possible to the door of Room 134.

When their blindfolds and handcuffs had been removed, Joe and Jerry were carried in the room, placed on separate beds and covered with faded western bedspreads. Will thought he might have seen something crawling on one of the blankets, but when he looked again, whatever it was had disappeared.

Charley folded the tarp and tied it down to the truck bed as Smoky locked the motel room from the outside. After wiping any fingerprints from the key, he threw it into a sludge-filled, green-slime-topped swimming pool and waited for a splash when the key hit the water. Instead, he heard a sound like some prehistoric monster burped.

Herb drove the semi into the outskirts of Boulder City, then turned right on Route 93 South and continued on to Kingman, Arizona. He stopped at a flourishing cattle ranch on a side road near Dolan Springs, where fifteen "special passengers" were loaded aboard.

The ranch owner, sixty-five-year-old Don Coleman, wore a genuine Stetson, faded blue jeans and muddy/shitty boots as he helped Herb, Skinny and Alan load fourteen large contented heifers. The cows displayed heavy udders hanging down to rival those of the sweetheart of the Do D o Inn.

The fifteenth passenger was a tremendously large bull that was meaner than a junkyard dog.

Loading the cows was easy, but the bull was something else. Old "Satan" didn't want to cooperate in any way, shape or form. He snorted, kicked and bucked. When Don applied an electric cattle prod to Satan's ass to help him on his way, it only pissed him off.

It took over an hour of hard work before the stupid stud was finally settled inside the cage at the rear of the trailer. As they shut the door, Satan was still snorting fire, pissing brimstone and glaring at them with smoldering red eyes.

Don looked their rig over and said, "I like the way you modified your trailer. It makes sense to haul the cattle facing forward. Plus you have more room to store your feed. The stall you built for old Satan is large enough to let him roam around without getting hurt or injuring another cow."

"Yeah," Herb said. "We like it too. I hope he behaves back there. I don't want him to get loose."

"I know what you mean," Don said. "Satan riles easily, but the cage looks strong enough. I hate to lose him, but the price your boss offered was too good to pass up. The old guy still has lots of lead in his pencil. I think half those cows are knocked up."

Herb laughed.

"That means more profit for my boss. Let's go guys. We have to get on the road."

After shaking hands all around, Herb and his crew climbed into the cab and pulled out with a fully loaded rig.

Two miles down the road, Herb pulled to the side of the deserted, sandblasted blacktop, and Skinny got out carrying his own electric cattle prod. Alan helped him open one of the rear doors.

Skinny hit Satan in the flank with a hot load of electricity and the bull reacted accordingly. He kicked the cage and spun around in circles, legs and horns flying in every direction. Skinny hit him again and Satan snorted smoke as he charged toward the front of the trailer.

At the rear of the cage, his head and horns hit a previously and purposely weakened board. It and two beneath splintered into kindling wood, as Satan sprinted into the interior. When his wicked horns scraped against the side of the truck, sparks flew.

"Good Boy," Skinny said, as he and Alan shut and locked the door. They heard Satan's hooves pound toward them and the door shook as the head of the dimwitted bull hit the reinforced cage.

"Good Boy," Skinny repeated, and Alan laughed.

They climbed back into the cab, where Herb sat smiling, and Skinny said, "Worked like a charm."

Herb put the truck in gear, and they headed for New Mexico.

While Herb and his helpers were loading cattle, two flea-bitten Brinks employees awakened from their drug induced sleep. Soaked in sweat, they found they were in a sleazy, hot, run-down room of the Do D o Inn.

Chapter 20

The phone rang in Clyde Rhodes' office and his secretary, Angie Rose, answered the call. She listened a moment, then pointed to Jake and said, "It's for you, Agent Polk."

Jake answered the phone in the required manner and listened for a few moments. Whatever the caller said, it must have pissed him off. Jake's face was beet red as he stood up and kicked a trash can across the room.

Reacting to the noise, Clyde ran out of his office and asked, "What the hell's going on?" Then he saw the color of Jake's face, knew something was radically wrong and waited to see what Jake would do next.

Jake was still listening to someone on the phone. It was two minutes before he spoke.

"Yes, Sir, I understand, Sir. I'll get right out to Las Vegas. Thank you, Sir."

After hanging up, Jake slumped wearily down in his seat like Joe Louis after a fifteen round title fight. Then he turned his swivel chair to face Clyde.

"I'm sorry, Clyde. You won't believe it, but Brinks lost another truck. This time it was a truck out of Laughlin, Nevada, with a payload of seventeen million. Man, I don't believe these people. Who the hell are they?"

"Calm down, Jake."

Jake took a couple of deep breaths, and his natural color returned.

"Okay Jake, take it easy and tell me what your supervisor

said. By the look on your face, I know it was him. He's not too happy, is he?"

"No, and he's looking for a whipping boy. Can you believe it? He relieved me and put one of his fair-haired youngsters in charge. Now I have to fly to Las Vegas and report to this punk kid."

Clyde shook his head.

"I'm sorry to hear that, Jake. You made good progress here. Your supervisor should remember it was you who figured out how the trucks were stopped. If he was smart enough to put the word out, maybe this latest robbery wouldn't have happened."

Jake looked up and said, "Thanks, Clyde."

Clyde nodded to say "You're welcome," and said, "Even though you're not in charge anymore, take it easy. Step back and look at this case again. Sometimes you can't see the horny toads for the sand."

"Thanks again, Clyde. I have a strange feeling I overlooked something right in front of my nose, but can't put my finger on it."

"Did your boss say anything about the guard and driver of the third truck?"

"I'm sorry; I forgot to tell you. They woke up this morning in a sleazy motel outside of Boulder City – said they were stopped by a phony detour. The bogus workers threatened them with an RPG, while a truck and car hemmed them in, so there was nowhere to go.

"Rather than die for Brinks, they gave up, were blindfolded, handcuffed and injected with something that put them out like a light. Several hours later they woke up and called the police."

Clyde expressed his appreciation of the report. "The good news is this time they let the men go free. Maybe their crime spree is over and we can relax."

"Not me," Jake said. "I'll catch these guys or die trying."

When Tim answered the phone, Harold said, "Good news, Mister Wythe. The driver and guard from the third missing armored truck have been found, safe and well. We still don't know where the truck is, but we do know the location of the robbery. The truck was hijacked on Nelson Road, a side road off Highway 95 approximately halfway between Laughlin and Boulder City.

"My men are there now. When the troopers searched Highway 95, they noticed the road was barricaded. Construction signs indicated a flagger was on duty, but they didn't see one. The troopers noted the problem, but continued to search for the truck."

Tim sighed.

"I doubt the robbers were anywhere near Nelson Road at the time. Your report coincides with an estimate of the location from my signal officer."

"Then it all ties together. Now all we have to do is find the missing truck and money."

"It may take some time," Tim said. "The New Mexico State Police searched for days and don't have a clue as to the location of anything or anybody. The third truck is probably on its way out of state."

"What about your transponder?"

"It's still functioning, but I doubt if we'll ever find it. My signal officer says the device is somewhere in the southern part of Boulder City, but I know it's not the truck."

"We'll keep searching," Harold said.

"Thanks, Captain. Good luck."

"I have the feeling we'll need all the luck we can get."

("Damn – there go my Major leafs.")

Ramon Hernandez was an acne scarred, mandatory mustachioed green-carder Mexican American, whose arms displayed seven tattoos. In addition, five of his body parts were pierced with different-sized, chromed accessories. If Ramon ever had to fly, he'd create havoc at the metal detector.

As a twelve year BMI veteran, Ramon drove a big blue monster garbage truck with two steel tusks. This morning he sat in his battered, but still shiny vehicle in a parking lot of a Quick Stop convenience store in southern Boulder City and cursed aloud.

"Damn it old lady; move it or park it."

When the white-haired bitch finally moved her BMW, Ramon headed for a stinking dumpster at the rear of the store, where he toggled a switch, and the steel hooks slid into slots with a loud grinding noise.

With practiced ease, prettily-pictured-and-private-parts-painfully-pierced Ramon increased pressure on one of his polished knobs. The dumpster shook like a hog in heat, rose into the air, turned over and allowed the stained lids to fall open.

With a sound like thunder, most of the congested contents fell into the hopper, including the heavy-duty battery and fragile transponder. As they landed inside, the wires snapped and the signal stopped. An hour later, the never-to-be-recovered device became part of a large landfill outside town.

While whistling a happy tune, Ramon turned out of the parking lot and moved on to his next customer.

With a heavy heart, Luke walked across the hall to Tim's office, where he said, "We lost the signal from the transponder, Tim. It suddenly quit transmitting."

Tim ran his nail-bitten fingers through thinning hair and sighed.

"It's just as well. We never would have found it anyway, but I'll let the authorities know."

Chapter 21

While Roger used his cell phone to keep track of their movement and location, each truck returned to the ranch by a different route. Since they had to stop periodically to give the cattle water and hay, the big rig took more time to make the journey.

During the return trip, Roger also maintained contact with the troops at the ranch. The next time he talked to A. J., he said, "Man the place is booming. If business continues to grow, we'll need more pens."

Roger smiled at his enthusiasm and asked, "How are our guests?"

A. J. laughed.

"Fred says they're still upset, but taking it like men. Larry continues to bitch, but what's new? Fred shuts off the mike and lets him rant and rave."

"Tomorrow, let the guards and drivers know they'll go home in a few days. It'll give them something to look forward to."

When they left the robbery site, Roger was worried about the weight of the armored truck combined with that of the cattle. He was relieved after Herb reported clear sailing through the first of several weigh stations.

Within an eight hour time span, all the pickups returned to the Crossed X ranch, where the men unloaded the luggage and drank a cold one to celebrate. Taking their drinks with them, they sat on the edge of the porch or parked their weary frames on the top rail of the corral and talked in hushed tones.

As they sat, watched and waited for their gold mine to come driving down the potholed ranch road, they resembled buzzards waiting for a break in traffic to get to some road kill on a busy highway.

Everything went well until the eighteen-wheeler reached Las Cruces, where Herb, Alan and Skinny stopped for diesel and lunch. When they tried to enter the freeway, they encountered a little elderly blue-haired lady named Florence White, driving a 1984 Buick Skylark.

Florence was a slight woman, eighty-two years of age. Although her eyesight wasn't what it once was, Flo was still feisty and loved to drive her old car to town and back occasionally.

When he met Florence, Herb was making a right turn onto Highway 70.

As she crept along at a steady fifteen miles an hour in the right lane, Flo was thinking, "To hell with what the doc says. If I stay on the access road, I can see well enough to find my street. I'm a good driver. I just have to watch for fools and idiots on the road nowadays."

On her car stereo, Freddy Fender sang "Lonely Days and Lonely Nights". As she peeked between the black plastic spokes of her steering wheel to see where she was headed, Flo's loose top partial plate clacked in time against what few real teeth she still possessed.

It was impossible for Herb to turn right from the first lane without running over the curb, so he was in the second lane, with his right turn signal blinking out a warning.

Posted on the right rear of the cattle trailer is a large sign in living color. In graphic detail, it displays how a car can be caught between the truck and curb.

Maybe Flo couldn't see it; perhaps she just ignored the warning, or didn't give a damn either way. When the light turned green, Herb began a slow gentle right turn.

Then Florence gave her car the gas, drove straight ahead and ran the bird-crap-covered hood of her beloved Buick into the undercarriage of the trailer. The left front fender of her jalopy hit the unforgiving metal and was impaled like a tomato on a skewer.

For such a mild mannered woman, Flo knew some abusive and slandering language. She also knew when to use it to the best advantage. This was one of those times, so she yelled, "You damned idiot."

Alan looked out the window and said, "Great, this is all we need when we're so close to home."

"When the cops arrive, play dumb," Herb said. "Let me do the talking."

Flo shook her fist with an upraised middle finger at Herb. When he saw her in his side view mirror, Herb knew she wasn't calling him number one on her hit parade.

An alert, (and mind-other-people's-business-for-them), driver notified the Las Cruces Police of the accident. When they arrived, they found Flo's bruised Buick was stuck so firmly it would require a wrecker or heavy-duty jack to extract her damaged vehicle.

As Herb and Sam set out warning flares and orange colored cones, the next few minutes were punctuated by Flo uttering a list of foul words and a few more hand signals. Then the city cops arrived, assessed the damage and called for a wrecker.

A portly policeman with a blue and white name tag reading; Sergeant Thinner, (a contradiction of self-apparent facts), informed Flo she'd receive a citation for improper lane usage.

"Your lane is clearly marked in white paint: RIGHT TURN ONLY," the overweight and underpaid cop said.

Flo was fighting mad and it might have turned ugly, but a bad scene was avoided when Skinny handed her a cold soda pop. In the middle of a tirade, Flo stopped, looked up at Skinny and said sweetly, "Thank you, young man."

A battered and badly-in-need-of-an-oil-change wrecker arrived, driven by a beer-bellied driver, wearing sloppy, greasy overhauls two sizes too small, with "Ted" sewn in red over his left pocket.

The weight of the truck as it sat on Flo's old bucket of bolts proved to be too much for Ted's wrecker. The fat policeman listened over his shoulder, as Ted asked, "What in hell have you got inside this truck?"

Herb shrugged and waved his hand in the general direction of his trailer.

"Fourteen cows and a big old bastard of a bull. Plus we got a shit pot full of feed. Hell, the bull weighs as much as the old gal's car."

Fat Sergeant Thinner looked perplexed, but then had a seemingly heavenly inspiration.

"Can you unload anything to lighten the load?"

Herb shrugged again.

"I don't know how. Without a ramp or chute, there's no way to get the cattle off, and I don't even want to think about trying to move the damn bull. He's been banging around back there for two days."

His bulging stomach gurgled like Mount Haleakala spewing forth lava, as Sergeant Thinner asked, "Were any of the animals injured?"

Herb looked exasperated.

"Hell, I didn't think to check."

After walking around the trailer and counting cows, Herb said, "All fourteen are standing up and eating, so I don't think they're injured."

"What about the bull?" Ted asked.

Herb pointed toward the rear doors and said, "I can open the door, but watch out for Satan. You've never seen a stud like this one. He's hung like an elephant and thinks his shit don't smell."

Skinny helped him unlock and open one of the doors. As it swung open, an upset and irritated to no end Satan stood there. Satan took one look at Skinny and remembering the last time he saw him, he charged. When his empty-brained head and curved sharp, pointed horns collided with the unforgiving and uncaring steel cage, it was enough to make even the bravest soul crap his pants.

Everyone jumped back in fright, and Herb said, "Damn; look what the crazy son of a bitch did. He broke down his stall. Now I can't get to the hay unless I crawl over those frigging cows. What a mess."

"You're right," a frightened Sergeant Thinner said. "I

wouldn't try to get inside that truck for all the money in the world. Lock up the beast again."

With his face red from embarrassment or fright, Sergeant Thinner turned to Ted and said, "Let's get a jack in place and get this rig out of here."

Herb tried not to laugh as he said, "I'm with you. I'm running late, and my boss isn't going to like the damage the bastard did. He'll probably dock my pay for it. Damn, this is just great."

Ted's partner, Mickey, according to his no-longer-white name tag, arrived with a hydraulic house jack. With his help, they raised the trailer high enough to remove Flo's battered Buick.

Herb and Skinny inspected the undercarriage and declared it fit to drive. Two cops with less weight on their blue uniformed bodies then Sergeant Thinner, who had been directing traffic around the wreck until their arms felt like they were going to fall off, were happy to see the rig depart.

Disgusted, but resigned to the fact fate crapped on her one more time, Flo sat in the rear seat of a black and white, sucking warm Coke through a plastic straw. Cursing under her breath, she lamented her bad luck.

"Damn it anyway."

The overhead red, white and blue lights flashed like a fourth of July parade, but Flo wasn't in a mood to notice.

As they drove up the on-ramp, Alan said, "That was good acting, Herb. Thank God for Satan and his foul temper."

"Thank Roger for planning for any possibility. He put Satan on the truck in case we got stopped for weight violations. With a badass bull running loose, no inspector would want to look inside. We were fine on weight, but just now old Satan saved our butts."

The remainder of the trip was uneventful. At seven twenty-eight p.m., a jovial Herb and his worn-out passengers rolled into Roswell. Following a bathroom break, and after procuring a fresh thermos of coffee, they headed north on Highway 285. An hour and ten minutes later they arrived at the ranch, where Herb checked in with Roger by cell phone and discovered all the men and vehicles had returned safely.

"Lock the gate behind you, Herb," Roger said. "There aren't any deliveries scheduled for tonight. Welcome home."

"We're glad to be here. Remind me to tell you about our run-in with Florence in Las Cruces."

"Is it anything we should worry about?"

"Nah," Herb replied. "It was funny. I'll tell you about it later tonight. I hope Wes has some food waiting."

"How does a porterhouse steak and baked potato sound?"

"You're a lifesaver."

Herb eased the big rig through the gate, and Alan dropped out to run back and lock the gate. He returned quickly, and they drove on to the ranch house.

As they topped a small rise, they saw the lights of the ranch shining like a beacon in the darkness, and Skinny said, "I never thought I'd miss this place, but I did. It's good to be home."

Chapter 22

"As of today, the cell phone ban goes back into effect," Roger said. "Alan, make sure everyone turns in their cells and the instruments are locked up."

Six months ago, when the team assembled on the ranch, Roger invoked a ban on cell phone use. Out of necessity, they utilized the phones on the Nevada trip, but now it was time to return to the old system.

"My phone and Carl's will be locked in the office," Roger said. "If someone has an emergency, we can use them and monitor the conversation. Make sure the men know."

"Will do," Alan said.

Late in the evening of the day Herb and the big rig returned, the final slot in the garage was filled. As the cattle were led down a manure-stained ramp and placed in an empty feed lot, Satan was still snorting fire and brimstone, so it was necessary to tranquilize him with a dart gun. Afterward, Slim tied a rope around his horns and led him to his new private corral. Satan stumbled along like a sleepwalker, docile as a kitten.

Pete and Clete looked on, and Pete said, "The old bull don't look too mean to me."

Never one to waste words, his brother, Clete said, "Nah."

By this time, the men were adept at removing the dirt, steel supports and four-by-four barriers. For the last time, Herb backed the trailer close to the remaining empty slot, and Carl drove the third truck into its final resting place.

Four weary hours later the job was completed, but it wasn't

time to celebrate yet. Since everyone was tired and needed their rest, Roger decided to forgo any display of wealth.

"Close the trap door and put some fresh manure on top."

All the way from Boulder City, Skinny pestered Herb about driving the big rig.

"Remember? You promised I could drive when we got back. Please let me move the truck."

Finally, Herb gave in. After the armored truck was parked, he gave Skinny the keys and said, "Drive to the rear of the mound and park it. I'll ride along, so show me you can do a good job."

Spaced-out Skinny was ecstatic with his new toy. He eased the truck away from the garage area and turned left. Enthralled, he made the first turn successfully, but on the second left turn Skinny swung the rig too short.

Herb shouted, "Whoa. Stop and back up a little. Remember what I told you about swinging wide? If you kept on the way you were, you'd run the trailer up on the side of the mound and get stuck."

Looking crestfallen, Skinny said, "I'm sorry."

"Don't look so sad. It's a mistake all rookies make. Next time, remember to swing wider."

"You mean you'll still let me drive? I thought you'd be pissed."

"Nah," Herb said. "When I was your age I made the same mistake. Now take your time and park it like a pro."

The next afternoon, after they were handcuffed, blindfolded and sedated with another fifty CCs of serum, Roger released his four prisoners.

When he was sure the guards and drivers were unconscious, Carl removed four seats from the van and they laid the sleeping men on the floor. A. J. covered them with a tarp.

With Carl driving and A. J. riding shotgun, they headed north on Highway 285, then turned left onto Route 60 through Pedernal Hills, where a blacktop road winds through the Manzano Mountain range southeast of Albuquerque.

Forty miles into the forest, Carl pulled off onto a deserted logging road and followed the potholed trail deep into the trees until it changed to a winding, narrow gravel path.

He stopped the van, and they surveyed the surrounding area, but saw no one. A. J. raised the rear hatch, and after uncovering their human cargo, he and Carl worked carefully, but paid strict attention to details.

The four sleeping beauties were hauled with their legs dangling to a clearing under a towering fir tree, where their handcuffs and blindfolds were removed. The night before their original uniforms and shoes were returned. Now Carl and A. J. replaced the Brinks employees' watches, belts and personal items.

After a final check, Carl closed the hatch and turned the van around. As he drove slowly down the path, A. J. followed behind, walking backward and sweeping away tire tracks. When they reached the blacktop, A. J. threw the broom into the woods and climbed into the front seat. While wiping perspiration from his brow with a white handkerchief, he said, "Let's head for home."

During their absence, changes were made to the jail. The bunks and chairs were torn apart and buried deep in a dry arroyo. The double entry addition and entire front of the building were removed and burned to ash, while the steel door was lowered into the depths of the garage.

Three new windows were installed, and red cedar lap and gap siding was nailed on and painted a dull white. Wes stood back, looked at the nearly finished product and said, "The place is beginning to look like my mom's house in Wisconsin."

Standing beside him, Herb said, "I didn't know you had a mother. I thought you were found under a rock in east Texas."

"Nah," Wes said, "that was slim."

The water-stained sink, commode and drain joined the electronic equipment in the dark, stinking garage. The air conditioning vent was removed and the hole in the ceiling patched, but the air conditioner/heater was disconnected and left in place. The ceiling was covered with white tile, and pale green linoleum was laid.

A tan colored paint was applied to the walls and allowed to

dry overnight. Then the new storage shed was filled with bales of hay.

Fred stood back, admired their work and said, "If those guys saw the shed today, they'd never know it was their jail."

A special burial party was assembled. After the RPG firing mechanism was rendered useless by the application of a five-pound sledgehammer, it and the still dangerous warhead were encased in four-hundred pounds of concrete.

The two leaders and several members of the gang stood at a loose attention and watched as Casey lowered the heavy coffin-shaped object into a ten-foot deep hole he had dug with the backhoe.

A. J. saluted and said, "Thank God we didn't have to use it."

Roscoe nodded and said, "Rest in pieces, good buddy."

"Amen," Roger added. "Bury it well and put three large stones on top – one for each job."

"You got it, Boss," Casey said with a smile.

The cattle trailer was steam cleaned and the special cage left in place for future use. The remaining equipment joined the other articles in the garage.

Fred and two other men cleaned the pickups, inside and out. At last, after a thorough inspection, the two leaders declared the ranch secure.

Today was a beautiful day, with the sun shining brightly and small white clouds drifting by overhead. No shipments of cattle were due, so there wasn't much work to keep everyone busy.

This was the type of day for some high jinks from the Crawford twins, Pete and Clete, better known as Pete and Repeat. What trouble one couldn't get into, the other was sure to find. It was anyone's guess what they would do next.

So far only three instances of their type of humor were reported to Roger. Someone put instant glue on one of the toilet seats; Cookie's bright red underwear was found flying from the flagstaff instead of Old Glory, and while the twins were assisting in the mess, someone switched chocolate chips for X-lax, which gave the entire camp, (except the twins), the running shits for three days.

Every time the two nuts met someone new, and were asked about their being twins, Pete would say, "I was born first and Clete stuck around in our mom's womb for another week to see what it was like not to have to share the tiny space with another body."

It was amazing how many people actually believed the big lie.

Until the day they set fire to a barn full of hay, they raised hell and made their parents' lives a living one. Clete claimed his ass hurt for four years afterward from the "lickin'" they got at their old man's hand.

It seemed to straighten them out for a short time, but when Pete and Clete enlisted in the National Guard, and their unit was called up to duty three months later, everyone in Possum's Slick, Arkansas was glad to see them leave.

One of their neighbors said, "It couldn't have happened to two more deserving guys."

Another claimed Saddam had better watch his ass. "With the Crawford boys on his case, the war will be over in two weeks."

To no one's surprise, when the fighting was called off after ten days, the entire community figured it was because Pete and Clete ran out of bad guys to kill.

When recalling their efforts, Roger said, "They were ambitious, tenacious and rambunctious."

Out front in every battle, Pete and Clete led the way up the road of death, shooting anything that moved, (and a whole hell of a lot that didn't). They loved to hear the big gun on the tank fire and went through more .50 caliber ammo than any other three tanks.

On the outside of their turret, an artist in the company drew a picture of an Iraqi soldier. Next to it was a line of Roman numeral Xs several feet long, indicating the number of enemy dead attributed to their marksmanship. Also pictured were seventeen camels, six Arab tents and three oil wells.

When Pete and Repeat weren't fighting the enemy, they were trying to outdo each other in every endeavor. A significant amount of money was won or lost by betting on one or the other. It was a nice break from the war.

Somewhere along the line, (no one knew where), the twins picked up some carpentry and masonry skills. Charley was probably the only man in the world who could get the two to cooperate long enough to get a building built, before they tried to tear it down again.

"When you can keep them apart, they both do the work of two people," Charley said. "Keeping them separated is the key. Let them put their heads together for some shenanigans, and you've got a world of hurt on your hands."

Charley passed the lesson on to Slim, and so far, he managed to get ten hours of work out of every eight hour day from both Pete and Repeat. It was too bad Slim was in town buying supplies. Maybe if he had been around, nothing would have happened, but no one would have bet on it.

Today Pete had his eyes on Satan. He had been measuring the stud bull since the day they led him down a ramp and into his new corral.

So had Repeat.

"The sucker doesn't look so mean," Pete said.

"Nah," Repeat said.

"I'll bet I could ride him," Pete bragged.

"Nah," Repeat repeated.

"Ya wanta bet?"

"Yeah; how much?"

"Fifty bucks says I can stay on his back for eight seconds."

"With no rope?"

"How the hell would I get a rope on him?" Pete asked. "Sure, without a rope. I'll just hang onto his ears and horns."

"You're on," Repeat said.

That's when the manure really hit the oscillating device.

When he saw Pete and Repeat with a rope made into a lasso, Garret Haggerty asked, "What in hell are you two up to?"

Garret was the same age as the twins, twenty-four, and served with them in Iraq as a tank mechanic. It was he who came up with the idea of keeping count of the kills credited to their tank he named "Old Ironsides".

When the Crawford boys headed west to join Roger and Carl, Garret was one step behind. He left the carpenter he was working for with a roof half shingled and rain on the horizon.

As they headed for Satan's corral, Repeat said, "Nothing."

Garret knew better. Shaking his head, he said, "You better stay away from the bull."

Pete smiled and bragged, "I'm going to ride him."

"You're crazier than hell. Satan will eat your balls for lunch."

Uttering the longest sentence he used in weeks, Repeat said, "Just keep shoveling shit, Garret, and let us be."

After much discussion between the brothers, it was decided a rope would be necessary after all. There was no way Satan would stand still long enough for Pete to jump up on him. Satan's ears and horns were also a long way from his back.

The twins figured they could lasso Satan and tie him off to the corral. Then they'd let Pete climb up, grab the rope and make his play. How Pete was going to get off never entered the equation. No one ever said Pete and Repeat were long on brains.

Garret decided to tag along to see what happened.

Satan eyed the trio with distrust as they approached his private roaming space. Not blessed with many brains himself, Satan was easy prey for Pete and Repeat.

Pete held out a carrot while Repeat hid the lasso behind his back. Garret took a seat on a nearby watering trough to watch the proceedings.

Satan moved closer and reached out for the carrot, only to find a lasso thrown over his horns and head. As he ate the treat, the noose didn't bother Satan too much. But then Repeat tied the rope to an upright and cinched Satan's head close to the corral. Satan didn't like that one damn bit.

Swinging his head to and fro, he tried to bust loose, but Repeat held on tight, while Pete climbed onto the top railing and jumped aboard.

In one swift motion, Repeat untied the rope and threw it to Pete, who yelled, "Start counting."

Satan didn't do anything for the first two seconds. Turning his massive head, he looked at the insignificant, skinny apparition sitting on his back and seemed to be asking, "Are you out of your mind?"

Then he took two small steps backward. Pete sat there, in his best bull rider pose; his left hand high above his head, holding the rope loosely in his right hand, with a big smile on his face.

Repeat reached the number "one thousand and four", and Pete figured he had it made; money in the bank and fame and fortune in the future. But he didn't stand a chance.

Satan seemed to rise up into the air on all four feet and pitched off the fly on his back with one twisting lunge.

Later, Garret estimated Pete flew at least ten feet into the air and fifteen feet forward. He landed across the corral fence and broke through two stout wooden bars, (not to mention shattering his left leg in two places below the knee).

Satan saw his chance, smashed through the two remaining bars and headed out to who knows where, with his head and horns downward and bellowing like the bull stud he was. One of his flying hooves caught Repeat up alongside his head, knocking him sideways and unconscious for four hours.

When the smoke cleared, Roger was down two men. Pete wound up in the hospital with pins in his leg. Repeat had a concussion that kept him out of work for a week.

Satan was missing in action for two days before they found him, winded and worn from roaming the range, looking for heifers to jump that weren't there. When they finally got Satan back into his repaired corral, he looked as relieved as Roger felt.

It was the first serious accident of the campaign. If there was a silver lining to the farce, it came at a time when they didn't need every man, so wasn't as serious as it could have been.

Slim was pissed at the twins. That evening he gave a long-winded dissertation to the rest of the men, concerning the fact that even though it was a contradiction of terms, there was no place for horseplay on a working ranch.

To everyone's continued amazement, the feeding station prospered. During the next two weeks, two additional pens were established in a flat area behind the ranch house, and more feeders and water troughs were delivered. The new business was such a beehive of activity it became hectic to keep up with demand.

Finally Roger called a halt to unannounced deliveries, telling his present and prospective customers, "We'll accept cattle only when an appointment is scheduled five days in advance, and won't accept night delivery after six p.m."

With an influx of additional cattle, the manure pile continued to grow. The shit gave off an aroma as foul as the rice fields of Vietnam. A fertilizer dealer agreed to dispatch trucks to pick up the manure, but the ranch owners would use their backhoe to load the trucks.

Roger also decided to sell the dump truck and trailer.

"We haven't used them since the second robbery, so they set there idle. Someone might see them and put two and two together. Get rid of them, A. J."

A. J. took the vehicles into town and put them on a consignment lot with a ridiculously low asking price. Within a week both items were snapped up by a construction firm from Arizona.

Several men approached Carl, and their spokesman, Wiley Jenkins asked, "When are we going to have this 'mother of all parties' Roger promised us? It's been two weeks since the last job and we need some down time."

Wiley was an ex-First Sergeant, proud of the stripes running nearly halfway up his sleeves from his elbows to his shoulders. He was a scrounger deluxe, able to steal anything not tied down if it bettered the living conditions of his troops.

In Iraq he took some shrapnel in his chest during one battle, losing three ribs and some other insignificant bones. After recuperating, the powers to be decided Wiley should sit out the next war, so they booted him from the ranks and out of the Army.

Wiley had fourteen years in by then and didn't know anything else but the military. Civilian life and the need to find a job hit him hard. There wasn't much call for a First Sergeant in any civilian asshole company.

When Carl called, Wiley was down to his last few dollars in the bank. The prospect of a million dollar payoff didn't interest him as much as helping run a semi-military operation again. He was back in the saddle and loving it.

"I'll give Roger your message," Carl said. "When he feels the time is right, we'll have the biggest party you ever attended. We stopped late deliveries, so we have more time to throw the blowout in the evening. Pass the word I said it would be soon, real soon."

Chapter 23

In response to Jake's question, a secretary pointed across the room and said, "That's Agent Hefner over there. He's in charge of the Las Vegas Brinks investigation."

"Thanks," Jake said and ambled over to where Agent Hefner sat with his feet up on a desk, reading a report.

"Howdy, I'm Jake Polk. Agent Mudd told me to report to you."

Agent Hefner took his feet off the desk, laid the report on the desktop, stood up and shook Jake's hand.

"Oh yeah, Bill told me about you. Welcome to Las Vegas. Call me Kris."

Kris was a youngster. Jake owned shoes older than he was. His new supervisor wore a two-piece brown suit with a light tan shirt. His blond hair was a little longer than regulation, but neatly trimmed and combed. Kris looked a lot smarter then good old Bill. In fact, he looked like he had his shit together.

As Jake sat down without being asked, he thought, "So it's 'Bill' and he told you about me. I'll bet you're thrilled to see me."

"What's going on, Kris? Is there anything new?"

"Not much. We're glad you found out how the trucks were stopped. That was a nice piece of investigative work."

"Thanks," Jake said while thinking, "Maybe you're okay, Kris. Let's wait and see."

"There are two other guys from the bureau working with me," Kris said. "You can assist them. Is that okay with you?"

"Sure. What's your slant on this latest caper?"

Kris picked up the report and read from it.

"The focus of the investigation is now on Las Vegas and the surrounding towns. We believe the two robberies in New Mexico were only a warm-up for this job. The perps may plan an even bigger one in the near future, so I'm glad they sent you here. I doubt there's anything new to be learned in Roswell or any other town in New Mexico."

"I'm happy to be here," Jake said, (but didn't mean it).

For the next two weeks, Jake checked with the state police and Brinks personnel in Las Vegas and Laughlin. He visited the crime scene twice and was surprised to see the crooks left the traffic signs and cones behind.

("Maybe this truck was the last job after all. Then again, the crooks know the construction caper is old news. Hell, they probably left this crap behind to muddy the waters. Whoever their leader is, he's smart.")

The crime scene provided him with no new information. There were tire tracks in the sand, but the constant, blowing wind had altered them.

As Jake talked with Joe and Jerry, he thought, "We could be the three stooges."

The robbery scenario and their abduction were similar to the crimes in New Mexico. The fact Jerry and Joe were sedated and left in a motel room was a change, but really meant nothing in the scheme of things.

After fourteen days of heat, sweat, frustration and too many lousy hamburgers, Jake was no closer to solving any of the crimes. His aching stomach rumbled constantly. It felt like there was a whole cow including hide, hooves and horns inside his protesting, bloated stomach.

The three trucks were still missing, but shortly after Jake arrived in Las Vegas, the four drivers and guards from the first two were released unharmed. Bill Mudd sent other "more qualified" agents to interview them. Jake stayed where he was.

So far, Jake had done little except spin his wheels. Finally he could take his position in life no longer.

In his motel bathtub, Jake was floating in a mound of

lavender scented bath bubbles. His aching stomach protruded above the white foam, looking like a breaching whale. Jake was on his fourth glass of Jim Beam and coke since quitting time and feeling no pain, when suddenly he made up his mind.

"Piss on it. I'm calling good old Bill."

Sticking a soggy wrinkled hand through the bubbles, he picked up his cell phone from the top of the shitter and got two wrong numbers before getting through to Agent Mudd.

In his New York nasal twang, Bill asked, "What is it, Jake?"

"I'm not accomplishing anything here. Agent Hefner has things under control, but hasn't been able to locate the trucks. Let me go back to Roswell and nose around. What can it hurt?"

Earlier in the evening, Bill and a couple of friends had a few drinks, so he was also feeling no pain. In an alcoholic haze, Bill felt magnanimous toward his old nemesis.

"I'll give you one more week and that's it. Our computer models tell us we can expect another robbery very soon, and you'll only be in the way in Las Vegas.

"When you get to Roswell, stay away from two other agents I've assigned there. They're working out of the sheriff's office and I don't want you to bother them. You established a connection with the Brinks personnel, so work out of their office. Am I making myself clear?"

Swallowing what little pride he had left, Jake said, "Yes, you are. Thank you," but thought, "Up yours."

After trying for several minutes to balance his strong drink in a plastic cup on his floating round-topped protrusion and failing, Jake said, "To hell with it," and downed the drink in one long, satisfying gulp.

Early the next morning Jake left for Roswell, where he moved his junk into his old desk in the Brinks office with Clyde and Alice.

During the next few days, Jake spent several more frustrating and uneventful hours along Highway 285, checking the area thoroughly. The drivers and guards were willing to cooperate, so they spent several hours at the crime scene.

They told Jake the same story as the Las Vegas employees. There was no new information except for the fact they felt sure they were held somewhere within the Albuquerque city limits. Jake thanked them for their time, and they returned to Roswell.

In the course of his ramblings, Jake passed the sign and entrance to the Crossed X Ranch several times. He noted a large number of cattle trucks and other vehicles exiting or entering the property and thought, "Whoever owns the ranch does a land office business. They must be making a fortune."

For the fiftieth time, Jake reviewed the threadbare transcript of the transponder tapes. He had read and re-read it, and every time, a nagging doubt gnawed at his gut.

After Herb and his buddy, Skinny finished unloading two hundred bales of hay they picked up in Vaughan, they were tired and sweaty. Herb sat down on a bale, took a big swig of water from a pail and said, "Whew, I don't want to do this again very soon."

Skinny joined him on the hay and asked, "Would it be okay if I parked the rig again? I'll take my time and remember what you told me."

"Yeah, what the hell, you have to learn sometime. Here's the key. I'm too bushed to ride along. Lock up the rig and bring the key back."

"Thanks, Herb," Skinny said and walked away with a big smile on his face and a swagger to his hips.

After taking another big gulp of water, Herb shook his head, lay back against the barn and shut his eyes against the sun's glare.

He was almost asleep when he heard Skinny fire up the engine of the eighteen-wheeler. Herb pushed himself up and waved as the kid drove by on his way to park the rig behind the mound so they could wash it tomorrow. Then laying his head back in the shade, he closed his eyes again for a short nap before Skinny returned.

Skinny thought he had learned his lesson the last time, but being young and foolish, made the same mistake. But this time he swung too wide.

In his haste to compensate for his error, Skinny cranked the wheel hard to the left. As the truck ran three feet up on the mound, the left front tire ran over the methane evacuating vent and crushed it to the ground.

Skinny felt the pull of the sand on his wheels and attempted to adjust his angle to where Herb usually parked. He thought he compensated for his mistake, so applied the brakes and stopped the tractor. Skinny was too full of himself to notice what he had done.

Without knowing it, he parked the second set of dual tires on top of the outlet pipe. Now it was flatter than a corn fritter at a Mexican feast. There was no way for the methane gas to escape.

After locking the tractor door, Skinny walked back around the mound, whistling a merry tune as he waved to Herb.

Herb returned the greeting and smiled proudly at his prodigy. He had no idea what his short nap would wind up costing him.

It was now three weeks since the eighteen-wheeler returned to the ranch. Jake had only two more days left to snoop around, so decided to walk the entire length of the crime scenes.

By now he knew the robbery area by heart and had visited all the checkpoints. The idea of three stops ran in and out of Jake's mind, and then out of the blue, he discovered his mistake.

("During the robbery there were two stops, not three you dummy. The trucks didn't stop at the first checkpoint. The flagger let them pass. The third stop has to be a few miles up the highway.")

That afternoon Jake returned to the Brinks office he was beginning to think of as his second home and asked, "Alice, can you figure out the location of the last stop both trucks made on Highway 285? I need to know exactly where those trucks stopped for a minute."

"What could they accomplish in a single minute?" He thought and then the answer appeared as crystal clear as the waters of Barton Springs.

("It was the transponder. The perps removed it somehow after the armored truck was loaded aboard some other vehicle. But when and where?")

Like a Buick Riviera, Jake's mind shifted into overdrive and he knew.

("Okay, the crooks load the truck into a big rig, hook up a battery and cut off the transponder. The truck stops long enough to let a guy get out. Juan Gonzales said the man he saw was waiting for someone. Ah ha; that's how the device got to Cline's Corner and onto Hank's truck.")

Jake looked at his drawing of the crime scene and wondered, "Did the big rig turn off Highway 285 or keep on going? Hell, how do I know? Was it just coincidence they stopped at the same place both times? I don't believe in coincidence. On these jobs, everything was planned for a reason.

"Questions, questions, always more questions.

"Tomorrow, after Alice finishes her evaluation, I'll find the spot where the trucks stopped. If there are any clues, I'll follow wherever the trail leads."

As he left for his motel, Jake felt better than anytime in the past month and thought, "Maybe my luck's changing."

The next day, the sky was clear and the forecast called for no rain, so Roger decided the party should go on. Wes and his assistants prepared a side of beef and impaled the meat on a spit.

Since they planned a menu of roast beef, BBQ, fajitas, tacos and enchiladas, they raided the pantry and freezer. For side dishes, baked potatoes, French fries, slaw, baked beans and roasted corn were selected.

Slim drove into Roswell to buy several cases of beer and an assortment of hard liquor. He returned with a truckload of booze and five hundred pounds of ice.

Word quickly spread that the party was on for tomorrow evening. The scuttlebutt was first they'd eat a fantastic meal and drink as much as they wanted. Then deep within the walls of the hidden garage, Roger would hold a meeting with all the men.

The news improved their disposition and morale, but before the party could begin, unwelcome guests arrived.

Following Alice's new assessment, Jake discovered the trail ended at the gate to the Crossed X Ranch. He decided to pay a visit to the owners, and as a precaution, asked the local police chief for several men to assist him.

With one ear tuned to radio calls on a scanner, Chief Howard, "Howie", Andrews sat at his desk, chewing on a toothpick and listening to Jake's request with the other.

Looking up at Jake inquisitively, he asked, "Do you have a search warrant?"

"No, but I don't think the owners will mind if I drop by for an unofficial visit. If they have nothing to hide, why would they complain? I'll just look around for a few minutes."

Chief Andrews reversed his toothpick and a small piece of something white was attached to the end now pointing at Jake. It appeared Howie ate rice for lunch. He continued to gnaw the damp wood and a drop of saliva dribbled from the right corner of his mouth.

Over the past sixteen years, Howie clawed his way up the promotion ladder, beginning as a rookie patrolman driving a black and white, while separating drunks on Saturday nights. He was known far and wide for his snazzy Stetson hat, jeans and custom-made boots, plus a toothpick he kept in constant motion in his mouth, flicking it from side to side.

Although he appeared to be a cowboy, Howie had never ridden a horse in his life. One bit him when he was a kid, and ever since, he hated the damn beasts.

For the last four years, he served as Chief of Police and watched Roswell grow and prosper. The welfare of the merchants in town and surrounding area was his first concern. They paid the taxes, which paid Howie and his men. They deserved the best police protection money could buy.

Howie was pissed at the Feds for sending in three men to run roughshod over anyone who looked sideways.

("I've heard about this yahoo's obsession with the missing Brinks trucks. I'm also aware the new cattle feeding station has added big bucks to our economy. Do I want this jerk to poke around where he shouldn't and cause friction? I hate to let him harass the owners.

"Technically he should have asked for help from the county sheriff, but I know his boss doesn't want Jake messing around over there. Aw, to hell with it; I'll send my two rookies out there with him.")

When he heard Howie's reply, Jake complained, "I may need more than rookies."

Howie stood up and pointed his finger at the door. "Take 'em or leave 'em. You may be the FBI, but I have to live here after you're long gone. These people are an asset to the community and I don't want you to harass them unnecessarily. If the owners tell you to take a hike, my men will escort you from the ranch. I hope you understand me."

"I do," Jake said while thinking, "I'm tired of getting the runaround from the local cops. Obsessed, hell; I want to solve a crime. Isn't that what I'm supposed to do?"

Although a heavy bank of dark clouds hung over far off mountains, the next morning dawned hot and dry. After Jake phoned the ranch to receive permission for his visit, he took Officers Keith Erby and Lynn Griffith with him.

"Come on; you two. Climb in; keep your eyes open and your mouths shut. If I want something from you, I'll yank your chain. Until then, stay out of my way and don't cause waves."

Chapter 24

When the phone rang, Roger was working on a list of supplies.

He answered the call, "Crossed X Ranch."

"Is this the owner?"

"My name is Roger Booth, and yes, I'm one of the owners. How may I help you?"

"This is Agent Polk of the FBI. I'm investigating the disappearance of two Brinks armored trucks in the Roswell area. Could I stop by this morning to speak with you about the case?"

Roger was surprised, but covered it well.

"I've been following the investigation in the newspaper and it's quite a mystery. My business partner and I will be happy to be of service to the FBI. I don't know how we can help, but you're welcome to stop by today and visit for a spell."

"Would ten a.m. be too soon?" Jake asked. ("I like this guy's voice and professional manner. But the leader of this gang would be as smart as he appears to be.")

Roger made a note of the time on his desk pad. "We'll be here all day. The front gate is unlocked, but be sure to close it behind you. We don't want our cattle on the highway. I look forward to making your acquaintance."

Roger walked to the doorway and called across the parking lot to Carl, who was speaking with Roscoe.

"Carl, the law, in the form of the FBI is coming for a visit. Tell everyone to be on their best behavior. Keep the men busy with the cattle and send Slim in to see me."

"Will do, Roger."

A few minutes later, Slim sauntered into Roger's office.

"I hear the law is on the rampage."

"The FBI is coming to visit," Roger said. "Do you want to stick around, or should I send you into town on an errand?"

"I'll hang around. Hell, the FBI don't scare me none. I'll act like a stupid cowboy who doesn't know shit from Shinola."

Roger smiled at Slim's remark.

"I think Agent Polk's a smart man and he may have picked up a clue somewhere. If he asks you something, answer him as truthfully as possible."

Slim shrugged.

"Okay, I'll help Carl spread the word. We have lots of beef to feed, so we won't be play acting. When the FBI shows up, we'll be working hard."

"Good," Roger said. "I want him to see we're making money. We don't need to rob any Brinks trucks, do we?"

Slim grinned slyly and said, "Not us."

As Roger continued to work on his feed list, he knew except for the hidden garage, there was nothing to find on the ranch. He doubted Agent Polk was that smart.

("We'll see what we shall see.")

An hour later, Jake drove up in a dusty rental car with two young policemen. It was obvious the cops were window dressing. The real worry would be Agent Polk.

Roger walked out to greet his guests, introduced himself to the oldest of the three and shook his hand. "I'm Roger Booth. I take it you're Agent Polk. You're the first FBI agent I've met. Welcome to the Crossed X Ranch."

Agent Polk's handshake was firm.

"Thank you, Mister Booth. This is Officer Erby and Officer Griffith from the Roswell Police Department. Everyone in town says your feeding station is a big success."

"Yes, it is. We came to Roswell with an idea and not much knowledge, but we're fast learners."

"How did you get started in the cattle feeding business?" Jake asked.

"I read about one in a western magazine and the idea caught my fancy. My business partner, Carl James, wanted to get away from the hustle and bustle of the big city, so here we are."

Jake noted the many workers and said, "You have a large crew of men. Where did you recruit them all?"

"That was the easy part of the operation. Most of these guys are from our old Army unit when we fought together in the Kuwaiti War. After being discharged, many found they had no jobs to return to. I inherited a good deal of money and wanted to share my luck with the men I trust the most. These guys kept me alive over there. I couldn't let them down."

As they got to know each other, Jake was beginning to like this guy Roger more and more. Since he was a Vietnam vet himself, Jake knew what Roger was talking about.

"You're to be commended."

As if he could read his mind, Roger asked, "Did you serve in Vietnam?"

Jake seemed to swell up with pride when he answered, "Yes, I did, and proudly. I spent two tours flying artillery spotter planes in Pleiku. I was one of the lucky ones who walked away without a scratch."

"Our foreman is a Vietnam Vet," Roger said. "His name's Slim Miles. He's the main reason the ranch runs so smoothly. Slim taught us everything we know about cattle. You wouldn't happen to know him?"

Jake shook his head.

"No, I don't think so. Vietnam was a big place, a sea of green and tan uniforms."

"If Slim isn't tied up, I'll introduce you. But I know you didn't come all the way out here to make small talk. How may I help you?"

"I've been studying the tapes from the transponders," Jake said.

"I saw the name in the paper. What does it do?"

Jake wanted to get on with the search, but took time for a quick explanation.

"The one Brinks has on board tells them where the truck is, whether it's moving, or if it stopped somewhere and for how long."

"What will they think of next?" Roger asked. "High tech is a little too much for me. As close as I come is when I use a computer, and then I always lose my material."

Jake was anxious to begin and hated the interruption, but then remembering the Sheriff's warning, kept his cool.

"We were discussing the transponder. The devices were removed from the two missing trucks and placed on another vehicle to confuse the police and FBI."

Roger interrupted again and chuckled before he spoke, "Excuse me for saying so. From what I read it did the trick."

Jake frowned.

"Yes, it's true, but let's cut to the chase. The tapes show both trucks stopped at your front gate for a minute and then moved on. Why do you suppose they did that?"

Roger sounded dubious.

"I have no idea. A lot of vehicles pull into our driveway because it's one of the biggest on the highway. We widened the area not too long ago to make it easier for the big rigs. If the trucks you're chasing stopped for some reason, I wouldn't know when or why. From where the ranch house sits, we can't see the front gate."

"I noticed that fact, so maybe you're right. I can't think of any other reason for the trucks to stop there; however it's my theory they weren't really the armored trucks. I think they were hidden inside other vehicles.

"The thieves removed the transponder and hooked the device to a car battery. The trucks stopped at your gate long enough to move them to another vehicle and throw us off the track."

It appeared Jake had enough of small talk, when he suddenly asked, "Would you mind if my men and I looked around your ranch?"

Roger shrugged and said, "Not at all. We have nothing to hide. Just because someone used our driveway for illegal purposes doesn't mean we were involved."

"I haven't accused you of anything and hope you don't take any offense, Mister Booth. I'm sure you understand we have to check out every lead."

Waving his hand to encompass the entire ranch, Roger said, "No problem. I'll ask Slim to show you the ranch. Take your time and look around."

Roger, Jake and the two police officers walked out to the corral, where Slim and two other cowboys were cleaning manure-caked hay from the chutes.

"Slim," Roger said, "this is Agent Polk of the FBI. His two assistants, Officers Erby and Griffith, are from the Roswell Police Department."

After taking off his gloves to shake hands, Slim said, "Pleased to meet all of you. Excuse the smell of the cow shit. When the wind blows just right, it clogs up our sinus cavities."

Everyone laughed, and as he gestured toward the pile, Jake said, "It is pretty stout. What do you do with the manure?"

"We sell it to a fertilizer company. They tone down the smell, mix in some dirt, bag it and sell it as potting soil."

Jake laughed.

"I can see why the cattle feeding business is so good. First you pay for the feed and charge the ranchers for it. In the end, literally, you get the feed back as manure and make a profit on the cow shit too."

Roger couldn't resist the chance to pull Jake's chain when he said, "You'd be surprised at the amount of money there is in manure."

"Enough talk about cow shit, gentlemen," Slim said. "What can I do for you?"

"Agent Polk is investigating the armored truck robberies," Roger said. "He and his men would like to look around the ranch. Take them anywhere they want to go and show them anything they want to see. By the way, Agent Polk is a Vietnam Vet."

Slim nodded at Jake and remarked, "It was a hell of a war, wasn't it? Sure, I'll show you around. Just watch where you step. It's the first rule of the cattle business."

Roger excused himself.

"I have to finish my list of feed for next month. Stop by before you leave and let me know if you find anything interesting."

"Thanks, Mister Booth," Jake said.

"Hell, we aren't formal out here. Call me Roger."

"Okay; thank you, Roger. My name's Jake."

They shook hands again and Slim led the lawmen away toward the cattle pens to give Jake and the two policemen the fifty dollar tour. At the feeding pens, Slim introduced the lawmen to Carl and several workers.

"I'm sorry we're so loaded with work," Carl said. "I'd like to show you around, but Slim knows the ranch better than I. If I have time, I'll stop by the office and we can have a cold one."

"Thanks," Jake said. "It is hot out here. I hope to see you later."

Slim led them on a tour of the barn and storage sheds. Without knowing it, Jake and the two policemen visited the jail. Jake took notice of everything, but the two policemen said very little.

When he saw the eighteen-wheeler parked behind the mound, with a cattle trailer and extra enclosed trailer parked beside it, Jake walked around the mound for a closer look. Both trailers had been swept and washed, and displayed a three colored decal of the Crossed X brand on each side.

Herb was polishing the tractor as Skinny wiped dust from the front wheel rims. Slim introduced them to the three lawmen, and Officer Erby said, "I like the Crossed X Brand."

"Yeah," Herb said. "We're proud of what we accomplished here. Roger and Carl gave us a chance to make something of ourselves. The least we can do in return is keep their equipment looking good."

"Everyone we met thinks the sun rises and sets on your bosses," Jake said.

"Yeah," Slim said, "they're swell people. I'm an ex-con. I was drunk, tried to rob a convenience store and got put away for two years. I did my time and changed my ways, but these two fellows were the only ones who would give me a second chance. Hell, I'd walk through fire to help them."

"Very commendable," Jake said, but thought, "It's interesting Slim has a police record, but he didn't hide the fact."

The young policeman, Lynn Griffith, was studying the mound. For some reason, it stirred a memory. Lynn was new to the police force and wanted to excel in his new job. In the past he worked at a variety of mundane tasks, but couldn't find his niche in life. Now, for the first time, Lynn felt like he was part of something important.

Throughout his police training, his instructors drilled it into his head that most crimes were solved by paying attention to minor details. He thought of how one instructor kept harping on the point. "The smallest thing you see may be the clue to solve a case. A good memory for facts and the ability to check and double-check will make your job easier."

Lynn took his mind off the mound and looked around the ranch.

("I still think I've been here before. The place looks familiar, but it's been changed a lot. Maybe I'm trying too hard to be Sherlock Holmes.")

Nothing came to mind, so he shrugged, sighed and listened to the conversation between Jake, Herb and Slim, as Jake asked, "What do you use the eighteen-wheeler for?"

"Sometimes we pick up cattle from ranches," Herb replied. "Other times we haul hay from the feedlot. Last week we brought in two hundred bales from Vaughn. At the rate the cattle are chomping it down, we'll have to look for more next week."

Jake pointed to where Satan stood pawing the ground and digging holes deep enough to hide a small Volkswagen.

"You've got a hell of a big bull. What do you use him for?"

Slim smiled knowingly and asked in return, "What do you think we use him for? We raise our own cattle and old Satan is our stud. We picked him up a couple weeks ago along with fourteen heifers. Half the cows were knocked up, and now they're all in the family way. Satan knows what's expected of him."

"Where did you buy the bull," Officer Erby asked.

"We picked him and the cows up out in Kingman, Arizona. Roger's computer expert found him and the girls for sale on the internet of all places. Hell, what won't they think of next. Imagine selling cows on a computer."

"It's interesting the eighteen-wheeler was in Arizona at the time of the robbery," Jake thought. It was another fact, or coincidence, but Jake still didn't believe in the latter.

"We've taken up enough of your time, Slim," Jake said. "I didn't think I would find anything here, but we have to check out every lead or we're not doing our job. Thanks for your help. It was nice meeting you."

As he shook Jake's hand, Slim said, "And you. I sure hope you catch the crooks pulling these robberies. They're pretty good at what they do. Hell, they might start stealing cattle next."

"I hope not. I intend to put a stop to their careers."

Slim shook the hands of the two policemen and said, "Nice meeting you guys. If you get tired of being inside writing reports, we can always use strong young men out here."

"We'll keep it in mind," Officer Erby said.

As Jake and the two cops walked back to their car, Slim rejoined the workers. Roger had watched their progress around the ranch house area through the office window. Now he stood up from his desk and walked outside.

Knowing the answer in advance, still he asked, "Did you have any luck?"

"No," Jake said. "I'm sorry to inconvenience you and your men. I hope our visit hasn't upset you."

"Not at all. I understand. You have a puzzle on your hands and I don't envy you."

"I intend to stick with it until I catch the crooks," Jake said. "Thanks again. Your men speak highly of you. I'm impressed."

"Thank you, Jake. I wish you luck. Next time I'm in town, maybe we could get together and you can tell me more about these robberies. Reading about them is fascinating."

"Thanks for the invite," Jake said, "but my week is up. My boss wants me back in Albuquerque. I leave tomorrow morning."

"This is a nice ranch you have," Officer Griffith said.

Roger shook his hand and said, "Thank you, Officer Griffith. We're trying to make it the best."

Slim watched the trio leave. Then he, Carl and Roger discussed the questions Jake posed.

"Everyone was honest," Carl said. "Slim even told him he

was an ex-con, which was smart. If Jake checks, Slim told him the truth ahead of time. It makes us look like we have nothing to hide."

Roger nodded.

"I wish Jake hadn't learned about the last place Satan worked, but Herb was honest about that too. I don't think Jake found anything. In fact, I'd say his visit was good for us."

"Is the party still on for tonight?" Slim asked. "The men are looking forward to letting their hair down."

Roger grinned.

"Yeah, I see no reason why we can't celebrate tonight. Tell Wes to continue with his plans and ice down the beer somewhere. We'll lock the gate at 1800 hours and eat at 1900."

Chapter 25

As Jake and his two new police buddies made their way back to Roswell, the sun took a short coffee break behind a thick wall of dark clouds and the sky turned from blue to purple.

Off in the distance, streaks of heat lightning reflected from low-hanging, grey rain clouds. Small drops of water splattered against the dusty windshield, making a pattern as if Jake was looking through a sponge. The dismal weather matched his mood.

Officer Erby took a stab at conversation, but Jake ignored most of what he had to say. The other cop possessed enough sense to keep his mouth shut. Officer Griffith seemed to be lost in thought, and Jake thanked God for one small miracle today.

Jake wasn't pleased with the lack of initiative on the part of the two rookies. During the visit, neither said enough words to fill a piss pot. They didn't strike out on their own to look things over, but stayed by Jake's side like they were Siamese triplets, joined at the hip.

Jake punched a button on the steering wheel and the cruise control took over the driving. Glancing down at his right foot resting on the floor mat midway between the brake and gas pedal, Jake thought, "Damn, I must have stepped in some cow shit. The rental agency's gonna love it."

Then he glanced sideways at Officer Erby in the right hand seat.

("Listen to this young long-winded whelp. He's talking his fool head off, while all I want is peace and quiet to think things through.")

"I thought they ran a great operation," Officer Erby said. "Just think; those two guys came out here to buy a ranch so they could help their Army buddies. They didn't know jack squat about how to run a spread or a feeder station, but look at them now. I think it would make a great human interest story."

"What do you mean by, 'they didn't know anything about ranching'?" Jake asked. "Where did you hear that?"

"My Uncle owned the ranch and sold it to them," Erby said. "He told me about Mister Booth and his partner. Said they were nuts to try something they didn't know anything about. I guess what we saw today proves him wrong."

The restless clouds above broke into their reserves and rain poured down in buckets. After taking the cruise control off, Jake let the vehicle slow itself, as he cranked up the windshield wipers to the max. It didn't do much good against the deluge, so he slowed to a crawl.

He was concentrating on keeping the car between the white lines, when Officer Griffith spoke up, "I think I was on the ranch before."

Jake thought, "Oh, no. Now the other one wants to join in. I'd give my right nut for some peace and quiet."

"Were you a cowboy?" Erby asked.

"No, but for some reason I recognized some of the buildings."

"At least you were observant," Jake said.

"Still, there was something missing from the picture I have in my mind. The place didn't look the same, but I just can't put my finger on it."

"Sherlock Holmes himself," Jake thought. "Why did I have to take these two rookies along? Damn Chief Andrews anyway." But he said, "Keep concentrating and maybe you'll make a connection."

The reserve ran low and the downpour slowed from fifty gallons a minute to around twenty. The windshield wipers sounded as if they were trying to commit suicide by beating themselves to death, so Jake reached up and turned them down.

Staring for a moment at the rookie in his rearview mirror,

Jake saw his face was screwed up and his brow wrinkled as a prune as he tried to come up with something new.

("At least he stopped talking. Now if only the other cop would shut up.")

A few minutes later Jake's wish came true. The hum of the tires combined with the sound of falling rain lulled Officer Erby into a light sleep. His head dropped down onto his chest and he snored softly.

By the time they reached Roswell, the rain had abated. From the looks of things it poured here too. Potholes were running over and large mud puddles had formed in litter-clogged gutters.

The smell from his shoes was beginning to get to Jake and he thought, "It's the perfect ending to a shitty day."

He dropped the two cops off at their station. As far as he was concerned, the Crossed X was just another well-run cattle operation. Although the police chief gave him grief about disturbing Roger and his men, it was worth the trip,

Driving up to his motel room, Jake thought, "But it was another useless journey and another dead end. Damn this case anyway.

The rain missed the ranch. Wes watched dark clouds and streaks of lightning off in the distance.

("After all this work, all I need is a thunderstorm.")

Over a glowing fire, a heifer on a spit was slowly turning a beautiful shade of brown. Sweet, sticky juices ran in rivulets down the sides and held on until gravity took control. Then they dripped onto red-hot coals below. With a smoky hiss, they were gone forever. The aroma was tantalizing, and Wes couldn't wait any longer.

Holding his carving knife like a mother holds the hand of a child; Wes sliced a thin piece of meat from the flank, tasted it and said, "Fantastic."

At six p.m. sharp, A. J. locked the gate behind the last cattle truck of the day. It was a long hot one for the entire crew. First thing this morning the FBI and a couple young cops showed up, nosed around and found nothing.

The men were under a lot of stress and tension for the past

month, and it was beginning to show, so they needed some downtime. Tonight, Roger promised them the mother of all parties, and A. J. was looking forward to the celebration.

("Yesterday was a month exactly from the day I had my last brew. Man, a cold one would taste good now.")

Thinking aloud, he said, "Crazy old Slim came up with a neat idea and said, 'Let's use the bucket on the backhoe to ice down the booze.'"

After loading everything aboard, Slim moved the backhoe under a large tree in front of the ranch house. By now the beer should be ice cold. Driving toward the ranch house, A. J. smacked his lips in anticipation.

When he climbed out of the pickup, he was met by Fred, holding two cold cans of Coors Light. Without a word, Fred tossed him one. A. J. popped the flip top and took a big swig. The cold beer slid down his throat like pure honey and tasted twice as sweet.

"Thanks, Fred. It's been a month since I drank a beer."

Tilting the can up again, he swiftly downed half the contents, as cold, frothy foam ran down his chin.

Sitting or standing in small groups, the entire gang was gathered by the ranch house. Their chatter was loud as they talked about the successful completion of the jobs or the way the cattle business was growing. Everyone was looking forward to their well-deserved payoff.

On the way to dinner, Roger stopped to talk to Ghost and asked, "Felt any bad vibes lately?"

Ghost seemed to shiver.

"Yeah, I still have the feeling someone's out there watching. A couple of nights ago, I took a walk, but didn't see anyone. Maybe I'm just imagining things, because nothing happened."

Roger patted Ghost on the back and said, "I'm glad it hasn't. I'll see you at the garage."

Wes and the other cooks recruited several men to carry chairs and tables. After hauling the furniture from the dining hall to a space under a large tree, they formed the tables into a large U.

The assistant cooks carried large bowls of side dishes from

the kitchen and placed them around the tables. Then Wes shouted, "Come and get it!"

The men moved to the pit, where Wes and his helpers piled their plates high with roast beef. If they were so inclined, a large crock of sweet-smelling barbecue sauce simmered slowly over dwindling coals.

Roger and Carl took their places at the center. One by one, the other men selected places and sat down to eat. Most carried their favorite beverage.

Ralph Hoyt, an ammunition loader on one of Roger's tanks gave a blessing, and they chowed down.

Ralph was a Deacon in the Baptist Church, who joined the National Guard to help make ends meet. He lost his faith in Iraq and was attempting to find it again by helping Roger. Ralph didn't take part in the actual robberies, but stayed behind at the ranch doing what he could to make things run smoothly.

Since the men couldn't go into Roswell for church services, Ralph held a nondenominational service in the barn on Sunday mornings and Bible study on Wednesday evenings. If anyone needed spiritual or religious guidance, he was always available.

When he received his share of the money, Ralph planned to build his own church for ex-servicemen. Maybe then, the good Lord would forgive him for all the men he sent to hell in Iraq.

Jensen smacked his lips and wiped barbeque sauce from his nose.

"The food in Roger's Army is a hell of a lot better than MREs, (Meals Ready to Eat)."

Three hours of food and drink debauchery followed. Then Roger stood up and asked, "Is everybody ready to see what we accomplished?"

His announcement was met with a loud cheer.

"Follow me to the garage. I want everyone to see what we worked so hard for."

As they made their way to the garage entrance, several men were feeling no pain, but it didn't stop anyone from joining this part of the party.

The men cheered him on, as Slim jumped on the backhoe and drove it slowly up the ramp to the entrance. When he parked the machine, the big bucket hung over the hidden doorway, where a scrap piece of one-by-four held the door open. The men walked by, reached into the bucket and snatched a chilled brew to take along.

Slim shouted above the din.

"I'll just leave it here so you won't have far to walk for a cold one."

One of the more tipsy men tipped his cowboy hat to Slim, and slurred, "Thank you, kind shir."

Although the door was opened earlier, a rancid smell came from below, but nothing was going to keep the men from receiving their just reward. Speaking for them all, Whitey said, "To hell with the stink."

Pete was released from the hospital three days ago and still had a hell of a time with his crutches. Clete helped his brother climb onto the slimy roof of the garage and said, "Be careful, if you get shit inside your cast, you're sleeping outside."

Charley overheard Clete's longwinded statement and said, "Clete's right, Pete. Give him hell, Repeat."

Pete hobbled down the stairs, looked back at Charley and said, "Up yours, Charley."

When the men were assembled, Carl counted heads to insure everyone was present. He wasn't worried because no one remained above ground. The gate was locked and there were no late deliveries scheduled.

After everyone gathered in front of the last Brinks truck, Carl climbed on top of a table, clapped his hands to get their attention and shouted, "Hold it down."

The men quieted and Carl pointed toward Roger while saying, "Let me introduce the genius who thought up our little scheme. Come up and take a bow, Roger."

The men cheered and raised their drinks in a salute, but Roger raised his hands to silence them and said, "Thanks, Carl, and all of you. Everyone worked hard to make this venture a success, so give yourselves a big hand."

There was another round of applause and cheering. Then as he and Carl grabbed the ends of a large tarp covering a heavily laden table, Roger shouted, "Now I want you to see your reward."

With a flourish worthy of a matador, they raised the camouflaged tarp and pulled it aside. Underneath was a table piled high with money bags from all the trucks. Earlier in the week Alan and Jensen counted the money again.

Including the amount Roger sent to Mister Remualdi, their final tally was thirty-four million, eight hundred fifty-seven thousand, three hundred and forty-seven dollars. Atop the pile, a large red-lettered sign on a white background indicated the tremendous amount of money they had stolen.

By this time, heavy drinking had taken its toll and some of the more inebriated men acted like small children at a picnic.

Someone yelled, "Go out for a long one."

Before anyone could stop him, a bag of money sailed through the air like a football, hit a pole, split open and packets of bills ballooned out like small bombs. Other bags joined the first and like litter at a county fair, bundles of one, five, ten, twenty, fifty and one-hundred-dollar bills scattered across the grimy floor.

Suddenly, there was a loud crash from the area of the stairway.

Chapter 26

Jake was settled in for the evening. His third Jack Daniels of the evening was melting the ice in a half empty glass like snow on an Eskimo's nose. It was Jake's last night in Roswell and he had made his final report to good old Bill Mudd. In the morning, he would drive back to Albuquerque.

Listening half-heartedly to Bill bitch about Jake's failure to produce anything for the amount of money he was costing the agency; Jake thought, "Maybe the horse's ass is right. The fact is there are no more clues to be found here. My visit to the Crossed X ranch was a frigging bust. It's time to retire. Hell, let the young squirts solve the crimes. Let's go fishing, Jake."

The green numbers on a digital clock in Jake's room glowed out warmly, telling Jake it was eleven forty-seven.

("It's time to hit the sack.")

It had been a long, tiring day, and Jake was ready to fall asleep and dream of something else besides this crazy investigation. His daydreams were filled with thoughts of being the Captain of his own fishing boat.

("I'll make a hell of a skipper. At least I won't have to put up with a horse's ass like Bill Mudd anymore.")

His thoughts were interrupted by the ringing of the phone.

"Who the hell can it be at this hour?" Jake said aloud, as he climbed out of bed and stumbled across the room.

He barked into the phone, "Agent Polk."

"Sir, this is Officer Griffith."

"This better be important, Griffith."

"I think it is, Sir. I finally remembered what was missing at the Crossed X Ranch."

"What was it?" Jake asked. ("Come on, Sherlock; let me have it.")

"A three-car garage," Griffith replied.

"What do you mean, by a 'three-car garage'?"

"It isn't there anymore."

"So, they tore it down," Jake said. "So what?"

Officer Griffith was insistent;

"Sir, they just built it a few months ago. It was poured concrete, and would take months to tear down. Why would they?"

The booze had dulled Jake's mind, and he couldn't see Griffith's point.

"Griffith, you're not making sense. How the hell can a three-car concrete garage disappear? I'm having a hard enough time trying to figure out how three armored trucks vanished."

The words were barely out of Jake's mouth before he realized what Griffith was saying.

Griffith started to reply, "Sir. . ."

Jake interrupted him and exclaimed, "Holy Mother of God, three trucks and a three-car garage! Griffith, you're a genius. How did you figure it out?"

"I knew something was wrong. Then I remembered I was on the ranch because I used to drive a concrete truck. I thought the company I worked for provided material for the floor and roof. Just to be sure, I called my old boss and he met me at his office. We went over the invoices and sure enough, it was the Crossed X Ranch."

Jake's breath was coming in gulps as he asked, "Where was the garage on the ranch?"

"It was built into the mound where the cow manure is stored. I remembered another thing about the building – there was a doorway built into the top. At the time I thought it was strange, but now I see its how they get into the garage."

Jake's face was flushed with excitement as he exclaimed once again, "My God, Griffith, you're brilliant."

"Thank you, sir. Do you think the garage is where the three

trucks are hidden?"

Jake was pumped up like a hot air balloon.

"Hell, buddy, they can't be anywhere else. Where are you?"

"I'm downtown at the police station."

"I'll be there in ten minutes," Jake said. "Call the Chief and tell him I want him to meet me there. Don't let him give you any static. Tell him it's an emergency."

"He's standing next to me," Griffith said.

"Put him on the phone."

"Chief Andrews."

"Did Griffith explain the situation, Chief?"

"Yeah, he did. For a rookie, Griffith displayed amazing insight. You owe him big time."

Jake agreed.

"Yeah, I do. Now, I need a search warrant and all your men."

Howie laughed and corrected him.

"No; you need a search warrant and all the Sheriff's men. The Crossed X Ranch is seventy-five miles north of Roswell. My jurisdiction ends at the city line."

"Thank God I forgot it this morning," Jake said. "If Griffith wasn't with me, we would never have discovered where the missing trucks are."

"You're sure they're there?"

"Yeah; I'm positive. Why in the world would you cover up a three-car garage? This guy, Roger Booth is a genius. It was the perfect plan."

Darrin was pissed at himself. He had overslept – didn't even hear the alarm go off.

("The frigging weather must be getting to me. I've spent too many days lying out in the sun watching these jaybirds. From what I saw yesterday, they must be going to have a party tonight. I about died of hunger as I smelled the damn cow cooking all day.")

The weather, the scent of good food and time spent watching got to him late last night. Darrin fell asleep, waking just in time to see Jake and two Roswell cops arrive.

Fascinated, he watched as the lawmen roamed around the ranch and met with various members of Roger's gang. It appeared Jake had discovered a clue and felt obliged to visit the ranch. After an hour of poking around, he came up empty, just as Darrin knew he would. After shaking hands with Roger and Carl, Jake and the lawmen left the ranch.

Darrin had enough of lying around on hard ground. His sore back cried out for a soft bed and clean sheets. He headed into town to catch a few hours of shuteye, and planned to return just before sundown. But he goofed and either didn't set the alarm or slept through the jangle. Anyway you cut it, he was late.

Climbing into his sand colored fatigues, he grabbed his burlap cover. There wasn't any moon tonight so he didn't think he needed the second item, but you never knew.

The tall guy who spooked Darrin was an ex-Ranger. Darrin made it a point to send the guy's picture to a friend in Washington, DC, who identified him as Tom, "Ghost", Clark. No wonder Darrin got bad vibes from the Ghost. He hoped the Ghost wouldn't take it upon himself to come looking for an intruder.

Darrin could take care of himself in a fight, but Mister Murdock didn't want anyone to know about what he was doing for the man. If Ghost came sniffing, Darrin would run, hide and evade.

It was just a few minutes before ten p.m. when he crawled into what he often thought of as his second home; a dry arroyo leading to a small rise where he could scope out the ranch house and surrounding area.

From the sounds of things, the party was in full swing.

Through his night scope, he watched the men follow Slim and his backhoe up the incline to the garage, where Roger and Carl were waiting to lead them down into the interior.

Slim parked the backhoe close to the garage, leaving the bucket hanging over the open door. Several men grabbed fresh brews as they descended into the garage. Since Darrin was downwind, the smell from the manure was almost overpowering.

Finally everyone was inside. Darrin heard loud cheering and applause rise on the evil-smelling wind.

("I guess they're reveling in their newly acquired wealth. I wonder if the total of over thirty-four million is correct. Damn, these guys are good.")

Suddenly, a loud "bang" came from the area of the garage and the noise startled him. The sounds from the interior were shut off as if someone chopped the conversation in two with a dull axe.

("What the hell happened?")

Looking closely, he noted the door was now closed tight against the frame, with the heavily laden bucket setting on top of it.

("Was that supposed to happen? I don't think so. I've heard about cow shit and the poisonous fumes the crap puts off as it decays. I hope those guys have a way out.")

Over the noise of the men, Roger shouted "What the hell was that?"

Charley waved it off as nothing to worry about as he explained, "The door brace must have slipped on cow shit again. It's happened before, and the door is heavier than hell, but we always managed to raise it. Don't sweat it. I'll take care of it."

Unknown to anyone, several days ago a hydraulic line controlling the bucket of the backhoe developed a pinhole-sized leak. Fluid dripped slowly from the line and oozed out, but in the warm desert air, dissipated quickly and no one detected the trouble. The level of fluid in the reservoir eventually dwindled to nearly nothing. Each time the bucket was raised, the strain on the hydraulic lines increased.

After Slim moved the backhoe, the bucket hovered above the door for another fifteen minutes. Then suddenly the pressure became too much and the hydraulic line ruptured. The small amount of remaining fluid exploded from the line. Following the law of gravity, the heavy bucket slid downward. The weight broke the one-by-four brace and the door slammed shut. Now the men were trapped.

Slim noticed several men were passed out. At first he wrote it off as too much booze. But then he thought of the methane gas and wondered, "Are we breathing poisonous gas from the cow shit? Is that why everyone's acting dizzy?"

Charley called out to Roger and Carl, "I can't raise the door. I need help."

They and several others joined him on the steps and tried to push the door upward, but their efforts were in vain. Truly frightened for the first time in his life, Carl yelled, "Come on guys; we need help with the door. If we can't get out of here, we'll all die!"

The gas made everyone drowsy and affected their mental state, but someone came up with a brilliant idea to use the truck jacks to raise the door.

As they feverishly levered jack handles against the stubborn door; their body heat combined with fear of death drenched the men in sweat. When the stair treads bent downward, the well-conceived plan was shot down like an Iraqi airplane. The overhead weight was too much. The door wouldn't budge. They were trapped and there was no way out.

One by one, they men succumbed, until only Carl remained conscious. If they weren't found soon, their fate was sealed. The front gate to the ranch was securely locked and no cattle delivery was scheduled, so it looked hopeless.

Carl's senses were dulled, but his mind raced on like a runaway locomotive on a downhill run to destruction. "Why did Roger and I leave our cell phones locked in the ranch house? God, I can't go on. My eyes won't stay open."

"Damn the bureaucratic crap," Jake said under his breath to Officer Griffith. Jake was frustrated. He wanted to rush out to the Crossed X Ranch and arrest Roger and his men.

("Damn this little hick town. First, I told the entire story to the Sheriff. Then he woke up the county judge. To get a search warrant, I had to tell the whole frigging story again. The backwoods judge needed more proof, so we woke up Griffith's old boss, who fetched the invoices from his office and showed them to the judge.")

Even that wasn't enough. Jake was sworn in and questioned by the judge about the existence of this supposed three-car garage. Finally at one a.m., His Honor was convinced of their evidence and issued a search warrant.

Warrant in hand, Jake called the Sheriff. He and ten of his men plus the other two FBI agents met Jake at the Brinks Office in five patrol vehicles. The flashing lights reminded Jake of a time in Saigon, when he drank too much and woke up in a whorehouse while it was being raided by MPs.

Finally, at one-thirty in the morning, the lawmen set out for the Crossed X Ranch.

Chapter 27

There was no way around it, Carl James was dying. Glancing around the cold, damp pit soon to be his grave, Carl saw the bodies of twenty-nine men, all members of his gang of thieves. Listening to the rasp of their lungs crying out for air, he knew his and their time on mother earth was dwindling.

With only minutes left until he too, would be overcome, his mind was dulled by the silent killer slowly taking control of his body.

"Why did you choose me, Lord?" He wondered aloud. "Why am I the last one still standing? Why should we all die now, when the game is over and we've won?"

When Carl's trembling legs could no longer carry the weight of his body, his knees buckled. He fell forward toward a table covered with bulging bags of money totaling more than thirty million dollars. In his present condition, the loot could do him about as much good as an anvil in the pocket of a condemned man on his way to the gallows.

Slipping forward and downward, he landed with his elbows on an edge of the table. His hands were clasped in front of him and he looked like a Tibetan monk praying for divine intervention.

Carl wasn't a monk, and not from that Asian country across the sea, but was praying; hoping someone could somehow miraculously save him and his comrades; but knew in his heart it was useless. It would be hours before anyone knew anything was wrong. By that time, the methane gas would kill them all.

Carl's best friend, Roger, lay nearby on a dirty floor littered with bundles and single bills of all denominations like green confetti at a high school prom. Carl watched Roger's chest slowly rise and fall as his lungs continued to suck in the noxious poison slowly seeping into his body.

Suddenly Carl's eyes filled with hot, scalding tears in fear of the unknown, and his heartbeat raced with dread. Glancing at his watch, he saw the time was one-seventeen a.m., and cried out again, "Why now Lord?"

Looking down at Roger, he shook his head in hopelessness and said, "It's been a hell of a ride, buddy. I hope we'll meet again somewhere." Then he clasped his hands tightly together and began to pray, "Our father who art...", but never finished. His eyes closed for the final time, and Carl slipped slowly to the floor to join his companions in peaceful slumber.

As his body fell, his left hand brushed against an open money bag perched precariously on an edge of the table, and it tipped over. Slowly, one bill at a time, with a sound no one but God heard, the filthy lucre slipped from the bag and drifted for a moment in the putrid air like lazy butterflies, until finding their final resting place on Carl's unconscious form.

Except for the sound of an occasional drop of water falling from the roof and splashing into a puddle below, there was an eerie silence in this unknown tomb of these ex-soldiers.

The party was over.

It had been four long hours since the door slammed down and Darrin was beginning to worry. He heard noises like someone banging on the steel door and scraping sounds, but so far the trapped men hadn't been able to break out of the garage.

His mind raced.

"I wonder how much longer I can wait. God, I can't be responsible for these guys dying, but what the hell can I do? If I move the backhoe and pull the bucket off, they'll know someone was here."

An hour ago, he realized no one was above ground. The cow on the spit was charred and beginning to smoke badly. It looked as if the entire gang was trapped.

Taking a chance, he crawled to the garage and laid his ear against the stinking door in an attempt to see if he could hear any sounds from below. If the men were still alive, he'd have to try something soon, or who knew what the results might be.

Suddenly, he heard the far-off wail of sirens and saw a large group of red and blue lights flashing in the direction of the gate to the ranch. Hurriedly, Darrin turned and ran back to his hidey-hole where he could watch what happened.

Two hours later, he watched as the last of the ambulances, accompanied by most of the police and sheriff's cruisers left for Roswell. Four officers stayed behind to provide security for the ranch.

Darrin crawled back down the arroyo and reached his Bronco. It had been an exhausting night. He was sure at least three men were dead and felt it was his fault.

Reaching into his vehicle, he retrieved his cell phone and called Mister Murdock. When he answered sleepily, Richard asked, "Making another early morning call, 'eh, Darrin?"

Darrin didn't have time for niceties.

"I'm sorry; Sir, but the shit just hit the fan here. Early this morning, Roger, Carl and all their gang were captured by the FBI and Sheriff's men."

"How the hell did the law get wind of their operation?"

"I don't know, Sir. Yesterday morning, an FBI agent visited the ranch. He's Jake Polk, who has been dogging Roger and Carl since the first truck was robbed. I was sure he didn't find anything, because they seemed to part as new friends."

"Was anyone injured?" Richard asked.

"Three of Roger's men died from gas poisoning. I probably could have prevented it from happening, but waited too long."

"Don't blame yourself," Richard said. "All these men knew what might happen."

"I know, Sir, but still feel badly."

"Come back to Houston as soon as you find out where the law is holding Roger and Carl. I look forward to your complete report. Again, don't blame yourself. I'll see you soon."

"Thank you, Sir," Darrin said and disconnected.

When Roger opened his eyes again, he thought he would see either Saint Peter and the Pearly Gates, or the Devil breathing fire and waving his pointed tail around in glee.

Instead, the first thing he saw was the stern face of Agent Polk staring down at him. Jake didn't resemble Saint Peter, but did look like hell. His eyes were bloodshot and his rumpled clothes made him appear a ragamuffin.

Checking his surroundings, Roger found he was in a hospital bed, wearing a too short white hospital gown with slanted grey stripes. His head felt like a woodpecker was trying to pound its beak through his skull.

Attempting to raise his left arm, Roger got it halfway to his head before it stopped abruptly and the chain of a handcuff rattled merrily against the railing.

Glancing around the white tiled, painted white hospital room, he saw a familiar face.

Carl waved and his manacles rattled as he said, "Welcome back from the dead."

"Good, Roger," Jake said, "you're coming around. I need to ask you some questions."

"Where am I?"

"You're in the Roswell hospital. So are most of your men. You're among the lucky ones. Three of your gang didn't make it."

The news hit Roger hard and he asked, "What happened? The last thing I remember, we were trapped in the garage."

"I told you – you were lucky. Another hour and we would have hauled twenty-eight bodies out of the stinking hole."

Roger shook his head to clear his mind. He was still confused.

("A few hours a go I thought I was dying, but now here I am, alive. From the looks of things we're all under arrest. Well, it's better than being dead.")

"Who bought the farm?" He asked.

"Slim, Fred Smith and a guy named Casey," Jake said. "I'm sorry."

Roger wiped his damp eyes with the sleeve of his gown.

"Not as sorry as I am. Those guys were all good men and their deaths are on my shoulders. Are the others okay?"

Jake nodded.

"They will be, but they'll have monumental hangovers. When we hauled them out of the garage we didn't have enough handcuffs to go around."

"What put you on to us?"

"Fate," Jake replied. "It was the fickle finger of Fate. We also had a little luck thrown in for good measure."

"What do you mean?"

Jake tapped his head, pointed to nothing in particular and asked, "Remember Officer Griffith? He used to drive a concrete truck and hauled the last load of concrete for your garage. When he couldn't find it, Griffith put two and two together. The strange or funny thing, depending on your point of view, is that Officer Griffith shouldn't have been with me yesterday."

"Why not?"

"Technically, your ranch is in the county, and Griffith works for the city. Their jurisdiction ends at the city limits sign. I wasn't thinking. I should have gone to the Sheriff's office instead. You see what I mean about fate and luck?"

Realizing the irony in Jake's words, Roger said, "Yeah, I do. But how did you know where to find us?"

"The gate was locked, but it didn't stop us. We had a search warrant, so we broke the lock and drove in, sirens screaming and guns drawn to find a deserted party scene. There was food on the table, a cow turning black on a spit and beer cans everywhere.

"We searched your place and the bunk house, but there was no one around. All your vehicles were there, so where could you have gone?

"Then somebody thought of the garage, where the Sheriff's men found the backhoe and the bucket full of beer on top of the door.

"We hooked up the tractor from your eighteen-wheeler, dragged the bucket off and found you and your men with the trucks and money. They tell me it'll take days to count it all. Was the total on the piece of cardboard correct?"

Roger grinned and said, "Yeah, it was. We took Brinks to a

cleaning. It was the perfect plan."

From across the room, where he was listening to their conversation, Carl called out, "Don't you know there's nothing perfect in this world?"

"I do now," Roger said, and they both laughed, but Jake wasn't amused.

Chapter 28

Although Julie and Maria knew each other and met several times while dating Carl and Roger, Julie was blissfully unaware of their true calling as thieves. She continued to believe the lies Carl told her concerning the cattle feeding station.

This morning Julie sat at her dining room table with her mouth wide-open, staring at Maria. She couldn't believe what her friend just told her. Suddenly her eyes filled with tears and she gave into her emotions, laid her head on her arms and sobbed.

Reaching across the table, Maria took Julie's manicured hand in hers. She expected this reaction to her news, but it hurt to see the younger woman cry. "Damn, I'm sorry, Julie."

Julie shook her head to say she couldn't speak and continued to cry. Moments later she released Maria's hand and sobbed, "It's not your fault."

Maria's eyes misted over. She waited for Julie to recover and reached for a tissue to wipe her own cheeks while thinking, "We're in the same boat now."

Two days ago, in Roswell, New Mexico, their boyfriends, Roger and Carl were arrested and charged as ringleaders in the robberies of three Brinks armored trucks.

Maria got the bad news from her father, Giacomo Remualdi, one of the leading Mafia bosses in the twelve western states. The Don learned of their capture from an associate, and the first person he notified was his daughter.

Maria's mind raced back in time, remembering her days and

nights with Roger; how they met and fell in love. She didn't know what lay ahead, but no matter what; she'd be there for him.

("Where does this situation leave me? God, I can't live without Roger. I have to find a way to get him out of jail, but I need help. I pray Julie will go along with me. My father is our only hope.")

Across the table, Julie's mind was on her lover, Carl. After reading the report of his arrest, she cried, knowing the newspaper couldn't be telling the truth. Carl wasn't the criminal type. He was too kind and considerate. The police must be wrong.

But now, she just received the truth about Carl and Roger from Maria and knew they did rob those trucks.

She also remembered the day of the accident and how she and Carl met, dated and fell in love. She remained positive their love was real. Carl couldn't fool her in that respect.

("We talked on the phone and he said things were going well. I dreamed every night of his return. How we'd get married and make babies. Now I know it was all lies to cover up the robberies. Carl's a crazy fool.

"But regardless, I love him. I must be stupid, but I do. Carl may be a fool, but he's my fool, and I won't stand by and let him rot in prison. What the hell are Maria and I going to do?")

Finally, Julie's tears stopped flowing.

Maria handed her a tissue and asked, "Feeling better now?"

"Not really. I was just thinking; what the hell are we going to do now?"

"I'm not sure," Maria said. "I only know I'm not going to stand by and see the love of my life locked away in a cell. How about you? How hung up on Carl are you?"

Julie's tears began again, as she sobbed, "I love him."

"Do you mean you're with me?" Maria asked.

"I guess so. What else can I do?"

"I don't want you guessing," Maria said. "Stop crying and tell me. Are you with me, come hell or high water, or not?"

"Yes, I am."

"Good," Maria said. "Let's go see my father."

Don Giacomo knew of Maria's love affair, but received her

news in a stoic manner. He also knew his daughter. If Maria wanted something as badly as she wanted Roger, there was no stopping her. Rather than see Maria and Julie arrested for attempting to free their men, the Don took action on their behalf.

"I'll do what I can behind the scenes," he said. "But regardless, your boyfriends must serve a year or two in prison. The press has had a field day with their capture. Their plan was nearly perfect, but fate stepped in. In time, the notoriety will die down and I can take action to have them released. In the meantime, you must be patient."

Chapter 29

In Courtroom Four, Gerard reached across the table and shook Carl's shoulder. He thought Carl had fallen asleep and wasn't aware he was only reminiscing about the past year.

Carl straightened his posture and looked around him. He caught Julie's eye for a moment and she smiled, but he knew she was anxious and worried about his chances.

While daydreaming, Carl hadn't realized several witnesses were called to testify, but their testimonies were shot down in flames by Gerard. Since the robbers were all masked or otherwise disguised, the so-called witnesses could not positively identify anyone.

"Score one for the good guys, (or the bad guys in this case)," Carl thought.

Roger whispered in his ear.

"Gerard's doing a good job. Try to stay awake or you'll piss off the judge."

Defending himself, Carl muttered softly, "I wasn't sleeping, just thinking about the past."

Glancing at the witness stand, Carl was surprised to see the driver of the last truck, Jerry Pribble, seated there. When he recognized Jerry, Carl tried to keep from smiling and listened to Gerard's cross examination.

"So, Mister Pribble, you and your fellow drivers and guards don't recognize anyone in the courtroom as your kidnappers or assailants. Am I correct?"

Jerry looked crestfallen, but answered truthfully, "No, Sir. It was dark and they were masked. No one said anything. All I saw was the message board telling us to exit the vehicle or die. Once we were outside our vehicle, they drugged us immediately."

Turning to the defense table, Gerard asked, "Mister Booth and Mister James, would you please stand?"

Roger and Carl did as he requested.

Gerard pointed to each of them individually and asked the witness, "Have you ever seen the defendants before?"

"Yes, Sir," Jerry replied.

"When?"

"At the lineups we attended?"

"How many lineups did the prosecutor arrange for you and the other Brinks employees?" Gerard asked.

"Seven."

"Did I hear you correctly; seven?" Gerard asked incredulously.

"Yes, Sir," Jerry replied.

Gerard turned to the other attorneys representing the remaining twenty-three defendants and asked, "Would you mind having your clients stand up, one at a time and give their names?"

"No problem," the lead attorney, Bill Brace, said.

Each stood and said his name as requested. When they were all standing, Gerard turned back to Jerry.

"How many people were you able to positively identify as part of the robbery team at these seven fiascos?"

"Objection," Gene shouted. "I take offense at Mister Bannister's labeling of the lineups as fiascos."

"Overruled," Judge Becker said. "It appears to me that if you weren't able to find one witness, the lineups were exactly what Mister Bannister called them. Answer the question please, Mister Pribble."

"None," Jerry said. "I told you. They were all masked."

"Did the prosecutor ask if you could identify their voices?" Gerard asked.

"Yes," Jerry said.

"And could you?"

"No, Sir. No one said anything in our presence. The voices

on the loudspeaker in our cell were muffled, so none of the others could identify anyone."

Turning to the judge and prosecutor, Gerard said, "I move for dismissal of the kidnapping charges against my clients. The state has failed to find one witness to support their claims."

Judge Becker called for a side bar and after a few minutes of discussion, told the attorneys to return to their seats. Then he announced, "The motion to dismiss the kidnapping charges is approved."

The courtroom erupted in applause by some and cries of disbelief of others. Jake couldn't believe his ears and whispered to Griff, "The fix has to be in."

To tell the truth, at this point and time, Jake didn't really give a damn. He had done his job. Now let the young hotrods old Bill Mudd was always raving about pick up the pieces and look under their own cow shit.

Judge Becker beat his gavel on his desk and cried out, "Order in the court. Another outburst and I'll find you all in contempt."

Gerard smiled at Roger and Carl. There was no way for them to know the judge was in the pocket of Don Giacomo.

Then Gene stood up, addressed the court and said, "I ask the charges be reinstated as simple assault. The facts of this case speak for themselves."

"Granted," Judge Becker said.

Gerard objected, but was overruled.

The trial dragged on for another week, but the wind had been taken out of the sails of the prosecutor's case. Gene was able to tie Roger and Carl and their associates to the stolen money and trucks, thereby giving credence to the assault and robbery charges. But the remainder of his case went nowhere in the eyes of the audience, or the Judge.

As their lawyers thought, the charges against the other twenty-three defendants were reduced to possession of stolen property. They were found guilty and sentenced to a period of from one to two years in prison. With time off for good behavior, most did less than a year, were released and resumed their past lives as if nothing happened.

All of them waited to see what Don Giacomo had in mind for their leaders. The loss of their million dollar payoff was not the fault of these two brilliant planners. If Roger and Carl were freed, somehow, every man was willing to take part in another adventure with them.

As soon as the guilty verdicts for Roger and Carl were returned, Jake intended to retire. He had already purchased the fishing boat he always dreamed of owning. Jake still admired his old adversaries, but knew they must pay for their crimes.

When the jury found the pair not guilty of assault, Jake was surprised. When they did return guilty verdicts for the robbery charges, he was relieved.

Judge Becker sentenced Roger and Carl to ten years in prison. As they were led from the courtroom, Roger and Carl stopped to shake Jake's hand, and to his surprise, wished him well.

"Don't feel badly for us, Jake," Roger said. "We did the crime and we'll do the time."

"Yeah," Carl added. "Have a happy retirement. Catch lots of fish."

Darrin reported to Mister Murdock, "Roger and Carl just received ten years in prison. What do I do now?"

"Was Mister Remualdi or his daughter in the courtroom?" Richard asked.

"The Don never showed, but his daughter, Maria, was there every day. She tried not to show it, but it wasn't hard to tell she's in love with Roger. Another woman, a blonde who I identified as Julie Frazier was with Maria. I think Julie's in love with Carl."

"Good work," Richard said. "Find out where this Don Giacomo lives and follow his daughter and her female friend. I have the feeling Mister Remualdi won't let Roger and Carl rot in prison."

"Am I still on the payroll?"

"For as long as it takes," Richard said. "Years, perhaps; are you up to the challenge?"

"Yes, Sir," Darrin said. "I'm your man."

"Very good, Darrin. Keep in touch and don't let the women out of your sight."

Although it was Gerard's first loss, when he considered the possible penalties his clients could have faced, (life in prison without parole or death by injection), he counted it as a victory. Besides, Gerard was knowledgeable of the plans Don Giacomo had for the future. With those in mind, he smiled as he shook Gene's hand and congratulated him on his victory.

The FBI impounded the Crossed X cattle feeding station, and six months later, sold the operation at public auction to a stranger from Dallas for five hundred thousand dollars. A new crew of cowboys was hired, and despite the notoriety, the business continued to expand.

It was difficult for the new owner to keep the public from trespassing on his newly purchased property. Morbid crime fans wanted to see the empty garage and feel the magic of the moment. The garage was almost as popular as the mythical, but very real, Field of Dreams baseball field in Kansas.

Finally the owner purchased three old, obsolete Brinks trucks and installed them in the garage. Now on weekends, he charges ten dollars a head admission to satisfy the curiosity of the idiots. The feeding station continues to show a good profit every year, and the extra money produced by the "side show" is icing on the cake.

Roger and Carl were model prisoners. Roger worked in the kitchen while Carl made license plates in the main workroom. Under threat of severe retaliation from Don Giacomo, they weren't harassed by other prisoners.

In fact, their hi-jinks made Roger and Carl very popular inmates. Many incarcerated men came to them with plans for spectacular robberies of their own. Roger listened to them all, and Carl helped him soften the blow when pointing out errors in their tactics.

In the evenings, Roger and Carl wrote the story of their sordid crimes, for which they were offered an advance of five hundred thousand dollars upon delivery, but the first draft wasn't completed before Don Giacomo made his move on their behalf.

Two years after the trial, Roger and Carl were transferred to a minimum security prison. Through the grapevine, Jake heard money changed hands to insure the switch, but didn't give a damn. He was retired now and very happy as the captain of his own boat.

Two months later, Roger and Carl calmly walked off the prison grounds and were never seen again. Met by the Don's men, they were transported to San Francisco overnight. The next morning they boarded an old decrepit freighter bound for Sicily.

While working as deckhands, they both enjoyed the freedom on the ship, being able to walk for more than twelve feet at a time, plus fresh air and sunshine.

Captain Sam Napolitano showed no favoritism to his "special passengers". They were taking the place of two crewmen and would work their way through the Panama Canal and across the Atlantic.

Sixteen days later, late at night, the ship was met by a high-speed "cigar boat". Roger and Carl, sunburned and tired, but feeling better than they had in two years, were offloaded and smuggled into the small town of Reggio di Calabria on the southern tip of Italy.

Captain Napolitano and his crew shared a substantial bonus for the safe transport of the two young men. They also received a detailed warning of the punishment they could expect if they spoke of their fellow deckhands. No one needed to be warned twice. The name of Don Giacomo was known, respected, (and feared), throughout the region.

Roger and Carl still rank as numbers one and two on the list of the FBI's ten most wanted criminals.

Shortly after Carl was imprisoned, Julie quit her job at the bank, telling her friends, "I'm moving to another state."

From the address she provided, several letters have been

returned with the notation: "Unknown at This Address".

In Dallas a young blonde woman moved into Maria Remualdi's apartment. Two years later both ladies departed for a trip to Europe, from which they have not returned. On the first of each month, Don Giacomo makes sure the rent on the apartment is paid by courier.

In a small town on the Southern tip of Italy, two young women recently leased an estate from a member of the local Mafia. It consists of two large villas setting high on a steep craggy cliff overlooking the azure blue waters of the Mediterranean.

The estate is surrounded on three sides by tall walls with glass imbedded on top and five strands of barbed wire to discourage any unwanted visitors. The fourth side is a high grassy ledge open to the sea.

Armed guards patrol the perimeter of the property and anyone inquiring of the owners is told to mind his own business. Since it is rumored the two ladies are under the protection of Don Giacomo, no one has to be told twice. It is enough to insure they are not disturbed.

So far no one has learned the names of the two lovely young women, but maids will gossip. They have said one woman is a radiant blonde with blue eyes and a figure to turn the head of any young man. The other is a stunning black-haired beauty who speaks fluent Italian and has fire in her black eyes.

Two months later, the gossipmongers found more to talk about, when without knowledge of the village elders, two young men arrived on the scene and took up residence in the villas. Once again, they turned to the maids, who discovered the men were engaged to the two gorgeous girls.

Shortly thereafter, a highly ranked member of the Mafia presented the necessary papers, asking a local priest to perform a double wedding ceremony on the grounds of the estate. Although the marriages were a small family affair, the servants reported Don Giacomo himself, his wife, Teresa, and most of their families were in attendance.

It was a festive occasion with many bottles of wine, and toasts to the newly married couples made by the Don and other noted officials of the community.

The maids report no honeymoons are planned.

The End

Postscript:

Roger, Carl and their new brides might have lived the rest of their lives quietly in Reggio, but two years later, they decided their notoriety had died down sufficiently for them to take a chance. At the urging of Maria and Julie, they went on a cruise, which turned out to be a disaster and pissed Roger off to no end.

As a result, a year later, hell broke out on one of the seven seas.

But then, that's another story...

(See "The Cyrus Caper" by Karl Boyd – coming soon.)

THE TALES OF CHEKHOV
VOLUME 5

THE WIFE
AND OTHER STORIES

THE TALES OF CHEKHOV

THE WIFE
AND OTHER STORIES

By
ANTON CHEKHOV

Translated By
CONSTANCE GARNETT

The Ecco Press
New York

Copyright © 1918, 1942, 1972 by Macmillan Company

All rights reserved
First published by The Ecco Press in 1985
26 West 17th Street, New York, N.Y. 10011
This edition is reprinted by arrangement with Macmillan Publishing Co., Inc.

PRINTED IN THE UNITED STATES OF AMERICA

The Ecco Press logo by Ahmed Yacoubi

Library of Congress Cataloging in Publication Data
Chekhov, Anton Pavlovich, 1860–1904.
The wife and other stories.
(The tales of Chekhov; vol. 5)
Reprint. Originally published: New York: Macmillan, 1918.
Contents: The wife–Difficult people–The grasshopper–[etc.]
1. Chekhov, Anton Pavlovich, 1860–1904 –Translations, English.
I. Title. II. Series: Chekhov, Anton Pavlovich, 1860–1904.
Short stories. English; vol. 5
PG3456.A15G3   1984   vol. 5   891.73'3s   84-13678
ISBN 0-88001-052-5 (pbk.)   [891.73'3]

SECOND PRINTING, 1988

CONTENTS

THE WIFE

THE TALES OF CHEKHOV

THE WIFE

I

I RECEIVED the following letter:

" DEAR SIR, PAVEL ANDREITCH!
" Not far from you — that is to say, in the
village of Pestrovo — very distressing incidents are
taking place, concerning which I feel it my duty to
write to you. All the peasants of that village sold
their cottages and all their belongings, and set off
for the province of Tomsk, but did not succeed in
getting there, and have come back. Here, of
course, they have nothing now; everything belongs
to other people. They have settled three or four
families in a hut, so that there are no less than fifteen persons of both sexes in each hut, not counting
the young children; and the long and the short of
it is, there is nothing to eat. There is famine and
there is a terrible pestilence of hunger, or spotted,
typhus; literally every one is stricken. The doctor's
assistant says one goes into a cottage and what does
one see? Every one is sick, every one delirious,
some laughing, others frantic; the huts are filthy;
there is no one to fetch them water, no one to give

3

them a drink, and nothing to eat but frozen potatoes. What can Sobol (our Zemstvo doctor) and his lady assistant do when more than medicine the peasants need bread which they have not? The District Zemstvo refuses to assist them, on the ground that their names have been taken off the register of this district, and that they are now reckoned as inhabitants of Tomsk; and, besides, the Zemstvo has no money.

"Laying these facts before you, and knowing your humanity, I beg you not to refuse immediate help.

"Your well-wisher."

Obviously the letter was written by the doctor with the animal name [1] or his lady assistant. Zemstvo doctors and their assistants go on for years growing more and more convinced every day that they can do *nothing,* and yet continue to receive their salaries from people who are living upon frozen potatoes, and consider they have a right to judge whether I am humane or not.

Worried by the anonymous letter and by the fact that peasants came every morning to the servants' kitchen and went down on their knees there, and that twenty sacks of rye had been stolen at night out of the barn, the wall having first been broken in, and by the general depression which was fostered by conversations, newspapers, and horrible weather — worried by all this, I worked listlessly and ineffectively. I was writing " A History of Railways ";

[1] *Sobol* in Russian means " sable-marten."— TRANSLATOR'S NOTE.

I had to read a great number of Russian and foreign books, pamphlets, and articles in the magazines, to make calculations, to refer to logarithms, to think and to write; then again to read, calculate, and think; but as soon as I took up a book or began to think, my thoughts were in a muddle, my eyes began blinking, I would get up from the table with a sigh and begin walking about the big rooms of my deserted country-house. When I was tired of walking about I would stand still at my study window, and, looking across the wide courtyard, over the pond and the bare young birch-trees and the great fields covered with recently fallen, thawing snow, I saw on a low hill on the horizon a group of mud-coloured huts from which a black muddy road ran down in an irregular streak through the white field. That was Pestrovo, concerning which my anonymous correspondent had written to me. If it had not been for the crows who, foreseeing rain or snowy weather, floated cawing over the pond and the fields, and the tapping in the carpenter's shed, this bit of the world about which such a fuss was being made would have seemed like the Dead Sea; it was all so still, motionless, lifeless, and dreary!

My uneasiness hindered me from working and concentrating myself; I did not know what it was, and chose to believe it was disappointment. I had actually given up my post in the Department of Ways and Communications, and had come here into the country expressly to live in peace and to devote myself to writing on social questions. It had long been my cherished dream. And now I had to say

good-bye both to peace and to literature, to give
up everything and think only of the peasants.   And
that was inevitable, because I was convinced that
there was abslouetly nobody in the district except
me to help the starving.   The people surrounding
me were uneducated, unintellectual, callous, for the
most part dishonest, or if they were honest, they
were unreasonable and unpractical like my wife,
for instance.   It was impossible to rely on such people, it was impossible to leave the peasants to their
fate, so that the only thing left to do was to submit
to necessity and see to setting the peasants to rights
myself.

I began by making up my mind to give five thousand roubles to the assistance of the starving peasants.   And that did not decrease, but only aggra-
vated my uneasiness.   As I stood by the window or
walked about the rooms I was tormented by the
question which had not occurred to me before: how
this money was to be spent.   To have bread bought
and to go from hut to hut distributing it was more
than one man could do, to say nothing of the risk
that in your haste you might give twice as much to
one who was well-fed or to one who was making,
money out of his fellows as to the hungry.   I had
no faith in the local officials.   All these district captains and tax inspectors were young men, and I
distrusted them as I do all young people of today,
who are materialistic and without ideals.   The District Zemstvo, the Peasant Courts, and all the local
institutions, inspired in me not the slightest desire
to appeal to them for assistance.   I knew that all

these institutions who were busily engaged in picking out plums from the Zemstvo and the Government pie had their mouths always wide open for a
bite at any other pie that might turn up.

The idea occurred to me to invite the neighbouring landowners and suggest to them to organize
in my house something like a committee or a centre
to which all subscriptions could be forwarded, and
from which assistance and instructions could be distributed throughout the district; such an organization, which would render possible frequent consulta-
tions and free control on a big scale, would completely meet my views. But I imagined the lunches,
the dinners, the suppers and the noise, the waste of
time, the verbosity and the bad taste which that
mixed provincial company would inevitably bring
into my house, and I made haste to reject my
idea.

As for the members of my own household, the last
thing I could look for was help or support from
them. Of my father's household, of the household of my childhood, once a big and noisy family,
no one remained but the governess Mademoiselle
Marie, or, as she was now called, Marya Gerasimovna, an absolutely insignificant person. She was
a precise little old lady of seventy, who wore a
light grey dress and a cap with white ribbons, and
looked like a china doll. She always sat in the
drawing-room reading.

Whenever I passed by her, she would say, knowing the reason for my brooding:

"What can you expect, Pasha? I told you how

it would be before.   You can judge from our servants."

My wife, Natalya Gavrilovna, lived on the lower
storey, all the rooms of which she occupied.   She
slept, had her meals, and received her visitors downstairs in her own rooms, and took not the slightest
interest in how I dined, or slept, or whom I saw.
Our relations with one another were simple and
not strained, but cold, empty, and dreary as relations are between people who have been so long
estranged, that even living under the same roof
gives no semblance of nearness.   There was no
trace now of the passionate and tormenting love —
at one time sweet, at another bitter as wormwood —
which I had once felt for Natalya Gavrilovna.
There was nothing left, either, of the outbursts of
the past — the loud altercations, upbraidings, complaints, and gusts of hatred which had usually ended
in my wife's going abroad or to her own people,
and in my sending money in small but frequent in-
stalments that I might sting her pride oftener.
(My proud and sensitive wife and her family live
at my expense, and much as she would have liked
to do so, my wife could not refuse my money: that
afforded me satisfaction and was one comfort in
my sorrow.)   Now when we chanced to meet in
the corridor downstairs or in the yard, I bowed,
she smiled graciously.   We spoke of the weather,
said that it seemed time to put in the double windows, and that some one with bells on their harness
had driven over the dam.   And at such times I read
in her face: " I am faithful to you and am not dis-

gracing your good name which you think so much about; you are sensible and do not worry me; we are quits."

I assured myself that my love had died long ago, that I was too much absorbed in my work to think seriously of my relations with my wife. But, alas! that was only what I imagined. When my wife talked aloud downstairs I listened intently to her voice, though I could not distinguish one word. When she played the piano downstairs I stood up and listened. When her carriage or her saddle-horse was brought to the door, I went to the window and waited to see her out of the house; then I watched her get into her carriage or mount her horse and ride out of the yard. I felt that there was something wrong with me, and was afraid the expression of my eyes or my face might betray me. I looked after my wife and then watched for her to come back that I might see again from the window her face, her shoulders, her fur coat, her hat. I felt dreary, sad, infinitely regretful, and felt inclined in her absence to walk through her rooms, and longed that the problem that my wife and I had not been able to solve because our characters were incompatible, should solve itself in the natural way as soon as possible — that is, that this beautiful woman of twenty-seven might make haste and grow old, and that my head might be grey and bald.

One day at lunch my bailiff informed me that the Pestrovo peasants had begun to pull the thatch off the roofs to feed their cattle. Marya Gerasimovna looked at me in alarm and perplexity.

" What can I do? " I said to her.   " One cannot
fight single-handed, and I have never experienced
such loneliness as I do now.   I would give a great
deal to find one man in the whole province on
whom I could rely."

" Invite Ivan Ivanitch," said Marya Gerasimovna.

" To be sure! " I thought, delighted.   " That is
an idea!   *C'est raison,*" I hummed, going to my
study to write to Ivan Ivanitch.   " *C'est raison, c'est
raison.*"

II

Of all the mass of acquaintances who, in this house
twenty-five to thirty-five years ago, had eaten, drunk,
masqueraded, fallen in love, married,bored us with
accounts of their splendid packs of hounds and
horses, the only one still living was Ivan Ivanitch
Bragin.   At one time he had been very active, talk-
ative, noisy, and given to falling in love, and had
been famous for his extreme views and for the peculiar charm of his face, which fascinated men as
well as women; now he was an old man, had grown
corpulent, and was living out his days with neither
views nor charm.   He came the day after getting
my letter, in the evening just as the samovar was
brought into the dining-room and little Marya Gerasimovna had begun slicing the lemon.

" I am very glad to see you, my dear fellow," I
said gaily, meeting him.   " Why, you are stouter
than ever."

"It isn't getting stout; it's swelling," he answered. "The bees must have stung me."

With the familiarity of a man laughing at his own fatness, he put his arms round my waist and laid on my breast his big soft head, with the hair combed down on the forehead like a Little Russian's, and went off into a thin, aged laugh.

"And you go on getting younger," he said through his laugh. "I wonder what dye you use for your hair and beard; you might let me have some of it." Sniffing and gasping, he embraced me and kissed me on the cheek. "You might give me some of it," he repeated. "Why, you are not forty, are you?"

"Alas, I am forty-six!" I said, laughing.

Ivan Ivanitch smelt of tallow candles and cooking, and that suited him. His big, puffy, slow-moving body was swathed in a long frock-coat like a coachman's full coat, with a high waist, and with hooks and eyes instead of buttons, and it would have been strange if he had smelt of eau-de-Cologne, for instance. In his long, unshaven, bluish double chin, which looked like a thistle, his goggle eyes, his shortness of breath, and in the whole of his clumsy, slovenly figure, in his voice, his laugh, and his words, it was difficult to recognize the graceful, interesting talker who used in old days to make the husbands of the district jealous on account of their wives.

"I am in great need of your assistance, my friend," I said, when we were sitting in the dining-room, drinking tea. "I want to organize relief for the starving peasants, and I don't know how to set about it. So perhaps you will be so kind as to advise me."

"Yes, yes, yes," said Ivan Ivanitch, sighing. "To be sure, to be sure, to be sure. . . ."

" I would not have worried you, my dear fellow, but really there is no one here but you I can appeal to. You know what people are like about here."

"To be sure, to be sure, to be sure. . . . Yes."

I thought that as we were going to have a serious, business consultation in which any one might take part, regardless of their position or personal relations, why should I not invite Natalya Gavrilovna.

"*Tres faciunt collegium*," I said gaily. "What if we were to ask Natalya Gavrilovna? What do you think? Fenya," I said, turning to the maid, " ask Natalya Gavrilovna to come upstairs to us, if possible at once. Tell her it's a very important matter."

A little later Natalya Gavrilovna came in. I got up to meet her and said:

"Excuse us for troubling you, Natalie. We are discussing a very important matter, and we had the happy thought that we might take advantage of your good advice, which you will not refuse to give us. Please sit down."

Ivan Ivanitch kissed her hand while she kissed his forehead; then, when we all sat down to the table, he, looking at her tearfully and blissfully, craned forward to her and kissed her hand again. She was dressed in black, her hair was carefully arranged, and she smelt of fresh scent. She had evidently dressed to go out or was expecting somebody. Coming into the dining-room, she held out her hand to me with simple friendliness, and smiled to me as graciously as she did to Ivan Ivanitch — that pleased me; but as she talked she moved her fingers, often and abruptly leaned back in her chair and talked rapidly, and this jerkiness in her words and movements irritated me and reminded me of her native town — Odessa, where the society, men and women alike, had wearied me by its bad taste.

" I want to do something for the famine-stricken peasants," I began, and after a brief pause I went on : " Money, of course, is a great thing, but to confine oneslf to subscribing money, and with that to be satisfied, would be evading the worst of the trouble. Help must take the form of money, but the most important thing is a proper and sound organization. Let us think it over, my friends, and do something."

Natalya Gavrilovna looked at me inquiringly and shrugged her shoulders as though to say, " What do I know about it ? "

" Yes, yes, famine . . ." muttered Ivan Ivanitch. " Certainly . . . yes."

" It's a serious position," I said, " and assistance is needed as soon as possible. I imagine the first point among the principles which we must work out ought to be promptitude. We must act on the military principles of judgment, promptitude, and energy."

" Yes, promptitude . . ." repeated Ivan Ivanitch in a drowsy and listless voice, as though he

were dropping asleep. "Only one can't do anything. The crops have failed, and so what's the
use of all your judgment and energy? . . . It's the
elements. . . . You can't go against God and
fate. . . ."

"Yes, but that's what man has a head for, to
contend against the elements."

"Eh? Yes . . . that's so, to be sure. . . .
Yes."

Ivan Ivanitch sneezed into his handkerchief,
brightened up, and as though he had just woken
up, looked round at my wife and me.

"My crops have failed, too." He laughed a
thin little laugh and gave a sly wink as though this
were really funny. "No money, no corn, and a
yard full of labourers like Count Sheremetyev's. I
want to kick them out, but I haven't the heart to."

Natalya Gavrilovna laughed, and began questioning him about his private affairs. Her presence
gave me a pleasure such as I had not felt for a
long time, and I was afraid to look at her for fear
my eyes would betray my secret feeling. Our relations were such that that feeling might seem surprising and ridiculous.

She laughed and talked with Ivan Ivanitch without being in the least disturbed that she was in my
room and that I was not laughing.

"And so, my friends, what are we to do?" I
asked after waiting for a pause. "I suppose before
we do anything else we had better immediately
open a subscription-list. We will write to our
friends in the capitals and in Odessa, Natalie, and

ask them to subscribe. When we have got together
a little sum we will begin buying corn and fodder
for the cattle; and you, Ivan Ivanitch, will you be
so kind as to undertake distributing the relief?
Entirely relying on your characteristic tact and efficiency, we will only venture to express a desire that
before you give any relief you make acquaintance
with the details of the case on the spot, and also,
which is very important, you should be careful that
corn should be distributed only to those who are
in genuine need, and not to the drunken, the idle,
or the dishonest."

"Yes, yes, yes . . ." muttered Ivan Ivanitch.
"To be sure, to be sure."

"Well, one won't get much done with that slob-
bering wreck," I thought, and I felt irritated.

"I am sick of these famine-stricken peasants,
bother them! It's nothing but grievances with
them!" Ivan Ivanitch went on, sucking the rind of
the lemon. "The hungry have a grievance against
those who have enough, and those who have enough
have a grievance against the hungry. Yes . . .
hunger stupefies and maddens a man and makes
him savage; hunger is not a potato. When a man
is starving he uses bad language, and steals, and
may do worse. . . . One must realize that."

Ivan Ivanitch choked over his tea, coughed, and
shook all over with a squeaky, smothered laughter.

"'There was a battle at Pol . . . Poltava,'" he
brought out, gesticulating with both hands in protest
against the laughter and coughing which prevented
him from speaking. "'There was a battle at

Poltava!'   When three years after the Emancipation we had famine in two districts here, Fyodor
Fyodoritch came and invited me to go to him.
'Come along, come along,' he persisted, and nothing else would satisfy him.   'Very well, let us go,'
I said.   And, so we set off.   It was in the evening;
there was snow falling.   Towards night we were
getting near his place, and suddenly from the wood
came 'bang!' and another time 'bang!' 'Oh,
damn it all!' . . . I jumped out of the sledge,
and I saw in the darkness a man running up to me,
knee-deep in the snow.   I put my arm round his
shoulder, like this, and knocked the gun out of his
hand.   Then another one turned up; I fetched him
a knock on the back of his head so that he grunted
and flopped with his nose in the snow.   I was a
sturdy chap then, my fist was heavy; I disposed of
two of them, and when I turned round Fyodor was
sitting astride of a third.   We did not let our three
fine fellows go; we tied their hands behind their
backs so that they might not do us or themselves
any harm, and took the fools into the kitchen.   We
were angry with them and at the same time ashamed
to look at them; they were peasants we knew, and
were good fellows; we were sorry for them.   They
were quite stupid with terror.   One was crying and
begging our pardon, the second looked like a wild
beast and kept swearing, the third knelt down and
began to pray.   I said to Fedya: 'Don't bear
them a grudge; let them go, the rascals!'   He fed
them, gave them a bushel of flour each, and let
them go: 'Get along with you,' he said.   So that's

what he did. . . . The Kingdom of Heaven be
his and everlasting peace! He understood and did
not bear them a grudge; but there were some who
did, and how many people they ruined! Yes. . . .
Why, over the affair at the Klotchkovs' tavern
eleven men were sent to the disciplinary battalion.
Yes. . . . And now, look, it's the same thing.
Anisyin, the investigating magistrate, stayed the
night with me last Thursday, and he told me about
some landowner. . . . Yes. . . . They took the
wall of his barn to pieces at night and carried off
twenty sacks of rye. When the gentleman heard
that such a crime had been committed, he sent a
telegram to the Governor and another to the police
captain, another to the investigating magistrate!
. . . Of course, every one is afraid of a man who
is fond of litigation. The authorities were in a flutter and there was a general hubbub. Two villages
were searched."

"Excuse me, Ivan Ivanitch," I said. "Twenty
sacks of rye were stolen from me, and it was I
who telegraphed to the Governor. I telegraphed
to Petersburg, too. But it was by no means out
of love for litigation, as you are pleased to express
it, and not because I bore them a grudge. I look
at every subject from the point of view of principle.
From the point of view of the law, theft is the same
whether a man is hungry or not."

"Yes, yes . . ." muttered Ivan Ivanitch in confusion. "Of course. . . To be sure, yes."

Natalya Gavrilovna blushed.

"There are people . . ." she said and stopped;

she made an effort to seem indifferent, but she could not keep it up, and looked into my eyes with the hatred that I know so well. "There are people," she said, "for whom famine and human suffering exist simply that they may vent their hateful and despicable temperaments upon them."

I was confused and shrugged my shoulders.

"I meant to say generally," she went on, "that there are people who are quite indifferent and completely devoid of all feeling of sympathy, yet who do not pass human suffering by, but insist on meddling for fear people should be able to do without them. Nothing is sacred for their vanity."

"There are people," I said softly, "who have an angelic character, but who express their glorious ideas in such a form that it is difficult to distinguish the angel from an Odessa market-woman."

I must confess it was not happily expressed.

My wife looked at me as though it cost her a great effort to hold her tongue. Her sudden outburst, and then her inappropriate eloquence on the subject of my desire to help the famine-stricken peasants, were, to say the least, out of place; when I had invited her to come upstairs I had expected quite a different attitude to me and my intentions.. I cannot say definitely what I had expected, but I had been agreeably agitated by the expectation. Now I saw that to go on speaking about the famine would be difficult and perhaps stupid.

"Yes . . ." Ivan Ivanitch muttered inappropriately. "Burov, the merchant, must have four hundred thousand at least. I said to him: 'Hand

over one or two thousand to the famine.   You can't
take it with you when you die, anyway.'   He was
offended.   But we all have to die, you know.
Death is not a potato."

A silence followed again.

" So there's nothing left for me but to reconcile
myself to loneliness," I sighed.   " One cannot fight
single-handed.   Well, I will try single-handed.
Let us hope that my campaign against the famine
will be more successful than my campaign against
indifference."

" I am expected downstairs," said Natalya Gavrilovna.

She got up from the table and turned to Ivan
Ivanitch.

" So you will look in upon me downstairs for a
minute?   I won't say good-bye to you."

And she went away.

Ivan Ivanitch was now drinking his seventh glass
of tea, choking, smacking his lips, and sucking
sometimes his moustache, sometimes the lemon.
He was muttering something drowsily and listlessly,
and I did not listen but waited for him to go.   At
last, with an expression that suggested that he had
only come to me to take a cup of tea, he got up
and began to take leave.   As I saw him out I said:

" And so you have given me no advice."

" Eh?   I am a feeble, stupid old man," he answered.   " What use would my advice be?   You
shouldn't worry yourself. . . . I really don't know
why you worry yourself.   Don't disturb yourself,
my dear fellow!   Upon my word, there's no need,"

he whispered genuinely and affectionately, soothing me as though I were a child. " Upon my word, there's no need."

" No need? Why, the peasants are pulling the thatch off their huts, and they say there is typhus somewhere already."

" Well, what of it? If there are good crops next year, they'll thatch them again, and if we die of typhus others will live after us. Anyway, we have to die — if not now, later. Don't worry yourself, my dear."

" I can't help worrying myself," I said irritably.

We were standing in the dimly lighted vestibule. Ivan Ivanitch suddenly took me by the elbow, and, preparing to say something evidently very important, looked at me in silence for a couple of minutes.

" Pavel Andreitch! " he said softly, and suddenly in his puffy, set face and dark eyes there was a gleam of the expression for which he had once been famous and which was truly charming. " Pavel Andreitch, I speak to you as a friend: try to be different! One is ill at ease with you, my dear fellow, one really is! "

He looked intently into my face; the charming expression faded away, his eyes grew dim again, and he sniffed and muttered feebly:

" Yes, yes. . . . Excuse an old man. . . . It's all nonsense . . . yes."

As he slowly descended the staircase, spreading out his hands to balance himself and showing me his huge, bulky back and red neck, he gave me the unpleasant impression of a sort of crab.

"You ought to go away, your Excellency," he muttered. "To Petersburg or abroad. . . . Why should you live here and waste your golden days? You are young, wealthy, and healthy. . . . Yes. . . . Ah, if I were younger I would whisk away like a hare, and snap my fingers at everything."

III

My wife's outburst reminded me of our married life together. In old days after every such outburst we felt irresistibly drawn to each other; we would meet and let off all the dynamite that had accumulated in our souls. And now after Ivan Ivanitch had gone away I had a strong impulse to go to my wife. I wanted to go downstairs and tell her that her behaviour at tea had been an insult to me, that she was cruel, petty, and that her plebeian mind had never risen to a comprehension of what *I* was saying and of what *I* was doing. I walked about the rooms a long time thinking of what I would say to her and trying to guess what she would say to me.

That evening, after Ivan Ivanitch went away, I felt in a peculiarly irritating form the uneasiness which had worried me of late. I could not sit down or sit still, but kept walking about in the rooms that were lighted up and keeping near to the one in which Marya Gerasimovna was sitting. I had a feeling very much like that which I had on the North Sea during a storm when every one thought that our ship, which had no freight nor ballast, would overturn. And that evening I understood that my uneasiness was not disappointment, as I had supposed, but a different feeling, though what exactly I could not say, and that irritated me more than ever.

" I will go to her," I decided. " I can think of a pretext. I shall say that I want to see Ivan Ivanitch; that will be all."

I went downstairs and walked without haste over the carpeted floor through the vestibule and the hall. Ivan Ivanitch was sitting on the sofa in the drawing-room; he was drinking tea again and muttering something. My wife was standing opposite to him and holding on to the back of a chair. There was a gentle, sweet, and docile expression on her face, such as one sees on the faces of people listening to crazy saints or holy men when a peculiar hidden significance is imagined in their vague words and mutterings. There was something morbid, something of a nun's exaltation, in my wife's expression and attitude; and her low-pitched, half-dark rooms with their old-fashioned furniture, with her birds asleep in their cages, and with a smell of geranium, reminded me of the rooms of some abbess or pious old lady.

I went into the drawing-room. My wife showed neither surprise nor confusion, and looked at me calmly and serenely, as though she had known I should come.

" I beg your pardon," I said softly. " I am so glad you have not gone yet, Ivan Ivanitch. I forgot to ask you, do you know the Christian name of the president of our Zemstvo?"

"Andrey Stanislavovitch. Yes. . . ."

"*Merci*," I said, took out my notebook, and wrote it down.

There followed a silence during which my wife and Ivan Ivanitch were probably waiting for me to go; my wife did not believe that I wanted to know the president's name — I saw that from her eyes.

"Well, I must be going, my beauty," muttered Ivan Ivanitch, after I had walked once or twice across the drawing-room and sat down by the fireplace.

"No," said Natalya Gavrilovna quickly, touching his hand. "Stay another quarter of an hour. . . . Please do!"

Evidently she did not wish to be left alone with me without a witness.

"Oh, well, I'll wait a quarter of an hour, too," I thought.

"Why, it's snowing!" I said, getting up and looking out of window. "A good fall of snow! Ivan Ivanitch"— I went on walking about the room —"I do regret not being a sportsman. I can imagine what a pleasure it must be coursing hares or hunting wolves in snow like this!"

My wife, standing still, watched my movements, looking out of the corner of her eyes without turning her head. She looked as though she thought I had a sharp knife or a revolver in my pocket.

" Ivan Ivanitch, do take me out hunting some day," I went on softly. " I shall be very, very grateful to you."

At that moment a visitor came into the room. He was a tall, thick-set gentleman whom I did not know, with a bald head, a big fair beard, and little eyes. From his baggy, crumpled clothes and his manners I took him to be a parish clerk or a teacher, but my wife introduced him to me as Dr. Sobol.

" Very, very glad to make your acquaintance," said the doctor in a loud tenor voice, shaking hands with me warmly, with a naïve smile. " Very glad ! "

He sat down at the table, took a glass of tea, and said in a loud voice :

" Do you happen to have a drop of rum or brandy ? Have pity on me, Olya, and look in the cupboard; I am frozen," he said, addressing the maid.

I sat down by the fire again, looked on, listened, and from time to time put in a word in the general conversation. My wife smiled graciously to the visitors and kept a sharp lookout on me, as though I were a wild beast. She was oppressed by my presence, and this aroused in me jealousy, annoyance, and an obstinate desire to wound her. " Wife, these snug rooms, the place by the fire," I thought, " are mine, have been mine for years, but some crazy Ivan Ivanitch or Sobol has for some reason more right to them than I. Now I see my wife, not out of window, but close at hand, in or-dinary home surroundings that I feel the want of

tomorrow, that's all; and that will
our quarrel."
r past one I went to bed.
visitors downstairs gone?" I asked
was undressing me.
they've gone."
were they shouting hurrah?"
Dmitritch Mahonov subscribed for the
a thousand bushels of flour and a
ubles. And the old lady — I don't
me — promised to set up a soup kitchen
e to feed a hundred and fifty people.
. . . . Natalya Gavrilovna has been
rrange that all the gentry should as-
Friday."
mble here, downstairs?"
. Before supper they read a list: since
to today Natalya Gavrilovna has col-
thousand roubles, besides corn. Thank
What I think is that if our mistress
rouble for the salvation of her soul, she
ollect a lot. There are plenty of rich
e."
ng Alexey, I put out the light and drew
hes over my head.
all, why am I so troubled?" I thought.
rce draws me to the starving peasants
erfly to a flame? I don't know them, I
rstand them; I have never seen them and
e them. Why this uneasiness?"
nly crossed myself under the quilt.
hat a woman she is!" I said to myself,

now I am growing older, and, in spite of her hatred
for me, I miss her as years ago in my childhood I
used to miss my mother and my nurse. And I feel
that now, on the verge of old age, my love for her
is purer and loftier than it was in the past; and that
is why I want to go up to her, to stamp hard on
her toe with my heel, to hurt her and smile as I
do it."

"Monsieur Marten," I said, addressing the
doctor, "how many hospitals have we in the district?"

"Sobol," my wife corrected.

"Two," answered Sobol.

"And how many deaths are there every year in
each hospital?"

"Pavel Andreitch, I want to speak to you," said
my wife.

She apologized to the visitors and went to the
next room. I got up and followed her.

"You will go upstairs to your own rooms this
minute," she said.

"You are ill-bred," I said to her.

"You will go upstairs to your own rooms this
very minute," she repeated sharply, and she looked
into my face with hatred.

She was standing so near that if I had stooped
a little my beard would have touched her face.

"What is the matter?" I asked. "What harm
have I done all at once?"

Her chin quivered, she hastily wiped her eyes,
and, with a cursory glance at the looking-glass,
whispered:

" The old story is beginning all over again. Of course you won't go away. Well, do as you like. I'll go away myself, and you stay."

We returned to the drawing-room, she with a resolute face, while I shrugged my shoulders and tried to smile. There were some more visitors — an elderly lady and a young man in spectacles. Without greeting the new arrivals or taking leave of the others, I went off to my own rooms.

After what had happened at tea and then again downstairs, it became clear to me that our " family happiness," which we had begun to forget about in the course of the last two years, was through some absurd and trivial reason beginning all over again, and that neither I nor my wife could now stop ourselves; and that next day or the day after, the outburst of hatred would, as I knew by experience of past years, be followed by something revolting which would upset the whole order of our lives. " So it seems that during these two years we have grown no wiser, colder, or calmer," I thought as I began walking about the rooms. " So there will again be tears, outcries, curses, packing up, going abroad, then the continual sickly fear that she will disgrace me with some coxcomb out there, Italian or Russian, refusing a passport, letters, utter loneliness, missing her, and in five years old age, grey hairs." I walked about, imagining what was really impossible — her, grown handsomer, stouter, embracing a man I did not know. By now convinced that that would certainly happen, " Why," I asked myself, " Why, in one of our long past quar-

rels, had
not at th
have had
this anxie
quietly, wc

A carria
then a big
evidently h

Till mid
and I hear
sound of m
So there was
and through
to be shouti
already aslee
upper storey;
insignificant p
of the drawin
in the window
feeling of jeal
downstairs, I l
here; if I like,
fine crew." B
sense, that I cou
" master " had
self master, m
much as one lik
what it means.

After supper
in a tenor voice.

" Why, nothin
persuade myself.

go downstairs
be the end of

At a quarte
" Have the
Alexey as he
" Yes, sir,
" And why
" Alexey
famine fund
thousand ro
know her na
on her estat
Thank God
pleased to
semble ever

" To ass
" Yes, si
August up
lected eight
God. . . .
does take t
will soon
people her

Dismissi
the bedclot
" After
" What f
like a butt
don't und
I don't lik

I sudde
" But

thinking of my wife. " There's a regular committee held in the house without my knowing. Why this secrecy? Why this conspiracy? What have I done to them? Ivan Ivanitch is right — I must go away."

Next morning I woke up firmly resolved to go away. The events of the previous day — the conversation at tea, my wife, Sobol, the supper, my apprehensions — worried me, and I felt glad to think of getting away from the surroundings which reminded me of all that. While I was drinking my coffee the bailiff gave me a long report on various matters. The most agreeable item he saved for the last.

" The thieves who stole our rye have been found," he announced with a smile. " The magistrate arrested three peasants at Pestrovo yesterday."

" Go away! " I shouted at him; and à propos of nothing, I picked up the cake-basket and flung it on the floor.

IV

After lunch I rubbed my hands, and thought I must go to my wife and tell her that I was going away. Why? Who cared? Nobody cares, I answered, but why shouldn't I tell her, especially as it would give her nothing but pleasure? Besides, to go away after our yesterday's quarrel without saying a word would not be quite tactful: she might think that I was frightened of her, and perhaps the thought that she has driven me out of my house may weigh upon her. It would be just as well, too, to tell her that I subscribe five thousand, and to give her some advice about the organization, and to warn her that her inexperience in such a complicated and responsible matter might lead to most lamentable results. In short, I wanted to see my wife, and while I thought of various pretexts for going to her, I had a firm conviction in my heart that I should do so.

It was still light when I went in to her, and the lamps had not yet been lighted. She was sitting in her study, which led from the drawing-room to her bedroom, and, bending low over the table, was writing something quickly. Seeing me, she started, got up from the table, and remained standing in an attitude such as to screen her papers from me.

"I beg your pardon, I have only come for a minute," I said, and, I don't know why, I was overcome with embarrassment. "I have learnt by chance that you are organizing relief for the famine, Natalie."

"Yes, I am. But that's my business," she answered.

"Yes, it is your business," I said softly. "I am glad of it, for it just fits in with my intentions. I beg your permission to take part in it."

"Forgive me, I cannot let you do it," she said in response, and looked away.

"Why not, Natalie?" I said quietly. "Why not? I, too, am well fed and I, too, want to help the hungry."

"I don't know what it has to do with you," she

said with a contemptuous smile, shrugging her
shoulders. " Nobody asks you."

" Nobody asks you, either, and yet you have got
up a regular committee in *my* house," I said.

" I am asked, but you can have my word for it
no one will ever ask you. Go and help where you
are not known."

" For God's sake, don't talk to me in that tone."
I tried to be mild, and besought myself most earnestly not to lose my temper. For the first few
minutes I felt glad to be with my wife. I felt an
atmosphere of youth, of home, of feminine softness, of the most refined elegance — exactly what
was lacking on my floor and in my life altogether.
My wife was wearing a pink flannel dressing-gown;
it made her look much younger, and gave a softness
to her rapid and sometimes abrupt movements.
Her beautiful dark hair, the mere sight of which
at one time stirred me to passion, had from sitting
so long with her head bent come loose from the
comb and was untidy, but, to my eyes, that only
made it look more rich and luxuriant. All this,
though is banal to the point of vulgarity. Before
me stood an ordinary woman, perhaps neither beautiful nor elegant, but this was my wife with whom
I had once lived, and with whom I should have been
living to this day if it had not been for her unfortunate character; she was the one human being on
the terrestrial globe whom I loved. At this moment, just before going away, when I knew that
I should no longer see her even through the window,
she seemed to me fascinating even as she was, cold

and forbidding, answering me with a proud and contemptuous mockery. I was proud of her, and confessed to myself that to go away from her was terible and impossible.

" Pavel Andreitch," she said after a brief silence, " for two years we have not interfered with each other but have lived quietly. Why do you suddenly feel it necessary to go back to the past? Yesterday you came to insult and humiliate me," she went on, raising her voice, and her face flushed and her eyes flamed with hatred; " but restrain yourself; do not do it, Pavel Andreitch! Tomorrow I will send in a petition and they will give me a passport, and I will go away; I will go, I will go! I'll go into a convent, into a widows' home, into an almshouse. . . ."

" Into a lunatic asylum! " I cried, not able to restrain myself.

" Well, even into a lunatic asylum! That would be better, that would be better," she cried, with flashing eyes. " When I was in Pestrovo today I envied the sick and starving peasant women because they are not living with a man like you. They are free and honest, while, thanks to you, I am a parasite, I am perishing in idleness, I eat your bread, I spend your money, and I repay you with my liberty and a fidelity which is of no use to any one. Because you won't give me a passport, I must respect your good name, though it doesn't exist."

I had to keep silent. Clenching my teeth, I walked quickly into the drawing-room, but turned back at once and said:

" I beg you earnestly that there should be no more
assemblies, plots, and meetings of conspirators in
my house! I only admit to my house those with
whom I am acquainted, and let all your crew find
another place to do it if they want to take up philanthropy. I can't allow people at midnight in my
house to be shouting hurrah at successfully exploit-
ing an hysterical woman like you! "

My wife, pale and wringing her hands, took a
rapid stride across the room, uttering a prolonged
moan as though she had toothache. With a wave
of my hand, I went into the drawing-room. I was
choking with rage, and at the same time I was trembling with terror that I might not restrain myself,
and that I might say or do something which I might
regret all my life. And I clenched my hands tight,
hoping to hold myself in.

After drinking some water and recovering my
calm a little, I went back to my wife. She was
standing in the same attitude as before, as though
barring my approach to the table with the papers.
Tears were slowly trickling down her pale, cold face.
I paused then and said to her bitterly but without
anger:

" How you misunderstand me! How unjust you
are to me! I swear upon my honour I came to you
with the best of motives, with nothing but the desire
to do good! "

" Pavel Andreitch! " she said, clasping her hands
on her bosom, and her face took on the agonized,
imploring expression with which frightened, weeping children beg not to be punished, " I know per-

fectly well that you will refuse me, but still I beg
you. Force yourself to do one kind action in your
life. I entreat you, go away from here! That's
the only thing you can do for the starving peasants.
Go away, and I will forgive you everything, everything! "

" There is no need for you to insult me, Natalie,"
I sighed, feeling a sudden rush of humility. " I had
already made up my mind to go away, but I won't
go until I have done something for the peasants.
It's my duty! "

" Ach! " she said softly with an impatient frown.
" You can make an excellent bridge or railway, but
you can do nothing for the starving peasants. Do
understand! "

" Indeed? Yesterday you reproached me with
indifference and with being devoid of the feeling
of compassion. How well you know me! " I
laughed. " You believe in God — well, God is my
witness that I am worried day and night. . . ."

" I see that you are worried, but the famine and
compassion have nothing to do with it. You are
worried because the starving peasants can get on
without you, and because the Zemstvo, and in fact
every one who is helping them, does not need your
guidance."

I was silent, trying to suppress my irritation.
Then I said:

" I came to speak to you on business. Sit down.
Please sit down."

She did not sit down.

"I beg you to sit down," I repeated, and I motioned her to a chair.

She sat down. I sat down, too, thought a little, and said:

"I beg you to consider earnestly what I am saying. Listen. . . . Moved by love for your fellow-creatures, you have undertaken the organization of famine relief. I have nothing against that, of course; I am completely in sympathy with you, and am prepared to co-operate with you in every way, whatever our relations may be. But, with all my respect for your mind and your heart . . . and your heart," I repeated, "I cannot allow such a difficult, complex, and responsible matter as the organization of relief to be left in your hands entirely. You are a woman, you are inexperienced, you know nothing of life, you are too confiding and expansive. You have surrounded yourself with assistants whom you know nothing about. I am not exaggerating if I say that under these conditions your work will inevitably lead to two deplorable consequences. To begin with, our district will be left unrelieved; and, secondly, you will have to pay for your mistakes and those of your assistants, not only with your purse, but with your reputation. The money deficit and other losses I could, no doubt, make good, but who could restore you your good name? When through lack of proper supervision and oversight there is a rumour that you, and consequently I, have made two hundred thousand over the famine fund, will your assistants come to your aid?"

She said nothing.

"Not from vanity, as you say," I went on, "but simply that the starving peasants may not be left unrelieved and your reputation may not be injured, I feel it my moral duty to take part in your work."

"Speak more briefly," said my wife.

"You will be so kind," I went on, "as to show me what has been subscribed so far and what you have spent. Then inform me daily of every fresh subscription in money or kind, and of every fresh outlay. You will also give me, Natalie, the list of your helpers. Perhaps they are quite decent people; I don't doubt it; but, still, it is absolutely necessary to make inquiries."

She was silent. I got up, and walked up and down the room.

"Let us set to work, then," I said, and I sat down to her table.

"Are you in earnest?" she asked, looking at me in alarm and bewilderment.

"Natalie, do be reasonable!" I said appealingly, seeing from her face that she meant to protest. "I beg you, trust my experience and my sense of honour."

"I don't understand what you want."

"Show me how much you have collected and how much you have spent."

"I have no secrets. Any one may see. Look."

On the table lay five or six school exercise books, several sheets of notepaper covered with writing, a map of the district, and a number of pieces of paper of different sizes. It was getting dusk. I lighted a candle.

"Excuse me, I don't see anything yet," I said, turning over the leaves of the exercise books. "Where is the account of the receipt of money subscriptions?"

"That can be seen from the subscription lists."

"Yes, but you must have an account," I said, smiling at her naïveté. "Where are the letters accompanying the subscriptions in money or in kind? *Pardon,* a little practical advice, Natalie: it's absolutely necessary to keep those letters. You ought to number each letter and make a special note of it in a special record. You ought to do the same with your own letters. But I will do all that myself."

"Do so, do so . . ." she said.

I was very much pleased with myself. Attracted by this living interesting work, by the little table, the naïve exercise books and the charm of doing this work in my wife's society, I was afraid that my wife would suddenly hinder me and upset everything by some sudden whim, and so I was in haste and made an effort to attach no consequence to the fact that her lips were quivering, and that she was looking about her with a helpless and frightened air like a wild creature in a trap.

"I tell you what, Natalie," I said without looking at her; "let me take all these papers and exercise books upstairs to my study. There I will look through them and tell you what I think about it tomorrow. Have you any more papers?" I asked, arranging the exercise books and sheets of papers in piles.

" Take them, take them all! " said my wife, helping me to arrange them, and big tears ran down her cheeks. " Take it all! That's all that was left me in life. . . . Take the last."

" Ach! Natalie, Natalie! " I sighed reproachfully.

She opened the drawer in the table and began flinging the papers out of it on the table at random, poking me in the chest with her elbow and brushing my face with her hair; as she did so, copper coins kept dropping upon my knees and on the floor.

" Take everything! " she said in a husky voice.

When she had thrown out the papers she walked away from me, and putting both hands to her head, she flung herself on the couch. I picked up the money, put it back in the drawer, and locked it up that the servants might not be led into dishonesty; then I gathered up all the papers and went off with them. As I passed my wife I stopped, and, looking at her back and shaking shoulders, I said:

" What a baby you are, Natalie! Fie, fie! Listen, Natalie: when you realize how serious and responsible a business it is you will be the first to thank me. I assure you you will."

In my own room I set to work without haste. The exercise books were not bound, the pages were not numbered. The entries were put in all sorts of handwritings; evidently any one who liked had a hand in managing the books. In the record of the subscriptions in kind there was no note of their money value. But, excuse me, I thought, the rye which is now worth one rouble fifteen kopecks may be worth two roubles fifteen kopecks in two months' time! Was that the way to do things? Then, " Given to A. M. Sobol 32 roubles." When was it given? For what purpose was it given? Where was the receipt? There was nothing to show, and no making anything of it. In case of legal proceedings, these papers would only obscure the case.

" How naïve she is! " I thought with surprise. " What a child! "

I felt both vexed and amused.

V

My wife had already collected eight thousand; with my five it would be thirteen thousand. For a start that was very good. The business which had so worried and interested me was at last in my hands; I was doing what the others would not and could not do; I was doing my duty, organizing the relief fund in a practical and businesslike way.

Everything seemed to be going in accordance with my desires and intentions; but why did my feeling of uneasiness persist? I spent four hours over my wife's papers, making out their meaning and correcting her mistakes, but instead of feeling soothed, I felt as though some one were standing behind me and rubbing my back with a rough hand. What was it I wanted? The organization of the relief fund had come into trustworthy hands, the hungry would be fed — what more was wanted?

The four hours of this light work for some reason

exhausted me, so that I could not sit bending over the table nor write. From below I heard from time to time a smothered moan; it was my wife sobbing. Alexey, invariably meek, sleepy, and sanctimonious, kept coming up to the table to see to the candles, and looked at me somewhat strangely.

"Yes, I must go away," I decided at last, feeling utterly exhausted. "As far as possible from these agreeable impressions! I will set off tomorrow."

I gathered together the papers and exercise books, and went down to my wife. As, feeling quite worn out and shattered, I held the papers and the exercise books to my breast with both hands, and passing through my bedroom saw my trunks, the sound of weeping reached me through the floor.

"Are you a kammer-junker?" a voice whispered in my ear. "That's a very pleasant thing. But yet you are a reptile."

"It's all nonsense, nonsense, nonsense," I muttered as I went downstairs. "Nonsense . . . and it's nonsense, too, that I am actuated by vanity or a love of display. . . . What rubbish! Am I going to get a decoration for working for the peasants or be made the director of a department? Nonsense, nonsense! And who is there to show off to here in the country?"

I was tired, frightfully tired, and something kept whispering in my ear: "Very pleasant. But, still, you are a reptile." For some reason I remembered a line out of an old poem I knew as a child: "How pleasant it is to be good!"

My wife was lying on the couch in the same atti-

The Wife   41

tude, on her face and with her hands clutching her
head. She was crying. A maid was standing beside her with a perplexed and frightened face. I
sent the maid away, laid the papers on the table,
thought a moment and said:

"Here are all your papers, Natalie. It's all in
order, it's all capital, and I am very much pleased.
I am going away tomorrow."

She went on crying. I went into the drawing-
room and sat there in the dark. My wife's sobs,
her sighs, accused me of something, and to justify
myself I remembered the whole of our quarrel,
starting from my unhappy idea of inviting my wife
to our consultation and ending with the exercise
books and these tears. It was an ordinary attack of
our conjugal hatred, senseless and unseemly, such as
had been frequent during our married life, but what
had the starving peasants to do with it? How could
it have happened that they had become a bone of
contention between us? It was just as though pursuing one another we had accidentally run up to the
altar and had carried on a quarrel there.

"Natalie," I said softly from the drawing-room,
"hush, hush!"

To cut short her weeping and make an end of this
agonizing state of affairs, I ought to have gone up
to my wife and comforted her, caressed her, or
apologized; but how could I do it so that she would
believe me? How could I persuade the wild duck,
living in captivity and hating me, that it was dear to
me, and that I felt for its sufferings? I had never
known my wife, so I had never known how to talk

to her or what to talk about. Her appearance I knew very well and appreciated it as it deserved, but her spiritual, moral world, her mind, her outlook on life, her frequent changes of mood, her eyes full of hatred, her disdain, the scope and variety of her reading which sometimes struck me, or, for instance, the nun-like expression I had seen on her face the day before — all that was unknown and incomprehensible to me. When in my collisions with her I tried to define what sort of a person she was, my psychology went no farther than deciding that she was giddy, impractical, ill-tempered, guided by feminine logic; and it seemed to me that that was quite sufficient. But now that she was crying I had a passionate desire to know more.

The weeping ceased. I went up to my wife. She sat up on the couch, and, with her head propped in both hands, looked fixedly and dreamily at the fire.

" I am going away tomorrow morning," I said.

She said nothing. I walked across the room, sighed, and said:

" Natalie, when you begged me to go away, you said: ' I will forgive you everything, everything. . . . So you think I have wronged you. I beg you calmly and in brief terms to formulate the wrong I've done you."

" I am worn out. Afterwards, some time . . ." said my wife.

" How am I to blame? " I went on. " What have I done? Tell me: you are young and beautiful, you want to live, and I am nearly twice your age and hated by you, but is that my fault? I didn't

marry you by force. But if you want to live in freedom, go; I'll give you your liberty. You can go
and love whom you please. . . . I will give you a
divorce."

" That's not what I want," she said. " You know
I used to love you and always thought of myself
as older than you. That's all nonsense. . . . You
are not to blame for being older or for my being
younger, or that I might be able to love some one
else if I were free; but because you are a difficult
person, an egoist, and hate every one."

" Perhaps so. I don't know," I said.

" Please go away. You want to go on at me
till the morning, but I warn you I am quite worn out
and cannot answer you. You promised me to go to
town. I am very grateful; I ask nothing more."

My wife wanted me to go away, but it was not
easy for me to do that. I was dispirited and I
dreaded the big, cheerless, chill rooms that I was so
weary of. Sometimes when I had an ache or a pain
as a child, I used to huddle up to my mother or my
nurse, and when I hid my face in the warm folds
of their dress, it seemed to me as though I were hiding from the pain. And in the same way it seemed
to me now that I could only hide from my uneasiness
in this little room beside my wife. I sat down and
screened away the light from my eyes with my hand.
. . . There was a stillness.

" How are you to blame? " my wife said after a
long silence, looking at me with red eyes that
gleamed with tears. " You are very well educated
and very well bred, very honest, just, and high-

principled, but in you the effect of all that is that
wherever you go you bring suffocation, oppression,
something insulting and humiliating to the utmost
degree.   You have a straightforward way of looking at things, and so you hate the whole world.   You
hate those who have faith, because faith is an expression of ignorance and lack of culture, and at the
same time you hate those who have no faith for having no faith and no ideals; you hate old people for
being conservative and behind the times, and young
people for free-thinking.   The interests of the peasantry and of Russia are dear to you, and so you hate
the peasants because you suspect every one of them
of being a thief and a robber.   You hate every
one.   You are just, and always take your stand on
your legal rights, and so you are always at law with
the peasants and your neighbours.   You have had
twenty bushels of rye stolen, and your love of order
has made you complain of the peasants to the Governor and all the local authorities, and to send a complaint of the local authorities to Petersburg.   Legal
justice!" said my wife, and she laughed.   "On the
ground of your legal rights and in the interests of
morality, you refuse to give me a passport.   Law
and morality is such that a self-respecting healthy
young woman has to spend her life in idleness, in depression, and in continual apprehension, and to receive in return board and lodging from a man she
does not love.   You have a thorough knowledge of
the law, you are very honest and just, you respect
marriage and family life, and the effect of all that
is that all your life you have not done one kind

action, that every one hates you, that you are on bad
terms with every one, and the seven years that you
have been married you've only lived seven months
with your wife. You've had no wife and I've had
no husband. To live with a man like you is impossible; there is no way of doing it. In the early years
I was frightened with you, and now I am ashamed.
. . . That's how my best years have been wasted.
When I fought with you I ruined my temper, grew
shrewish, coarse, timid, mistrustful. . . . Oh, but
what's the use of talking! As though you wanted to
understand! Go upstairs, and God be with you!"
My wife lay down on the couch and sank into
thought.

"And how splendid, how enviable life might have
been!" she said softly, looking reflectively into the
fire. "What a life it might have been! There's
no bringing it back now."

Any one who has lived in the country in winter and
knows those long dreary, still evenings when even
the dogs are too bored to bark and even the clocks
seem weary of ticking, and any one who on such
evenings has been troubled by awakening conscience
and has moved restlessly about, trying now to
smother his conscience, now to interpret it, will understand the distraction and the pleasure my wife's
voice gave me as it sounded in the snug little room,
telling me I was a bad man. I did not understand
what was wanted of me by my conscience, and my
wife, translating it in her feminine way, made clear
to me in the meaning of my agitation. As often before in the moments of intense uneasiness, I guessed

that the whole secret lay, not in the starving peasants, but in my not being the sort of a man I ought to be.

My wife got up with an effort and came up to me.

"Pavel Andreitch," she said, smiling mournfully, "forgive me, I don't believe you: you are not going away, but I will ask you one more favour. Call this "— she pointed to her papers —" self-deception, feminine logic, a mistake, as you like; but do not hinder me. It's all that is left me in life." She turned away and paused. "Before this I had nothing. I have wasted my youth in fighting with you. Now I have caught at this and am living; I am happy. . . . It seems to me that I have found in this a means of justifying my existence."

"Natalie, you are a good woman, a woman of ideas," I said, looking at my wife enthusiastically, "and everything you say and do is intelligent and fine."

I walked about the room to conceal my emotion.

"Natalie," I went on a minute later, "before I go away, I beg of you as a special favour, help me to do something for the starving peasants!"

"What can I do?" said my wife, shrugging her shoulders. "Here's the subscription list."

She rummaged among the papers and found the subscription list.

"Subscribe some money," she said, and from her tone I could see that she did not attach great importance to her subscription list; "that is the only way in which you can take part in the work."

I took the list and wrote: "Anonymous, 5,000."

In this " anonymous " there was something wrong,
false, conceited, but I only realized that when I noticed that my wife flushed very red and hurriedly
thrust the list into the heap of papers. We both
felt ashamed; I felt that I must at all costs efface
this clumsiness at once, or else I should feel ashamed
afterwards, in the train and at Petersburg. But
how efface it? What was I to say?

" I fully approve of what you are doing, Natalie,"
I said genuinely, " and I wish you every success.
But allow me at parting to give you one piece of
advice, Natalie; be on your guard with Sobol, and
with your assistants generally, and don't trust them
blindly. I don't say they are not honest, but they
are not gentlefolks; they are people with no ideas,
no ideals, no faith, with no aim in life, no definite
principles, and the whole object of their life is comprised in the rouble. Rouble, rouble, rouble ! " I
sighed. " They are fond of getting money easily,
for nothing, and in that respect the better educated
they are the more they are to be dreaded."

My wife went to the couch and lay down.

" Ideas," she brought out, listlessly and reluctantly, " ideas, ideals, objects of life, principles . . .
you always used to use those words when you wanted
to insult or humiliate some one, or say something
unpleasant. Yes, that's your way: if with your
views and such an attitude to people you are allowed
to take part in anything, you would destroy it from
the first day. It's time you understand that."

She sighed and paused.

" It's coarseness of character, Pavel Andreitch,"

she said. "You are well-bred and educated, but what a . . . Scythian you are in reality! That's because you lead a cramped life full of hatred, see no one, and read nothing but your engineering books. And, you know, there are good people, good books! Yes . . . but I am exhausted and it wearies me to talk. I ought to be in bed."

"So I am going away, Natalie," I said.

"Yes . . . yes. . . . *Merci.* . . ."

I stood still for a little while, then went upstairs. An hour later — it was half-past one — I went downstairs again with a candle in my hand to speak to my wife. I didn't know what I was going to say to her, but I felt that I must say something very important and necessary. She was not in her study, the door leading to her bedroom was closed.

"Natalie, are you asleep?" I asked softly.

There was no answer.

I stood near the door, sighed, and went into the drawing-room. There I sat down on the sofa, put out the candle, and remained sitting in the dark till the dawn.

VI

I went to the station at ten o'clock in the morning. There was no frost, but snow was falling in big wet flakes and an unpleasant damp wind was blowing.

We passed a pond and then a birch copse, and then began going uphill along the road which I could see from my window. I turned round to take a last look at my house, but I could see nothing for the

snow. Soon afterwards dark huts came into sight
ahead of us as in a fog. It was Pestrovo.

" If I ever go out of my mind, Pestrovo will be
the cause of it," I thought. " It persecutes me."

We came out into the village street. All the roofs
were intact, not one of them had been pulled to
pieces; so my bailiff had told a lie. A boy was pulling along a little girl and a baby in a sledge. Another boy of three, with his head wrapped up like a
peasant woman's and with huge mufflers on his
hands, was trying to catch the flying snowflakes on his
tongue, and laughing. Then a wagon loaded with
fagots came toward us and a peasant walking beside
it, and there was no telling whether his beard was
white or whether it was covered with snow. He
recognized my coachman, smiled at him and said
something, and mechanically took off his hat to me.
The dogs ran out of the yards and looked inquisitively at my horses. Everything was quiet, ordinary,
as usual. The emigrants had returned, there was
no bread; in the huts " some were laughing, some
were delirious "; but it all looked so ordinary that
one could not believe it really was so. There were
no distracted faces, no voices whining for help, no
weeping, nor abuse, but all around was stillness,
order, life, children, sledges, dogs with dishevelled
tails. Neither the children nor the peasant we met
were troubled; why was I so troubled?

Looking at the smiling peasant, at the boy with
the huge mufflers, at the huts, remembering my wife,
I realized there was no calamity that could daunt
this people; I felt as though there were already a

breath of victory in the air.   I felt proud and felt
ready to cry out that I was with them too; but the
horses were carrying us away from the village into
the open country, the snow was whirling, the wind
was howling, and I was left alone with my thoughts.
Of the million people working for the peasantry,
life itself had cast me out as a useless, incompetent,
bad man.   I was a hindrance, a part of the people's
calamity; I was vanquished, cast out, and I was
hurrying to the station to go away and hide myself in
Petersburg in a hotel in Bolshaya Morskaya.

An hour later we reached the station.   The coachman and a porter with a disc on his breast carried my
trunks into the ladies' room.   My coachman Nikanor, wearing high felt boots and the skirt of his
coat tucked up through his belt, all wet with the
snow and glad I was going away, gave me a friendly
smile and said:

"A fortunate journey, your Excellency.   God
give you luck."

Every one, by the way, calls me "your Excellency," though I am only a collegiate councillor and
a kammer-junker.   The porter told me the train had
not yet left the next station; I had to wait.   I went
outside, and with my head heavy from my sleepless
night, and so exhausted I could hardly move my legs,
I walked aimlessly towards the pump.   There was
not a soul anywhere near.

"Why am I going?" I kept asking myself.
"What is there awaiting me there?   The acquaintances from whom I have come away, loneliness, restaurant dinners, noise, the electric light, which makes

my eyes ache. Where am I going, and what am I going for? What am I going for? "

And it seemed somehow strange to go away without speaking to my wife. I felt that I was leaving her in uncertainty. Going away, I ought to have told that she was right, that I really was a bad man.

When I turned away from the pump, I saw in the doorway the station-master, of whom I had twice made complaints to his superiors, turning up the collar of his coat, shrinking from the wind and the snow. He came up to me, and putting two fingers to the peak of his cap, told me with an expression of helpless confusion, strained respectfulness, and hatred on his face, that the train was twenty minutes late, and asked me would I not like to wait in the warm?

" Thank you," I answered, " but I am probably not going. Send word to my coachman to wait; I have not made up my mind."

I walked to and fro on the platform and thought, should I go away or not? When the train came in I decided not to go. At home I had to expect my wife's amazement and perhaps her mockery, the dismal upper storey and my uneasiness; but, still, at my age that was easier and as it were more homelike than travelling for two days and nights with strangers to Petersburg, where I should be conscious every minute that my life was of no use to any one or to anything, and that it was approaching its end. No, better at home whatever awaited me there. . . . I went out of the station. It was awkward by daylight to return home, where every one was so glad at my going. I might spend the rest of the day till evening at some neighbour's, but with whom? With some of them I was on strained relations, others I did not know at all. I considered and thought of Ivan Ivanitch.

"We are going to Bragino!" I said to the coachman, getting into the sledge.

"It's a long way," sighed Nikanor; "it will be twenty miles, or maybe twenty-five."

"Oh, please, my dear fellow," I said in a tone as though Nikanor had the right to refuse. "Please let us go!"

Nikanor shook his head doubtfully and said slowly that we really ought to have put in the shafts, not Circassian, but Peasant or Siskin; and uncertainly, as though expecting I should change my mind, took the reins in his gloves, stood up, thought a moment, and then raised his whip.

"A whole series of inconsistent actions . . ." I thought, screening my face from the snow. "I must have gone out of my mind. Well, I don't care. . . ."

In one place, on a very high and steep slope, Nikanor carefully held the horses in to the middle of the descent, but in the middle the horses suddenly bolted and dashed downhill at a fearful rate; he raised his elbows and shouted in a wild, frantic voice such as I had never heard from him before:

"Hey! Let's give the general a drive! If you come to grief he'll buy new ones, my darlings! Hey! look out! We'll run you down!"

Only now, when the extraordinary pace we were

going at took my breath away, I noticed that he was
very drunk. He must have been drinking at the
station. At the bottom of the descent there was the
crash of ice; a piece of dirty frozen snow thrown up
from the road hit me a painful blow in the face.

The runaway horses ran up the hill as rapidly as
they had downhill, and before I had time to shout
to Nikanor my sledge was flying along on the level
in an old pine forest, and the tall pines were stretching out their shaggy white paws to me from all directions.

" I have gone out of my mind, and the coachman's
drunk," I thought. " Good ! "

I found Ivan Ivanitch at home. He laughed till
he coughed, laid his head on my breast, and said
what he always did say on meeting me :

" You grow younger and younger. I don't know
what dye you use for your hair and your beard; you
might give me some of it."

" I've come to return your call, Ivan Ivanitch,"
I said untruthfully. " Don't be hard on me; I'm a
townsman, conventional; I do keep count of calls."

" I am delighted, my dear fellow. I am an old
man; I like respect. . . . Yes."

From his voice and his blissfully smiling face, I
could see that he was greatly flattered by my visit.
Two peasant women helped me off with my coat in
the entry, and a peasant in a red shirt hung it on a
hook, and when Ivan Ivanitch and I went into his
little study, two barefooted little girls were sitting on
the floor looking at a picture-book; when they saw
us they jumped up and ran away, and a tall, thin old

woman in spectacles came in at once, bowed gravely
to me, and picking up a pillow from the sofa and a
picture-book from the floor, went away.   From the
adjoining rooms we heard incessant whispering and
the patter of bare feet.

"I am expecting the doctor to dinner," said Ivan
Ivanitch.   "He promised to come from the relief
centre.   Yes.   He dines with me every Wednesday,
God bless him."   He craned towards me and kissed
me on the neck.   "You have come, my dear fellow,
so you are not vexed," he whispered, sniffing.
"Don't be vexed, my dear creature.   Yes.   Perhaps it is annyoing, but don't be cross.   My only
prayer to God before I die is to live in peace and
harmony with all in the true way.   Yes."

"Forgive me, Ivan Ivanitch, I will put my feet
on a chair," I said, feeling that I was so exhausted I
could not be myself; I sat further back on the sofa
and put up my feet on an arm-chair.   My face was
burning from the snow and the wind, and I felt as
though my whole body were basking in the warmth
and growing weaker from it.

"It's very nice here," I went on —"warm, soft,
snug . . . and goose-feather pens," I laughed, looking at the writing-table; "sand instead of blotting-
paper."

"Eh? Yes . . . yes. . . . The   writing-table
and the mahogany cupboard here were made for my
father by a self-taught cabinet-maker — Glyeb
Butyga, a serf of General Zhukov's.   Yes . . . a
great artist in his own way."

Listlessly and in the tone of a man dropping

asleep, he began telling me about cabinet-maker Butyga. I listened. Then Ivan Ivanitch went into the next room to show me a polisander wood chest of drawers remarkable for its beauty and cheapness. He tapped the chest with his fingers, then called my attention to a stove of patterned tiles, such as one never sees now. He tapped the stove, too, with his fingers. There was an atmosphere of good-natured simplicity and well-fed abundance about the chest of drawers, the tiled stove, the low chairs, the pictures embroidered in wool and silk on canvas in solid, ugly frames. When one remembers that all those objects were standing in the same places and precisely in the same order when I was a little child, and used to come here to name-day parties with my mother, it is simply unbelievable that they could ever cease to exist.

I thought what a fearful difference between Butyga and me! Butyga who made things, above all, solidly and substantially, and seeing in that his chief object, gave to length of life peculiar significance, had no thought of death, and probably hardly believed in its possibility; I, when I built my bridges of iron and stone which would last a thousand years, could not keep from me the thought, " It's not for long . . . it's no use." If in time Butyga's cupboard and my bridge should come under the notice of some sensible historian of art, he would say: " These were two men remarkable in their own way: Butyga loved his fellow-creatures and would not admit the thought that they might die and be annihilated, and so when he made his furniture he had the immortal

man in his mind.   The engineer Asorin did not love
life or his fellow-creatures; even in the happy moments of creation, thoughts of death, of finiteness
and dissolution, were not alien to him, and we see
how insignificant and finite, how timid and poor, are
these lines of his. . . ."

"I only heat these rooms," muttered Ivan Ivanitch, showing me his rooms.   "Ever since my wife
died and my son was killed in the war, I have kept
the best rooms shut up.   Yes . . . see . . ."

He opened a door, and I saw a big room with four
columns, an old piano, and a heap of peas on the
floor; it smelt cold and damp.

"The garden seats are in the next room . . ."
muttered Ivan Ivanitch.   "There's no one to dance
the mazurka now. . . . I've shut them up."

We heard a noise.   It was Dr. Sobol arriving.
While he was rubbing his cold hands and stroking
his wet beard, I had time to notice in the first place
that he had a very dull life, and so was pleased to
see Ivan Ivanitch and me; and, secondly, that he was
a naïve and simple-hearted man.   He looked at me
as though I were very glad to see him and very much
interested in him.

"I have not slept for two nights," he said, looking at me naïvely and stroking his beard.   "One
night with a confinement, and the next I stayed at a
peasant's with the bugs biting me all night.   I am as
sleepy as Satan, do you know."

With an expression on his face as though it could
not afford me anything but pleasure, he took me by
the arm and led me to the dining-room.   His naïve

eyes, his crumpled coat, his cheap tie and the smell of
iodoform made an unpleasant impression upon me;
I felt as though I were in vulgar company. When
we sat down to table he filled my glass with vodka,
and, smiling helplessly, I drank it; he put a piece
of ham on my plate and I ate it submissively.

"*Repetitia est mater studiorum,*" said Sobol,
hastening to drink off another wineglassful.
"Would you believe it, the joy of seeing good people
has driven away my sleepiness? I have turned into
a peasant, a savage in the wilds; I've grown coarse,
but I am still an educated man, and I tell you in good
earnest, it's tedious without company."

They served first for a cold course white sucking-
pig with horse-radish cream, then a rich and very hot
cabbage soup with pork on it, with boiled buckwheat,
from which rose a column of steam. The doctor
went on talking, and I was soon convinced that he
was a weak, unfortunate man, disorderly in external
life. Three glasses of vodka made him drunk; he
grew unnaturally lively, ate a great deal, kept clearing his throat and smacking his lips, and already addressed me in Italian, "Eccellenza." Looking
naïvely at me as though he were convinced that I was
very glad to see and hear him, he informed me that
he had long been separated from his wife and gave
her three-quarters of his salary; that she lived in the
town with his children, a boy and a girl, whom he
adored; that he loved another woman, a widow, well
educated, with an estate in the country, but was
rarely able to see her, as he was busy with his work
from morning till night and had not a free moment.

" The whole day long, first at the hospital, then on my rounds," he told us; " and I assure you, Eccellenza, I have not time to read a book, let alone going to see the woman I love. I've read nothing for ten years! For ten years, Eccellenza. As for the financial side of the question, ask Ivan Ivanitch: I have often no money to buy tobacco."

" On the other hand, you have the moral satisfaction of your work," I said.

" What? " he asked, and he winked. " No," he said, " better let us drink."

I listened to the doctor, and, after my invariable habit, tried to take his measure by my usual classification — materialist, idealist, filthy lucre, gregarious instincts, and so on; but no classification fitted him even approximately; and strange to say, while I simply listened and looked at him, he seemed perfectly clear to me as a person, but as soon as I began trying to classify him he became an exceptionally complex, intricate, and incomprehensible character in spite of all his candour and simplicity. " Is that man," I asked myself, " capable of wasting other people's money, abusing their confidence, being disposed to sponge on them? " And now this question, which had once seemed to me grave and important, struck me as crude, petty, and coarse.

Pie was served; then, I remember, with long intervals between, during which we drank home-made liquors, they gave us a stew of pigeons, some dish of giblets, roast sucking-pig, partridges, cauliflower, curd dumplings, curd cheese and milk, jelly, and finally pancakes and jam. At first I ate with great

relish, especially the cabbage soup and the buckwheat, but afterwards I munched and swallowed mechanically, smiling helplessly and unconscious of the
taste of anything. My face was burning from the
hot cabbage soup and the heat of the room. Ivan
Ivanitch and Sobol, too, were crimson.

" To the health of your wife," said Sobol. " She
likes me. Tell her her doctor sends her his re-
spects."

" She's fortunate, upon my word," sighed Ivan
Ivanitch. " Though she takes no trouble, does not
fuss or worry herself, she has become the most important person in the whole district. Almost the
whole business is in her hands, and they all gather
round her, the doctor, the District Captains, and the
ladies. With people of the right sort that happens
of itself. Yes. . . . The apple-tree need take no
thought for the apple to grow on it; it will grow of
itself."

" It's only people who don't care who take no
thought," said I.

" Eh? Yes . . . " muttered Ivan Ivanitch, not
catching what I said, " that's true. . . . One must
not worry oneself. Just so, just so. . . . Only do
your duty towards God and your neighbour, and then
never mind what happens."

" Eccellenza," said Sobol solemnly, " just look at
nature about us: if you poke your nose or your ear
out of your fur collar it will be frost-bitten; stay in
the fields for one hour, you'll be buried in the snow;
while the village is just the same as in the days of
Rurik, the same Petchenyegs and Polovtsi. It's

nothing but being burnt down, starving, and struggling against nature in every way. What was I saying? Yes! If one thinks about it, you know, looks into it and analyses all this hotchpotch, if you will allow me to call it so, it's not life but more like a fire in a theatre! Any one who falls down or screams with terror, or rushes about, is the worst enemy of good order; one must stand up and look sharp, and not stir a hair! There's no time for whimpering and busying oneself with trifles. When you have to deal with elemental forces you must put out force against them, be firm and as unyielding as a stone. Isn't that right, grandfather?" He turned to Ivan Ivanitch and laughed. "I am no better than a woman myself; I am a limp rag, a flabby creature, so I hate flabbiness. I can't endure petty feelings! One mopes, another is frightened, a third will come straight in here and say: 'Fie on you! Here you've guzzled a dozen courses and you talk about the starving!' That's petty and stupid! A fourth will reproach you, Eccellenza, for being rich. Excuse me, Eccellenza," he went on in a loud voice, laying his hand on his heart, "but your having set our magistrate the task of hunting day and night for your thieves — excuse me, that's also petty on your part. I am a little drunk, so that's why I say this now, but you know, it is petty!"

"Who's asking him to worry himself? I don't understand!" I said, getting up.

I suddenly felt unbearably ashamed and mortified, and I walked round the table.

" Who asks him to worry himself? I didn't ask
him to. . . . Damn him! "

" They have arrested three men and let them go
again. They turned out not to be the right ones,
and now they are looking for a fresh lot," said Sobol,
laughing. " It's too bad! "

" I did not ask him to worry himself," said I, almost crying with excitement. " What's it all for?
What's it all for? Well, supposing I was wrong,
supposing I have done wrong, why do they try to put
me more in the wrong? "

" Come, come, come, come! " said Sobol, trying to
soothe me. " Come! I have had a drop, that is
why I said it. My tongue is my enemy. Come,"
he sighed, " we have eaten and drunk wine, and now
for a nap."

He got up from the table, kissed Ivan Ivanitch on
the head, and staggering from repletion, went out of
the dining-room. Ivan Ivanitch and I smoked in
silence.

" I don't sleep after dinner, my dear," said Ivan
Ivanitch, " but you have a rest in the lounge-room."

I agreed. In the half-dark and warmly heated
room they called the lounge-room, there stood
against the walls long, wide sofas, solid and heavy,
the work of Butyga the cabinet maker; on them lay
high, soft, white beds, probably made by the old
woman in spectacles. On one of them Sobol, without
his coat and boots, already lay asleep with his face
to the back of the sofa; another bed was awaiting
me. I took off my coat and boots, and, overcome by

fatigue, by the spirit of Butyga which hovered over the quiet lounge-room, and by the light, caressing snore of Sobol, I lay down submissively.

And at once I began dreaming of my wife, of her room, of the station-master with his· face full of hatred, the heaps of snow, a fire in the theatre. . . . I dreamed of the peasants who had stolen twenty sacks of rye out of my barn. . . .

" Anyway, it's a good thing the magistrate let them go," I said.

I woke up at the sound of my own voice, looked for a moment in perplexity at Sobol's broad back, at the buckles of his waistcoat, at his thick heels, then lay down again and fell asleep.

When I woke up the second time it was quite dark. Sobol was asleep. There was peace in my heart, and I longed to make haste home. I dressed and went out of the lounge-room. Ivan Ivanitch was sitting in a big arm-chair in his study, absolutely motionless, staring at a fixed point, and it was evident that he had been in the same state of petrifaction all the while I had been asleep.

" Good! " I said, yawning. " I feel as though I had woken up after breaking the fast at Easter. I shall often come and see you now. Tell me, did my wife ever dine here ? "

" So-ome-ti-mes . . . sometimes," muttered Ivan Ivanitch, making an effort to stir. " She dined here last Saturday. Yes. . . . She likes me."

After a silence I said:

" Do you remember, Ivan Ivanitch, you told me I had a disagreeable character and that it was difficult to get on with me? But what am I to do to make my character different?"

" I don't know, my dear boy. . . . I'm a feeble old man, I can't advise you. . . . Yes. . . . But I said that to you at the time because I am fond of you and fond of your wife, and I was fond of your father. . . . Yes. I shall soon die, and what need have I to conceal things from you or to tell you lies? So I tell you: I am very fond of you, but I don't respect you. No, I don't respect you."

He turned towards me and said in a breathless whisper:

" It's impossible to respect you, my dear fellow. You look like a real man. You have the figure and deportment of the French President Carnot — I saw a portrait of him the other day in an illustrated paper . . . yes. . . . You use lofty language, and you are clever, and you are high up in the service beyond all reach, but haven't real soul, my dear boy . . . there's no strength in it."

" A Scythian, in fact," I laughed. " But what about my wife? Tell me something about my wife; you know her better."

I wanted to talk about my wife, but Sobol came in and prevented me.

" I've had a sleep and a wash," he said, looking at me naïvely. " I'll have a cup of tea with some rum in it and go home."

VII

It was by now past seven.   Besides Ivan Ivanitch, women servants, the old dame in spectacles, the little girls and the peasant, all accompanied us from the hall out on to the steps, wishing us good-bye and all sorts of blessings, while near the horses in the darkness there were standing and moving about men with lanterns, telling our coachmen how and which way to drive, and wishing us a lucky journey.   The horses, the men, and the sledges were white.

" Where do all these people come from? " I asked as my three horses and the doctor's two moved at a walking pace out of the yard.

" They are all his serfs," said Sobol.   " The new order has not reached him yet.   Some of the old servants are living out their lives with him, and then there are orphans of all sorts who have nowhere to go; there are some, too, who insist on living there, there's no turning them out.   A queer old man! "

Again the flying horses, the strange voice of drunken Nikanor, the wind and the persistent snow, which got into one's eyes, one's mouth, and every fold of one's fur coat. . . .

" Well, I am running a rig," I thought, while my bells chimed in with the doctor's, the wind whistled, the coachmen shouted; and while this frantic uproar was going on, I recalled all the details of that strange wild day, unique in my life, and it seemed to me that I really had gone out of my mind or become a different man. It was as though the man I had been till that day were already a stranger to me.

The doctor drove behind and kept talking loudly with his coachman. From time to time he overtook me, drove side by side, and always, with the same naïve confidence that it was very pleasant to me, offered me a cigarette or asked for the matches. Or, overtaking me, he would lean right out of his sledge, and waving about the sleeves of his fur coat, which were at least twice as long as his arms, shout:

"Go it, Vaska! Beat the thousand roublers! Hey, my kittens!"

And to the accompaniment of loud, malicious laughter from Sobol and his Vaska the doctor's kittens raced ahead. My Nikanor took it as an affront, and held in his three horses, but when the doctor's bells had passed out of hearing, he raised his elbows, shouted, and our horses flew like mad in pursuit. We drove into a village, there were glimpses of lights, the silhouettes of huts. Some one shouted: "Ah, the devils!" We seemed to have galloped a mile and a half, and still it was the village street and there seemed no end to it. When we caught up the doctor and drove more quietly, he asked for matches and said:

"Now try and feed that street! And, you know, there are five streets like that, sir. Stay, stay," he shouted. "Turn in at the tavern! We must get warm and let the horses rest."

They stopped at the tavern.

"I have more than one village like that in my

district," said the doctor, opening a heavy door with a squeaky block, and ushering me in front of him. " If you look in broad daylight you can't see to the end of the street, and there are side-streets, too, and one can do nothing but scratch one's head. It's hard to do anything."

We went into the best room where there was a strong smell of table-cloths, and at our entrance a sleepy peasant in a waistcoat and a shirt worn outside his trousers jumped up from a bench. Sobol asked for some beer and I asked for tea.

" It's hard to do anything," said Sobol. " Your wife has faith; I respect her and have the greatest reverence for her, but I have no great faith myself. As long as our relations to the people continue to have the character of ordinary philanthropy, as shown in orphan asylums and almshouses, so long we shall only be shuffling, shamming, and deceiving ourselves, and nothing more. Our relations ought to be businesslike, founded on calculation, knowledge, and justice. My Vaska has been working for me all his life; his crops have failed, he is sick and starving. If I give him fifteen kopecks a day, by so so doing I try to restore him to his former condition as a workman; that is, I am first and foremost looking after my own interests, and yet for some reason I call that fifteen kopecks relief, charity, good works. Now let us put it like this. On the most modest computation, reckoning seven kopecks a soul and five souls a family, one needs three hundred and fifty roubles a day to feed a thousand families. That sum is fixed by our practical duty to a thousand families. Meanwhile we give not three hundred and fifty a day, but only ten, and say that that is relief, charity, that that makes your wife and all of us exceptionally good people and hurrah for our humaneness. That is it, my dear soul! Ah! if we would talk less of being humane and calculated more, reasoned, and took a conscientious attitude to our duties! How many such humane, sensitive people there are among us who tear about in all good faith with subscription lists, but don't pay their tailors or their cooks. There is no logic in our life; that's what it is! No logic!"

We were silent for a while. I was making a mental calculation and said:

"I will feed a thousand families for two hundred days. Come and see me tomorrow to talk it over."

I was pleased that this was said quite simply, and was glad that Sobol answered me still more simply:

"Right."

We paid for what we had and went out of the tavern.

"I like going on like this," said Sobol, getting into the sledge. "Eccellenza, oblige me with a match. I've forgotten mine in the tavern."

A quarter of an hour later his horses fell behind, and the sound of his bells was lost in the roar of the snow-storm. Reaching home, I walked about my rooms, trying to think things over and to define my position clearly to myself; I had not one word, one phrase, ready for my wife. My brain was not working.

But without thinking of anything, I went downstairs to my wife. She was in her room, in the same pink dressing-gown, and standing in the same attitude as though screening her papers from me. On her face was an expression of perplexity and irony, and it was evident that having heard of my arrival, she had prepared herself not to cry, not to entreat me, not to defend herself, as she had done the day before, but to laugh at me, to answer me contemptuously, and to act with decision. Her face was saying: " If that's how it is, good-bye."

" Natalie, I've not gone away," I said, " but it's not deception. I have gone out of my mind; I've grown old, I'm ill, I've become a different man — think as you like. . . . I've shaken off my old self with horror, with horror; I despise him and am ashamed of him, and the new man who has been in me since yesterday will not let me go away. Do not drive me away, Natalie ! "

She looked intently into my face and believed me, and there was a gleam of uneasiness in her eyes. Enchanted by her presence, warmed by the warmth of her room, I muttered as in delirium, holding out my hands to her:

" I tell you, I have no one near to me but you. I have never for one minute ceased to miss you, and only obstinate vanity prevented me from owning it. The past, when we lived as husband and wife, cannot be brought back, and there's no need; but make me your servant, take all my property, and give it away to any one you like. I am at peace, Natalie, I am content. . . . I am at peace."

My wife, looking intently and with curiosity into

my face, suddenly uttered a faint cry, burst into tears, and ran into the next room. I went upstairs to my own storey.

An hour later I was sitting at my table, writing my "History of Railways," and the starving peasants did not now hinder me from doing so. Now I feel no uneasiness. Neither the scenes of disorder which I saw when I went the round of the huts at Pestrovo with my wife and Sobol the other day, nor malignant rumours, nor the mistakes of the people around me, nor old age close upon me — nothing disturbs me. Just as the flying bullets do not hinder soldiers from talking of their own affairs, eating and cleaning their boots, so the starving peasants do not hinder me from sleeping quietly and looking after my personal affairs. In my house and far around it there is in full swing the work which Dr. Sobol calls "an orgy of philanthropy." My wife often comes up to me and looks about my rooms uneasily, as though looking for what more she can give to the starving peasants "to justify her existence," and I see that, thanks to her, there will soon be nothing of our property left and we shall be poor; but that does not trouble me, and I smile at her gaily. What will happen in the future I don't know.

1892

DIFFICULT PEOPLE

DIFFICULT PEOPLE

YEVGRAF IVANOVITCH SHIRYAEV, a small farmer, whose father, a parish priest, now deceased, had received a gift of three hundred acres of land from Madame Kuvshinnikov, a general's widow, was standing in a corner before a copper washing-stand, washing his hands. As usual, his face looked anxious and ill-humoured, and his beard was uncombed.

"What weather!" he said. "It's not weather, but a curse laid upon us. It's raining again!"

He grumbled on, while his family sat waiting at table for him to have finished washing his hands before beginning dinner. Fedosya Semyonovna, his wife, his son Pyotr, a student, his eldest daughter Varvara, and three small boys, had been sitting waiting a long time. The boys — Kolka, Vanka, and Arhipka — grubby, snub-nosed little fellows with chubby faces and tousled hair that wanted cutting, moved their chairs impatiently, while their elders sat without stirring, and apparently did not care whether they ate their dinner or waited. . . .

As though trying their patience, Shiryaev deliberately dried his hands, deliberately said his prayer, and sat down to the table without hurrying himself. Cabbage-soup was served immediately. The sound of carpenters' axes (Shiryaev was having a new barn built) and the laughter of Fomka, their labourer, teasing the turkey, floated in from the courtyard.

Big, sparse drops of rain pattered on the window.

Pyotr, a round-shouldered student in spectacles, kept exchanging glances with his mother as he ate his dinner. Several times he laid down his spoon and cleared his throat, meaning to begin to speak, but after an intent look at his father he fell to eating again. At last, when the porridge had been served, he cleared his throat resolutely and said:

"I ought to go tonight by the evening train. I out to have gone before; I have missed a fortnight as it is. The lectures begin on the first of September."

"Well, go," Shiryaev assented; "why are you lingering on here? Pack up and go, and good luck to you."

A minute passed in silence.

"He must have money for the journey, Yevgraf Ivanovitch," the mother observed in a low voice.

"Money? To be sure, you can't go without money. Take it at once, since you need it. You could have had it long ago!"

The student heaved a faint sigh and looked with relief at his mother. Deliberately Shiryaev took a pocket-book out of his coat-pocket and put on his spectacles.

"How much do you want?" he asked.

"The fare to Moscow is eleven roubles forty-two kopecks. . . ."

"Ah, money, money!" sighed the father. (He always sighed when he saw money, even when he

was receiving it.)   " Here are twelve roubles for
you.   You will have change out of that which will
be of use to you on the journey."

" Thank you."

After waiting a little, the student said:

" I did not get lessons quite at first last year.   I
don't know how it will be this year; most likely it
will take me a little time to find work.   I ought
to ask you for fifteen roubles for my lodging and
dinner."

Shiryaev thought a little and heaved a sigh.

" You will have to make ten do," he said.
" Here, take it."

The student thanked him.   He ought to have
asked him for something more, for clothes, for lecture fees, for books, but after an intent look at his
father he decided not to pester him further.

The mother, lacking in diplomacy and prudence,
like all mothers, could not restrain herself, and said:

" You ought to give him another six roubles, Yevgraf Ivanovitch, for a pair of boots.   Why, just
see, how can he go to Moscow in such wrecks ? "

" Let him take my old ones; they are still quite
good."

" He must have trousers, anyway; he is a disgrace
to look at."

And immediately after that a storm-signal showed
itself, at the sight of which all the family trembled.

Shiryaev's short, fat neck turned suddenly red as
a beetroot.   The colour mounted slowly to his ears,
from his ears to his temples, and by degrees suffused
his whole face.   Yevgraf Ivanovitch shifted in his

chair and unbuttoned his shirt-collar to save himself from choking. He was evidently struggling with the feeling that was mastering him. A deathlike silence followed. The children held their breath. Fedosya Semyonovna, as though she did not grasp what was happening to her husband, went on:

"He is not a little boy now, you know; he is ashamed to go about without clothes."

Shiryaev suddenly jumped up, and with all his might flung down his fat pocket-book in the middle of the table, so that a hunk of bread flew off a plate. A revolting expression of anger, resentment, avarice — all mixed together — flamed on his face.

"Take everything!" he shouted in an unnatural voice; "plunder me! Take it all! Strangle me!"

He jumped up from the table, clutched at his head, and ran staggering about the room.

"Strip me to the last thread!" he shouted in a shrill voice. "Squeeze out the last drop! Rob me! Wring my neck!"

The student flushed and dropped his eyes. He could not go on eating. Fedosya Semyonovna, who had not after twenty-five years grown used to her husband's difficult character, shrank into herself and muttered something in self-defence. An expression of amazement and dull terror came into her wasted and birdlike face, which at all times looked dull and scared. The little boys and the elder daughter Varvara, a girl in her teens, with a pale ugly face, laid down their spoons and sat mute.

Shiryaev, growing more and more ferocious, uttering words each more terrible than the one before, dashed up to the table and began shaking the notes out of his pocket-book.

"Take them!" he muttered, shaking all over. "You've eaten and drunk your fill, so here's money for you too! I need nothing! Order yourself new boots and uniforms!"

The student turned pale and got up.

"Listen, papa," he began, gasping for breath. "I . . . I beg you to end this, for . . ."

"Hold your tongue!" the father shouted at him, and so loudly that the spectacles fell off his nose; "hold your tongue!"

"I used . . . I used to be able to put up with such scenes, but . . . but now I have got out of the way of it. Do you understand? I have got out of the way of it!"

"Hold your tongue!" cried the father, and he stamped with his feet. "You must listen to what I say! I shall say what I like, and you hold your tongue. At your age I was earning my living, while you . . . Do you know what you cost me, you scoundrel? I'll turn you out! Wastrel!"

"Yevgraf Ivanovitch," muttered Fedosya Semyonovna, moving her fingers nervously; "you know he . . . you know Petya . . . !"

"Hold your tongue!" Shiryaev shouted out to her, and tears actually came into his eyes from anger. "It is you who have spoilt them — you! It's all your fault! He has no respect for us, does not say his prayers, and earns nothing! I am only one against the ten of you! I'll turn you out of the house!"

The daughter Varvara gazed fixedly at her mother with her mouth open, moved her vacant-looking eyes to the window, turned pale, and, uttering a loud shriek, fell back in her chair. The father, with a curse and a wave of the hand, ran out into the yard.

This was how domestic scenes usually ended at the Shiryaevs'. But on this occasion, unfortunately, Pyotr the student was carried away by overmastering anger. He was just as hasty and ill-tempered as his father and his grandfather the priest, who used to beat his parishioners about the head with a stick. Pale and clenching his fists, he went up to his mother and shouted in the very highest tenor note his voice could reach:

"These reproaches are loathsome! sickening to me! I want nothing from you! Nothing! I would rather die of hunger than eat another mouthful at your expense! Take your nasty money back! take it!"

The mother huddled against the wall and waved her hands, as though it were not her son, but some phantom before her.

"What have I done?" she wailed. "What?"

Like his father, the boy waved his hands and ran into the yard. Shiryaev's house stood alone on a ravine which ran like a furrow for four miles along the steppe. Its sides were overgrown with oak saplings and alders, and a stream ran at the bottom. On one side the house looked towards the ravine, on the other towards the open country, there were no fences nor hurdles. Instead there were farm-build-

ings of all sorts close to one another, shutting in a
small space in front of the house which was regarded
as the yard, and in which hens, ducks, and pigs ran
about.

Going out of the house, the student walked along
the muddy road towards the open country. The air
was full of a penetrating autumn dampness. The
road was muddy, puddles gleamed here and there,
and in the yellow fields autumn itself seemed looking
out from the grass, dismal, decaying, dark. On the
right-hand side of the road was a vegetable-garden
cleared of its crops and gloomy-looking, with here
and there sunflowers standing up in it with hanging
heads already black.

Pyotr thought it would not be a bad thing to walk
to Moscow on foot; to walk just as he was, with
holes in his boots, without a cap, and without a
farthing of money. When he had gone eighty miles
his father, frightened and aghast, would overtake
him, would begin begging him to turn back or take
the money, but he would not even look at him, but
would go on and on. . . . Bare forests would be
followed by desolate fields, fields by forests again;
soon the earth would be white with the first snow,
and the streams would be coated with ice. . . .
Somewhere near Kursk or near Serpuhovo, exhausted and dying of hunger, he would sink down
and die. His corpse would be found, and there
would be a paragraph in all the papers saying that
a student called Shiryaev had died of hunger. . . .

A white dog with a muddy tail who was wandering about the vegetable-garden looking for some-

thing gazed at him and sauntered after him. . . .

He walked along the road and thought of death, of the grief of his family, of the moral sufferings of his father, and then pictured all sorts of adventures 'on the road, each more marvellous than the one before — picturesque places, terrible nights, chance encounters. He imagined a string of pilgrims, a hut in the forest with one little window shining in the darkness; he stands before the window, begs for a night's lodging. . . . They let him in, and suddenly he sees that they are robbers. Or, better still, he is taken into a big manor-house, where, learning who he is, they give him food and drink, play to him on the piano, listen to his complaints, and the daughter of the house, a beauty, falls in love with him.

Absorbed in his bitterness and such thoughts, young Shiryaev walked on and on. Far, far ahead he saw the inn, a dark patch against the grey background of cloud. Beyond the inn, on the very horizon, he could see a little hillock; this was the railway-station. That hillock reminded him of the connection existing between the place where he was now standing and Moscow, where street-lamps were burning and carriages were rattling in the streets, where lectures were being given. And he almost wept with depression and impatience. The solemn landscape, with its order and beauty, the deathlike stillness all around, revolted him and moved him to despair and hatred!

"Look out!" He heard behind him a loud voice.

An old lady of his acquaintance, a landowner of

the neighbourhood, drove past him in a light, elegant landau. He bowed to her, and smiled all over his face. And at once he caught himself in that smile, which was so out of keeping with his gloomy mood. Where did it come from if his whole heart was full of vexation and misery? And he thought nature itself had given man this capacity for lying, that even in difficult moments of spiritual strain he might be able to hide the secrets of his nest as the fox and the wild duck do. Every family has its joys and its horrors, but however great they may be, it's hard for an outsider's eye to see them; they are a secret. The father of the old lady who had just driven by, for instance, had for some offence lain for half his lifetime under the ban of the wrath of Tsar Nicolas I.; her husband had been a gambler; of her four sons, not one had turned out well. One could imagine how many terrible scenes there must have been in her life, how many tears must have been shed. And yet the old lady seemed happy and satisfied, and she had answered his smile by smiling too. The student thought of his comrades, who did not like talking about their families; he thought of his mother, who almost always lied when she had to speak of her husband and children. . . .

Pyotr walked about the roads far from home till dusk, abandoning himself to dreary thoughts. When it began to drizzle with rain he turned homewards. As he walked back he made up his mind at all costs to talk to his father, to explain to him, once and for all, that it was dreadful and oppressive to live with him.

He found perfect stillness in the house. His sister Varvara was lying behind a screen with a headache, moaning faintly. His mother, with a look of amazement and guilt upon her face, was sitting beside her on a box, mending Arhipka's trousers. Yevgraf Ivanovitch was pacing from one window to another, scowling at the weather. From his walk, from the way he cleared his throat, and even from the back of his head, it was evident he felt himself to blame.

" I suppose you have changed your mind about going today? " he asked.

The student felt sorry for him, but immediately suppressing that feeling, he said:

" Listen . . . I must speak to you seriously . . . yes, seriously. I have always respected you, and . . . and have never brought myself to speak to you in such a tone, but your behaviour . . . your last action . . ."

The father looked out of the window and did not speak. The student, as though considering his words, rubbed his forehead and went on in great excitement:

" Not a dinner or tea passes without your making an uproar. Your bread sticks in our throat . . . nothing is more bitter, more humiliating, than bread that sticks in one's throat. . . . Though you are my father, no one, neither God nor nature, has given you the right to insult and humiliate us so horribly, to vent your ill-humour on the weak. You have worn my mother out and made a slave of her, my sister is hopelessly crushed, while I . . ."

" It's not your business to teach me," said his father.

" Yes, it is my business! You can quarrel with me as much as you like, but leave my mother in peace! I will not allow you to torment my mother! " the student went on, with flashing eyes. " You are spoilt because no one has yet dared to oppose you. They tremble and are mute towards you, but now that is over! Coarse, ill-bred man! You are coarse . . . do you understand? You are coarse, ill-humoured, unfeeling. And the peasants can't endure you! "

The student had by now lost his thread, and was not so much speaking as firing off detached words. Yevgraf Ivanovitch listened in silence, as though stunned; but suddenly his neck turned crimson, the colour crept up his face, and he made a movement.

" Hold your tongue! " he shouted.

" That's right! " the son persisted; " you don't like to hear the truth! Excellent! Very good! begin shouting! Excellent! "

" Hold your tongue, I tell you! " roared Yevgraf Ivanovitch.

Fedosya Semyonovna appeared in the doorway, very pale, with an astonished face; she tried to say something, but she could not, and could only move her fingers.

" It's all your fault! " Shiryaev shouted at her. " You have brought him up like this! "

" I don't want to go on living in this house!" shouted the student, crying, and looking angrily at his mother. " I don't want to live with you! "

Varvara uttered a shriek behind the screen and broke into loud sobs. With a wave of his hand, Shiryaev ran out of the house.

The student went to his own room and quietly lay down. He lay till midnight without moving or opening his eyes. He felt neither anger nor shame, but a vague ache in his soul. He neither blamed his father nor pitied his mother, nor was he tormented by stings of conscience; he realized that every one in the house was feeling the same ache, and God only knew which was most to blame, which was suffering most. . . .

At midnight he woke the labourer, and told him to have the horse ready at five o'clock in the morning for him to drive to the station; he undressed and got into bed, but could not get to sleep. He heard how his father, still awake, paced slowly from window to window, sighing, till early morning. No one was asleep; they spoke rarely, and only in whispers. Twice his mother came to him behind the screen. Always with the same look of vacant wonder, she slowly made the cross over him, shaking nervously.

At five o'clock in the morning he said good-bye to them all affectionately, and even shed tears. As he passed his father's room, he glanced in at the door. Yevgraf Ivanovitch, who had not taken off his clothes or gone to bed, was standing by the window, drumming on the panes.

" Good-bye; I am going," said his son.

" Good-bye . . . the money is on the round table . . ." his father answered, without turning round.

A cold, hateful rain was falling as the labourer drove him to the station. The sunflowers were drooping their heads still lower, and the grass seemed darker than ever.

1886

THE GRASSHOPPER

THE GRASSHOPPER

I

ALL Olga Ivanovna's friends and acquaintances were at her wedding.

" Look at him; isn't it true that there is something in him? " she said to her friends, with a nod towards her husband, as though she wanted to explain why she was marrying a simple, very ordinary, and in no way remarkable man.

Her husband, Osip Stepanitch Dymov, was a doctor, and only of the rank of a titular councillor. He was on the staff of two hospitals: in one a ward-surgeon and in the other a dissecting demonstrator. Every day from nine to twelve he saw patients and was busy in his ward, and after twelve o'clock he went by tram to the other hospital, where he dissected. His private practice was a small one, not worth more than five hundred roubles a year. That was all. What more could one say about him? Meanwhile, Olga Ivanovna and her friends and acquaintances were not quite ordinary people. Every one of them was remarkable in some way, and more or less famous; already had made a reputation and was looked upon as a celebrity; or if not yet a celebrity, gave brilliant promise of becoming one. There was an actor from the Dramatic Theatre, who was a great talent of established reputation, as well as an elegant, intelligent, and modest man, and a capital elocutionist, and who taught Olga Ivanovna to recite; there was a singer from the opera, a good-natured, fat man who assured Olga Ivanovna, with a sigh, that she was ruining herself, that if she would take herself in hand and not be lazy she might make a remarkable singer; then there were several artists, and chief among them Ryabovsky, a very handsome, fair young man of five-and-twenty who painted genre pieces, animal studies, and landscapes, was successful at exhibitions, and had sold his last picture for five hundred roubles. He touched up Olga Ivanovna's sketches, and used to say she might do something. Then a violoncellist, whose instrument used to sob, and who openly declared that of all the ladies of his acquaintance the only one who could accompany him was Olga Ivanovna; then there was a literary man, young but already well known, who had written stories, novels, and plays. Who else? Why, Vassily Vassilyitch, a landowner and amateur illustrator and vignettist, with a great feeling for the old Russian style, the old ballad and epic. On paper, on china, and on smoked plates, he produced literally marvels. In the midst of this free artistic company, spoiled by fortune, though refined and modest, who recalled the existence of doctors only in times of illness, and to whom the name of Dymov sounded in no way different from Sidorov or Tarasov — in the midst of this company Dymov seemed strange, not wanted, and small, though he was tall and broad-shouldered. He looked as though he had on somebody else's coat, and his beard was like a shopman's. Though if he had been a writer or an artist, they would have said that his beard reminded them of Zola.

An artist said to Olga Ivanovna that with her flaxen hair and in her wedding-dress she was very much like a graceful cherry-tree when it is covered all over with delicate white blossoms in spring.

" Oh, let me tell you," said Olga Ivanovna, taking his arm, " how it was it all came to pass so suddenly. Listen, listen! . . . I must tell you that my father was on the same staff at the hospital as Dymov. When my poor father was taken ill, Dymov watched for days and nights together at his bedside. Such self-sacrifice! Listen, Ryabovsky! You, my writer, listen; it is very interesting! Come nearer. Such self-sacrifice, such genuine sympathy! I sat up with my father, and did not sleep for nights, either. And all at once — the princess had won the hero's heart — my Dymov fell head over ears in love. Really, fate is so strange at times! Well, after my father's death he came to see me sometimes, met me in the street, and one fine evening, all at once he made me an offer . . . like snow upon my head. . . . I lay awake all night, crying, and fell hellishly in love myself. And here, as you see, I am his wife. There really is something strong, powerful, bearlike about him, isn't there? Now his face is turned three-quarters towards us in a bad light, but when he turns round look at his forehead. Ryabovsky, what do you say to that forehead? Dymov, we are talking about you! " she called to her husband. " Come

here; hold out your honest hand to Ryabovsky. . . .
That's right, be friends."

Dymov, with a naïve and good-natured smile, held
out his hand to Ryabovsky, and said:

" Very glad to meet you. There was a Ryabovsky in my year at the medical school. Was he a
relation of yours? "

II

Olga Ivanovna was twenty-two, Dymov was
thirty-one. They got on splendidly together when
they were married. Olga Ivanovna hung all her
drawing-room walls with her own and other people's
sketches, in frames and without frames, and near the
piano and furniture arranged picturesque corners
with Japanese parasols, easels, daggers, busts, photographs, and rags of many colours. . . . In the dining-room she papered the walls with peasant wood-
cuts, hung up bark shoes and sickles, stood in a corner a scythe and a rake, and so achieved a dining-
room in the Russian style. In her bedroom she
draped the ceiling and the walls with dark cloths to
make it like a cavern, hung a Venetian lantern over
the beds, and at the door set a figure with a halberd.
And every one thought that the young people had a
very charming little home.

When she got up at eleven o'clock every morning,
Olga Ivanovna played the piano or, if it were sunny,
painted something in oils. Then between twelve and
one she drove to her dressmaker's. As Dymov and
she had very little money, only just enough, she and

her dressmaker were often put to clever shifts to
enable her to appear constantly in new dresses and
make a sensation with them. Very often out of an
old dyed dress, out of bits of tulle, lace, plush, and
silk, costing nothing, perfect marvels were created,
something bewitching — not a dress, but a dream.
From the dressmaker's Olga Ivanovna usually drove
to some actress of her acquaintance to hear the latest
theatrical gossip, and incidentally to try and get hold
of tickets for the first night of some new play or for
a benefit performance. From the actress's she had
to go to some artist's studio or to some exhibition or
to see some celebrity — either to pay a visit or to
give an invitation or simply to have a chat. And
everywhere she met with a gay and friendly welcome, and was assured that she was good, that she
was sweet, that she was rare. . . . Those whom she
called great and famous received her as one of
themselves, as an equal, and predicted with one
voice that, with her talents, her taste, and her intelligence, she would do great things if she concentrated
herself. She sang, she played the piano, she painted
in oils, she carved, she took part in amateur per-
formances; and all this not just anyhow, but all with
talent, whether she made lanterns for an illumination
or dressed up or tied somebody's cravat — everything she did was exceptionally graceful, artistic, and
charming. But her talents showed themselves in
nothing so clearly as in her faculty for quickly becoming acquainted and on intimate terms with celebrated people. No sooner did any one become ever
so little celebrated, and set people talking about him,

than she made his acquaintance, got on friendly terms the same day, and invited him to her house. Every new acquaintance she made was a veritable fête for her. She adored celebrated people, was proud of them, dreamed of them every night. She craved for them, and never could satisfy her craving. The old ones departed and were forgotten, new ones came to replace them, but to these, too, she soon grew accustomed or was disappointed in them, and began eagerly seeking for fresh great men, finding them and seeking for them again. What for?

Between four and five she dined at home with her husband. His simplicity, good sense, and kind-heartedness touched her and moved her up to enthusiasm. She was constantly jumping up, impulsively hugging his head and showering kisses on it.

" You are a clever, generous man, Dymov," she used to say, " but you have one very serious defect. You take absolutely no interest in art. You don't believe in music or painting."

" I don't understand them," he would say mildly. " I have spent all my life in working at natural science and medicine, and I have never had time to take an interest in the arts."

" But, you know, that's awful, Dymov ! "

" Why so ? Your friends don't know anything of science or medicine, but you don't reproach them with it. Every one has his own line. I don't understand landscapes and operas, but the way I look at it is that if one set of sensible people devote their whole lives to them, and other sensible people pay immense sums for them, they must be of use. I don't understand them, but not understanding does not imply disbelieving in them."

" Let me shake your honest hand! "

After dinner Olga Ivanovna would drive off to see her friends, then to a theatre or to a concert, and she returned home after midnight. So it was every day.

On Wednesdays she had " At Homes." At these " At Homes " the hostess and her guests did not play cards and did not dance, but entertained themselves with various arts. An actor from the Dramatic Theatre recited, a singer sang, artists sketched in the albums of which Olga Ivanovna had a great number, the violoncellist played, and the hostess herself sketched, carved, sang, and played accompaniments. In the intervals between the recitations, music, and singing, they talked and argued about literature, the theatre, and painting. There were no ladies, for Olga Ivanovna considered all ladies wearisome and vulgar except actresses and her dressmaker. Not one of these entertainments passed without the hostess starting at every ring at the bell, and saying, with a triumphant expression, " It is he," meaning by " he," of course, some new celebrity. Dymov was not in the drawing-room, and no one remembered his existence. But exactly at half-past eleven the door leading into the dining-room opened, and Dymov would appear with his good-natured, gentle smile and say, rubbing his hands:

" Come to supper, gentlemen."

They all went into the dining-room, and every

time found on the table exactly the same things: a dish of oysters, a piece of ham or veal, sardines, cheese, caviare, mushrooms, vodka, and two decanters of wine.

" My dear *maître d' hôtel!* " Olga Ivanovna would say, clasping her hands with enthusiasm, " you are simply fascinating! My friends, look at his forehead! Dymov, turn your profile. Look! he has the face of a Bengal tiger and an expression as kind and sweet as a gazelle. Ah, the darling! "

The visitors ate, and, looking at Dymov, thought, " He really is a nice fellow "; but they soon forgot about him, and went on talking about the theatre, music, and painting.

The young people were happy, and their life flowed on without a hitch.

The third week of their honeymoon was spent, however, not quite happily — sadly, indeed. Dymov caught erysipelas in the hospital, was in bed for six days, and had to have his beautiful black hair cropped. Olga Ivanovna sat beside him and wept bitterly, but when he was better she put a white handkerchief on his shaven head and began to paint him as a Bedouin. And they were both in good spirits. Three days after he had begun to go back to the hospital he had another mischance.

" I have no luck, little mother," he said one day at dinner. " I had four dissections to do today, and I cut two of my fingers at one. And I did not notice it till I got home."

Olga Ivanovna was alarmed. He smiled, and

told her that it did not matter, and that he often cut his hands when he was dissecting.

" I get absorbed, little mother, and grow careless."

Olga Ivanovna dreaded symptoms of blood-poisoning, and prayed about it every night, but all went well. And again life flowed on peaceful and happy, free from grief and anxiety. The present was happy, and to follow it spring was at hand, already smiling in the distance, and promising a thousand delights. There would be no end to their happiness. In April, May and June a summer villa a good distance out of town; walks, sketching, fishing, nightingales; and then from July right on to autumn an artist's tour on the Volga, and in this tour Olga Ivanovna would take part as an indispensable member of the society. She had already had made for her two travelling dresses of linen, had bought paints, brushes, canvases, and a new palette for the journey. Almost every day Ryabovsky visited her to see what progress she was making in her painting; when she showed him her painting, he used to thrust his hands deep into his pockets, compress his lips, sniff, and say:

" Ye—es . . . ! That cloud of yours is screaming: it's not in the evening light. The foreground is somehow chewed up, and there is something, you know, not the thing. . . . And your cottage is weighed down and whines pitifully. That corner ought to have been taken more in shadow, but on the whole it is not bad; I like it."

And the more incomprehensible he talked, the more readily Olga Ivanovna understood him.

III

After dinner on the second day of Trinity week, Dymov bought some sweets and some savouries and went down to the villa to see his wife. He had not seen her for a fortnight, and missed her terribly. As he sat in the train and afterwards as he looked for his villa in a big wood, he felt all the while hungry and weary, and dreamed of how he would have supper in freedom with his wife, then tumble into bed and to sleep. And he was delighted as he looked at his parcel, in which there was caviare, cheese, and white salmon.

The sun was setting by the time he found his villa and recognized it. The old servant told him that her mistress was not at home, but that most likely she would soon be in. The villa, very uninviting in appearance, with low ceilings papered with writing-paper and with uneven floors full of crevices, consisted only of three rooms. In one there was a bed, in the second there were canvases, brushes, greasy papers, and men's overcoats and hats lying about on the chairs and in the windows, while in the third Dymov found three unknown men; two were dark-haired and had beards, the other was clean-shaven and fat, apparently an actor. There was a samovar boiling on the table.

"What do you want? " asked the actor in a bass voice, looking at Dymov ungraciously. " Do you want Olga Ivanovna? Wait a minute; she will be here directly."

Dymov sat down and waited. One of the dark-haired men, looking sleepily and listlessly at him, poured himself out a glass of tea, and asked:

" Perhaps you would like some tea? "

Dymov was both hungry and thirsty, but he refused tea for fear of spoiling his supper. Soon he heard footsteps and a familiar laugh; a door slammed, and Olga Ivanovna ran into the room, wearing a wide-brimmed hat and carrying a box in her hand; she was followed by Ryabovsky, rosy and good-humoured, carrying a big umbrella and a camp-stool.

" Dymov! " cried Olga Ivanovna, and she flushed crimson with pleasure. " Dymov! " she repeated, laying her head and both arms on his bosom. " Is that you? Why haven't you come for so long? Why? Why? "

" When could I, little mother? I am always busy, and whenever I am free it always happens somehow that the train does not fit."

" But how glad I am to see you! I have been dreaming about you the whole night, the whole night, and I was afraid you must be ill. Ah! if you only knew how sweet you are! You have come in the nick of time! You will be my salvation! You are the only person who can save me! There is to be a most original wedding here tomorrow," she went on, laughing, and tying her husband's cravat. " A young telegraph clerk at the station, called Tchikeld-yeev, is going to be married. He is a handsome

young man and — well, not stupid, and you know
there is something strong, bearlike in his face . . .
you might paint him as a young Norman. We summer vistors take a great interest in him, and have
promised to be at his wedding. . . . He is a lonely,
timid man, not well off, and of course it would be a
shame not to be sympathetic to him. Fancy! the
wedding will be after the service; then we shall all
walk from the church to the bride's lodgings . . .
you see the wood, the birds singing, patches of sun-
light on the grass, and all of us spots of different
colours against the bright green background — very
original, in the style of the French impressionists.
But, Dymov, what am I to go to the church in? "
said Olga Ivanovna, and she looked as though she
were going to cry. " I have nothing here, literally
nothing! no dress, no flowers, no gloves . . . you
must save me. Since you have come, fate itself bids
you save me. Take the keys, my precious, go home
and get my pink dress from the wardrobe. You remember it; it hangs in front. . . . Then, in the
storeroom, on the floor, on the right side, you will
see two cardboard boxes. When you open the top
one you will see tulle, heaps of tulle and rags of all
sorts, and under them flowers. Take out all the
flowers carefully, try not to crush them, darling; I
will choose among them later. . . . And buy me
some gloves."

"Very well," said Dymov; " I will go tomorrow
and send them to you."

"Tomorrow? " asked Olga Ivanovna, and she
looked at him surprised. " You won't have time to-

morrow. The first train goes tomorrow at nine, and the wedding's at eleven. No, darling, it must be today; it absolutely must be today. If you won't be able to come tomorrow, send them by a messenger. Come, you must run along. . . . The passenger train will be in directly; don't miss it, darling."

" Very well."

" Oh, how sorry I am to let you go ! " said Olga Ivanovna, and tears came into her eyes. " And why did I promise that telegraph clerk, like a silly ? "

Dymov hurriedly drank a glass of tea, took a cracknel, and, smiling gently, went to the station. And the caviare, the cheese, and the white salmon were eaten by the two dark gentlemen and the fat actor.

IV

On a still moonlight night in July Olga Ivanovna was standing on the deck of a Volga steamer and looking alternately at the water and at the picturesque banks. Beside her was standing Ryabovsky, telling her the black shadows on the water were not shadows, but a dream, that it would be sweet to sink into forgetfulness, to die, to become a memory in the sight of that enchanted water with the fantastic glimmer, in sight of the fathomless sky and the mournful, dreamy shores that told of the vanity of our life and of the existence of something higher, blessed, and eternal. The past was vulgar and uninteresting, the future was trivial, and that marvellous night, unique in a lifetime, would soon be over, would blend with eternity; then, why live?

And Olga Ivanovna listened alternately to Ryabovsky's voice and the silence of the night, and
thought of her being immortal and never dying.
The turquoise colour of the water, such as she had
never seen before, the sky, the river-banks, the black
shadows, and the unaccountable joy that flooded her
soul, all told her that she would make a great artist,
and that somewhere in the distance, in the infinite
space beyond the moonlight, success, glory, the love
of the people, lay awaiting her. . . . When she
gazed steadily without blinking into the distance,
she seemed to see crowds of people, lights, triumphant strains of music, cries of enthusiasm, she herself in a white dress, and flowers showered upon her
from all sides. She thought, too, that beside her,
leaning with his elbows on the rail of the steamer,
there was standing a real great man, a genius, one
of God's elect. . . . All that he had created up to
the present was fine, new, and extraordinary, but
what he would create in time, when with maturity his
rare talent reached its full development, would be
astounding, immeasurably sublime; and that could
be seen by his face, by his manner of expressing himself and his attitude to nature. He talked of shadows, of the tones of evening, of the moonlight, in a
special way, in a language of his own, so that one
could not help feeling the fascination of his power
over nature. He was very handsome, original, and
his life, free, independent, aloof from all common
cares, was like the life of a bird.

"It's growing cooler," said Olga Ivanovna, and
she gave a shudder.

Ryabovsky wrapped her in his cloak, and said mournfully:

" I feel that I am in your power; I am a slave. Why are you so enchanting today? "

He kept staring intently at her, and his eyes were terrible. And she was afraid to look at him.

" I love you madly," he whispered, breathing on her cheek. " Say one word to me and I will not go on living; I will give up art . . ." he muttered in violent emotion. " Love me, love . . ."

" Don't talk like that," said Olga Ivanovna, covering her eyes. " It's dreadful! How about Dymov? "

" What of Dymov? Why Dymov? What have I to do with Dymov? The Volga, the moon, beauty, my love, ecstasy, and there is no such thing as Dymov. . . . Ah! I don't know . . . I don't care about the past; give me one moment, one instant! "

Olga Ivanovna's heart began to throb. She tried to think about her husband, but all her past, with her wedding, with Dymov, and with her " At Homes," seemed to her petty, trivial, dingy, unnecessary, and far, far away. . . . Yes, really, what of Dymov? Why Dymov? What had she to do with Dymov? Had he any existence in nature, or was he only a dream?

" For him, a simple and ordinary man the happiness he has had already is enough," she thought, covering her face with her hands. " Let them condemn me, let them curse me, but in spite of them all I will go to my ruin; I will go to my ruin! . . . One must experience everything in life.   My God! how terrible and how glorious!"

"Well?   Well?" muttered the artist, embracing her, and greedily kissing the hands with which she feebly tried to thrust him from her.   "You love me? Yes? Yes? Oh, what a night! marvellous night!"

"Yes, what a night!" she whispered, looking into his eyes, which were bright with tears.

Then she looked round quickly, put her arms round him, and kissed him on the lips.

"We are nearing Kineshmo!" said some one on the other side of the deck.

They heard heavy footsteps; it was a waiter from the refreshment-bar.

"Waiter," said Olga Ivanovna, laughing and crying with happiness, "bring us some wine."

The artist, pale with emotion, sat on the seat, looking at Olga Ivanovna with adoring, grateful eyes; then he closed his eyes, and said, smiling languidly:

"I am tired."

And he leaned his head against the rail.

V

On the second of September the day was warm and still, but overcast.   In the early morning a light mist had hung over the Volga, and after nine o'clock it had begun to spout with rain.   And there seemed no hope of the sky clearing.   Over their morning tea Ryabovsky told Olga Ivanovna that painting was the

most ungrateful and boring art, that he was not an
artist, that none but fools thought that he had any
talent, and all at once, for no rhyme or reason, he
snatched up a knife and with it scraped over his very
best sketch. After his tea he sat plunged in gloom
at the window and gazed at the Volga. And now
the Volga was dingy, all of one even colour without
a gleam of light, cold-looking. Everything, everything recalled the approach of dreary, gloomy
autumn. And it seemed as though nature had removed now from the Volga the sumptuous green
covers from the banks, the brilliant reflections of the
sunbeams, the transparent blue distance, and all its
smart gala array, and had packed it away in boxes
till the coming spring, and the crows were flying
above the Volga and crying tauntingly, " Bare,
bare ! "

Ryabovsky heard their cawing, and thought he
had already gone off and lost his talent, that everything in this world was relative, conditional, and
stupid, and that he ought not to have taken up with
this woman. . . . In short, he was out of humour
and depressed.

Olga Ivanovna sat behind the screen on the bed,
and, passing her fingers through her lovely flaxen
hair, pictured herself first in the drawing-room, then
in the bedroom, then in her husband's study; her
imagination carried her to the theatre, to the dressmaker, to her distinguished friends. Were they
getting something up now ? Did they think of her ?
The season had begun by now, and it would be time
to think about her " At Homes." And Dymov ?

Dear Dymov! with what gentleness and childlike pathos he kept begging her in his letters to make haste and come home! Every month he sent her seventy-five roubles, and when she wrote him that she had lent the artists a hundred roubles, he sent that hundred too. What a kind, generous-hearted man! The travelling wearied Olga Ivanovna; she was bored; and she longed to get away from the peasants, from the damp smell of the river, and to cast off the feeling of physical uncleanliness of which she was conscious all the time, living in the peasants' huts and wandering from village to village. If Ryabovsky had not given his word to the artists that he would stay with them till the twentieth of September, they might have gone away that **very day**. And how nice that would have been!

"My God!" moaned Ryabovsky. "Will the sun ever come out? I can't go on with a sunny landscape without the sun. . . ."

"But you have a sketch with a cloudy sky," said Olga Ivanovna, coming from behind the screen. "Do you remember, in the right foreground forest trees, on the left a herd of cows and geese? You might finish it now."

"Aie!" the artist scowled. "Finish it! Can you imagine I am such a fool that I don't know what I want to do?"

"How you have changed to me!" sighed Olga Ivanovna.

"Well, a good thing too!"

Olga Ivanovna's face quivered; she moved away to the stove and began to cry.

" Well, that's the last straw — crying! Give
over! I have a thousand reasons for tears, but I
am not crying."

" A thousand reasons!" cried Olga Ivanovna.
" The chief one is that you are weary of me. Yes!"
she said, and broke into sobs. " If one is to tell the
truth, you are ashamed of our love. You keep trying to prevent the artists from noticing it, though it
is impossible to conceal it, and they have known all
about it for ever so long."

" Olga, one thing I beg you," said the artist in an
imploring voice, laying his hand on his heart —" one
thing; don't worry me! I want nothing else from
you!"

" But swear that you love me still!"

" This is agony!" the artist hissed through his
teeth, and he jumped up. " It will end by my throwing myself in the Volga or going out of my mind!
Let me alone!"

" Come, kill me, kill me!" cried Olga Ivanovna.
" Kill me!"

She sobbed again, and went behind the screen.
There was a swish of rain on the straw thatch of
the hut. Ryabovsky clutched his head and strode
up and down the hut; then with a resolute face, as
though bent on proving something to somebody, put
on his cap, slung his gun over his shoulder, and went
out of the hut.

After he had gone, Olga Ivanovna lay a long time
on the bed, crying. At first she thought it would be
a good thing to poison herself, so that when Ryabovsky came back he would find her dead; then her

imagination carried her to her drawing-room, to her husband's study, and she imagined herself sitting motionless beside Dymov and enjoying the physical peace and cleanliness, and in the evening sitting in the theatre, listening to Mazini. And a yearning for civilization, for the noise and bustle of the town, for celebrated people sent a pang to her heart. A peasant woman came into the hut and began in a leisurely way lighting the stove to get the dinner. There was a smell of charcoal fumes, and the air was filled with bluish smoke. The artists came in, in muddy high boots and with faces wet with rain, examined their sketches, and comforted themselves by saying that the Volga had its charms even in bad weather. On the wall the cheap clock went " tic-tic-tic." . . . The flies, feeling chilled, crowded round the ikon in the corner, buzzing, and one could hear the cockroaches scurrying about among the thick portfolios under the seats. . . .

Ryabovsky came home as the sun was setting. He flung his cap on the table, and, without removing his muddy boots, sank pale and exhausted on the bench and closed his eyes.

" I am tired . . ." he said, and twitched his eyebrows, trying to raise his eyelids.

To be nice to him and to show she was not cross, Olga Ivanovna went up to him, gave him a silent kiss, and passed the comb through his fair hair. She meant to comb it for him.

" What's that? " he said, starting as though something cold had touched him, and he opened his eyes. " What is it? Please let me alone."

He thrust her off, and moved away. And it seemed to her that there was a look of aversion and annoyance on his face.

At that time the peasant woman cautiously carried him, in both hands, a plate of cabbage-soup. And Olga Ivanovna saw how she wetted her fat fingers in it. And the dirty peasant woman, standing with her body thrust forward, and the cabbage-soup which Ryabovsky began eating greedily, and the hut, and their whole way of life, which she at first had so loved for its simplicity and artistic disorder, seemed horrible to her now. She suddenly felt insulted, and said coldly:

" We must part for a time, or else from boredom we shall quarrel in earnest. I am sick of this; I am going today."

" Going how? Astride on a broomstick? "

" Today is Thursday, so the steamer will be here at half-past nine."

" Eh? Yes, yes. . . . Well, go, then . . ." Ryabovsky said softly, wiping his mouth with a towel instead of a dinner napkin. " You are dull and have nothing to do here, and one would have to be a great egoist to try and keep you. Go home, and we shall meet again after the twentieth."

Olga Ivanovna packed in good spirits. Her cheeks positively glowed with pleasure. Could it really be true, she asked herself, that she would soon be writing in her drawing-room and sleeping in her bedroom, and dining with a cloth on the table? A weight was lifted from her heart, and she no longer felt angry with the artist.

" My paints and brushes I will leave with you, Ryabovsky," she said. " You can bring what's left. . . . Mind, now, don't be lazy here when I am gone; don't mope, but work. You are such a splendid fellow, Ryabovsky ! "

At ten o'clock Ryabovsky gave her a farewell kiss, in order, as she thought, to avoid kissing her on the steamer before the artists, and went with her to the landing-stage. The steamer soon came up and carried her away.

She arrived home two and a half days later. Breathless with excitement, she went, without taking off her hat or waterproof, into the drawing-room and thence into the dining-room. Dymov, with his waistcoat unbuttoned and no coat, was sitting at the table sharpening a knife on a fork; before him lay a grouse on a plate. As Olga Ivanovna went into the flat she was convinced that it was essential to hide everything from her husband, and that she would have the strength and skill to do so; but now, when she saw his broad, mild, happy smile, and shining, joyful eyes, she felt that to deceive this man was as vile, as revolting, and as impossible and out of her power as to bear false witness, to steal, or to kill, and in a flash she resolved to tell him all that had happened. Letting him kiss and embrace her, she sank down on her knees before him and hid her face.

" What is it, what is it, little mother ? " he asked tenderly. " Were you homesick ? "

She raised her face, red with shame, and gazed at him with a guilty and imploring look, but fear

and shame prevented her from telling him the truth.
" Nothing," she said; " it's just nothing. . . ."
" Let us sit down," he said, raising her and seat-
ing her at the table. " That's right, eat the grouse.
You are starving, poor darling."
She eagerly breathed in the atmosphere of home
and ate the grouse, while he watched her with ten-
derness and laughed with delight.

VI

Apparently, by the middle of the winter Dymov
began to suspect that he was being deceived. As
though his conscience was not clear, he could not
look his wife straight in the face, did not smile with
delight when he met her, and to avoid being left
alone with her, he often brought in to dinner his
colleague, Korostelev, a little close-cropped man
with a wrinkled face, who kept buttoning and unbuttoning his reefer jacket with embarrassment when
he talked with Olga Ivanovna, and then with his
right hand nipped his left moustache. At dinner
the two doctors talked about the fact that a displace-
ment of the diaphragm was sometimes accompanied
by irregularities of the heart, or that a great number of neurotic complaints were met with of late, or
that Dymov had the day before found a cancer of
the lower abdomen while dissecting a corpse with
the diagnosis of pernicious anaemia. And it seemed
as though they were talking of medicine to give
Olga Ivanovna a chance of being silent — that is,
of not lying. After dinner Korostelev sat down to

the piano, while Dymov sighed and said to him:
" Ech, brother — well, well! Play something
melancholy."

Hunching up his shoulders and stretching his
fingers wide apart, Korostelev played some chords
and began singing in a tenor voice, " Show me the
abode where the Russian peasant would not groan,"
while Dymov sighed once more, propped his head
on his fist, and sank into thought.

Olga Ivanovna had been extremely imprudent in
her conduct of late.   Every morning she woke up
in a very bad humour and with the thought that she
no longer cared for Ryabovsky, and that, thank God,
it was all over now.   But as she drank her coffee
she reflected that Ryabovsky had robbed her of her
husband, and that now she was left with neither
her husband nor Ryabovsky; then she remembered
talks she had heard among her acquaintances of a
picture Ryabovsky was preparing for the exhibition,
something striking, a mixture of genre and landscape, in the style of Polyenov, about which every
one who had been into his studio went into raptures;
and this, of course, she mused, he had created under
her influence, and altogether, thanks to her influence,
he had greatly changed for the better.   Her influence was so beneficent and essential that if she were
to leave him he might perhaps go to ruin.   And she
remembered, too, that the last time he had come to
see her in a great-coat with flecks on it and a new
tie, he had asked her languidly:

" Am I beautiful? "

And with his elegance, his long curls, and his blue

eyes, he really was very beautiful (or perhaps it only seemed so), and he had been affectionate to her.

Considering and remembering many things Olga Ivanovna dressed and in great agitation drove to Ryabovsky's studio. She found him in high spirits, and enchanted with his really magnificent picture. He was dancing about and playing the fool and answering serious questions with jokes. Olga Ivanovna was jealous of the picture and hated it, but from politeness she stood before the picture for five minutes in silence, and, heaving a sigh, as though before a holy shrine, said softly:

" Yes, you have never painted anything like it before. Do you know, it is positively awe-inspiring? "

And then she began beseeching him to love her and not to cast her off, to have pity on her in her misery and her wretchedness. She shed tears, kissed his hands, insisted on his swearing that he loved her, told him that without her good influence he would go astray and be ruined. And, when she had spoilt his good-humour, feeling herself humiliated, she would drive off to her dressmaker or to an actress of her acquaintance to try and get theatre tickets.

If she did not find him at his studio she left a letter in which she swore that if he did not come to see her that day she would poison herself. He was scared, came to see her, and stayed to dinner. Regardless of her husband's presence, he would say rude things to her, and she would answer him in the same way. Both felt they were a burden to each other, that they were tyrants and enemies, and were wrathful, and in their wrath did not notice that their behaviour was unseemly, and that even Korostelev, with his close-cropped head, saw it all. After dinner Ryabovsky made haste to say good-bye and get away.

" Where are you off to? " Olga Ivanovna would ask him in the hall, looking at him with hatred.

Scowling and screwing up his eyes, he mentioned some lady of their acquaintance, and it was evident that he was laughing at her jealousy and wanted to annoy her. She went to her bedroom and lay down on her bed; from jealousy, anger, a sense of humiliation and shame, she bit the pillow and began sobbing aloud. Dymov left Korostelev in the drawing-room, went into the bedroom, and with a desperate and embarrassed face said softly:

" Don't cry so loud, little mother; there's no need. You must be quiet about it. You must not let people see. . . . You know what is done is done, and can't be mended."

Not knowing how to ease the burden of her jealousy, which actually set her temples throbbing with pain, and thinking still that things might be set right, she would wash, powder her tear-stained face, and fly off to the lady mentioned.

Not finding Ryabovsky with her, she would drive off to a second, then to a third. At first she was ashamed to go about like this, but afterwards she got used to it, and it would happen that in one evening she would make the round of all her female acquaintances in search of Ryabovsky, and they all understood it.

One day she said to Ryabovsky of her husband:

" That man crushes me with his magnanimity."

This phrase pleased her so much that when she met the artists who knew of her affair with Ryabovsky she said every time of her husband, with a vigorous movement of her arm:

" That man crushes me with his magnanimity."

Their manner of life was the same as it had been the year before. On Wednesdays they were " At Home "; an actor recited, the artists sketched. The violoncellist played, a singer sang, and invariably at half-past eleven the door leading to the dining-room opened and Dymov, smiling, said:

" Come to supper, gentlemen."

As before, Olga Ivanovna hunted celebrities, found them, was not satisfied, and went in pursuit of fresh ones. As before, she came back late every night; but now Dymov was not, as last year, asleep, but sitting in his study at work of some sort. He went to bed at three o'clock and got up at eight.

One evening when she was getting ready to go to the theatre and standing before the pier glass, Dymov came into her bedroom, wearing his dress-coat and a white tie. He was smiling gently and looked into his wife's face joyfully, as in old days; his face was radiant.

" I have just been defending my thesis," he said, sitting down and smoothing his knees.

" Defending? " asked Olga Ivanovna.

" Oh, oh! " he laughed, and he craned his neck to

see his wife's face in the mirror, for she was still standing with her back to him, doing up her hair. " Oh, oh," he repeated, " do you know it's very possible they may offer me the Readership in General Pathology? It seems like it."

It was evident from his beaming, blissful face that if Olga Ivanovna had shared with him his joy and triumph he would have forgiven her everything, both the present and the future, and would have forgotten everything, but she did not understand what was meant by a " readership " or by " general pathology "; besides, she was afraid of being late for the theatre, and she said nothing.

He sat there another two minutes, and with a guilty smile went away.

VII

It had been a very troubled day.

Dymov had a very bad headache; he had no breakfast, and did not go to the hospital, but spent the whole time lying on his sofa in the study. Olga Ivanovna went as usual at midday to see Ryabovsky, to show him her still-life sketch, and to ask him why he had not been to see her the evening before. The sketch seemed to her worthless, and she had painted it only in order to have an additional reason for going to the artist.

She went in to him without ringing, and as she was taking off her goloshes in the entry she heard a sound as of something running softly in the studio, with a feminine rustle of skirts; and as she hastened to peep in she caught a momentary glimpse of a bit of brown petticoat, which vanished behind a big picture draped, together with the easel, with black calico, to the floor. There could be no doubt that a woman was hiding there. How often Olga Ivanovna herself had taken refuge behind that picture!

Ryabovsky, evidently much embarrassed, held out both hands to her, as though surprised at her arrival, and said with a forced smile:

"Aha! Very glad to see you! Anything nice to tell me?"

Olga Ivanovna's eyes filled with tears. She felt ashamed and bitter, and would not for a million roubles have consented to speak in the presence of the outsider, the rival, the deceitful woman who was standing now behind the picture, and probably giggling malignantly.

"I have brought you a sketch," she said timidly in a thin voice, and her lips quivered. "*Nature morte.*"

"Ah — ah! . . . A sketch?"

The artist took the sketch in his hands, and as he examined it walked, as it were mechanically, into the other room.

Olga Ivanovna followed him humbly.

"*Nature morte* . . . first-rate sort," he muttered, falling into rhyme. "Kurort . . . sport . . . port . . ."

From the studio came the sound of hurried footsteps and the rustle of a skirt.

So she had gone. Olga Ivanovna wanted to

scream aloud, to hit the artist on the head with something heavy, but she could see nothing through her tears, was crushed by her shame, and felt herself, not Olga Ivanovna, not an artist, but a little insect.

"I am tired . . ." said the artist languidly, looking at the sketch and tossing his head as though struggling with drowsiness. "It's very nice, of course, but here a sketch today, a sketch last year, another sketch in a month . . . I wonder you are not bored with them. If I were you I should give up painting and work seriously at music or something. You're not an artist, you know, but a musician. But you can't think how tired I am! I'll tell them to bring us some tea, shall I?"

He went out of the room, and Olga Ivanovna heard him give some order to his footman. To avoid farewells and explanations, and above all to avoid bursting into sobs, she ran as fast as she could, before Ryabovsky came back, to the entry, put on her goloshes, and went out into the street; then she breathed easily, and felt she was free for ever from Ryabovsky and from painting and from the burden of shame which had so crushed her in the studio. It was all over!

She drove to her dressmaker's; then to see Barnay, who had only arrived the day before; from Barnay to a music-shop, and all the time she was thinking how she would write Ryabovsky a cold, cruel letter full of personal dignity, and how in the spring or the summer she would go with Dymov to the Crimea, free herself finally from the past there, and begin a new life.

On getting home late in the evening she sat down in the drawing-room, without taking off her things, to begin the letter. Ryabovsky had told her she was not an artist, and to pay him out she wrote to him now that he painted the same thing every year, and said exactly the same thing every day; that he was at a standstill, and that nothing more would come of him than had come already. She wanted to write, too, that he owed a great deal to her good influence, and that if he was going wrong it was only because her influence was paralysed by various dubious persons like the one who had been hiding behind the picture that day.

"Little mother!" Dymov called from the study, without opening the door.

"What is it?"

"Don't come· in to me, but only come to the door — that's right. . . . The day before yesterday I must have caught diphtheria at the hospital, and now . . . I am ill. Make haste and send for Korostelev."

Olga Ivanovna always called her husband by his surname, as she did all the men of her acquaintance; she disliked his Christian name, Osip, because it reminded her of the Osip in Gogol and the silly pun on his name. But now she cried:

"Osip, it cannot be!"

"Send for him; I feel ill," Dymov said behind the door, and she could hear him go back to the sofa and lie down. "Send!" she heard his voice faintly.

"Good Heavens!" thought Olga Ivanovna, turning chill with horror. "Why, it's dangerous!"

For no reason she took the candle and went into the bedroom, and there, reflecting what she must do, glanced casually at herself in the pier glass. With her pale, frightened face, in a jacket with sleeves high on the shoulders, with yellow ruches on her bosom, and with stripes running in unusual directions on her skirt, she seemed to herself horrible and disgusting. She suddenly felt poignantly sorry for Dymov, for his boundless love for her, for his young life, and even for the desolate little bed in which he had not slept for so long; and she remembered his habitual, gentle, submissive smile. She wept bitterly, and wrote an imploring letter to Korostelev. It was two o'clock in the night.

VIII

When towards eight o'clock in the morning Olga Ivanovna, her head heavy from want of sleep and her hair unbrushed, came out of her bedroom, looking unattractive and with a guilty expression on her face, a gentleman with a black beard, apparently the doctor, passed by her into the entry. There was a smell of drugs. Korostelev was standing near the study door, twisting his left moustache with his right hand.

"Excuse me, I can't let you go in," he said surlily

to Olga Ivanovna; " it's catching. Besides, it's no use, really; he is delirious, anyway."

" Has he really got diphtheria? " Olga Ivanovna asked in a whisper.

" People who wantonly risk infection ought to be hauled up and punished for it," muttered Korostelev, not answering Olga Ivanovna's question. Do you know why he caught it? On Tuesday he was sucking up the mucus through a pipette from a boy with diphtheria. And what for? It was stupid. . . . Just from folly. . . ."

" Is it dangerous, very? " asked Olga Ivanovna.

" Yes; they say it is the malignant form. We ought to send for Shrek really."

A little red-haired man with a long nose and a Jewish accent arrived; then a tall, stooping, shaggy individual, who looked like a head deacon; then a stout young man with a red face and spectacles. These were doctors who came to watch by turns beside their colleague. Korostelev did not go home when his turn was over, but remained and wandered about the rooms like an uneasy spirit. The maid kept getting tea for the various doctors, and was constantly running to the chemist, and there was no one to do the rooms. There was a dismal stillness in the flat.

Olga Ivanovna sat in her bedroom and thought that God was punishing her for having deceived her husband. That silent, unrepining, uncomprehended creature, robbed by his mildness of all personality and will, weak from excessive kindness, had been

suffering in obscurity somewhere on his sofa, and
had not complained.   And if he were to complain
even in delirium, the doctors watching by his bedside
would learn that diphtheria was not the only cause
of his sufferings.   They would ask Korostelev.   He
knew all about it, and it was not for nothing that he
looked at his friend's wife with eyes that seemed to
say that she was the real chief criminal and diphtheria was only her accomplice.   She did not think
now of the moonlight evening on the Volga, nor the
words of love, nor their poetical life in the peasant's
hut.   She thought only that from an idle whim,
from self-indulgence, she had sullied herself all over
from head to foot in something filthy, sticky, which
one could never wash off. . . .

   " Oh, how fearfully false I've been! " she thought,
recalling the troubled passion she had known with
Ryabovsky.   " Curse it all! . . ."

   At four o'clock she dined with Korostelev.   He
did nothing but scowl and drink red wine, and did
not eat a morsel.   She ate nothing, either.   At one
minute she was praying inwardly and vowing to God
that if Dymov recovered she would love him again
and be a faithful wife to him.   Then, forgetting
herself for a minute, she would look at Korostelev,
and think: " Surely it must be dull to be a humble,
obscure person, not remarkable in any way, especially with such a wrinkled face and bad manners! "
Then it seemed to her that God would strike her
dead that minute for not having once been in her
husband's study, for fear of infection.   And altogether she had a dull, despondent feeling and a con-

viction that her life was spoilt, and that there was no setting it right anyhow. . . .

After dinner darkness came on. When Olga Ivanovna went into the drawing-room Korostelev was asleep on the sofa, with a gold-embroidered silk cushion under his head.

" Khee-poo-ah," he snored —" khee-poo-ah."

And the doctors as they came to sit up and went away again did not notice this disorder. The fact that a strange man was asleep and snoring in the drawing-room, and the sketches on the walls and the exquisite decoration of the room, and the fact that the lady of the house was dishevelled and untidy — all that aroused not the slightest interest now. One of the doctors chanced to laugh at something, and the laugh had a strange and timid sound that made one's heart ache.

When Olga Ivanovna went into the drawing-room next time, Korostelev was not asleep, but sitting up and smoking.

" He has diphtheria of the nasal cavity," he said in a low voice, " and the heart is not working properly now. Things are in a bad way, really."

" But you will send for Shrek? " said Olga Ivanovna.

" He has been already. It was he noticed that the diphtheria had passed into the nose. What's the use of Shrek! Shrek's no use at all, really. He is Shrek, I am Korostelev, and nothing more."

The time dragged on fearfully slowly. Olga Ivanovna lay down in her clothes on her bed, that had not been made all day, and sank into a doze. She dreamed that the whole flat was filled up from floor to ceiling with a huge piece of iron, and that if they could only get the iron out they would all be light-hearted and happy. Waking, she realized that it was not the iron but Dymov's illness that was weighing on her.

"Nature morte, port . . ." she thought, sinking into forgetfulness again. "Sport . . . Kurort . . . and what of Shrek? Shrek . . . trek . . . wreck. . . . And where are my friends now? Do they know that we are in trouble? Lord, save . . . spare! Shrek . . . trek . . ."

And again the iron was there. . . . The time dragged on slowly, though the clock on the lower storey struck frequently. And bells were continually ringing as the doctors arrived. . . . The house-maid came in with an empty glass on a tray, and asked, " Shall I make the bed, madam? " and getting no answer, went away.

The clock below struck the hour. She dreamed of the rain on the Volga; and again some one came into her bedroom, she thought a stranger. Olga Ivanovna jumped up, and recognized Korostelev.

"What time is it? " she asked.

"About three."

"Well, what is it? "

"What, indeed! . . . I've come to tell you he is passing. . . ."

He gave a sob, sat down on the bed beside her, and wiped away the tears with his sleeve. She could not grasp it at once, but turned cold all over and began slowly crossing herself.

"He is passing," he repeated in a shrill voice, and again he gave a sob. "He is dying because he sacrificed himself. What a loss for science!" he said bitterly. "Compare him with all of us. He was a great man, an extraordinary man! What gifts! What hopes we all had of him!" Korostelev went on, wringing his hands: "Merciful God, he was a man of science; we shall never look on his like again. Osip Dymov, what have you done — aie, aie, my God!"

Korostelev covered his face with both hands in despair, and shook his head.

"And his moral force," he went on, seeming to grow more and more exasperated against some one. "Not a man, but a pure, good, loving soul, and clean as crystal. He served science and died for science. And he worked like an ox night and day — no one spared him — and with his youth and his learning he had to take a private practice and work at translations at night to pay for these . . . vile rags!"

Korostelev looked with hatred at Olga Ivanovna, snatched at the sheet with both hands and angrily tore it, as though it were to blame.

"He did not spare himself, and others did not spare him. Oh, what's the use of talking!"

"Yes, he was a rare man," said a bass voice in the drawing-room.

Olga Ivanovna remembered her whole life with

him from the beginning to the end, with all its details, and suddenly she understood that he really was an extraordinary, rare, and, compared with every one else she knew, a great man. And remembering how her father, now dead, and all the other doctors had behaved to him, she realized that they really had seen in him a future celebrity. The walls, the ceiling, the lamp, and the carpet on the floor, seemed to be winking at her sarcastically, as though they would say, "You were blind! you were blind!" With a wail she flung herself out of the bedroom, dashed by some unknown man in the drawing-room, and ran into her husband's study. He was lying motionless on the sofa, covered to the waist with a quilt. His face was fearfully thin and sunken, and was of a greyish-yellow colour such as is never seen in the living; only from the forehead, from the black eyebrows and from the familiar smile, could he be recognized as Dymov. Olga Ivanovna hurriedly felt his chest, his forehead, and his hands. The chest was still warm, but the forehead and hands were unpleasantly cold, and the half-open eyes looked, not at Olga Ivanovna, but at the quilt.

"Dymov!" she called aloud, "Dymov!" She wanted to explain to him that it had been a mistake, that all was not lost, that life might still be beauiful and happy, that he was an extraordinary, rare, great man, and that she would all her life worship him and bow down in homage and holy awe before him. . . .

"Dymov!" she called him, patting him on the

shoulder, unable to believe that he would never wake again. "Dymov! Dymov!"

In the drawing-room Korostelev was saying to the housemaid:

"Why keep asking? Go to the church beadle and enquire where they live. They'll wash the body and lay it out, and do everything that is necessary."

1892

A DREARY STORY

A DREARY STORY

FROM THE NOTEBOOK OF AN OLD MAN

I

THERE is in Russia an emeritus Professor Nikolay Stepanovitch, a chevalier and privy councillor; he has so many Russian and foreign decorations that when he has occasion to put them on the students nickname him " The Ikonstand." His acquaintances are of the most aristocratic; for the last twenty-five or thirty years, at any rate, there has not been one single distinguished man of learning in Russia with whom he has not been intimately acquainted. There is no one for him to make friends with nowadays; but if we turn to the past, the long list of his famous friends winds up with such names as Pirogov, Kavelin, and the poet Nekrasov, all of whom bestowed upon him a warm and sincere affection. He is a member of all the Russian and of three foreign universities. And so on, and so on. All that and a great deal more that might be said makes up what is called my " name."

That is my name as known to the public. In Russia it is known to every educated man, and abroad it is mentioned in the lecture-room with the addition " honoured and distinguished." It is one of those fortunate names to abuse which or to take which in vain, in public or in print, is considered a sign of bad taste. And that is as it should be. You see, my name is closely associated with the conception of a highly distinguished man of great gifts and unquestionable usefulness. I have the industry and power of endurance of a camel, and that is important, and I have talent, which is even more important. Moreover, while I am on this subject, I am a well-educated, modest, and honest fellow. I have never poked my nose into literature or politics; I have never sought popularity in polemics with the ignorant; I have never made speeches either at public dinners or at the funerals of my friends. . . . In fact, there is no slur on my learned name, and there is no complaint one can make against it. It is fortunate.

The bearer of that name, that is I, see myself as a man of sixty-two, with a bald head, with false teeth, and with an incurable tic douloureux. I am myself as dingy and unsightly as my name is brilliant and splendid. My head and my hands tremble with weakness; my neck, as Turgenev says of one of his heroines, is like the handle of a double bass; my chest is hollow; my shoulders narrow; when I talk or lecture, my mouth turns down at one corner; when I smile, my whole face is covered with aged-looking, deathly wrinkles. There is nothing impressive about my pitiful figure; only, perhaps, when I have an attack of tic douloureux my face wears a peculiar expression, the sight of which must have roused in every one the grim and impressive thought, " Evidently that man will soon die."

I still, as in the past, lecture fairly well; I can still, as in the past, hold the attention of my listeners for a couple of hours. My fervour, the literary skill of my exposition, and my humour, almost efface the defects of my voice, though it is harsh, dry, and monotonous as a praying beggar's. I write poorly. That bit of my brain which presides over the faculty of authorship refuses to work. My memory has grown weak; there is a lack of sequence in my ideas, and when I put them on paper it always seems to me that I have lost the instinct for their organic connection; my construction is monotonous; my language is poor and timid. Often I write what I do not mean; I have forgotten the beginning when I am writing the end. Often I forget ordinary words, and I always have to waste a great deal of energy in avoiding superfluous phrases and unnecessary parentheses in my letters, both unmistakable proofs of a decline in mental activity. And it is noteworthy that the simpler the letter the more painful the effort to write it. At a scientific article I feel far more intelligent and at ease than at a letter of congratulation or a minute of proceedings. Another point: I find it easier to write German or English than to write Russian.

As regards my present manner of life, I must give a foremost place to the insomnia from which I have suffered of late. If I were asked what constituted the chief and fundamental feature of my existence now, I should answer, Insomnia. As in the past, from habit I undress and go to bed exactly at midnight. I fall asleep quickly, but before two o'clock I wake up and feel as though I had not slept at all.   Sometimes I get out of bed and light a lamp. For an hour or two I walk up and down the room looking at the familiar photographs and pictures. When I am weary of walking about, I sit down to my table.   I sit motionless, thinking of nothing, conscious of no inclination; if a book is lying before me, I mechanically move it closer and read it without any interest — in that way not long ago I mechanically read through in one night a whole novel, with the strange title " The Song the Lark was Singing "; or to occupy my attention I force myself to count to a thousand; or I imagine the face of one of my colleagues and begin trying to remember in what year and under what circumstances he entered the service.   I like listening to sounds.   Two rooms away from me my daughter Liza says something rapidly in her sleep, or my wife crosses the drawing-room with a candle and invariably drops the match-box; or a warped cupboard creaks; or the burner of the lamp suddenly begins to hum — and all these sounds, for some reason, excite me.

To lie awake at night means to be at every moment conscious of being abnormal, and so I look forward with impatience to the morning and the day when I have a right to be awake.   Many wearisome hours pass before the cock crows in the yard. He is my first bringer of good tidings.   As soon as he crows I know that within an hour the porter will wake up below, and, coughing angrily, will go upstairs to fetch something.   And then a pale light

will begin gradually glimmering at the windows,
voices will sound in the street. . . .

The day begins for me with the entrance of my
wife. She comes in to me in her petticoat, before
she has done her hair, but after she has washed,
smelling of flower-scented eau-de-Cologne, looking
as though she had come in by chance. Every time
she says exactly the same thing: " Excuse me, I
have just come in for a minute. . . . Have you had
a bad night again? "

Then she puts out the lamp, sits down near the
table, and begins talking. I am no prophet, but
I know what she will talk about. Every morning
it is exactly the same thing. Usually, after anxious
inquiries concerning my health, she suddenly men-
tions our son who is an officer serving at Warsaw.
After the twentieth of each month we send him fifty
roubles, and that serves as the chief topic of our
conversation.

" Of course it is difficult for us," my wife would
sigh, " but until he is completely on his own feet it is
our duty to help him. The boy is among strangers,
his pay is small. . . . However, if you like, next
month we won't send him fifty, but forty. What
do you think? "

Daily experience might have taught my wife that
constantly talking of our expenses does not reduce
them, but my wife refuses to learn by experience,
and regularly every morning discusses our officer
son, and tells me that bread, thank God, is cheaper,
while sugar is a halfpenny dearer — with a tone and

an air as though she were communicating interesting news.

I listen, mechanically assent, and probably because I have had a bad night, strange and inappropriate thoughts intrude themselves upon me. I gaze at my wife and wonder like a child. I ask myself in perplexity, is it possible that this old, very stout, ungainly woman, with her dull expression of petty anxiety and alarm about daily bread, with eyes dimmed by continual brooding over debts and money difficulties, who can talk of nothing but expenses and who smiles at nothing but things getting cheaper — is it possible that this woman is no other than the slender Varya whom I fell in love with so passionately for her fine, clear intelligence, for her pure soul, her beauty, and, as Othello his Desdemona, for her " sympathy " for my studies? Could that woman be no other than the Varya who had once borne me a son?

I look with strained attention into the face of this flabby, spiritless, clumsy old woman, seeking in her my Varya, but of her past self nothing is left but her anxiety over my health and her manner of calling my salary " our salary," and my cap " our cap." It is painful for me to look at her, and, to give her what little comfort I can, I let her say what she likes, and say nothing even when she passes unjust criticisms on other people or pitches into me for not having a private practice or not publishing text-books.

Our conversation always ends in the same way. My wife suddenly remembers with dismay that I have not had my tea.

"What am I thinking about, sitting here?" she says, getting up. "The samovar has been on the table ever so long, and here I stay gossiping. My goodness! how forgetful I am growing!"

She goes out quickly, and stops in the doorway to say:

"We owe Yegor five months' wages. Did you know it? You mustn't let the servants' wages run on; how many times I have said it! It's much easier to pay ten roubles a month than fifty roubles every five months!"

As she goes out, she stops to say:

"The person I am sorriest for is our Liza. The girl studies at the Conservatoire, always mixes with people of good position, and goodness knows how she is dressed. Her fur coat is in such a state she is ashamed to show herself in the street. If she were somebody else's daughter it wouldn't matter, but of course every one knows that her father is a distinguished professor, a privy councillor."

And having reproached me with my rank and reputation, she goes away at last. That is how my day begins. It does not improve as it goes on.

As I am drinking my tea, my Liza comes in wearing her fur coat and her cap, with her music in her hand, already quite ready to go to the Conservatoire. She is two-and-twenty. She looks younger, is pretty, and rather like my wife in her young days. She kisses me tenderly on my forehead and on my hand, and says:

"Good-morning, papa; are you quite well?"

As a child she was very fond of ice-cream, and I used often to take her to a confectioner's. Ice-cream was for her the type of everything delightful. If she wanted to praise me she would say: "You are as nice as cream, papa." We used to call one of her little fingers "pistachio ice," the next, "cream ice," the third "raspberry," and so on. Usually when she came in to say good-morning to me I used to sit her on my knee, kiss her little fingers, and say:

"Creamy ice . . . pistachio . . . lemon. . . ."

And now, from old habit, I kiss Liza's fingers and mutter: "Pistachio . . . cream . . . lemon . . ." but the effect is utterly different. I am cold as ice and I am ashamed. When my daughter comes in to me and touches my forehead with her lips I start as though a bee had stung me on the head, give a forced smile, and turn my face away. Ever since I have been suffering from sleeplessness, a question sticks in my brain like a nail. My daughter often sees me, an old man and a distinguished man, blush painfully at being in debt to my footman; she sees how often anxiety over petty debts forces me to lay aside my work and to walk up and down the room for hours together, thinking; but why is it she never comes to me in secret to whisper in my ear: "Father, here is my watch, here are my bracelets, my earrings, my dresses. . . . Pawn them all; you want money . . ."? How is it that, seeing how her mother and I are placed in a false position and do our utmost to hide our poverty from people, she does not give up her expensive pleasure of music lessons? I would not accept her watch nor her bracelets, nor the sacrifice of her lessons — God forbid! That isn't what I want.

I think at the same time of my son, the officer at Warsaw. He is a clever, honest, and sober fellow. But that is not enough for me. I think if I had an old father, and if I knew there were moments when he was put to shame by his poverty, I should give up my officer's commission to somebody else, and should go out to earn my living as a workman. Such thoughts about my children poison me. What is the use of them? It is only a narrow-minded or embittered man who can harbour evil thoughts about ordinary people because they are not heroes. But enought of that!

At a quarter to ten I have to go and give a lecture to my dear boys. I dress and walk along the road which I have known for thirty years, and which has its history for me. Here is the big grey house with the chemist's shop; at this point there used to stand a little house, and in it was a beershop; in that beershop I thought out my thesis and wrote my first love-letter to Varya. I wrote it in pencil, on a page headed " Historia morbi." Here there is a grocer's shop; at one time it was kept by a little Jew, who sold me cigarettes on credit; then by a fat peasant woman, who liked the students because " every one of them has a mother "; now there is a red-haired shopkeeper sitting in it, a very stolid man who drinks tea from a copper teapot. And here are the gloomy gates of the University, which have long needed doing up; I see the bored porter in his sheep-skin, the

broom, the drifts of snow. . . . On a boy coming
fresh from the provinces and imagining that the
temple of science must really be a temple, such gates
cannot make a healthy impression. Altogether the
dilapidated condition of the University buildings, the
gloominess of the corridors, the griminess of the
walls, the lack of light, the dejected aspect of the
steps, the hat-stands and the benches, take a prominent position among predisposing causes in the history of Russian pessimism. . . . Here is our garden . . . I fancy it has grown neither better nor
worse since I was a student. I don't like it. It
would be far more sensible if there were tall pines
and fine oaks growing here instead of sickly-looking
lime-trees, yellow acacias, and skimpy pollard lilacs.
The student whose state of mind is in the majority
of cases created by his surroundings, ought in the
place where he is studying to see facing him at every
turn nothing but what is lofty, strong and elegant.
. . . God preserve him from gaunt trees, broken
windows, grey walls, and doors covered with torn
American leather!

When I go to my own entrance the door is flung
wide open, and I am met by my colleague, contem-
porary, and namesake, the porter Nikolay. As he
lets me in he clears his throat and says:

" A frost, your Excellency! "

Or, if my great-coat is wet:

" Rain, your Excellency! "

Then he runs on ahead of me and opens all the
doors on my way. In my study he carefully takes
off my fur coat, and while doing so manages to tell

me some bit of University news. Thanks to the
close intimacy existing between all the University
porters and beadles, he knows everything that goes
on in the four faculties, in the office, in the rector's
private room, in the library. What does he not
know? When in an evil day a rector or dean, for
instance, retires, I hear him in conversation with the
young porters mention the candidates for the post,
explain that such a one would not be confirmed by
the minister, that another would himself refuse to
accept it, then drop into fantastic details concerning
mysterious papers received in the office, secret conversations alleged to have taken place between the
minister and the trustee, and so on. With the exception of these details, he almost always turns out
to be right. His estimates of the candidates,
though original, are very correct, too. If one wants
to know in what year some one read his thesis, entered the service, retired, or died, then summon to
your assistance the vast memory of that soldier, and
he will not only tell you the year, the month and the
day, but will furnish you also with the details that
accompanied this or that event. Only one who loves
can remember like that.

He is the guardian of the University traditions.
From the porters who were his predecessors he has
inherited many legends of University life, has added
to that wealth much of his own gained during his
time of service, and if you care to hear he will tell
you many long and intimate stories. He can tell
one about extraordinary sages who knew *everything*,
about remarkable students who did not sleep for

weeks, about numerous martyrs and victims of science; with him good triumphs over evil, the weak always vanquishes the strong, the wise man the fool, the humble the proud, the young the old. There is no need to take all these fables and legends for sterling coin; but filter them, and you will have left what is wanted: our fine traditions and the names of real heroes, recognized as such by all.

In our society the knowledge of the learned world consists of anecdotes of the extraordinary absent-mindedness of certain old professors, and two or three witticisms variously ascribed to Gruber, to me, and to Babukin. For the educated public that is not much. If it loved science, learned men, and students, as Nikolay does, its literature would long ago have contained whole epics, records of sayings and doings such as, unfortunately, it cannot boast of now.

After telling me a piece of news, Nikolay assumes a severe expression, and conversation about business begins. If any outsider could at such times overhear Nikolay's free use of our terminology, he might perhaps imagine that he was a learned man disguised as a soldier. And, by the way, the rumours of the erudition of the University porters are greatly exaggerated. It is true that Nikolay knows more than a hundred Latin words, knows how to put the skeleton together, sometimes prepares the apparatus and amuses the students by some long, learned quotation, but the by no means complicated theory of the circulation of the blood, for instance, is as much a mystery to him now as it was twenty years ago.

At the table in my study, bending low over some book or preparation, sits Pyotr Ignatyevitch, my demonstrator, a modest and industrious but by no means clever man of five-and-thirty, already bald and corpulent; he works from morning to night, reads a lot, remembers well everything he has read — and in that way he is not a man, but pure gold; in all else he is a carthorse or, in other words, a learned dullard. The carthorse characteristics that show his lack of talent are these: his outlook is narrow and sharply limited by his specialty; outside his special branch he is simple as a child.

"Fancy! what a misfortune! They say Skobelev is dead."

Nikolay crosses himself, but Pyotr Ignatyevitch turns to me and asks:

"What Skobelev is that?"

Another time — somewhat earlier — I told him that Professor Perov was dead. Good Pyotr Ignatyevitch asked:

"What did he lecture on?"

I believe if Patti had sung in his very ear, if a horde of Chinese had invaded Russia, if there had been an earthquake, he would not have stirred a limb, but screwing up his eye, would have gone on calmly looking through his microscope. What is he to Hecuba or Hecuba to him, in fact? I would give a good deal to see how this dry stick sleeps with his wife at night.

Another characteristic is his fanatical faith in the infallibility of science, and, above all, of everything written by the Germans. He believes in himself, in his preparations; knows the object of life, and knows nothing of the doubts and disappointments that turn the hair of talent grey.   He has a slavish reverence for authorities and a complete lack of any desire for independent thought.   To change his convictions is difficult, to argue with him impossible.   How is one to argue with a man who is firmly persuaded that medicine is the finest of sciences, that doctors are the best of men, and that the traditions of the medical profession are superior to those of any other?   Of the evil past of medicine only one tradition has been preserved — the white tie still worn by doctors; for a learned — in fact, for any educated man the only traditions that can exist are those of the University as a whole, with no distinction between medicine, law, etc.   But it would be hard for Pyotr Ignatye-vitch to accept these facts, and he is ready to argue with you till the day of judgment.

I have a clear picture in my mind of his future. In the course of his life he will prepare many hundreds of chemicals of exceptional purity; he will write a number of dry and very accurate memoranda, will make some dozen conscientious translations, but he won't do anything striking.   To do that one must have imagination, inventiveness, the gift of insight, and Pyotr Ignatyevitch has nothing of the kind.   In short, he is not a master in science, but a journeyman.

Pyotr Ignatyevitch, Nikolay, and I, talk in subdued tones.   We are not quite ourselves.   There is always a peculiar feeling when one hears through the doors a murmur as of the sea from the lecture-theatre. In the course of thirty years I have not grown accustomed to this feeling, and I experience it every morning. I nervously button up my coat, ask Nikolay unnecessary questions, lose my temper. . . . It is just as though I were frightened; it is not timidity, though, but something different which I can neither describe nor find a name for.

Quite unnecessarily, I look at my watch and say: " Well, it's time to go in."

And we march into the room in the following order: foremost goes Nikolay, with the chemicals and apparatus or with a chart; after him I come; and then the carthorse follows humbly, with hanging head; or, when necessary, a dead body is carried in first on a stretcher, followed by Nikolay, and so on. On my entrance the students all stand up, then they sit down, and the sound as of the sea is suddenly hushed. Stillness reigns.

I know what I am going to lecture about, but I don't know how I am going to lecture, where I am going to begin or with what I am going to end. I haven't a single sentence ready in my head. But I have only to look round the lecture-hall (it is built in the form of an amphitheatre) and utter the stereotyped phrase, " Last lecture we stopped at . . ." when sentences spring up from my soul in a long string, and I am carried away by my own eloquence. I speak with irresistible rapidity and passion, and it seems as though there were no force which could check the flow of my words. To lecture well — that is, with profit to the listeners and without boring them — one must have, besides tal-

ent, experience and a special knack; one must possess
a clear conception of one's own powers, of the audience to which one is lecturing, and of the subject of
one's lecture.   Moreover, one must be a man who
knows what he is doing; one must keep a sharp lookout, and not for one second lose sight of what lies
before one.

A good conductor, interpreting the thought of
the composer, does twenty things at once: reads the
score, waves his baton, watches the singer, makes
a motion sideways, first to the drum then to the
wind-instruments, and so on.   I do just the same
when I lecture.   Before me a hundred and fifty
faces, all unlike one another; three hundred eyes all
looking straight into my face.   My object is to
dominate this many-headed monster.   If every moment as I lecture I have a clear vision of the degree
of its attention and its power of comprehension, it
is in my power.   The other foe I have to overcome
is in myself.   It is the infinite variety of forms,
phenomena, laws, and the multitude of ideas of my
own and other people's conditioned by them.   Every
moment I must have the skill to snatch out of that
vast mass of material what is most important and
necessary, and, as rapidly as my words flow, clothe
my thought in a form in which it can be grasped by
the monster's intelligence, and may arouse its attention, and at the same time one must keep a sharp
lookout that one's thoughts are conveyed, not just as
they come, but in a certain order, essential for the
correct composition of the picture I wish to sketch.
Further, I endeavour to make my diction literary,

my definitions brief and precise, my wording, as far
as possible, simple and eloquent. Every minute I
have to pull myself up and remember that I have
only an hour and forty minutes at my disposal. In
short, one has one's work cut out. At one and the
same minute one has to play the part of savant and
teacher and orator, and it's a bad thing if the orator
gets the upper hand of the savant or of the teacher
in one, or *vice versa.*

You lecture for a quarter of an hour, for half an
hour, when you notice that the students are beginning
to look at the ceiling, at Pyotr Ignatyevitch; one is
feeling for his handkerchief, another shifts in his
seat, another smiles at his thoughts. . . . That
means that their attention is flagging. Something
must be done. Taking advantage of the first opportunity, I make some pun. A broad grin comes on to
a hundred and fifty faces, the eyes shine brightly, the
sound of the sea is audible for a brief moment. . . .
I laugh too. Their attention is refreshed, and I can
go on.

No kind of sport, no kind of game or diversion,
has ever given me such enjoyment as lecturing.
Only at lectures have I been able to abandon myself
entirely to passion, and have understood that inspiration is not an invention of the poets, but exists in real
life, and I imagine Hercules after the most piquant
of his exploits felt just such voluptuous exhaustion as
I experience after every lecture.

That was in old times. Now at lectures I feel
nothing but torture. Before half an hour is over I
am conscious of an overwhelming weakness in my

legs and my shoulders.   I sit down in my chair, but
I am not accustomed to lecture sitting down; a minute
later I get up and go on standing, then sit down
again.   There is a dryness in my mouth, my voice
grows husky, my head begins to go round. . . . To
conceal my condition from my audience I continually
drink water, cough, often blow my nose as though I
were hindered by a cold, make puns inappropriately,
and in the end break off earlier than I ought to.   But
above all I am ashamed.

My conscience and my intelligence tell me that
the very best thing I could do now would be to deliver a farewell lecture to the boys, to say my last
word to them, to bless them, and give up my post to
a man younger and stronger than me.   But, God,
be my judge, I have not manly courage enough to act
according to my conscience.

Unfortunately, I am not a philosopher and not a
theologian.   I know perfectly well that I cannot
live more than another six months; it might be supposed that I ought now to be chiefly concerned with
the question of the shadowy life beyond the grave,
and the visions that will visit my slumbers in the
tomb.   But for some reason my soul refuses to
recognize these questions, though my mind is fully
alive to their importance.   Just as twenty, thirty
years ago, so now, on the threshold of death, I am
interested in nothing but science.   As I yield up my
last breath I shall still believe that science is the
most important, the most splendid, the most essential
thing in the life of man; that it always has been and

will be the highest manifestation of love, and that only by means of it will man conquer himself and nature. This faith is perhaps naïve and may rest on false assumptions, but it is not my fault that I believe that and nothing else; I cannot overcome in myself this belief.

But that is not the point. I only ask people to be indulgent to my weakness, and to realize that to tear from the lecture-theatre and his pupils a man who is more interested in the history of the development of the bone medulla than in the final object of creation would be equivalent to taking him and nailing him up in his coffin without waiting for him to be dead.

Sleeplessness and the consequent strain of combating increasing weakness leads to something strange in me. In the middle of my lecture tears suddenly rise in my throat, my eyes begin to smart, and I feel a passionate, hysterical desire to stretch out my hands before me and break into loud lamentation. I want to cry out in a loud voice that I, a famous man, have been sentenced by fate to the death penalty, that within some six months another man will be in control here in the lecture-theatre. I want to shriek that I am poisoned; new ideas such as I have not known before have poisoned the last days of my life, and are still stinging my brain like mosquitoes. And at that moment my position seems to me so awful that I want all my listeners to be horrified, to leap up from their seats and to rush in panic terror, with desperate screams, to the exit.

It is not easy to get through such moments.

II

After my lecture I sit at home and work. I read journals and monographs, or prepare my next lecture; sometimes I write something. I work with interruptions, as I have from time to time to see visitors.

There is a ring at the bell. It is a colleague come to discuss some business matter with me. He comes in to me with his hat and his stick, and, holding out both these objects to me, says:

" Only for a minute! Only for a minute! Sit down, *collega!* Only a couple of words."

To begin with, we both try to show each other that we are extraordinarily polite and highly delighted to see each other. I make him sit down in an easy-chair, and he makes me sit down; as we do so, we cautiously pat each other on the back, touch each other's buttons, and it looks as though we were feeling each other and afraid of scorching our fingers. Both of us laugh, though we say nothing amusing. When we are seated we bow our heads towards each other and begin talking in subdued voices. However affectionately disposed we may be to one another, we cannot help adorning our conversation with all sorts of Chinese mannerisms, such as " As you so justly observed," or " I have already had the honour to inform you "; we cannot help laughing if one of us makes a joke, however unsuccessfully. When we have finished with business my colleague gets up impulsively and, waving his hat in the direc-

tion of my work, begins to say good-bye. Again we
paw one another and laugh. I see him into the hall;
when I assist my colleague to put on his coat, while
he does all he can to decline this high honour. Then
when Yegor opens the door my colleague declares
that I shall catch cold, while I make a show of being
ready to go even into the street with him. And
when at last I go back into my study my face still
goes on smiling, I suppose from inertia.

A little later another ring at the bell. Somebody
comes into the hall, and is a long time coughing and
taking off his things. Yegor announces a student.
I tell him to ask him in. A minute later a young
man of agreeable appearance comes in. For the last
year he and I have been on strained relations; he
answers me disgracefully at the examinations, and I
mark him one. Every year I have some seven such
hopefuls whom, to express it in the students' slang,
I " chivy " or " floor." Those of them who fail in
their examination through incapacity or illness usually bear their cross patiently and do not haggle
with me; those who come to the house and haggle
with me are always youths of sanguine temperament,
broad natures, whose failure at examinations spoils
their appetites and hinders them from visiting the
opera with their usual regularity. I let the first class
off easily, but the second I chivy through a whole
year.

" Sit down," I say to my visitor; " what have you
to tell me? "

" Excuse me, professor, for troubling you," he begins, hesitating, and not looking me in the face. " I

would not have ventured to trouble you if it had not
been . . . I have been up for your examination five
times, and have been ploughed. . . . I beg you, be
so good as to mark me for a pass, because . . ."

The argument which all the sluggards bring forward on their own behalf is always the same; they
have passed well in all their subjects and have only
come to grief in mine, and that is the more surprising because they have always been particularly interested in my subject and knew it so well; their failure has always been entirely owing to some incomprehensible misunderstanding.

" Excuse me, my friend," I say to the visitor; " I
cannot mark you for a pass.   Go and read up the
lectures and come to me again.   Then we shall see."

A pause.   I feel an impulse to torment the student
a little for liking beer and the opera better than
science, and I say, with a sigh:

" To my mind, the best thing you can do now is to
give up medicine altogether.   If, with your abilities,
you cannot succeed in passing the examination, it's
evident that you have neither the desire nor the
vocation for a doctor's calling."

The sanguine youth's face lengthens.

" Excuse me, professor," he laughs, " but that
would be odd of me, to say the least of it.   After
studying for five years, all at once to give it up."

" Oh, well!   Better to have lost your five years
than have to spend the rest of your life in doing
work you do not care for."

But at once I feel sorry for him, and I hasten to
add:

" However, as you think best. And so read a
little more and come again."

" When ? " the idle youth asks in a hollow voice.

" When you like. Tomorrow if you like."

And in his good-natured eyes I read:

" I can come all right, but of course you will
plough me again, you beast ! "

" Of course," I say, " you won't know more
science for going in for my examination another
fifteen times, but it is training your character, and
you must be thankful for that."

Silence follows. I get up and wait for my visitor
to go, but he stands and looks towards the window,
fingers his beard, and thinks. It grows boring.

The sanguine youth's voice is pleasant and mellow,
his eyes are clever and ironical, his face is genial,
though a little bloated from frequent indulgence in
beer and overlong lying on the sofa; he looks as
though he could tell me a lot of interesting things
about the opera, about his affairs of the heart, and
about comrades whom he likes. Unluckily, it is not
the thing to discuss these subjects, or else I should
have been glad to listen to him.

" Professor, I give you my word of honour that if
you mark me for a pass I . . . I'll . . ."

As soon as we reach the " word of honour " I
wave my hands and sit down to the table. The student ponders a minute longer, and says dejectedly:

" In that case, good-bye. . . . I beg your pardon."

" Good-bye, my friend. Good luck to you."

He goes irresolutely into the hall, slowly puts on

his outdoor things, and, going out into the street, probably ponders for some time longer; unable to think of anything, except " old devil," inwardly addressed to me, he goes into a wretched restaurant to dine and drink beer, and then home to bed. " Peace be to thy ashes, honest toiler."

A third ring at the bell. A young doctor, in a pair of new black trousers, gold spectacles, and of course a white tie, walks in. He introduces himself. I beg him to be seated, and ask what I can do for him. Not without emotion, the young devotee of science begins telling me that he has passed his examination as a doctor of medicine, and that he has now only to write his dissertation. He would like to work with me under my guidance, and he would be greatly obliged to me if I would give him a subject for his dissertation.

" Very glad to be of use to you, colleague," I say, " but just let us come to an understanding as to the meaning of a dissertation. That word is taken to mean a composition which is a product of independent creative effort. Is that not so? A work written on another man's subject and under another man's guidance is called something different. . . ."

The doctor says nothing. I fly into a rage and jump up from my seat.

" Why is it you all come to me? " I cry angrily. " Do I keep a shop? I don't deal in subjects. For the thousand and oneth time I ask you all to leave me in peace! Excuse my brutality, but I am quite sick of it! "

The doctor remains silent, but a faint flush is apparent on his cheek-bones. His face expresses a profound reverence for my fame and my learning, but from his eyes I can see he feels a contempt for my voice, my pitiful figure, and my nervous gesticulation. I impress him in my anger as a queer fish.

" I don't keep a shop," I go on angrily. " And it is a strange thing! Why don't you want to be independent? Why have you such a distaste for independence? "

I say a great deal, but he still remains silent. By degrees I calm down, and of course give in. The doctor gets a subject from me for his theme not worth a halfpenny, writes under my supervision a dissertation of no use to any one, with dignity defends it in a dreary discussion, and receives a degree of no use to him.

The rings at the bell may follow one another endlessly, but I will confine my description here to four of them. The bell rings for the fourth time, and I hear familiar footsteps, the rustle of a dress, a dear voice. . . .

Eighteen years ago a colleague of mine, an oculist, died leaving a little daughter Katya, a child of seven, and sixty thousand roubles. In his will he made me the child's guardian. Till she was ten years old Katya lived with us as one of the family, then she was sent to a boarding-school, and only spent the summer holidays with us. I never had time to look after her education. I only superintended it at leisure moments, and so I can say very little about her childhood.

The first thing I remember, and like so much in

remembrance, is the extraordinary trustfulness with which she came into our house and let herself be treated by the doctors, a trustfulness which was always shining in her little face. She would sit somewhere out of the way, with her face tied up, invariably watching something with attention; whether she watched me writing or turning over the pages of a book, or watched my wife bustling about, or the cook scrubbing a potato in the kitchen, or the dog playing, her eyes invariably expressed the same thought — that is, " Everything that is done in this world is nice and sensible." She was curious, and very fond of talking to me. Sometimes she would sit at the table opposite me, watching my movements and asking questions. It interested her to know what I was reading, what I did at the University, whether I was not afraid of the dead bodies, what I did with my salary.

" Do the students fight at the University? " she would ask.

" They do, dear."

" And do you make them go down on their knees? "

" Yes, I do."

And she thought it funny that the students fought and I made them go down on their knees, and she laughed. She was a gentle, patient, good child. It happened not infrequently that I saw something taken away from her, saw her punished without reason, or her curiosity repressed; at such times a look of sadness was mixed with the invariable expression of trustfulness on her face — that was all. I did not know how to take her part; only when I saw her sad I had an inclination to draw her to me and to commiserate her like some old nurse: "My poor little orphan one!"

I remember, too, that she was fond of fine clothes and of sprinkling herself with scent. In that respect she was like me. I, too, am fond of pretty clothes and nice scent.

I regret that I had not time nor inclination to watch over the rise and development of the passion which took complete possession of Katya when she was fourteen or fifteen. I mean her passionate love for the theatre. When she used to come from boarding-school and stay with us for the summer holidays, she talked of nothing with such pleasure and such warmth as of plays and actors. She bored us with her continual talk of the theatre. My wife and children would not listen to her. I was the only one who had not the courage to refuse to attend to her. When she had a longing to share her transports, she used to come into my study and say in an imploring tone:

"Nikolay Stepanovitch, do let me talk to you about the theatre!"

I pointed to the clock, and said:

"I'll give you half an hour — begin."

Later on she used to bring with her dozens of portraits of actors and actresses which she worshipped; then she attempted several times to take part in private theatricals, and the upshot of it all was that when she left school she came to me and announced that she was born to be an actress.

I had never shared Katya's inclinations for the theatre. To my mind, if a play is good there is no need to trouble the actors in order that it may make the right impression; it is enough to read it. If the play is poor, no acting will make it good.

In my youth I often visited the theatre, and now my family takes a box twice a year and carries me off for a little distraction. Of course, that is not enough to give me the right to judge of the theatre. In my opinion the theatre has become no better than it was thirty or forty years ago. Just as in the past, I can never find a glass of clean water in the corridors or foyers of the theatre. Just as in the past, the attendants fine me twenty kopecks for my fur coat, though there is nothing reprehensible in wearing a warm coat in winter. As in the past, for no sort of reason, music is played in the intervals, which adds something new and uncalled-for to the impression made by the play. As in the past, men go in the intervals and drink spirits in the buffet. If no progress can be seen in trifles, I should look for it in vain in what is more important. When an actor wrapped from head to foot in stage traditions and conventions tries to recite a simple ordinary speech, " To be or not to be," not simply, but invariably with the accompaniment of hissing and convulsive movements all over his body, or when he tries to convince me at all costs that Tchatsky, who talks so much with fools and is so fond of folly, is a very clever man, and that " Woe from Wit " is not a dull play, the stage gives me the same feeling of conventionality which bored me so much forty years ago when I was regaled with the classical howling and beating on the breast. And every time I come out of the theatre more conservative than I go in.

The sentimental and confiding public may be persuaded that the stage, even in its present form, is a school; but any one who is familiar with a school in its true sense will not be caught with that bait. I cannot say what will happen in fifty or a hundred years, but in its actual condition the theatre can serve only as an entertainment. But this entertainment is too costly to be frequently enjoyed. It robs the state of thousands of healthy and talented young men and women, who, if they had not devoted themselves to the theatre, might have been good doctors, farmers, schoolmistresses, officers; it robs the public of the evening hours — the best time for intellectual work and social intercourse. I say nothing of the waste of money and the moral damage to the spectator when he sees murder, fornication, or false witness unsuitably treated on the stage.

Katya was of an entirely different opinion. She assured me that the theatre, even in its present condition, was superior to the lecture-hall, to books, or to anything in the world. The stage was a power that united in itself all the arts, and actors were missionaries. No art nor science was capable of producing so strong and so certain an effect on the soul of man as the stage, and it was with good reason that an actor of medium quality enjoys greater popularity than the greatest savant or artist. And no sort of public service could provide such enjoyment and gratification as the theatre.

And one fine day Katya joined a troupe of actors, and went off, I believe to Ufa, taking away with her a good supply of money, a store of rainbow hopes, and the most aristocratic views of her work.

Her first letters on the journey were marvellous. I read them, and was simply amazed that those small sheets of paper could contain so much youth, purity of spirit, holy innocence, and at the same time subtle and apt judgments which would have done credit to a fine masculine intellect.   It was more like a rapturous pæan of praise she sent me than a mere description of the Volga, the country, the towns she visited, her companions, her failures and successes; every sentence was fragrant with that confiding trustfulness I was accustomed to read in her face — and at the same time there were a great many grammatical mistakes, and there was scarcely any punctuation at all.

Before six months had passed I received a highly poetical and enthusiastic letter beginning with the words, " I have come to love . . ." This letter was accompanied by a photograph representing a young man with a shaven face, a wide-brimmed hat, and a plaid flung over his shoulder.   The letters that followed were as splendid as before, but now commas and stops made their appearance in them, the grammatical mistakes disappeared, and there was a distinctly masculine flavour about them.   Katya began writing to me how splendid it would be to build a great theatre somewhere on the Volga, on a co-operative system, and to attract to the enterprise the rich merchants and the steamer owners; there would

be a great deal of money in it; there would be vast
audiences; the actors would play on co-operative
terms. . . . Possibly all this was really excellent,
but it seemed to me that such schemes could only
originate from a man's mind.

However that may have been, for a year and a
half everything seemed to go well: Katya was in
love, believed in her work, and was happy; but then
I began to notice in her letters unmistakable signs of
falling off. It began with Katya's complaining of
her companions — this was the first and most ominous symptom; if a young scientific or literary man
begins his career with bitter complaints of scientific
and literary men, it is a sure sign that he is worn out
and not fit for his work. Katya wrote to me that
her companions did not attend the rehearsals and
never knew their parts; that one could see in every
one of them an utter disrespect for the public in the
production of absurd plays, and in their behaviour
on the stage; that for the benefit of the Actors' Fund,
which they only talked about, actresses of the serious
drama demeaned themselves by singing chansonettes,
while tragic actors sang comic songs making fun of
deceived husbands and the pregnant condition of un-
faithful wives, and so on. In fact, it was amazing
that all this had not yet ruined the provincial stage,
and that it could still maintain itself on such a rotten
and unsubstantial footing.

In answer I wrote Katya a long and, I must confess, a very boring letter. Among other things, I
wrote to her:

" I have more than once happened to converse

with old actors, very worthy men, who showed a friendly disposition towards me; from my conversations with them I could understand that their work was controlled not so much by their own intelligence and free choice as by fashion and the mood of the public. The best of them had had to play in their day in tragedy, in operetta, in Parisian farces, and in extravaganzas, and they always seemed equally sure that they were on the right path and that they were of use. So, as you see, the cause of the evil must be sought, not in the actors, but, more deeply, in the art itself and in the attitude of the whole of society to it."

This letter of mine only irritated Katya. She answered me:

"You and I are singing parts out of different operas. I wrote to you, not of the worthy men who showed a friendly disposition to you, but of a band of knaves who have nothing worthy about them. They are a horde of savages who have got on the stage simply because no one would have taken them elsewhere, and who call themselves artists simply because they are impudent. There are numbers of dull-witted creatures, drunkards, intriguing schemers and slanderers, but there is not one person of talent among them. I cannot tell you how bitter it is to me that the art I love has fallen into the hands of people I detest; how bitter it is that the best men look on at evil from afar, not caring to come closer, and, instead of intervening, write ponderous commonplaces and utterly useless sermons. . . ." And so on, all in the same style.

A little time passed, and I got this letter: " I have been brutally deceived. I cannot go on living. Dispose of my money as you think best. I loved you as my father and my only friend. Good-bye."

It turned out that *he,* too, belongéd to the " horde of savages." Later on, from certain hints, I gathered that there had been an attempt at suicide. I believe Katya tried to poison herself. I imagine that she must have been seriously ill afterwards, as the next letter I got was from Yalta, where she had most probably been sent by the doctors. Her last letter contained a request to send her a thousand roubles to Yalta as quickly as possible, and ended with these words:

" Excuse the gloominess of this letter; yesterday I buried my child." After spending about a year in the Crimea, she returned home.

She had been about four years on her travels, and during those four years, I must confess, I had played a rather strange and unenviable part in regard to her. When in earlier days she had told me she was going on the stage, and then wrote to me of her love; when she was periodically overcome by extravagance, and I continually had to send her first one and then two thousand roubles; when she wrote to me of her intention of suicide, and then of the death of her baby, every time I lost my head, and all my sympathy for her sufferings found no expression except that, after prolonged reflection, I wrote long, boring letters which I might just as well not have written. And yet I took a father's place with her and loved her like a daughter!

Now Katya is living less than half a mile off.   She has taken a flat of five rooms, and has installed herself fairly comfortably and in the taste of the day. If any one were to undertake to describe her surroundings, the most characteristic note in the picture would be indolence.   For the indolent body there are soft lounges, soft stools; for indolent feet soft rugs; for indolent eyes faded, dingy, or flat colours; for the indolent soul the walls are hung with a number of cheap fans and trivial pictures, in which the originality of the execution is more conspicuous than the subject; and the room contains a multitude of little tables and shelves filled with utterly useless articles of no value, and shapeless rags in place of curtains. . . . All this, together with the dread of bright colours, of symmetry, and of empty space, bears witness not only to spiritual indolence, but also to a corruption of natural taste.   For days together Katya lies on the lounge reading, principally novels and stories.   She only goes out of the house once a day, in the afternoon, to see me.

I go on working while Katya sits silent not far from me on the sofa, wrapping herself in her shawl, as though she were cold.   Either because I find her sympathetic or because I was used to her frequent visits when she was a little girl, her presence does not prevent me from concentrating my attention. From time to time I mechanically ask her some question; she gives very brief replies; or, to rest for a minute, I turn round and watch her as she looks dreamily at some medical journal or review.   And at such moments I notice that her face has lost the

old look of confiding trustfulness. Her expression
now is cold, apathetic, and absent-minded, like that
of passengers who had to wait too long for a train.
She is dressed, as in old days, simply and beautifully,
but carelessly; her dress and her hair show visible
traces of the sofas and rocking-chairs in which she
spends whole days at a stretch. And she has lost the
curiosity she had in old days. She has ceased to ask
me questions now, as though she had experienced
everything in life and looked for nothing new
from it.

Towards four o'clock there begins to be sounds
of movement in the hall and in the drawing-room.
Liza has come back from the Conservatoire, and
has brought some girl-friends in with her. We hear
them playing on the piano, trying their voices and
laughing; in the dining-room Yegor is laying the
table, with the clatter of crockery.

"Good-bye," said Katya. "I won't go in and see
your people today. They must excuse me. I
haven't time. Come and see me."

While I am seeing her to the door, she looks me
up and down grimly, and says with vexation:

"You are getting thinner and thinner! Why
don't you consult a doctor? I'll call at Sergey Fyodorovitch's and ask him to have a look at you."

"There's no need, Katya."

"I can't think where your people's eyes are!
They are a nice lot, I must say!"

She puts on her fur coat abruptly, and as she does
so two or three hairpins drop unnoticed on the floor
from her carelessly arranged hair. She is too lazy

and in too great a hurry to do her hair up; she carelessly stuffs the falling curls under her hat, and goes away.

When I go into the dining-room my wife asks me:
" Was Katya with you just now? Why didn't she come in to see us? It's really strange . . ."

" Mamma," Liza says to her reproachfully, " let her alone, if she doesn't want to. We are not going down on our knees to her."

" It's very neglectful, anyway. To sit for three hours in the study without remembering our existence! But of course she must do as she likes."

Varya and Liza both hate Katya. This hatred is beyond my comprehension, and probably one would have to be a woman in order to understand it. I am ready to stake my life that of the hundred and fifty young men I see every day in the lecture-theatre, and of the hundred elderly ones I meet every week, hardly one could be found capable of understanding their hatred and aversion for Katya's past — that is, for her having been a mother without being a wife, and for her having had an illegitimate child; and at the same time I cannot recall one woman or girl of my acquaintance who would not consciously or unconsciously harbour such feelings. And this is not because woman is purer or more virtuous than man: why, virtue and purity are not very different from vice if they are not free from evil feeling. I attribute this simply to the backwardness of woman. The mournful feeling of compassion and the pang of conscience experienced by a modern man at the sight of suffering is, to my mind, far greater proof of culture and moral elevation than hatred and aversion. Woman is as tearful and as coarse in her feelings now as she was in the Middle Ages, and to my thinking those who advise that she should be educated like a man are quite right.

My wife also dislikes Katya for having been an actress, for ingratitude, for pride, for eccentricity, and for the numerous vices which one woman can always find in another.

Besides my wife and daughter and me, there are dining with us two or three of my daughter's friends and Alexandr Adolfovitch Gnekker, her admirer and suitor. He is a fair-haired young man under thirty, of medium height, very stout and broad-shouldered, with red whiskers near his ears, and little waxed moustaches which make his plump smooth face look like a toy. He is dressed in a very short reefer jacket, a flowered waistcoat, breeches very full at the top and very narrow at the ankle, with a large check pattern on them, and yellow boots without heels. He has prominent eyes like a crab's, his cravat is like a crab's neck, and I even fancy there is a smell of crab-soup about the young man's whole person. He visits us every day, but no one in my family knows anything of his origin nor of the place of his education, nor of his means of livelihood. He neither plays nor sings, but has some connection with music and singing, sells somebody's pianos somewhere, is frequently at the Conservatoire, is acquainted with all the celebrities, and is a steward at the concerts; he criticizes music with great authority, and I have noticed that people are eager to agree with him.

Rich people always have dependents hanging about them; the arts and sciences have the same. I believe there is not an art nor a science in the world free from " foreign bodies " after the style of this Mr. Gnekker. I am not a musician, and possibly I am mistaken in regard to Mr. Gnekker, of whom, indeed, I know very little. But his air of authority and the dignity with which he takes his stand beside the piano when any one is playing or singing strike me as very suspicious.

You may be ever so much of a gentleman and a privy councillor, but if you have a daughter you cannot be secure of immunity from that petty bourgeois atmosphere which is so often brought into your house and into your mood by the attentions of suitors, by matchmaking and marriage. I can never reconcile myself, for instance, to the expression of triumph on my wife's face every time Gnekker is in our company, nor can I reconcile myself to the bottles of Lafitte, port and sherry which are only brought out on his account, that he may see with his own eyes the liberal and luxurious way in which we live. I cannot tolerate the habit of spasmodic laughter Liza has picked up at the Conservatoire, and her way of screwing up her eyes whenever there are men in the room. Above all, I cannot understand why a creature utterly alien to my habits, my studies, my whole manner of life, completely different from the people I like, should come and see me every day, and every day should dine with me. My wife and my servants mysteriously whisper that he is a suitor, but still I don't understand his presence; it

rouses in me the same wonder and perplexity as if
they were to set a Zulu beside me at the table.   And
it seems strange to me, too, that my daughter, whom
I am used to thinking of as a child, should love that
cravat, those eyes, those soft cheeks. . . .

In the old days I used to like my dinner, or at least
was indifferent about it; now it excites in me no feeling but weariness and irritation.   Ever since I became an " Excellency " and one of the Deans of the
Faculty my family has for some reason found it
necessary to make a complete change in our menu
and dining habits.   Instead of the simple dishes to
which I was accustomed when I was a student and
when I was in practice, now they feed me with a
purée with little white things like circles floating
about in it, and kidneys stewed in madeira.   My
rank as a general and my fame have robbed me for
ever of cabbage-soup and savoury pies, and goose
with apple-sauce, and bream with boiled grain.
They have robbed me of our maid-servant Agasha,
a chatty and laughter-loving old woman, instead of
whom Yegor, a dull-witted and conceited fellow with
a white glove on his right hand, waits at dinner.
The intervals between the courses are short, but they
seem immensely long because there is nothing to
occupy them.   There is none of the gaiety of the
old days, the spontaneous talk, the jokes, the
laughter; there is nothing of mutual affection and the
joy which used to animate the children, my wife, and
me when in old days we met together at meals.   For
me, the celebrated man of science, dinner was a time
of rest and reunion, and for my wife and children a

fête — brief indeed, but bright and joyous — in which they knew that for half an hour I belonged, not to science, not to students, but to them alone. Our real exhilaration from one glass of wine is gone for ever, gone is Agasha, gone the bream with boiled grain, gone the uproar that greeted every little startling incident at dinner, such as the cat and dog fighting under the table, or Katya's bandage falling off her face into her soup-plate.

To describe our dinner nowadays is as uninteresting as to eat it. My wife's face wears a look of triumph and affected dignity, and her habitual expression of anxiety. She looks at our plates and says, " I see you don't care for the joint. Tell me; you don't like it, do you? " and I am obliged to answer: " There is no need for you to trouble, my dear; the meat is very nice." And she will say: " You always stand up for me, Nikolay Stepanovitch, and you never tell the truth. Why is Alexandr Adolfovitch eating so little? " And so on in the same style all through dinner. Liza laughs spasmodically and screws up her eyes. I watch them both, and it is only now at dinner that it becomes absolutely evident to me that the inner life of these two has slipped away out of my ken. I have a feeling as though I had once lived at home with a real wife and children and that now I am dining with visitors, in the house of a sham wife who is not the real one, and am lookin at a Liza who is not the real Liza. A startling change has taken place in both of them; I have missed the long process by which that change was effected, and it is no wonder that I can make nothing

of it. Why did that change take place? I don't
know. Perhaps the whole trouble is that God has
not given my wife and daughter the same strength of
character as me. From childhood I have been accustomed to resisting external influences, and have
steeled myself pretty thoroughly. Such catastrophes
in life as fame, the rank of a general, the transition
from comfort to living beyond our means, acquaintance with celebrities, etc., have scarcely affected me,
and I have remained intact and unashamed; but on
my wife and Liza, who have not been through the
same hardening process and are weak, all this has
fallen like an avalanche of snow, overwhelming them.
Gnekker and the young ladies talk of fugues, of
counterpoint, of singers and pianists, of Bach and
Brahms, while my wife, afraid of their suspecting
her of ignorance of music, smiles to them sympathet-
ically and mutters: "That's exquisite . . . really!
You don't say so! . . . Gnekker eats with solid dignity, jests with solid dignity, and condescendingly
listens to the remarks of the young ladies. From
time to time he is moved to speak in bad French, and
then, for some reason or other, he thinks it necessary
to address me as "*Votre Excellence.*"

And I am glum. Evidently I am a constraint to
them and they are a constraint to me. I have never
in my earlier days had a close knowledge of class an-
tagonism, but now I am tormented by something of
that sort. I am on the lookout for nothing but bad
qualities in Gnekker; I quickly find them, and am
fretted at the thought that a man not of my circle is
sitting here as my daughter's suitor. His presence

has a bad influence on me in other ways, too. As a rule, when I am alone or in the society of people I like, never think of my own achievements, or, if I do recall them, they seem to me as trivial as though I had only completed my studies yesterday; but in the presence of people like Gnekker my achievements in science seem to be a lofty mountain the top of which vanishes into the clouds, while at its foot Gnekkers are running about scarcely visible to the naked eye.

After dinner I go into my study and there smoke my pipe, the only one in the whole day, the sole relic of my old bad habit of smoking from morning till night. While I am smoking my wife comes in and sits down to talk to me. Just as in the morning, I know beforehand what our conversation is going to be about.

"I must talk to you seriously, Nikolay Stepanovitch," she begins. "I mean about Liza. . . . Why don't you pay attention to it?"

"To what?"

"You pretend to notice nothing. But that is not right. We can't shirk responsibility. . . . Gnekker has intentions in regard to Liza. . . . What do you say?"

"That he is a bad man I can't say, because I don't know him, but that I don't like him I have told you a thousand times already."

"But you can't . . . you can't!"

She gets up and walks about in excitement.

"You can't take up that attitude to a serious step," she says. "When it is a question of our daughter's happiness we must lay aside all personal feeling. I know you do not like him. . . . Very good . . . if we refuse him now, if we break it all off, how can you be sure that Liza will not have a grievance against us all her life? Suitors are not plentiful nowadays, goodness knows, and it may happen that no other match will turn up. . . . He is very much in love with Liza, and she seems. to like him. . . . Of course, he has no settled position, but that can't be helped. Please God, in time he will get one. He is of good family and well off."

" Where did you learn that? "

" He told us so. His father has a large house in Harkov and an estate in the neighbourhood. In short, Nikolay Stepanovitch, you absolutely must go to Harkov."

" What for? "

" You will find out all about him there. . . . You know the professors there; they will help you. I would go myself, but I am a woman. I cannot. . . ."

" I am not going to Harkov," I say morosely.

My wife is frightened, and a look of intense suffering comes into her face.

" For God's sake, Nikolay Stepanovitch," she implores me, with tears in her voice —" for God's sake, take this burden off me! I am so worried! "

It is painful for me to look at her.

" Very well, Varya," I say affectionately, " if you wish it, then certainly I will go to Harkov and do all you want."

She presses her handkerchief to her eyes and goes off to her room to cry, and I am left alone.

A little later lights are brought in. The arm-
chair and the lamp-shade cast familiar shadows that
have long grown wearisome on the walls and on the
floor, and when I look at them I feel as though the
night had come and with it my accursed sleeplessness. I lie on my bed, then get up and walk about
the room, then lie down again. As a rule it is after
dinner, at the approach of evening, that my nervous
excitement reaches its highest pitch. For no reason
I begin crying and burying my head in the pillow.
At such times I am afraid that some one may come
in; I am afraid of suddenly dying; I am ashamed of
my tears, and altogether there is something insuf-
ferable in my soul. I feel that I can no longer bear
the sight of my lamp, of my books, of the shadows
on the floor. I cannot bear the sound of the voices
coming from the drawing-room. Some force un-
seen, uncomprehended, is roughly thrusting me out
of my flat. I leap up hurriedly, dress, and cautiously, that my family may not notice, slip out into
the street. Where am I to go?

The answer to that question has long been ready
in my brain. To Katya.

III

As a rule she is lying on the sofa or in a lounge-
chair reading. Seeing me, she raises her read languidly, sits up, and shakes hands.

" You are always lying down," I say, after pausing
and taking breath. " That's not good for you.
You ought to occupy yourself with something."

" What ? "

" I say you ought to occupy yourself in some way."

" With what? A woman can be nothing but a simple workwoman or an actress."

" Well, if you can't be a workwoman, be an actress."

She says nothing.

" You ought to get married,'' I say, half in jest.

" There is no one to marry. There's no reason to, either."

" You can't live like this."

" Without a husband? Much that matters; I could have as many men as I like if I wanted to."

" That's ugly, Katya."

" What is ugly ? "

" Why, what you have just said."

Noticing that I am hurt and wishing to efface the disagreeable impression, Katya says:

" Let us go; come this way."

She takes me into a very snug little room, and says, pointing to the writing-table:

" Look . . . I have got that ready for you. You shall work here. Come here every day and bring your work with you. They only hinder you there at home. Will you work here? Will you like to?"

Not to wound her by refusing, I answer that I will work here, and that I like the room very much. Then we both sit down in the snug little room and begin talking.

The warm, snug surroundings and the presence of a sympathetic person does not, as in old days, arouse in me a feeling of pleasure, but an intense impulse to complain and grumble. I feel for some reason that if I lament and complain I shall feel better.

" Things are in a bad way with me, my dear — very bad. . . ."

" What is it? "

" You see how it is, my dear; the best and holiest right of kings is the right of mercy. And I have always felt myself a king, since I have made unlimited use of that right. I have never judged, I have been indulgent, I have readily forgiven every one, right and left. Where others have protested and expressed indignation, I have only advised and persuaded. All my life it has been my endeavour that my society should not be a burden to my family, to my students, to my colleagues, to my servants. And I know that this attitude to people has had a good influence on all who have chanced to come into contact with me. But now I am not a king. Something is happening to me that is only excusable in a slave; day and night my brain is haunted by evil thoughts, and feelings such as I never knew before are brooding in my soul. I am full of hatred, and contempt, and indignation, and loathing, and dread. I have become execessively severe, exacting, irritable, ungracious, suspicious. Even things that in old days would have provoked me only to an unnecessary jest and a good-natured laugh now arouse an oppressive feeling in me. My reasoning, too, has undergone a change: in old days I despised money; now I harbour an evil feeling, not towards money, but towards the rich as though they were to blame: in old days I hated violence and tyranny, but now I hate the men who make use of violence, as though they were alone to blame, and not all of us who do not know how to educate each other. What is the meaning of it? If these new ideas and new feelings have come from a change of convictions, what is that change due to? Can the world have grown worse and I better, or was I blind before and indifferent? If this change is the result of a general decline of physical and intellectual powers — I am ill, you know, and every day I am losing weight — my position is pitiable; it means that my new ideas are morbid and abnormal; I ought to be ashamed of them and think them of no consequence. . . ."

" Illness has nothing to do with it," Katya interrupts me; " it's simply that your eyes are opened, that's all. You have seen what in old days, for some reason, you refused to see. To my thinking, what you ought to do first of all, is to break with your family for good, and go away."

" You are talking nonsense."

" You don't love them; why should you force your feelings? Can you call them a family? Nonentities! If they died today, no one would notice their absence tomorrow."

Katya despises my wife and Liza as much as they hate her. One can hardly talk at this date of people's having a right to despise one another. But if one looks at it from Katya's standpoint and recognizes such a right, one can see she has as much right to despise my wife and Liza as they have to hate her.

" Nonentities," she goes on. " Have you had dinner today? How was it they did not forget to tell you it was ready? How is it they still remember your existence? "

" Katya," I say sternly, " I beg you to be silent."

" You think I enjoy talking about them? I should be glad not to know them at all. Listen, my dear: give it all up and go away. Go abroad. The sooner the better."

" What nonsense! What about the University? "

" The University, too. What is it to you? There's no sense in it, anyway. You have been lecturing for thirty years, and where are your pupils? Are many of them celebrated scientific men? Count them up! And to multiply the doctors who exploit ignorance and pile up hundreds of thousands for themselves, there is no need to be a good and talented man. You are not wanted."

" Good heavens! how harsh you are!" I cry in horror. " How harsh you are! Be quiet or I will go away! I don't know how to answer the harsh things you say! "

The maid comes in and summons us to tea. At the samovar our conversation, thank God, changes. After having had my grumble out, I have a longing to give way to another weakness of old age, reminiscences. I tell Katya about my past, and to my great astonishment tell her incidents which, till then, I did not suspect of being still preserved in my memory, and she listens to me with tenderness, with pride, holding her breath. I am particularly fond of tell-

ing her how I was educated in a seminary and
dreamed of going to the University.

" At times I used to walk about our seminary garden . . ." I would tell her. " If from some faraway tavern the wind floated sounds of a song and
the squeaking of an accordion, or a sledge with bells
dashed by the garden-fence, it was quite enough to
send a rush of happiness, filling not only my heart,
but even my stomach, my legs, my arms. . . . I
would listen to the accordion or the bells dying away
in the distance and imagine myself a doctor, and
paint pictures, one better than another. And here,
as you see, my dreams have come true. I have had
more than I dared to dream of. For thirty years
I have been the favourite professor, I have had
splendid comrades, I have enjoyed fame and honour.
I have loved, married from passionate love, have
had children. In fact, looking back upon it, I see my
whole life as a fine composition arranged with talent.
Now all that is left to me is not to spoil the end.
For that I must die like a man. If death is really
a thing to dread, I must meet it as a teacher, a man
of science, and a citizen of a Christian country ought
to meet it, with courage and untroubled soul. But
I am spoiling the end; I am sinking, I fly to you, I
beg for help, and you tell me ' Sink; that is what you
ought to do.' "

But here there comes a ring at the front-door.
Katya and I recognize it, and say:

" It must be Mihail Fyodorovitch."

And a minute later my colleague, the philologist
Mihail Fyodorovitch, a tall, well-built man of fifty,

clean-shaven, with thick grey hair and black eyebrows, walks in.   He is a good-natured man and an
excellent comrade.   He comes of a fortunate and
talented old noble family which has played a prominent part in the history of literature and enlighten-
ment.   He is himself intelligent, talented, and very
highly educated, but has his oddities.   To a certain
extent we are all odd and all queer fish, but in his
oddities there is something exceptional, apt to cause
anxiety among his acquaintances.   I know a good
many people for whom his oddities completely obscure his good qualities.

Coming in to us, he slowly takes off his gloves and
says in his velvety bass:

"Good-evening.   Are you having tea?   That's
just right.   It's diabolically cold."

Then he sits down to the table, takes a glass, and
at once begins talking.   What is most characteristic
in his manner of talking is the countinually jesting
tone, a sort of mixture of philosophy and drollery as
in Shakespeare's gravediggers.   He is always talking about serious things, but he never speaks seriously.   His judgments are always harsh and railing, but, thanks to his soft, even, jesting tone, the
harshness and abuse do not jar upon the ear, and one
soon grows used to them.   Every evening he brings
with him five or six anecdotes from the University,
and he usually begins with them when he sits down
to table.

"Oh, Lord!" he sighs, twitching his black eyebrows ironically.   "What comic people there are in
the world!"

" Well? " asks Katya.

" As I was coming from my lecture this morning I met that old idiot N. N—— on the stairs. . . . He was going along as usual, sticking out his chin like a horse, looking for some one to listen to his grumblings at his migraine, at his wife, and his students who won't attend his lectures. ' Oh,' I thought, ' he has seen me — I am done for now; it is all up. . . .' "

And so on in the same style. Or he will begin like this:

" I was yesterday at our friend Z. Z——'s public lecture. I wonder how it is our alma mater — don't speak of it after dark — dare display in public such noodles and patent dullards as that Z. Z——. Why, he is a European fool! Upon my word, you could not find another like him all over Europe! He lectures — can you imagine? — as though he were sucking a sugar-stick — sue, sue, sue; . . . he is in a nervous funk; he can hardly decipher his own manuscript; his poor little thoughts crawl along like a bishop on a bicycle, and, what's worse, you can never make out what he is trying to say. The deadly dulness is awful, the very flies expire. It can only be compared with the boredom in the assembly-hall at the yearly meeting when the traditional address is read — damn it! "

And at once an abrupt transition:

" Three years ago — Nikolay Stepanovitch here will remember it — I had to deliver that address. It was hot, stifling, my uniform cut me under the arms — it was deadly! I read for half an hour,

for an hour, for an hour and a half, for two hours.
. . . ' Come,' I thought; ' thank God, there are only
ten pages left ! ' And at the end there were four
pages that there was no need to read, and I reckoned
to leave them out. ' So there are only six really,'
I thought; ' that is, only six pages left to read.'
But, only fancy, I chanced to glance before me, and,
sitting in the front row, side by side, were a general
with a ribbon on his breast and a bishop. The poor
beggars were numb with boredom; they were staring
with their eyes wide open to keep awake, and yet
they were trying to put on an expression of attention
and to pretend that they understood what I was saying and liked it. ' Well,' I thought, ' since you like
it you shall have it ! I'll pay you out;' so I just
gave them those four pages too."

As is usual with ironical people, when he talks
nothing in his face smiles but his eyes and eyebrows.
At such times there is no trace of hatred or spite in
his eyes, but a great deal of humour, and that peculiar fox-like slyness which is only to be noticed in
very observant people. Since I am speaking about
his eyes, I notice another peculiarity in them.
When he takes a glass from Katya, or listens to her
speaking, or looks after her as she goes out of the
room for a moment, I notice in his eyes something
gentle, beseeching, pure. . . .

The maid-servant takes away the samovar and
puts on the table a large piece of cheese, some fruit,
and a bottle of Crimean champagne — a rather
poor wine of which Katya had grown fond in the
Crimea. Mihail Fyodorovitch takes two packs of

cards off the whatnot and begins to play patience. According to him, some varieties of patience require great concentration and attention, yet while he lays out the cards he does not leave off distracting his attention with talk. Katya watches his cards attentively, and more by gesture than by words helps him in his play. She drinks no more than a couple of wine-glasses of wine the whole evening; I drink four glasses, and the rest of the bottle falls to the share of Mihail Fyodorovitch, who can drink a great deal and never get drunk.

Over our patience we settle various questions, principally of the higher order, and what we care for most of all — that is, science and learning — is more roughly handled than anything.

" Science, thank God, has outlived its day," says Mihail Fyodorovitch emphatically. " Its song is sung. Yes, indeed. Mankind begins to feel impelled to replace it by something different. It has grown on the soil of superstition, been nourished by superstition, and is now just as much the quintessence of superstition as its defunct granddames, alchemy, metaphysics, and philospohy. And, after all, what has it given to mankind? Why, the difference between the learned Europeans and the Chinese who have no science is trifling, purely external. The Chinese know nothing of science, but what have they lost thereby? "

" Flies know nothing of science, either," I observe, " but what of that? "

" There is no need to be angry, Nikolay Stepanovitch. I only say this here between ourselves. . . .

I am more careful than you think, and I am not going to say this in public — God forbid! The superstition exists in the multitude that the arts and sciences are superior to agriculture, commerce, superior to handicrafts. Our sect is maintained by that superstition, and it is not for you and me to destroy it. God forbid!"

After patience the younger generation comes in for a dressing too.

"Our audiences have degenerated," sighs Mihail Fyodorovitch. "Not to speak of ideals and all the rest of it, if only they were capable of work and rational thought! In fact, it's a case of 'I look with mournful eyes on the young men of today.'"

"Yes; they have degenerated horribly," Katya agrees. "Tell me, have you had one man of distinction among them for the last five or ten years?"

"I don't know how it is with the other professors, but I can't remember any among mine."

"I have seen in my day many of your students and young scientific men and many actors — well, I have never once been so fortunate as to meet — I won't say a hero or a man of talent, but even an interesting man. It's all the same grey mediocrity, puffed up with self-conceit."

All this talk of degeneration always affects me as though I had accidentally overheard offensive talk about my own daughter. It offends me that these charges are wholesale, and rest on such worn-out commonplaces, on such wordy vapourings as degeneration and absence of ideals, or on references to the splendours of the past. Every accusation, even

if it is uttered in ladies' society, ought to be formu-
lated with all possible definiteness, or it is not an
accusation, but idle disparagement, unworthy of
decent people.

I am an old man, I have been lecturing for thirty
years, but I notice neither degeneration nor lack of
ideals, and I don't find that the present is worse
than the past. My porter Nikolay, whose experience of this subject has its value, says that the students of today are neither better nor worse than
those of the past.

If I were asked what I don't like in my pupils of
today, I should answer the question, not straight off
and not at length, but with sufficient definiteness.
I know their failings, and so have no need to resort
to vague generalities. I don't like their smoking,
using spirituous beverages, marrying late, and often
being so irresponsible and careless that they will let
one of their number be starving in their midst while
they neglect to pay their subscriptions to the Students' Aid Society. They don't know modern languages, and they don't express themselves correctly
in Russian; no longer ago than yesterday my colleague, the professor of hygiene, complained to me
that he had to give twice as many lectures, because
the students had a very poor knowledge of physics
and were utterly ignorant of meteorology. They
are readily carried away by the influence of the last
new writers, even when they are not first-rate, but
they take absolutely no interest in classics such as
Shakespeare, Marcus Aurelius, Epictetus, or Pascal,
and this inability to distinguish the great from the

small betrays their ignorance of practical life more than anything. All difficult questions that have more or less a social character (for instance the migration question) they settle by studying monographs on the subject, but not by way of scientific investigation or experiment, though that method is at their disposal and is more in keeping with their calling. They gladly become ward-surgeons, assistants, demonstrators, external teachers, and are ready to fill such posts until they are forty, though independence, a sense of freedom and personal initiative, are no less necessary in science than, for instance, in art or commerce. I have pupils and listeners, but no successors and helpers, and so I love them and am touched by them, but am not proud of them. And so on, and so on. . . .

Such shortcomings, however numerous they may be, can only give rise to a pessimistic or fault-finding temper in a faint-hearted and timid man. All these failings have a casual, transitory character, and are completely dependent on conditions of life; in some ten years they will have disappeared or given place to other fresh defects, which are all inevitable and will in their turn alarm the faint-hearted. The students' sins often vex me, but that vexation is nothing in comparison with the joy I have been experiencing now for the last thirty years when I talk to my pupils, lecture to them, watch their relations, and compare them with people not of their circle.

Mihail Fyodorovitch speaks evil of everything. Katya listens, and neither of them notices into what depths the apparently innocent diversion of finding

fault with their neighbours is gradually drawing
them. They are not conscious how by degrees simple talk passes into malicious mockery and jeering,
and how they are both beginning to drop into the
habits and methods of slander.

"Killing types one meets with," says Mihail Fyodorovitch. "I went yesterday to our friend Yegor
Petrovitch's, and there I found a studious gentleman, one of your medicals in his third year, I believe.
Such a face! . . . in the Dobrolubov style, the im-
print of profound thought on his brow; we got into
talk. 'Such doings, young man,' said I. 'I've
read,' said I, 'that some German — I've forgotten
his name — has created from the human brain a new
kind of alkaloid, idiotine.' What do you think?
He believed it, and there was positively an expression of respect on his face, as though to say, 'See
what we fellows can do!' And the other day I
went to the theatre. I took my seat. In the next
row directly in front of me were sitting two men:
one of 'us fellows' and apparently a law student,
the other a shaggy-looking figure, a medical student.
The latter was as drunk as a cobbler. He did not
look at the stage at all. He was dozing with his
nose on his shirt-front. But as soon as an actor
begins loudly reciting a monologue, or simply raises
his voice, our friend starts, pokes his neighbour in
the ribs, and asks, 'What is he saying? Is it
elevating?' 'Yes,' answers one of our fellows.
'B-r-r-ravo!' roars the medical student. 'Elevating! Bravo!' He had gone to the theatre, you
see, the drunken blockhead, not for the sake of art,

the play, but for elevation! He wanted noble senti·
ments."

Katya listens and laughs. She has a strange
laugh; she catches her breath in rhythmically regular
gasps, very much as though she were playing the
accordion, and nothing in her face is laughing but
her nostrils. I grow depressed and don't know
what to say. Beside myself, I fire up, leap up from
my seat, and cry:

" Do leave off! Why are you sitting here like
two toads, poisoning the air with your breath?
Give over! "

And without waiting for them to finish their gossip I prepare to go home. And, indeed, it is high
time: it is past ten.

" I will stay a little longer," says Mihail Fyodorovitch. " Will you allow me, Ekaterina Vladi-
mirovna ? "

" I will," answers Katya.

" *Bene!* In that case have up another little
bottle."

They both accompany me with candles to the hall,
and while I put on my fur coat, Mihail Fyodorovitch
says:

" You have grown dreadfully thin and older looking, Nikolay Stepanovitch. What's the matter with
you? Are you ill? "

" Yes; I am not very well."

" And you are not doing anything for it ˙. . ."
Katya puts in grimly.

" Why don't you? You can't go on like that!
God helps those who help themselves, my dear fel-

low. Remember me to your wife and daughter,
and make my apologies for not having been to see
them.   In a day or two, before I go abroad, I shall
come to say good-bye.   I shall be sure to.   I am
going away next week."

I come away from Katya, irritated and alarmed
by what has been said about my being ill, and dis-
satisfied with myself.   I ask myself whether I really
ought not to consult one of my colleagues.   And at
once I imagine how my colleague, after listening to
me, would walk away to the window without speaking, would think a moment, then would turn round
to me and, trying to prevent my reading the truth
in his face, would say in a careless tone: "So far
I see nothing serious, but at the same time, *collega*,
I advise you to lay aside your work. . . ."   And
that would deprive me of my last hope.

Who is without hope?   Now that I am diagnos-
ing my illness and prescribing for myself, from time
to time I hope that I am deceived by my own illness,
that I am mistaken in regard to the albumen and the
sugar I find, and in regard to my heart, and in
regard to the swellings I have twice noticed in the
mornings; when with the fervour of the hypochon-
driac I look through the textbooks of therapeutics
and take a different medicine every day, I keep
fancying that I shall hit upon something comforting.
All that is petty.

Whether the sky is covered with clouds or the
moon and the stars are shining, I turn my eyes towards it every evening and think that death is taking
me soon.   One would think that my thoughts at

such times ought to be deep as the sky, brilliant, striking. . . . But no! I think about myself, about my wife, about Liza, Gnekker, the students, people in general; my thoughts are evil, petty, I am insincere with myself, and at such times my theory of life may be expressed in the words the celebrated Araktcheev said in one of his intimate letters: " Nothing good can exist in the world without evil, and there is more evil than good." That is, everything is disgusting; there is nothing to live for, and the sixty-two years I have already lived must be reckoned as wasted. I catch myself in these thoughts, and try to persuade myself that they are accidental, temporary, and not deeply rooted in me, but at once I think:

" If so, what drives me every evening to those two toads? "

And I vow to myself that I will never go to Katya's again, though I know I shall go next evening.

Ringing the bell at the door and going upstairs, I feel that I have no family now and no desire to bring it back again. It is clear that the new Araktcheev thoughts are not casual, temporary visitors, but have possession of my whole being. With my conscience ill at ease, dejected, languid, hardly able to move my limbs, feeling as though tons were added to my weight, I get into bed and quickly drop asleep.

And then — insomnia!

IV

Summer comes on and life is changed.

One fine morning Liza comes in to me and says in a jesting tone:

"Come, your Excellency! We are ready."

My Excellency is conducted into the street, and seated in a cab. As I go along, having nothing to do, I read the signboards from right to left. The word "Traktir" reads "Ritkart"; that would just suit some baron's family: Baroness Ritkart. Farther on I drive through fields, by the graveyard, which makes absolutely no impression on me, though I shall soon lie in it; then I drive by forests and again by fields. There is nothing of interest. After two hours of driving, my Excellency is conducted into the lower storey of a summer villa and installed in a small, very cheerful little room with light blue hangings.

At night there is sleeplessness as before, but in the morning I do not put a good face upon it and listen to my wife, but lie in bed. I do not sleep, but lie in the drowsy, half-conscious condition in which you know you are not asleep, but dreaming. At midday I get up and from habit sit down at my table, but I do not work now; I amuse myself with French books in yellow covers, sent me by Katya. Of course, it would be more patriotic to read Russian authors, but I must confess I cherish no particular liking for them. With the exception of two or three of the older writers, all our literature of today strikes me as not being literature, but a special sort of home industry, which exists simply in order to be encouraged, though people do not readily make use of its products.   The very best of these home products cannot be called remarkable and cannot be sincerely praised without qualification.   I must say the same of all the literary novelties I have read during the last ten or fifteen years; not one of them is remarkable, and not one of them can be praised without a " but."   Cleverness, a good tone, but no talent; talent, a good tone, but no cleverness; or talent, cleverness, but not a good tone.

I don't say the French books have talent, cleverness, and a good tone.   They don't satisfy me, either. But they are not so tedious as the Russian, and it is not unusual to find in them the chief element of artistic creation — the feeling of personal freedom which is lacking in the Russian authors.   I don't remember one new book in which the author does not try from the first page to entangle himself in all sorts of conditions and contracts with his conscience.   One is afraid to speak of the naked body; another ties himself up hand and foot in psychological analysis; a third must have a " warm attitude to man "; a fourth purposely scrawls whole descriptions of nature that he may not be suspected of writing with a purpose. . . . One is bent upon being middleclass in his work, another must be a nobleman, and so on.   There is intentionalness, circumspection, and self-will, but they have neither the independence nor the manliness to write as they like, and therefore there is no creativeness.

All this applies to what is called belles-lettres.

As for serious treatises in Russian on sociology, for instance, on art, and so on, I do not read them simply from timidity. In my childhood and early youth I had for some reason a terror of doorkeepers and attendants at the theatre, and that terror has remained with me to this day. I am afraid of them even now. It is said that we are only afraid of what we do not understand. And, indeed, it is very difficult to understand why doorkeepers and theatre attendants are so dignified, haughty, and majestically rude. I feel exactly the same terror when I read serious articles. Their extraordinary dignity, their bantering lordly tone, their familiar manner to foreign authors, their ability to split straws with dignity — all that is beyond my understanding; it is intimidating and utterly unlike the quiet, gentlemanly tone to which I am accustomed when I read the works of our medical and scientific writers. It oppresses me to read not only the articles written by serious Russians, but even works translated or edited by them. The pretentious, edifying tone of the preface; the redundancy of remarks made by the translator, which prevent me from concentrating my attention; the question marks and " sic " in parenthesis scattered all over the book or article by the liberal translator, are to my mind an outrage on the author and on my independence as a reader.

Once I was summoned as an expert to a circuit court; in an interval one of my fellow-experts drew my attention to the rudeness of the public prosecutor to the defendants, among whom there were two ladies of good education.   I believe I did not exaggerate at all when I told him that the prosecutor's manner was no ruder than that of the authors of serious articles to one another.   Their manners are, indeed, so rude that I cannot speak of them without distaste.   They treat one another and the writers they criticize either with superfluous respect, at the sacrifice of their own dignity, or, on the contrary, with far more ruthlessness than I have shown in my notes and my thoughts in regard to my future son-in-law Gnekker.   Accusations of irrationality, of evil intentions, and, indeed, of every sort of crime, form an habitual ornament of serious articles.   And that, as young medical men are fond of saying in their monographs, is the *ultima ratio!*   Such ways must infallibly have an effect on the morals of the younger generation of writers, and so I am not at all surprised that in the new works with which our literature has been enriched during the last ten or fifteen years the heroes drink too much vodka and the heroines are not over-chaste.

I read French books, and I look out of the window which is open; I can see the spikes of my garden-fence, two or three scraggy trees, and beyond the fence the road, the fields, and beyond them a broad stretch of pine-wood.   Often I admire a boy and girl, both flaxen-headed and ragged, who clamber on the fence and laugh at my baldness.   In their shining little eyes I read, " Go up, go up, thou baldhead! " They are almost the only people who care nothing for my celebrity or my rank.

Visitors do not come to me every day now.   I

will only mention the visits of Nikolay and Pyotr
Ignatyevitch. Nikolay usually comes to me on holidays, with some pretext of business, though really
to see me. He arrives very much exhilarated, a
thing which never occurs to him in the winter.

"What have you to tell me?" I ask, going out
to him in the hall.

"Your Excellency!" he says, pressing his hand
to his heart and looking at me with the ecstasy of a
lover —"your Excellency! God be my witness!
Strike me dead on the spot! *Gaudeamus egitur ju-
ventus!*"

And he greedily kisses me on the shoulder, on the
sleeve, and on the buttons.

"Is everything going well?" I ask him.

"Your Excellency! So help me God! . . ."

He persists in grovelling before me for no sort
of reason, and soon bores me, so I send him away
to the kitchen, where they give him dinner.

Pyotr Ignatyevitch comes to see me on holidays,
too, with the special object of seeing me and sharing
his thoughts with me. He usually sits down near my
table, modest, neat, and reasonable, and does not
venture to cross his legs or put his elbows on the
table. All the time, in a soft, even, little voice, in
rounded bookish phrases, he tells me various, to his
mind, very interesting and piquant items of news
which he has read in the magazines and journals.
They are all alike and may be reduced to this type:
"A Frenchman has made a discovery; some one else,
a German, has denounced him, proving that the discovery was made in 1870 by some American; while a

third person, also a German, trumps them both by proving they both had made fools of themselves, mistaking bubbles of air for dark pigment under the microscope. Even when he wants to amuse me, Pyotr Ignatyevitch tells me things in the same lengthy, circumstantial manner as though he were defending a thesis, enumerating in detail the literary sources from which he is deriving his narrative, doing his utmost to be accurate as to the date and number of the journals and the name of every one concerned, invariably mentioning it in full — Jean Jacques Petit, never simply Petit. Sometimes he stays to dinner with us, and then during the whole of dinner-time he goes on telling me the same sort of piquant anecdotes, reducing every one at table to a state of dejected boredom. If Gnekker and Liza begin talking before him of fugues and counterpoint, Brahms and Bach, he drops his eyes modestly, and is overcome with embarrassment; he is ashamed that such trivial subjects should be discussed before such serious people as him and me.

In my present state of mind five minutes of him is enough to sicken me as though I had been seeing and hearing him for an eternity. I hate the poor fellow. His soft, smooth voice and bookish language exhaust me, and his stories stupefy me. . . . He cherishes the best of feelings for me, and talks to me simply in order to give me pleasure, and I repay him by looking at him as though I wanted to hypnotize him, and think, " Go, go, go! . . ." But he is not amenable to thought-suggestion, and sits on and on and on. . . .

While he is with me I can never shake off the thought, " It's possible when I die he will be appointed to succeed me," and my poor lecture-hall presents itself to me as an oasis in which the spring is died up; and I am ungracious, silent, and surly with Pyotr Ignatyevitch, as though he were to blame for such thoughts, and not I myself. When he begins, as usual, praising up the German savants, instead of making fun of him good-humouredly, as I used to do, I mutter sullenly:

" Asses, your Germans! . . ."

That is like the late Professor Nikita Krylov, who once, when he was bathing with Pirogov at Revel and vexed at the water's being very cold, burst out with, " Scoundrels, these Germans! " I behave badly with Pyotr Ignatyevitch, and only when he is going away, and from the window I catch a glimpse of his grey hat behind the garden-fence, I want to call out and say, " Forgive me, my dear fellow! "

Dinner is even drearier than in the winter. Gnekker, whom now I hate and despise, dines with us almost every day. I used to endure his presence in silence, now I aim biting remarks at him which make my wife and daughter blush. Carried away by evil feeling, I often say things that are simply stupid, and I don't know why I say them. So on one occasion it happened that I stared a long time at Gnekker, and, *à propos* of nothing, I fired off:

" An eagle may perchance swoop down below a cock,
  But never will the fowl soar upwards to the clouds. . . ."

And the most vexatious thing is that the fowl

Gnekker shows himself much cleverer than the eagle professor.   Knowing that my wife and daughter are on his side, he takes up the line of meeting my gibes with condescending silence, as though to say:

" The old chap is in his dotage; what's the use of talking to him? "

Or he makes fun of me good-naturedly.   It is wonderful how petty a man may become!   I am capable of dreaming all dinner-time of how Gnekker will turn out to be an adventurer, how my wife and Liza will come to see their mistake, and how I will taunt them — and such absurd thoughts at the time when I am standing with one foot in the grave!

There are now, too, misunderstandings of which in the old days I had no idea except from hearsay. Though I am ashamed of it, I will describe one that occurred the other day after dinner.

I was sitting in my room smoking a pipe; my wife came in as usual, sat down, and began saying what a good thing it would be for me to go to Harkov now while it is warm and I have free time, and there find out what sort of person our Gnekker is.

"Very good; I will go," I assented.

My wife, pleased with me, got up and was going to the door, but turned back and said:

" By the way, I have another favour to ask of you. I know you will be angry, but it is my duty to warn you. . . . Forgive my saying it, Nikolay Stepano-vitch, but all our neighbours and acquaintances have begun talking about your being so often at Katya's. She is clever and well-educated; I don't deny that her company may be agreeable; but at your age and with your social position it seems strange that you should find pleasure in her society. . . . Besides, she has such a reputation that . . ."

All the blood suddenly rushed to my brain, my eyes flashed fire, I leaped up and, clutching at my head and stamping my feet, shouted in a voice unlike my own:

" Let me alone! let me alone! let me alone! "

Probably my face was terrible, my voice was strange, for my wife suddenly turned pale and began shrieking aloud in a despairing voice that was utterly unlike her own. Liza, Gnekker, then Yegor, came running in at our shouts. . . .

" Let me alone! " I cried; " let me alone! Go away! "

My legs turned numb as though they had ceased to exist; I felt myself falling into some one's arms; for a little while I still heard weeping, then sank into a swoon which lasted two or three hours.

Now about Katya; she comes to see me every day towards evening, and of course neither the neighbours nor our acquaintances can avoid noticing it. She comes in for a minute and carries me off for a drive with her. She has her own horse and a new chaise bought this summer. Altogether she lives in an expensive style; she has taken a big detached villa with a large garden, and has taken all her town retinue with her — two maids, a coachman . . . I often ask her:

" Katya, what will you live on when you have spent your father's money? "

" Then we shall see," she answers.

" That money, my dear, deserves to be treated more seriously. It was earned by a good man, by honest labour."

" You have told me that already. I know it."

At first we drive through the open country, then through the pine-wood which is visible from my window. Nature seems to me as beautiful as it always has been, though some evil spirit whispers to me that these pines and fir trees, birds, and white clouds on the sky, wlll not notice my absence when in three or four months I am dead. Katya loves driving, and she is pleased that it is fine weather and that I am sitting beside her. She is in good spirits and does not say harsh things.

" You are a very good man, Nikolay Stepanovitch," she says. " You are a rare specimen, and there isn't an actor who would understand how to play you. Me or Mihail Fyodorovitch, for instance, any poor actor could do, but not you. And I envy you, I envy you horribly! Do you know what I stand for? What? "

She ponders for a minute, and then asks me:

" Nikolay Stepanovitch, I am a negative phenomenon! Yes? "

" Yes," I answer.

" H'm! what am I to do? "

What answer was I to make her? It is easy to say " work," or " give your possessions to the poor," or " know yourself," and because it is so easy to say that, I don't know what to answer.

My colleagues when they teach therapeutics advise " the individual study of each separate case."

One has but to obey this advice to gain the conviction that the methods recommended in the textbooks as the best and as providing a safe basis for treatment turn out to be quite unsuitable in individual cases. It is just the same in moral ailments.

But I must make some answer, and I say:

" You have too much free time, my dear; you absolutely must take up some occupation. After all, why shouldn't you be an actress again if it is your vocation? "

" I cannot! "

" Your tone and manner suggest that you are a victim. I don't like that, my dear; it is your own fault. Remember, you began with falling out with people and methods, but you have done nothing to make either better. You did not struggle with evil, but were cast down by it, and you are not the victim of the struggle, but of your own impotence. Well, of course you were young and inexperienced then; now it may all be different. Yes, really, go on the stage. You will work, you will serve a sacred art."

" Don't pretend, Nikolay Stepanovitch," Katya interrupts me.   " Let us make a compact once for all; we will talk about actors, actresses, and authors, but we will let art alone. You are a splendid and rare person, but you don't know enough about art sincerely to think it sacred. You have no instinct or feeling for art. You have been hard at work all your life, and have not had time to acquire that feeling. Altogether . . . I don't like talk about art," she goes on nervously. " I don't like it! And, my goodness, how they have vulgarized it! "

" Who has vulgarized it? "

" They have vulgarized it by drunkenness, the newspapers by their familiar attitude, clever people by philosophy."

" Philosophy has nothing to do with it."

" Yes, it has. If any one philosophizes about it, it shows he does not understand it."

To avoid bitterness I hasten to change the subject, and then sit a long time silent. Only when we are driving out of the wood and turning towards Katya's villa I go back to my former question, and say:

" You have still not answered me, why you don't want to go on the stage."

" Nikolay Stepanovitch, this is cruel!" she cries, and suddenly flushes all over. " You want me to tell you the truth aloud? Very well, if . . . if you like it! I have no talent! No talent and . . . and a great deal of vanity! So there! "

After making this confession she turns her face away from me, and to hide the trembling of her hands tugs violently at the reins.

As we are driving towards her villa we see Mihail Fyodorovitch walking near the gate, impatiently awaiting us.

" That Mihail Fyodorovitch again! " says Katya with vexation. " Do rid me of him, please! I am sick and tired of him . . . bother him! "

Mihail Fyodorovitch ought to have gone abroad long ago, but he puts off going from week to. week. Of late there have been certain changes in him. He looks, as it were, sunken, has taken to drinking until he is tipsy, a thing which never used to happen to

him, and his black eyebrows are beginning to turn
grey. When our chaise stops at the gate he does
not conceal his joy and his impatience. He fussily
helps me and Katya out, hurriedly asks questions,
laughs, rubs his hands, and that gentle, imploring,
pure expression, which I used to notice only in his
eyes, is now suffused all over his face. He is glad
and at the same time he is ashamed of his gladness,
ashamed of his habit of spending every evening with
Katya. And he thinks it necessary to explain his
visit by some obvious absurdity such as: " I was driving by, and I thought I would just look in for a
minute."

We all three go indoors; first we drink tea, then
the familiar packs of cards, the big piece of cheese,
the fruit, and the bottle of Crimean champagne are
put upon the table. The subjects of our conversation are not new; they are just the same as in the
winter. We fall foul of the University, the students, and literature and the theatre; the air grows
thick and stifling with evil speaking, and poisoned by
the breath, not of two toads as in the winter, but of
three. Besides the velvety baritone laugh and the
giggle like the gasp of a concertina, the maid who
waits upon us hears an unpleasant cracked " He,
he! " like the chuckle of a general in a vaudeville.

V

There are terrible nights with thunder, lightning,
rain, and wind, such as are called among the people

" sparrow nights." There has been one such night in my personal life. . . .

I woke up after midnight and leaped suddenly out of bed. It seemed to me for some reason that I was just immediately going to die. Why did it seem so? I had no sensation in my body that suggested my immediate death, but my soul was oppressed with terror, as though I had suddenly seen a vast menacing glow of fire.

I rapidly struck a light, drank some water straight out of the decanter, then hurried to the open window. The weather outside was magnificent. There was a smell of hay and some other very sweet scent. I could see the spikes of the fence, the gaunt, drowsy trees by the window, the road, the dark streak of woodland, there was a serene, very bright moon in the sky and not a single cloud, perfect stillness, not one leaf stirring. I felt that everything was looking at me and waiting for me to die. . . .

It was uncanny. I closed the window and ran to my bed. I felt for my pulse, and not finding it in my wrist, tried to find it in my temple, then in my chin, and again in my wrist, and everything I touched was cold and clammy with sweat. My breathing came more and more rapidly, my body was shivering, all my inside was in commotion; I had a sensation on my face and on my bald head as though they were covered with spiders' webs.

What should I do? Call my family? No; it would be no use. I could not imagine what my wife and Liza would do when they came in to me.

I hid my head under the pillow, closed my eyes,

and waited and waited. . . . My spine was cold; it seemed to be drawn inwards, and I felt as though death were coming upon me stealthily from behind. . . . .

" Kee-vee! kee-vee! " I heard a sudden shriek in the night's stillness, and did not know where it was —in my breast or in the street. " Kee-vee! kee-vee! "

" My God, how terrible! " I would have drunk some more water, but by then it was fearful to open my eyes and I was afraid to raise my head. I was possessed by unaccountable animal terror, and I cannot understand why I was so frightened: was it that I wanted to live, or that some new unknown pain was in store for me?

Upstairs, overhead, some one moaned or laughed. . . . I listened. Soon afterwards there was a sound of footsteps on the stairs. Some one came hurriedly down, then went up again. A minute later there was a sound of steps downstairs again; some one stopped near my door and listened.

" Who is there? " I cried.

The door opened. I boldly opened my eyes, and saw my wife. Her face was pale and her eyes were tear-stained.

" You are not asleep, Nikolay Stepanovitch? " she asked.

" What is it? "

" For God's sake, go up and have a look at Liza; there is something the matter with her. . . ."

" Very good, with pleasure," I muttered, greatly relieved at not being alone. " Very good, this minute. . . ."

I followed my wife, heard what she said to me, and was too agitated to understand a word. Patches of light from her candle danced about the stairs, our long shadows trembled. My feet caught in the skirts of my dressing-gown; I gasped for breath, and felt as though something were pursuing me and trying to catch me from behind.

"I shall die on the spot, here on the staircase," I thought. "On the spot. . . ." But we passed the staircase, the dark corridor with the Italian windows, and went into Liza's room. She was sitting on the bed in her nightdress, with her bare feet hanging down, and she was moaning.

"Oh, my God! Oh, my God!" she was muttering, screwing up her eyes at our candle. "I can't bear it."

"Liza, my child," I said, "what is it?"

Seeing me, she began crying out, and flung herself on my neck.

"My kind papa! . . ." she sobbed — "my dear, good papa . . . my darling, my pet, I don't know what is the matter with me. . . . I am miserable!"

She hugged me, kissed me, and babbled fond words I used to hear from her when she was a child.

"Calm yourself, my child. God be with you," I said. "There is no need to cry. I am miserable, too."

I tried to tuck her in; my wife gave her water, and we awkwardly stumbled by her bedside; my shoulder jostled against her shoulder, and meanwhile I was thinking how we used to give our children their bath together.

"Help her! help her!" my wife implored me. "Do something!"

What could I do? I could do nothing. There was some load on the girl's heart; but I did not understand, I knew nothing about it, and could only mutter:

"It's nothing, it's nothing; it will pass. Sleep, sleep!"

To make things worse, there was a sudden sound of dogs howling, at first subdued and uncertain, then loud, two dogs howling together. I had never attached significance to such omens as the howling of dogs or the shrieking of owls, but on that occasion it sent a pang to my heart, and I hastened to explain the howl to myself.

"It's nonsense," I thought, "the influence of one organism on another. The intensely strained condition of my nerves has infected my wife, Liza, the dog — that is all. . . . Such infection explains presentiments, forebodings. . . ."

When a little later I went back to my room to write a prescription for Liza, I no longer thought I should die at once, but only had such a weight, such a feeling of oppression in my soul that I felt actually sorry that I had not died on the spot. For a long time I stood motionless in the middle of the room, pondering what to prescribe for Liza. But the moans overhead ceased, and I decided to prescribe nothing, and yet I went on standing there. . . .

There was a deathlike stillness, such a stillness, as some author has expressed it, "it rang in one's ears." Time passed slowly; the streaks of moonlight on the window-sill did not 'shift their position, but seemed as though frozen. . . . It was still some time before dawn.

But the gate in the fence creaked, some one stole in and, breaking a twig from one of those scraggy trees, cautiously tapped on the window with it.

"Nikolay Stepanovitch," I heard a whisper. "Nikolay Stepanovitch."

I opened the window, and fancied I was dreaming: under the window, huddled against the wall, stood a woman in a black dress, with the moonlight bright upon her, looking at me with great eyes. Her face was pale, stern, and weird-looking in the moonlight, like marble, her chin was quivering.

"It is I," she said — "I . . . Katya."

In the moonlight all women's eyes look big and black, all people look taller and paler, and that was probably why I had not recognized her for the first minute.

"What is it?"

"Forgive me!" she said. "I suddenly felt un-bearably miserable . . . I couldn't stand it, so came here. There was a light in your window and . . . and I ventured to knock. . . . I beg your pardon. . . . Ah! if you knew how miserable I am! What are you doing just now?"

"Nothing. . . . I can't sleep."

"I had a feeling that there was something wrong, but that is nonsense."

Her brows were lifted, her eyes shone with tears, and her whole face was lighted up with the familiar look of trustfulness which I had not seen for so long.

" Nikolay Stepanovitch," she said imploringly, stretching out both hands to me, " my precious friend, I beg you, I implore you. . . . If you don't despise my affection and respect for you, consent to what I ask of you."

" What is it? "

" Take my money from me! "

" Come! what an idea! What do I want with your money? "

" You'll go away somewhere for your health. . . . You ought to go for your health. Will you take it? Yes? Nikolay Stepanovitch darling, yes? "

She looked greedily into my face and repeated: " Yes, you will take it? "

" No, my dear, I won't take it . . ." I said. " Thank you."

She turned her back upon me and bowed her head. Probably I refused her in a tone which made further conversation about money impossible.

" Go home to bed," I said. " We will see each other tomorrow."

" So you don't consider me your friend? " she asked dejectedly.

" I don't say that. But your money would be no use to me now."

" I beg your pardon . . ." she said, dropping her voice a whole octave. " I understand you . . . to be indebted to a person like me . . . a retired actress. . . . But, good-bye. . . ."

And she went away so quickly that I had not time even to say good-bye.

VI

I am in Harkov.

As it would be useless to contend against my present mood and, indeed, beyond my power, I have made up my mind that the last days of my life shall at least be irreproachable externally.   If I am unjust in regard to my wife and daughter, which I fully recognize, I will try and do as she wishes; since she wants me to go to Harkov, I go to Harkov.   Besides, I have become of late so indifferent to everything that it is really all the same to me where I go, to Harkov, or to Paris, or to Berditchev.

I arrived here at midday, and have put up at the hotel not far from the cathedral.   The train was jolting, there were draughts, and now I am sitting on my bed, holding my head and expecting tic douloureux.   I ought to have gone today to see some professors of my acquaintance, but I have neither strength nor inclination.

The old corridor attendant comes in and asks whether I have brought my bed-linen.   I detain him for five minutes, and put several questions to him about Gnekker, on whose account I have come here. The attendant turns out to be a native of Harkov; he knows the town like the fingers of his hand, but does not remember any household of the surname of Gnekker.   I question him about the estate — the same answer.

The clock in the corridor strikes one, then two, then three. . . . These last months in which I am waiting for death seem much longer than the whole of my life. And I have never before been so ready to resign myself to the slowness of time as now. In the old days, when one sat in the station and waited for a train, or presided in an examination-room, a quarter of an hour would seem an eternity. Now I can sit all night on my bed without moving, and quite unconcernedly reflect that tomorrow will be followed by another night as long and colourless, and the day after tomorrow.

In the corridor it strikes five, six, seven. . . . It grows dark.

There is a dull pain in my cheek, the tic beginning. To occupy myself with thoughts, I go back to my old point of view, when I was not so indifferent, and ask myself why I, a distinguished man, a privy councillor, am sitting in this little hotel room, on this bed with the unfamiliar grey quilt. Why am I looking at that cheap tin washing-stand and listening to the whirr of the wretched clock in the corridor? Is all this in keeping with my fame and my lofty position? And I answer these questions with a jeer. I am amused by the naïveté with which I used in my youth to exaggerate the value of renown and of the exceptional position which celebrities are supposed to enjoy. I am famous, my name is pronounced with reverence, my portrait has been both in the *Niva* and in the *Illustrated News of the World;* I have read my biography even in a German magazine. And what of all that? Here I am sitting utterly alone in a strange town, on a strange bed, rubbing my aching cheek with my hand. . . . Domestic wor-

ries, the hard-heartedness of creditors, the rudeness
of the railway servants, the inconveniences of the
passport system, the expensive and unwholesome
food in the refreshment-rooms, the general rudeness
and coarseness in social intercourse — all this, and a
great deal more which would take too long to reckon
up, affects me as much as any working man who is
famous only in his alley.   In what way does my exceptional position find expression?   Admitting that
I am celebrated a thousand times over, that I am a
hero of whom my country is proud.   They publish
bulletins of my illness in every paper, letters of sympathy come to me by post from my colleagues, my
pupils, the general public; but all that does not prevent me from dying in a strange bed, in misery, in
utter loneliness.   Of course, no one is to blame for
that; but I in my foolishness dislike my popularity.
I feel as though it had cheated me.

At ten o'clock I fall asleep, and in spite of the tic
I sleep soundly, and should have gone on sleeping
if I had not been awakened.   Soon after one came a
sudden knock at the door.

" Who is there? "

" A telegram."

" You might have waited till tomorrow," I say
angrily, taking the telegram from the attendant.
" Now I shall not get to sleep again."

" I am sorry.   Your light was burning, so I
thought you were not asleep."

I tear open the telegram and look first at the signature.   From my wife.

" What does she want? "

" Gnekker was secretly married to Liza yesterday. Return."

I read the telegram, and my dismay does not last long. I am dismayed, not by what Liza and Gnekker have done, but by the indifference with which I hear of their marriage. They say philosophers and the truly wise are indifferent. It is false: indifference is the paralysis of the soul; it is premature death.

I go to bed again, and begin trying to think of something to occupy my mind. What am I to think about? I feel as though everything had been thought over already and there is nothing which could hold my attention now.

When daylight comes I sit up in bed with my arms round my knees, and to pass the time I try to know myself. " Know thyself " is excellent and useful advice; it is only a pity that the ancients never thought to indicate the means of following this precept.

When I have wanted to understand somebody or myself I have considered, not the actions, in which everything is relative, but the desires.

" Tell me what you want, and I will tell you what manner of man you are."

And now I examine myself: what do I want?

I want our wives, our children, our friends, our pupils, to love in us, not our fame, not the brand and not the label, but to love us as ordinary men. Anything else? I should like to have had helpers and successors. Anything else? I should like to wake

up in a hundred years' time and to have just a peep
out of one eye at what is happeneing in science.   I
should have liked to have lived another ten years.
. . . What further?   Why, nothing further.   I
think and think, and can think of nothing more.
And however much I might think, and however far
my thoughts might travel, it is clear to me that there
is nothing vital, nothing of great importance in my
desires.   In my passion for science, in my desire to
live, in this sitting on a strange bed, and in this striving to know myself — in all the thoughts, feelings,
and ideas I form about everything, there is no common bond to connect it all into one whole.   Every
feeling and every thought exists apart in me; and in
all my criticisms of science, the theatre, literature,
my pupils, and in all the pictures my imagination
draws, even the most skilful analyst could not find
what is called a general idea, or the god of a living
man.

And if there is not that, then there is nothing.

In a state so poverty-stricken, a serious ailment,
the fear of death, the influences of circumstance and
men were enough to turn upside down and scatter
in fragments all which I had once looked upon as
my theory of life, and in which I had seen the meaning and joy of my existence.   So there is nothing
surprising in the fact that I have over-shadowed the
last months of my life with thoughts and feelings only
worthy of a slave and barbarian, and that now I am
indifferent and take no heed of the dawn.   When a
man has not in him what is loftier and mightier than
all external impressions a bad cold is really enough to

upset his equilibrium and make him begin to see an owl in every bird, to hear a dog howling in every sound. And all his pessimism or optimism with his thoughts great and small have at such times significance as symptoms and nothing more.

I am vanquished. If it is so, it is useless to think, it is useless to talk. I will sit and wait in silence for what is to come.

In the morning the corridor attendant brings me tea and a copy of the local newspaper. Mechanically I read the advertisements on the first page, the leading article, the extracts from the newspapers and journals, the chronicle of events. . . . In the latter I find, among other things, the following paragraph: " Our distinguished savant, Professor Nikolay Stepanovitch So-and-so, arrived yesterday in Harkov, and is staying in the So-and-so Hotel."

Apparently, illustrious names are created to live on their own account, apart from those that bear them. Now my name is promenading tranquilly about Harkov; in another three months, printed in gold letters on my monument, it will shine bright as the sun itself, while I shall be already under the moss.

A light tap at the door. Somebody wants me.

" Who is there? Come in."

The door opens, and I step back surprised and hurriedly wrap my dressing-gown round me. Before me stands Katya.

" How do you do? " she says, breathless with running upstairs. " You didn't expect me? I have come here, too. . . . I have come, too! "

She sits down and goes on, hesitating and not looking at me.

"Why don't you speak to me? I have come, too . . . today. . . . I found out that you were in this hotel, and have come to you."

"Very glad to see you," I say, shrugging my shoulders, "but I am surprised. You seem to have dropped from the skies. What have you come for?"

"Oh . . . I've simply come."

Silence. Suddenly she jumps up impulsively and comes to me.

"Nikolay Stepanovitch," she says, turning pale and pressing her hands on her bosom — "Nikolay Stepanovitch, I cannot go on living like this! I cannot! For God's sake tell me quickly, this minute, what I am to do! Tell me, what am I to do?"

"What can I tell you?" I ask in perplexity. "I can do nothing."

"Tell me, I beseech you," she goes on, breathing hard and trembling all over. "I swear that I cannot go on living like this. It's too much for me!"

She sinks on a chair and begins sobbing. She flings her head back, wrings her hands, taps with her feet; her hat falls off and hangs bobbing on its elastic; her hair is ruffled.

"Help me! help me!" she implores me. "I cannot go on!"

She takes her handkerchief out of her travelling-bag, and with it pulls out several letters, which fall from her lap to the floor. I pick them up, and on one of them I recognize the handwriting of Mihail

Fyodorovitch and accidentally read a bit of a word
" passionat . . ."

" There is nothing I can tell you, Katya," I say.

" Help me! " she sobs, clutching at my hand and
kissing it. " You are my father, you know, my only
friend! You are clever, educated; you have lived
so long; you have been a teacher! Tell me, what
am I to do? "

" Upon my word, Katya, I don't know. . . ."

I am utterly at a loss and confused, touched by her
sobs, and hardly able to stand.

" Let us have lunch, Katya," I say, with a forced
smile. " Give over crying."

And at once I add in a sinking voice:

" I shall soon be gone, Katya. . . ."

" Only one word, only one word! " she weeps,
stretching out her hands to me.

" What am I to do? "

" You are a queer girl, really . . ." I mutter. " I
don't understand it! So sensible, and all at once
. . . crying your eyes out. . . ."

A silence follows. Katya straightens her hair,
puts on her hat, then crumples up the letters and stuffs
them in her bag — and all this deliberately, in silence. Her face, her bosom, and her gloves are wet
with tears, but her expression now is cold and forbidding. . . . I look at her, and feel ashamed that
I am happier than she. The absence of what my
philosophic colleagues call a general idea I have detected in myself only just before death, in the decline
of my days, while the soul of this poor girl has known
and will know no refuge all her life, all her life!

"Let us have lunch, Katya," I say.

"No, thank you," she answers coldly.

Another minute passes in silence.

"I don't like Harkov," I say; "it's so grey here — such a grey town."

"Yes, perhaps. . . . It's ugly. I am here not for long, passing through. I am going on today."

"Where?"

"To the Crimea . . . that is, to the Caucasus."

"Oh! For long?"

"I don't know."

Katya gets up, and, with a cold smile, holds out her hand without looking at me.

I want to ask her, "Then, you won't be at my funeral?" but she does not look at me; her hand is cold and, as it were, strange. I escort her to the door in silence. She goes out, walks down the long corridor without looking back; she knows that I am looking after her, and most likely she will look back at the turn.

No, she did not look back. I've seen her black dress for the last time: her steps have died away. Farewell, my treasure!

1899

THE PRIVY COUNCILLOR

THE PRIVY COUNCILLOR

At the beginning of April in 1870 my mother, Klavdia Arhipovna, the widow of a lieutenant, received from her brother Ivan, a privy councillor in Petersburg, a letter in which, among other things, this passage occurred: " My liver trouble forces me to spend every summer abroad, and as I have not at the moment the money in hand for a trip to Marienbad, it is very possible, dear sister, that I may spend this summer with you at Kotchuevko. . . ."

On reading the letter my mother turned pale and began trembling all over; then an expression of mingled tears and laughter came into her face. She began crying and laughing. This conflict of tears and laughter always reminds me of the flickering and spluttering of a brightly burning candle when one sprinkles it with water. Reading the letter once more, mother called together all the household, and in a voice broken with emotion began explaining to us that there had been four Gundasov brothers: one Gundasov had died as a baby; another had gone to the war, and he, too, was dead; the third, without offence to him be it said, was an actor; the fourth . . .

" The fourth has risen far above us," my mother brought out tearfully. " My own brother, we grew up together; and I am all of a tremble, all of a

tremble! . . . A privy councillor with the rank of a
general! How shall I meet him, my angel brother?
What can I, a foolish, uneducated woman, talk to
him about? It's fifteen years since I've seen him!
Andryushenka," my mother turned to me, " you must
rejoice, little stupid! It's a piece of luck for you that
God is sending him to us! "

After we had heard a detailed history of the
Gundasovs, there followed a fuss and bustle in the
place such as I had been accustomed to see only before Christmas and Easter. The sky above and the
water in the river were all that escaped; everything
else was subjected to a merciless cleansing, scrubbing,
painting. If the sky had been lower and smaller and
the river had not flowed so swiftly, they would have
scoured them, too, with bath-brick and rubbed them,
too, with tow. Our walls were as white as snow, but
they were whitewashed; the floors were bright and
shining, but they were washed every day. The cat
Bobtail (as a small child I had cut off a good quarter
of his tail with the knife used for chopping the sugar,
and that was why he was called Bobtail) was carried off to the kitchen and put in charge of Anisya;
Fedka was told that if any of the dogs came near the
front-door " God would punish him." But no one
was so badly treated as the poor sofas, easy-chairs,
and rugs! They had never before been so violently
beaten as on this occasion in preparation for our
visitor. My pigeons took fright at the loud thud
of the sticks, and were continually flying up into the
sky.

The tailor Spiridon, the only tailor in the whole

district who ventured to make for the gentry, came over from Novostroevka. He was a hard-working capable man who did not drink and was not without a certain fancy and feeling for form, but yet he was an atrocious tailor. His work was ruined by hesitation. . . . The idea that his cut was not fashionable enough made him alter everything half a dozen times, walk all the way to the town simply to study the dandies, and in the end dress us in suits that even a caricaturist would have called *outré* and grotesque. We cut a dash in impossibly narrow trousers and in such short jackets that we always felt quite abashed in the presence of young ladies.

This Spiridon spent a long time taking my measure. He measured me all over lengthways and crossways, as though he meant to put hoops round me like a barrel; then he spent a long time noting down my measurements with a thick pencil on a bit of paper, and ticked off all the measurements with triangular signs. When he had finished with me he set to work on my tutor, Yegor Alexyevitch Pobyedimsky. My beloved tutor was then at the stage when young men watch the growth of their moustache and are critical of their clothes, and so you can imagine the devout awe with which Spiridon approached him. Yegor Alexyevitch had to throw back his head, to straddle his legs like an inverted V, first lift up his arms, then let them fall. Spiridon measured him several times, walking round him during the process like a love-sick pigeon round its mate, going down on one knee, bending double. . . . My mother, weary, exhausted by her exertions and heated by ironing, watched these lengthy proceedings, and said:

"Mind now, Spiridon, you will have to answer for it to God if you spoil the cloth! And it will be the worse for you if you don't make them fit!"

Mother's words threw Spiridon first into a fever, then into a perspiration, for he was convinced that he would not make them fit. He received one rouble twenty kopecks for making my suit, and for Pobyedimsky's two roubles, but we provided the cloth, the lining, and the buttons. The price cannot be considered excessive, as Novostroevka was about seven miles from us, and the tailor came to fit us four times. When he came to try the things on and we squeezed ourselves into the tight trousers and jackets adorned with basting threads, mother always frowned contemptuously and expressed her surprise:

"Goodness knows what the fashions are coming to nowadays! I am postively ashamed to look at them. If brother were not used to Petersburg I would not get you fashionable clothes!"

Spiridon, relieved that the blame was thrown on the fashion and not on him, shrugged his shoulders and sighed, as though to say:

"There's no help for it; it's the spirit of the age!"

The excitement with which we awaited the arrival of our guest can only be compared with the strained suspense with which spiritualists wait from minute to minute the appearance of a ghost. Mother went about with a sick headache, and was continually melting into tears. I lost my appetite, slept badly, and did not learn my lessons. Even in my dreams

I was haunted by an impatient longing to see a general — that is, a man with epaulettes and an embroidered collar sticking up to his ears, and with a naked sword in his hands, exactly like the one who hung over the sofa in the drawing-room and glared with terrible black eyes at everybody who dared to look at him. Pobyedimsky was the only one who felt himself in his element. He was neither terrified nor delighted, and merely from time to time, when he heard the history of the Gundasov family, said:

" Yes, it will be pleasant to have some one fresh to talk to."

My tutor was looked upon among us as an exceptional nature. He was a young man of twenty, with a pimply face, shaggy locks, a low forehead, and an unusually long nose. His nose was so big that when he wanted to look close at anything he had to put his head on one side like a bird. To our thinking, there was not a man in the province cleverer, more cultivated, or more stylish. He had left the high-school in the class next to the top, and had then entered a veterinary college, from which he was expelled before the end of the first half-year. The reason of his expulsion he carefully concealed, which enabled any one who wished to do so to look upon my instructor as an injured and to some extent a mysterious person. He spoke little, and only of intellectual subjects; he ate meat during the fasts, and looked with contempt and condescension on the life going on around him, which did not prevent him, however, from taking presents, such as suits of clothes, from my mother, and drawing funny faces with red teeth on my kites. Mother disliked him for his " pride," but stood in awe of his cleverness.

Our visitor did not keep us long waiting. At the beginning of May two wagon-loads of big boxes arrived from the station. These boxes looked so majestic that the drivers instinctively took off their hats as they lifted them down.

" There must be uniforms and gunpowder in those boxes," I thought.

Why " gunpowder " ? Probably the conception of a general was closely connected in my mind with cannons and gunpowder.

When I woke up on the morning of the tenth of May, nurse told me in a whisper that " my uncle had come." I dressed rapidly, and, washing after a fashion, flew out of my bedroom without saying my prayers. In the vestibule I came upon a tall, solid gentleman with fashionable whiskers and a foppish-looking overcoat. Half dead with devout awe, I went up to him and, remembering the ceremonial mother had impressed upon me, I scraped my foot before him, made a very low bow, and craned forward to kiss his hand; but the gentleman did not allow me to kiss his hand: he informed me that he was not my uncle, but my uncle's footman, Pyotr. The appearance of this Pyotr, far better dressed than Pobyedimsky or me, excited in me the utmost astonishment, which, to tell the truth, has lasted to this day. Can such dignified, respectable people with stern and intellectual faces really be footmen? And what for?

Pyotr told me that my uncle was in the garden with my mother.   I rushed into the garden.

Nature, knowing nothing of the history of the Gundasov family and the rank of my uncle, felt far more at ease and unconstrained than I.   There was a clamour going on in the garden such as one only hears at fairs.   Masses of starlings flitting through the air and hopping about the walks were noisily chattering as they hunted for cockchafers.   There were swarms of sparrows in the lilac-bushes, which threw their tender, fragrant blossoms straight in one's face. Wherever one turned, from every direction came the note of the golden oriole and the shrill cry of the hoopoe and the red-legged falcon.   At any other time I should have begun chasing dragon-flies or throwing stones at a crow which was sitting on a low mound under an aspen-tree, with its blunt beak turned away; but at that moment I was in no mood for mischief.   My heart was throbbing, and I felt a cold sinking at my stomach; I was preparing myself to confront a gentleman with epaulettes, with a naked sword, and with terrible eyes!

But imagine my disappointment!   A dapper little foppish gentleman in white silk trousers, with a white cap on his head, was walking beside my mother in the garden.   With his hands behind him and his head thrown back, every now and then running on ahead of mother, he looked quite young.   There was so much life and movement in his whole figure that I could only detect the treachery of age when I came close up behind and saw beneath his cap a fringe of

close-cropped silver hair.   Instead of the staid dignity and stolidity of a general, I saw an almost school-
boyish nimbleness; instead of a collar sticking up to
his ears, an ordinary light blue necktie.   Mother
and my uncle were walking in the avenue talking together.   I went softly up to them from behind, and
waited for one of them to look round.

"What a delightful place you have here, Klavdia!" said my uncle.   "How charming and lovely
it is!   Had I known before that you had such a
charming place, nothing would have induced me to
go abroad all these years."

My uncle stooped down rapidly and sniffed at a
tulip.   Everything he saw moved him to rapture
and excitement, as though he had never been in a
garden on a sunny day before.   The queer man
moved about as though he were on springs, and chat-
tered incessantly, without allowing mother to utter
a single word.   All of a sudden Pobyedimsky came
into sight from behind an elder-tree at the turn of the
avenue.   His appearance was so unexpected that my
uncle positively started and stepped back a pace.
On this occasion my tutor was attired in his best
Inverness cape with sleeves, in which, especially back-
view, he looked remarkably like a windmill.   He
had a solemn and majestic air.   Pressing his hat
to his bosom in Spanish style, he took a step towards
my uncle and made a bow such as a marquis makes
in a melodrama, bending forward, a little to one side.

"I have the honour to present myself to your
high excellency," he said aloud: "the teacher and
instructor of your nephew, formerly a pupil of the

veterinary institute, and a nobleman by birth, Pobyedimsky ! "

This politeness on the part of my tutor pleased my
mother very much.   She gave a smile, and waited
in thrilled suspense to hear what clever thing he
would say next; but my tutor, expecting his dignified
address to be answered with equal dignity — that is,
that my uncle would say " H'm ! " like a general and
hold out two fingers — was greatly confused and
abashed when the latter laughed genially and shook
hands with him.   He muttered something incoher-
ent, cleared his throat, and walked away.

" Come ! isn't that charming ? " laughed my uncle.
" Just look ! he has made his little flourish and thinks
he's a very clever fellow !   I do like that — upon my
soul I do !   What youthful aplomb, what life in that
foolish flourish !   And what boy is this ? " he asked,
suddenly turning and looking at me.

" That is my Andryushenka," my mother introduced me, flushing crimson.   " My consolation. . . ."

I made a scrape with my foot on the sand and
dropped a low bow.

" A fine fellow . . . a fine fellow . . ." muttered
my uncle, taking his hand from my lips and stroking
me on the head.   " So your name is Andrusha?
Yes, yes. . . . H'm ! . . . upon my soul ! . . . Do
you learn lessons ? "

My mother, exaggerating and embellishing as all
mothers do, began to describe my achievements in
the sciences and the excellence of my behaviour, and
I walked round my uncle and, following the cere-
morial laid down for me, I continued making low

bows. Then my mother began throwing out hints
that with my remarkable abilities it would not be
amiss for me to get a government nomination to the
cadet school; but at the point when I was to have
burst into tears and begged for my uncle's protection,
my uncle suddenly stopped and flung up his hands in
amazement.

"My goo-oodness! What's that?" he asked.

Tatyana Ivanovna, the wife of our bailiff, Fyodor
Petrovna, was coming towards us. She was carrying a starched white petticoat and a long ironing-
board. As she passed us she looked shyly at the visitor through her eyelashes and flushed crimson.

"Wonders will never cease . . ." my uncle filtered through his teeth, looking after her with
friendly interest. "You have a fresh surprise at
every step, sister . . . upon my soul!"

"She's a beauty . . ." said mother. "They
chose her as a bride for Fyodor, though she lived
over seventy miles from here. . . ."

Not every one would have called Tatyana a
beauty. She was a plump little woman of twenty,
with black eyebrows and a graceful figure, always
rosy and attractive-looking, but in her face and in her
whole person there was not one striking feature, not
one bold line to catch the eye, as though nature had
lacked inspiration and confidence when creating her.
Tatyana Ivanovna was shy, bashful, and modest in
her behaviour; she moved softly and smoothly, said
little, seldom laughed, and her whole life was as
regular as her face and as flat as her smooth, tidy
hair. My uncle screwed up his eyes looking after

her, and smiled.   Mother looked intently at his smiling face and grew serious.

"And so, brother, you've never married!" she
sighed.

"No; I've not married."

"Why not?" asked mother softly.

"How can I tell you?   It has happened so.   In
my youth I was too hard at work, I had no time to
live, and when I longed to live — I looked round —
and there I had fifty years on my back already.   I
was too late!   However, talking about it . . . is
depressing."

My mother and my uncle both sighed at once and
walked on, and I left them and flew off to find my
tutor, that I might share my impressions with him.
Pobyedimsky was standing in the middle of the yard,
looking majestically at the heavens.

"One can see he is a man of culture!" he said,
twisting his head round.   "I hope we shall get on
together."

An hour later mother came to us.

"I am in trouble, my dears!" she began, sighing.
"You see brother has brought a valet with him, and
the valet, God bless him, is not one you can put in
the kitchen or in the hall; we must give him a room
apart.   I can't think what I am to do!   I tell you
what, children, couldn't you move out somewhere —
to Fyodor's lodge, for instance — and give your
room to the valet?   What do you say?"

We gave our ready consent, for living in the lodge
was a great deal more free than in the house, under
mother's eye.

" It's a nuisance, and that's a fact! " said mother.
" Brother says he won't have dinner in the middle
of the day, but between six and seven, as they do in
Petersburg. I am simply distracted with worry!
By seven o'clock the dinner will be done to rags in
the oven. Really, men don't understand anything
about housekeeping, though they have so much intellect. Oh, dear! we shall have to cook two dinners
every day! You will have dinner at midday as before, children, while your poor old mother has to
wait till seven, for the sake of her brother."

Then my mother heaved a deep sigh, bade me try
and please my uncle, whose coming was a piece of
luck for me for which we must thank God, and hurried off to the kitchen. Pobyedimsky and I moved
into the lodge the same day. We were installed in
a room which formed the passage from the entry
to the bailiff's bedroom.

Contrary to my expectations, life went on just as
before, drearily and monotonously, in spite of my
uncle's arrival and our move into new quarters. We
were excused lessons " on account of the visitor."
Pobyedimsky, who never read anything or occupied
himself in any way, spent most of his time sitting on
his bed, with his long nose thrust into the air, thinking. Sometimes he would get up, try on his new
suit, and sit down again to relapse into contempla-
tion and silence. Only one thing worried him, the
flies, which he used mercilessly to squash between his
hands. After dinner he usually " rested," and his
snores were a cause of annoyance to the whole household. I ran about the garden from morning to

night, or sat in the lodge sticking my kites together. For the first two or three weeks we did not see my uncle often. For days together he sat in his own room working, in spite of the flies and the heat. His extraordinary capacity for sitting as though glued to his table produced upon us the effect of an inexplicable conjuring trick. To us idlers, knowing nothing of systematic work, his industry seemed simply miraculous. Getting up at nine, he sat down to his table, and did not leave it till dinner-time; after dinner he set to work again, and went on till late at night. Whenever I peeped through the keyhole I invariably saw the same thing: my uncle sitting at the table working. The work consisted in his writing with one hand while he turned over the leaves of a book with the other, and, strange to say, he kept moving all over — swinging his leg as though it were a pendulum, whistling, and nodding his head in time. He had an extremely careless and frivolous expression all the while, as though he were not working, but playing at noughts and crosses. I always saw him wearing a smart short jacket and a jauntily tied cravat, and he always smelt, even through the keyhole, of delicate feminine perfumery. He only left his room for dinner, but he ate little.

"I can't make brother out!" mother complained of him. "Every day we kill a turkey and pigeons on purpose for him, I make a *compote* with my own hands, and he eats a plateful of broth and a bit of meat the size of a finger and gets up from the table. I begin begging him to eat; he comes back and drinks a glass of milk. And what is there in that, in a glass

of milk? It's no better than washing up water!
You may die of a diet like that. . . . If I try to per-
suade him, he laughs and makes a joke of it. . . .
No; he does not care for our fare, poor dear!"

We spent the evenings far more gaily than the
days. As a rule, by the time the sun was setting and
long shadows were lying across the yard, we — that
is, Tatyana Ivanovna, Pobyedimsky, and I — were
sitting on the steps of the lodge. We did not talk till
it grew quite dusk. And, indeed, what is one to
talk of when every subject has been talked over already? There was only one thing new, my uncle's
arrival, and even that subject was soon exhausted.
My tutor never took his eyes off Tatyana Ivanovna's
face, and frequently heaved deep sighs. . . . At the
time I did not understand those sighs, and did not
try to fathom their significance; now they explain a
great deal to me.

When the shadows merged into one thick mass of
shade, the bailiff Fyodor would come in from shooting or from the field. This Fyodor gave me the impression of being a fierce and even a terrible man.
The son of a Russianized gipsy from Izyumskoe,
swarthy-faced and curly-headed, with big black eyes
and a matted beard, he was never called among our
Kotchuevko peasants by any name but "The Devil."
And, indeed, there was a great deal of the gipsy
about him apart from his appearance. He could
not, for instance, stay at home, and went off for days
together into the country or into the woods to shoot.
He was gloomy, ill-humoured, taciturn, was afraid
of nobody, and refused to recognize any authority.

He was rude to mother, addressed me familiarly, and was contemptuous of Pobyedimsky's learning. All this we forgave him, looking upon him as a hot-tempered and nervous man; mother liked him because, in spite of his gipsy nature, he was ideally honest and industrious. He loved his Tatyana Ivanovna passionately, like a gipsy, but this love took in him a gloomy form, as though it cost him suffering. He was never affectionate to his wife in our presence, but simply rolled his eyes angrily at her and twisted his mouth.

When he came in from the fields he would noisily and angrily put down his gun, would come out to us on the steps, and sit down beside his wife. After resting a little, he would ask his wife a few questions about household matters, and then sink into silence.

" Let us sing," I would suggest.

My tutor would tune his guitar, and in a deep deacon's bass strike up " In the midst of the valley." We would begin singing. My tutor took the bass, Fyodor sang in a hardly audible tenor, while I sang soprano in unison with Tatyana Ivanovna.

When the whole sky was covered with stars and the frogs had left off croaking, they would bring in our supper from the kitchen. We went into the lodge and sat down to the meal. My tutor and the gipsy ate greedily, with such a sound that it was hard to tell whether it was the bones crunching or their jaws, and Tatyana Ivanovna and I scarcely succeeded in getting our share. After supper the lodge was plunged in deep sleep.

One evening, it was at the end of May, we were

sitting on the steps, waiting for supper. A shadow suddenly fell across us, and Gundasov stood before us as though he had sprung out of the earth. He looked at us for a long time, then clasped his hands and laughed gaily.

" An idyll!" he said. " They sing and dream in the moonlight! It's charming, upon my soul! May I sit down and dream with you?"

We looked at one another and said nothing. My uncle sat down on the bottom step, yawned, and looked at the sky. A silence followed. Pobyedimsky, who had for a long time been wanting to talk to somebody fresh, was delighted at the opportunity, and was the first to break the silence. He had only one subject for intellectual conversation, the epizootic diseases. It sometimes happens that after one has been in an immense crowd, only some one countenance of the thousands remains long imprinted on the memory; in the same way, of all that Pobyedimsky had heard, during his six months at the veterinary institute, he remembered only one passage:

" The epizootics do immense damage to the stock of the country. It is the duty of society to work hand in hand with the government in waging war upon them."

Before saying this to Gundasov, my tutor cleared his throat three times, and several times, in his excitement, wrapped himself up in his Inverness. On hearing about the epizootics, my uncle looked intently at my tutor and made a sound between a snort and a laugh.

"Upon my soul, that's charming!" he said, scru-
tinizing us as though we were mannequins. "This
is actually life. . . . This is really what reality is
bound to be. Why are you silent, Pelagea Ivanovna?" he said, addressing Tatyana Ivanovna.

She coughed, overcome with confusion.

"Talk, my friends, sing . . . play! . . . Don't
lose time. You know, time, the rascal, runs away
and waits for no man! Upon my soul, before you
have time to look round, old age is upon you. . . .
Then it is too late to live! That's how it is, Pelagea
Ivanovna. . . . We mustn't sit still and be silent. . . ."

At that point supper was brought out from the
kitchen. Uncle went into the lodge with us, and
to keep us company ate five curd fritters and the wing
of a duck. He ate and looked at us. He was
touched and delighted by us all. Whatever silly
nonsense my precious tutor talked, and whatever
Tatyana Ivanovna did, he thought charming and delightful. When after supper Tatyana Ivanovna sat
quietly down and took up her knitting, he kept his
eyes fixed on her fingers and chatted away without
ceasing.

"Make all the haste you can to live, my friends
. . ." he said. "God forbid you should sacrifice
the present for the future! There is youth, health,
fire in the present; the future is smoke and deception!
As soon as you are twenty begin to live."

Tatyana Ivanovna dropped a knitting-needle.
My uncle jumped up, picked up the needle, and
handed it to Tatyana Ivanovna with a bow, and for

the first time in my life I learnt that there were people in the world more refined than Pobyedimsky.

"Yes . . ." my uncle went on, " love, marry, do silly things. Foolishness is a great deal more living and healthy than our straining and striving after rational life."

My uncle talked a great deal, so much that he bored us; I sat on a box listening to him and dropping to sleep. It distressed me that he did not once all the evening pay attention to me. He left the lodge at two o'clock, when, overcome with drowsiness, I was sound asleep.

From that time forth my uncle took to coming to the lodge every evening. He sang with us, had supper with us, and always stayed on till two o'clock in the morning, chatting incessantly, always about the same subject. His evening and night work was given up, and by the end of June, when the privy councillor had learned to eat mother's turkey and *compote*, his work by day was abandoned too. My uncle tore himself away from his table and plunged into " life." In the daytime he walked up and down the garden, he whistled to the workmen and hindered them from working, making them tell him their various histories. When his eye fell on Tatyana Ivanovna he ran up to her, and, if she were carrying anything, offered his assistance, which embarrassed her dreadfully.

As the summer advanced my uncle grew more and more frivolous, volatile, and careless. Pobyedimsky was completely disillusioned in regard to him.

" He is too one-sided," he said. " There is noth-

ing to show that he is in the very foremost ranks of
the service.   And he doesn't even know how to talk.
At every word it's 'upon my soul.'   No, I don't
like him!"

From the time that my uncle began visiting the
lodge there was a noticeable change both in Fyodor
and my tutor.   Fyodor gave up going out shooting,
came home early, sat more taciturn than ever, and
stared with particular ill-humour at his wife.   In
my uncle's presence my tutor gave up talking about
epizootics, frowned, and even laughed sarcastically.

" Here comes our little bantam cock! " he growled
on one occasion when my uncle was coming into the
lodge.

I put down this change in them both to their being offended with my uncle.   My absent-minded uncle mixed up their names, and to the very day of his
departure failed to distinguish which was my tutor
and which was Tatyana Ivanovna's husband.   Tatyana Ivanovna herself he sometimes called Nastasya,
sometimes   Pelagea,   and   sometimes   Yevdokia.
Touched and delighted by us, he laughed and behaved exactly as though in the company of small
children. . . . All this, of course, might well offend
young men.   It was not a case of offended pride,
however, but, as I realize now, subtler feelings.

I remember one evening I was sitting on the box
struggling with sleep.   My eyelids felt glued together and my body, tired out by running about all
day, drooped sideways.   But I struggled against
sleep and tried to look on.   It was about midnight.
Tatyana Ivanovna, rosy and unassuming as always,

was sitting at a little table sewing at her husband's shirt. Fyodor, sullen and gloomy, was staring at her from one corner, and in the other sat Pobyedimsky, snorting angrily and retreating into the high collar of his shirt. My uncle was walking up and down the room thinking. Silence reigned; nothing was to be heard but the rustling of the linen in Tatyana Ivanovna's hands. Suddenly my uncle stood still before Tatyana Ivanovna, and said:

"You are all so young, so fresh, so nice, you live so peacefully in this quiet place, that I envy you. I have become attached to your way of life here; my heart aches when I remember I have to go away. . . . You may believe in my sincerity!"

Sleep closed my eyes and I lost myself. When some sound waked me, my uncle was standing before Tatyana Ivanovna, looking at her with a softened expression. His cheeks were flushed.

"My life has been wasted," he said. "I have not lived! Your young face makes me think of my own lost youth, and I should be ready to sit here watching you to the day of my death. It would be a pleasure to me to take you with me to Petersburg."

"What for?" Fyodor asked in a husky voice.

"I should put her under a glass case on my worktable. I should admire her and show her to other people. You know, Pelagea Ivanovna, we have no women like you there. Among us there is wealth, distinction, sometimes beauty, but we have not this true sort of life, this healthy serenity. . . ."

My uncle sat down facing Tatyana Ivanovna and took her by the hand.

"So you won't come with me to Petersburg?" he
laughed. "In that case give me your little hand.
. . . A charming little hand! . . . You won't give
it? Come, you miser! let me kiss it, anyway. . . ."

At that moment there was the scrape of a chair.
Fyodor jumped up, and with heavy, measured steps
went up to his wife. His face was pale, grey, and
quivering. He brought his fist down on the table
with a bang, and said in a hollow voice:

"I won't allow it!"

At the same moment Pobyedimsky jumped up from
his chair. He, too, pale and angry, went up to Tatyana Ivanovna, and he, too, struck the table with his
fist.

"I . . . I won't allow it!" he said.

"What, what's the matter?" asked my uncle in
surprise.

"I won't allow it!" repeated Fyodor, banging on
the table.

My uncle jumped up and blinked nervously. He
tried to speak, but in his amazement and alarm
could not utter a word; with an embarrassed smile,
he shuffled out of the lodge with the hurried step of
an old man, leaving his hat behind. When, a little
later, my mother ran into the lodge, Fyodor and
Pobyedimsky were still hammering on the table like
blacksmiths and repeating, "I won't allow it!"

"What has happened here?" asked mother.
"Why has my brother been taken ill? What's the
matter?"

Looking at Tatyana's pale, frightened face and
at her infuriated husband, mother probably guessed

what was the matter.   She sighed and shook her head.

"Come! give over banging on the table!" she said.   "Leave off, Fyodor!   And why are you thumping, Yegor Alexyevitch?   What have you got to do with it?"

Pobyedimsky was startled and confused.   Fyodor looked intently at him, then at his wife, and began walking about the room.   When mother had gone out of the lodge, I saw what for long afterwards I looked upon as a dream.   I saw Fyodor seize my tutor, lift him up in the air, and thrust him out of the door.

When I woke up in the morning my tutor's bed was empty.   To my question where he was nurse told me in a whisper that he had been taken off early in the morning to the hospital, as his arm was broken.   Distressed at this intelligence and remembering the scene of the previous evening, I went out of doors.   It was a grey day.   The sky was covered with storm-clouds and there was a wind blowing dust, bits of paper, and feathers along the ground. . . . It felt as though rain were coming.   There was a look of boredom in the servants and in the animals.   When I went into the house I was told not to make such a noise with my feet, as mother was ill and in bed with a migraine.   What was I to do?   I went outside the gate, sat down on the little bench there, and fell to trying to discover the meaning of what I had seen and heard the day before.   From our gate there was a road which, passing the forge and the pool which never dried up, ran into the main road.   I looked at the telegraph-posts, about which clouds of dust were whirling, and at the sleepy birds sitting on the wires, and I suddenly felt so dreary that I began to cry.

A dusty wagonette crammed full of townspeople, probably going to visit the shrine, drove by along the main road. The wagonette was hardly out of sight when a light chaise with a pair of horses came into view. In it was Akim Nikititch, the police inspector, standing up and holding on to the coachman's belt. To my great surprise, the chaise turned into our road and flew by me in at the gate. While I was puzzling why the police inspector had come to see us, I heard a noise, and a carriage with three horses came into sight on the road. In the carriage stood the police captain, directing his coachman towards our gate.

" And why is he coming? " I thought, looking at the dusty police captain. " Most probably Pobyedimsky has complained of Fyodor to him, and they have come to take him to prison."

But the mystery was not so easily solved. The police inspector and the police captain were only the first instalment, for five minutes had scarcely passed when a coach drove in at our gate. It dashed by me so swiftly that I could only get a glimpse of a red beard.

Lost in conjecture and full of misgivings, I ran to the house. In the passage first of all I saw mother; she was pale and looking with horror towards the door, from which came the sounds of men's voices. The visitors had taken her by surprise in the very throes of migraine.

" Who has come, mother? " I asked.

" Sister," I heard my uncle's voice, " will you send in something to eat for the governor and me?"

" It is easy to say ' something to eat,' " whispered my mother, numb with horror. " What have I time to get ready now? I am put to shame in my old age! "

Mother clutched at her head and ran into the kitchen. The governor's sudden visit stirred and overwhelmed the whole household. A ferocious slaughter followed. A dozen fowls, five turkeys, eight ducks, were killed, and in the fluster the old gander, the progenitor of our whole flock of geese and a great favourite of mother's, was beheaded. The coachmen and the cook seemed frenzied, and slaughtered birds at random, without distinction of age or breed. For the sake of some wretched sauce a pair of valuable pigeons, as dear to me as the gander was to mother, were sacrificed. It was a long while before I could forgive the governor their death.

In the evening, when the governor and his suite, after a sumptuous dinner, had got into their carriages and driven away, I went into the house to look at the remains of the feast. Glancing into the drawing-room from the passage, I saw my uncle and my mother. My uncle, with his hands behind his back, was walking nervously up and down close to the wall, shrugging his shoulders. Mother, exhausted and looking much thinner, was sitting on the sofa and watching his movements with heavy eyes.

" Excuse me, sister, but this won't do at all," my

uncle grumbled, wrinkling up his face. "I introduced the governor to you, and you didn't offer to shake hands. You covered him with confusion, poor fellow! No, that won't do. . . . Simplicity is a very good thing, but there must be limits to it. . . . Upon my soul! And then that dinner! How can one give people such things? What was that mess, for instance, that they served for the fourth course?"

"That was duck with sweet sauce . . ." mother answered softly.

"Duck! Forgive me, sister, but . . . but here I've got heartburn! I am ill!"

My uncle made a sour, tearful face, and went on:

"It was the devil sent that governor! As though I wanted his visit! Pff! . . . heartburn! I can't work or sleep . . . I am completely out of sorts. . . . And I can't understand how you can live here without anything to do . . . in this boredom! Here I've got a pain coming under my shoulder-blade! . . ."

My uncle frowned, and walked about more rapidly than ever.

"Brother," my mother inquired softly, "what would it cost to go abroad?"

"At least three thousand . . ." my uncle answered in a tearful voice. "I would go, but where am I to get it? I haven't a farthing. Pff! . . . heartburn!"

My uncle stopped to look dejectedly at the grey, overcast prospect from the window, and began pacing to and fro again.

A silence followed. . . . Mother looked a long

while at the ikon, pondering something, then she began crying, and said:
" I'll give you the three thousand, brother. . . ."

Three days later the majestic boxes went off to the station, and the privy councillor drove off after them. As he said good-bye to mother he shed tears, and it was a long time before he took his lips from her hands, but when he got into his carriage his face beamed with childlike pleasure. . . . Radiant and happy, he settled himself comfortably, kissed his hand to my mother, who was crying, and all at once his eye was caught by me.   A look of the utmost astonishment came into his face.
" What boy is this? " he asked.
My mother, who had declared my uncle's coming was a piece of luck for which I must thank God, was bitterly mortified at this question.   I was in no mood for questions.   I looked at my uncle's happy face, and for some reason I felt fearfully sorry for him. I could not resist jumping up to the carriage and hugging that frivolous man, weak as all men are. Looking into his face and wanting to say something pleasant, I asked:
" Uncle, have you ever been in a battle? "
" Ah, the dear boy . . ." laughed my uncle, kissing me.   " A charming boy, upon my soul!   How natural, how living it all is, upon my soul! . . ."
The carriage set off. . . . I looked after him, and long afterwards that farewell " upon my soul " was ringing in my ears.

1886

THE MAN IN A CASE

THE MAN IN A CASE

AT the furthest end of the village of Mironositskoe some belated sportsmen lodged for the night in the elder Prokofy's barn. There were two of them, the veterinary surgeon Ivan Ivanovitch and the schoolmaster Burkin. Ivan Ivanovitch had a rather strange double-barrelled surname — Tchimsha-Himalaisky — which did not suit him at all, and he was called simply Ivan Ivanovitch all over the province. He lived at a stud-farm near the town, and had come out shooting now to get a breath of fresh air. Burkin, the high-school teacher, stayed every summer at Count P——'s, and had been thoroughly at home in this district for years.

They did not sleep. Ivan Ivanovitch, a tall, lean old fellow with long moustaches, was sitting outside the door, smoking a pipe in the moonlight. Burkin was lying within on the hay, and could not be seen in the darkness.

They were telling each other all sorts of stories. Among other things, they spoke of the fact that the elder's wife, Mavra, a healthy and by no means stupid woman, had never been beyond her native village, had never seen a town nor a railway in her life, and had spent the last ten years sitting behind the stove, and only at night going out into the street.

" What is there wonderful in that ! " said Burkin.

" There are plenty of people in the world, solitary by temperament, who try to retreat into their shell like a hermit crab or a snail.   Perhaps it is an instance of atavism, a return to the period when the ancestor of man was not yet a social animal and lived alone in his den, or perhaps it is only one of the diversities of human character — who knows?   I am not a natural science man, and it is not my business to settle such questions; I only mean to say that people like Mavra are not uncommon.   There is no need to look far; two months ago a man called Byelikov, a colleague of mine, the Greek master, died in our town.   You have heard of him, no doubt.   He was remarkable for always wearing goloshes and a warm wadded coat, and carrying an umbrella even in the very finest weather.   And his umbrella was in a case, and his watch was in a case made of grey chamois leather, and when he took out his penknife to sharpen his pencil, his penknife, too, was in a little case; and his face seemed to be in a case too, because he always hid it in his turned-up collar.   He wore dark spectacles and flannel vests, stuffed up his ears with cotton-wool, and when he got into a cab always told the driver to put up the hood.   In short, the man displayed a constant and insurmountable impulse to wrap himself in a covering, to make himself, so to speak, a case which would isolate him and protect him from external influences.   Reality irritated him, frightened him, kept him in continual agitation, and, perhaps to justify his timidity, his aversion for the actual, he always praised the past and what had never existed; and even the classical languages which he taught were in reality for him goloshes and umbrellas in which he sheltered himself from real life.

" ' Oh, how sonorous, how beautiful is the Greek language ! ' he would say, with a sugary expression; and as though to prove his words he would screw up his eyes and, raising his finger, would pronounce ' Anthropos ! '

" And Byelikov tried to hide his thoughts also in a case. The only things that were clear to his mind were government circulars and newspaper articles in which something was forbidden. When some proclamation prohibited the boys from going out in the streets after nine o'clock in the evening, or some article declared carnal love unlawful, it was to his mind clear and definite; it was forbidden, and that was enough. For him there was always a doubtful element, something vague and not fully expressed, in any sanction or permission. When a dramatic club or a reading-room or a tea-shop was licensed in the town, he would shake his head and say softly:

" ' It is all right, of course; it is all very nice, but I hope it won't lead to anything ! '

" Every sort of breach of order, deviation or departure from rule, depressed him, though one would have thought it was no business of his. If one of his colleagues was late for church or if rumours reached him of some prank of the high-school boys, or one of the mistresses was seen late in the evening in the company of an officer, he was much disturbed, and said he hoped that nothing would come of it. At the teachers' meetings he simply oppressed us with

his caution, his circumspection, and his characteristic
reflection on the ill-behaviour of the young people in
both male and female high-schools, the uproar in the
classes. . . .

" Oh, he hoped it would not reach the ears of the
authorities; oh, he hoped nothing would come of it;
and he thought it would be a very good thing if
Petrov were expelled from the second class and
Yegorov from the fourth. And, do you know, by
his sighs, his despondency, his black spectacles on his
pale little face, a little face like a pole-cat's, you
know, he crushed us all, and we gave way, reduced
Petrov's and Yegorov's marks for conduct, kept them
in, and in the end expelled them both. He had a
strange habit of visiting our lodgings. He would
come to a teacher's, would sit down, and remain
silent, as though he were carefully inspecting something. He would sit like this in silence for an hour
or two and then go away. This he called ' maintaining good relations with his colleagues '; and it was
obvious that coming to see us and sitting there was
tiresome to him, and that he came to see us simply
because he considered it his duty as our colleague.
We teachers were afraid of him. And even the
headmaster was afraid of him. Would you believe
it, our teachers were all intellectual, right-minded
people, brought up on Turgenev and Shtchedrin, yet
this little chap, who always went about with goloshes
and an umbrella, had the whole high-school under
his thumb for fifteen long years! High-school, indeed — he had the whole town under his thumb!
Our ladies did not get up private theatricals on Sat-

urdays for fear he should hear of it, and the clergy
dared not eat meat or play cards in his presence.
Under the influence of people like Byelikov we have
got into the way of being afraid of everything in our
town for the last ten or fifteen years. They are
afraid to speak aloud, afraid to send letters, afraid
to make acquaintances, afraid to read books, afraid
to help the poor, to teach people to read and
write. . . ."

Ivan Ivanovitch cleared his throat, meaning to
say something, but first lighted his pipe, gazed at the
moon, and then said, with pauses:

" Yes, intellectual, right minded people read
Shtchedrin and Turgenev, Buckle, and all the rest of
them, yet they knocked under and put up with it . . .
that's just how it is."

" Byelikov lived in the same house as I did,"
Burkin went on, " on the same storey, his door facing mine; we often saw each other, and I knew how
he lived when he was at home. And at home it was
the same story: dressing-gown, nightcap, blinds,
bolts, a perfect succession of prohibitions and restric-
tions of all sorts, and —' Oh, I hope nothing will
come of it! ' Lenten fare was bad for him, yet he
could not eat meat, as people might perhaps say
Byelikov did not keep the fasts, and he ate fresh-
water fish with butter — not a Lenten dish, yet one
could not say that it was meat. He did not keep a
female servant for fear people might think evil of
him, but had as cook an old man of sixty, called Afanasy, half-witted and given to tippling, who had once
been an officer's servant and could cook after a fash-

ion.   This Afanasy was usually standing at the door with his arms folded; with a deep sigh, he would mutter always the same thing:

" ' There are plenty of *them* about nowadays! '

" Byelikov had a little bedroom like a box; his bed had curtains.   When he went to bed he covered his head over; it was hot and stuffy; the wind battered on the closed doors; there was a droning noise in the stove and a sound of sighs from the kitchen — ominous sighs. . . . And he felt frightened under the bed-clothes.   He was afraid that something might happen, that Afanasy might murder him, that thieves might break in, and so he had troubled dreams all night, and in the morning, when we went together to the high-school, he was depressed and pale, and it was evident that the high-school full of people excited dread and aversion in his whole being, and that to walk beside me was irksome to a man of his solitary temperament.

" ' They make a great noise in our classes,' he used to say, as though trying to find an explanation for his depression.   ' It's beyond anything.'

" And the Greek master, this man in a case — would you believe it? — almost got married."

Ivan Ivanovitch glanced quickly into the barn, and said:

" You are joking! "

" Yes, strange as it seems, he almost got married. A new teacher of history and geography, Milhail Savvitch Kovalenko, a Little Russian, was appointed. He came, not alone, but with his sister Varinka.   He was a tall, dark young man with huge hands, and one could see from his face that he had a bass voice, and, in fact, he had a voice that seemed to come out of a barrel —' boom, boom, boom!'   And she was not so young, about thirty, but she, too, was tall, well-made, with black eyebrows and red cheeks — in fact, she was a regular sugar-plum, and so sprightly, so noisy; she was always singing Little Russian songs and laughing.   For the least thing she would go off into a ringing laugh —' Ha-ha-ha!'   We made our first thorough acquaintance with the Kovalenkos at the headmaster's name-day party.   Among the glum and intensely bored teachers who came even to the name-day party as a duty we suddenly saw a new Aphrodite risen from the waves; she walked with her arms akimbo, laughed, sang, danced. . . . She sang with feeling ' The Winds do Blow,' then another song, and another, and she fascinated us all — all, even Byelikov.   He sat down by her and said with a honeyed smile:

" ' The Little Russian reminds one of the ancient Greek in its softness and agreeable resonance.'

" That flattered her, and she began telling him with feeling and earnestness that they had a farm in the Gadyatchsky district, and that her mamma lived at the farm, and that they had such pears, such melons, such *kabaks!*   The Little Russians call pumpkins *kabaks* (*i.e.,* pothouses), while their pothouses they call *shinki,* and they make a beetroot soup with tomatoes and aubergines in it, ' which was so nice — awfully nice!'

" We listened and listened, and suddenly the same idea dawned upon us all:

" ' It would be a good thing to make a match of it,' the headmaster's wife said to me softly.

" We all for some reason recalled the fact that our friend Byelikov was not married, and it now seemed to us strange that we had hitherto failed to observe, and had in fact completely lost sight of, a detail so important in his life. What was his attitude to woman? How had he settled this vital question for himself? This had not interested us in the least till then; perhaps we had not even admitted the idea that a man who went out in all weathers in goloshes and slept under curtains could be in love.

" ' He is a good deal over forty and she is thirty,' the headmaster's wife went on, developing her idea. ' I believe she would marry him.'

" All sorts of things are done in the provinces through boredom, all sorts of unnecessary and nonsensical things! And that is because what is necessary is not done at all. What need was there, for instance, for us to make a match for this Byelikov, whom one could not even imagine married? The headmaster's wife, the inspector's wife, and all our high-school ladies, grew livelier and even better-looking, as though they had suddenly found a new object in life. The headmaster's wife would take a box at the theatre, and we beheld sitting in her box Varinka, with such a fan, beaming and happy, and beside her Byelikov, a little bent figure, looking as though he had been extracted from his house by pincers. I would give an evening party, and the ladies would insist on my inviting Byelikov and Varinka. In

short, the machine was set in motion.   It appeared
that Varinka was not averse to matrimony.   She
had not a very cheerful life with her brother; they
could do nothing but quarrel and scold one another
from morning till night.   Here is a scene, for instance.   Kovalenko would be coming along the
street, a tall, sturdy young ruffian, in an embroidered
shirt, his love-locks falling on his forehead under his
cap, in one hand a bundle of books, in the other a
thick knotted stick, followed by his sister, also with
books in her hand.

"'But you haven't read it, Mihalik!' she would
be arguing loudly.   'I tell you, I swear you have not
read it at all!'

"'And I tell you I have read it,' cries Kovalenko,
thumping his stick on the pavement.

"'Oh, my goodness, Mihalik! why are you so
cross?   We are arguing about principles.'

"'I tell you that I have read it!' Kovalenko
would shout, more loudly than ever.

"And at home, if there was an outsider present,
there was sure to be a skirmish.   Such a life must
have been wearisome, and of course she must have
longed for a home of her own.   Besides, there was
her age to be considered; there was no time left to
pick and choose; it was a case of marrying anybody,
even a Greek master.   And, indeed, most of our
young ladies don't mind whom they marry so long
as they do get married.   However that may be,
Varinka began to show an unmistakable partiality
for Byelikov.

"And Byelikov?   He used to visit Kovalenko just

as he did us. He would arrive, sit down, and remain silent. He would sit quiet, and Varinka would sing to him ' The Winds do Blow,' or would look pensively at him with her dark eyes, or would suddenly go off into a peal —' Ha-ha-ha! '

" Suggestion plays a great part in love affairs, and still more in getting married. Everybody — both his colleagues and the ladies — began assuring Byelikov that he ought to get married, that there was nothing left for him in life but to get married; we all congratulated him, with solemn countenances delivered ourselves of various platitudes, such as ' Marriage is a serious step.' Besides, Varinka was good-looking and interesting; she was the daughter of a civil councillor, and had a farm; and what was more, she was the first woman who had been warm and friendly in her manner to him. His head was turned, and he decided that he really ought to get married."

" Well, at that point you ought to have taken away his goloshes and umbrella," said Ivan Ivanovitch.

" Only fancy! that turned out to be impossible. He put Varinka's portrait on his table, kept coming to see me and talking about Varinka, and home life, saying marriage was a serious step. He was frequently at Kovalenko's, but he did not alter his manner of life in the least; on the contrary, indeed, his determination to get married seemed to have a depressing effect on him. He grew thinner and paler, and seemed to retreat further and further into his case.

" ' I like Varvara Savvishna,' he used to say to me, with a faint and wry smile, ' and I know that every one ought to get married, but . . . you know all this has happened so suddenly. . . . One must think a little.'

" ' What is there to think over? ' I used to say to him. ' Get married — that is all.'

" ' No; marriage is a serious step. One must first weigh the duties before one, the responsibilities . . . that nothing may go wrong afterwards. It worries me so much that I don't sleep at night. And I must confess I am afraid: her brother and she have a strange way of thinking; they look at things strangely, you know, and her disposition is very impetuous. One may get married, and then, there is no knowing, one may find oneself in an unpleasant position.'

" And he did not make an offer; he kept putting it off, to the great vexation of the headmaster's wife and all our ladies; he went on weighing his future duties and responsibilities, and meanwhile he went for a walk with Varinka almost every day — possibly he thought that this was necessary in his position — and came to see me to talk about family life. And in all probability in the end he would have proposed to her, and would have made one of those unnecessary, stupid marriages such as are made by thousands among us from being bored and having nothing to do, if it had not been for a *kolossalische scandal.* I must mention that Varinka's brother, Kovalenko, detested Byelikov from the first day of their acquaintance, and could not endure him.

" ' I don't understand,' he used to say to us, shrugging his shoulders —' I don't understand how you can put up with that sneak, that nasty phiz. Ugh! how can you live here! The atmosphere is stifling and unclean! Do you call yourselves schoolmasters, teachers? You are paltry government clerks. You keep, not a temple of science, but a department for red tape and loyal behaviour, and it smells as sour as a police-station. No, my friends; I will stay with you for a while, and then I will go to my farm and there catch crabs and teach the Little Russians. I shall go, and you can stay here with your Judas — damn his soul! '

" Or he would laugh till he cried, first in a loud bass, then in a shrill, thin laugh, and ask me, waving his hands:

" ' What does he sit here for? What does he want? He sits and stares.'

" He even gave Byelikov a nickname, ' The Spider.' And it will readily be understood that we avoided talking to him of his sister's being about to marry ' The Spider.'

" And on one occasion, when the headmaster's wife hinted to him what a good thing it would be to secure his sister's future with such a reliable, universally respected man as Byelikov, he frowned and muttered:

" ' It's not my business; let her marry a reptile if she likes. I don't like meddling in other people's affairs.'

" Now hear what happened next. Some mischievous person drew a caricature of Byelikov walking along in his goloshes with his trousers tucked up, under his umbrella, with Varinka on his arm; below, the inscription 'Anthropos in love.' The expression was caught to a marvel, you know. The artist must have worked for more than one night, for the teachers of both the boys' and girls' high-schools, the teachers of the seminary, the government officials, all received a copy. Byelikov received one, too. The caricature made a very painful impression on him.

" We went out together; it was the first of May, a Sunday, and all of us, the boys and the teachers, had agreed to meet at the high-school and then to go for a walk together to a wood beyond the town. We set off, and he was green in the face and gloomier than a storm-cloud.

" ' What wicked, ill-natured people there are! ' he said, and his lips quivered.

" I felt really sorry for him. We were walking along, and all of a sudden — would you believe it? — Kovalenko came bowling along on a bicycle, and after him, also on a bicycle, Varinka, flushed and exhausted, but good-humoured and gay.

" ' We are going on ahead,' she called. ' What lovely weather! Awfully lovely! '

" And they both disappeared from our sight. Byelikov turned white instead of green, and seemed petrified. He stopped short and stared at me. . . .

" ' What is the meaning of it? Tell me, please! ' he asked. ' Can my eyes have deceived me? Is it the proper thing for high-school masters and ladies to ride bicycles? '

" ' What is there improper about it? ' I said. ' Let them ride and enjoy themselves.'

" ' But how can that be? ' he cried, amazed at my calm.   ' What are you saying? '

" And he was so shocked that he was unwilling to go on, and returned home.

" Next day he was continually twitching and nervously rubbing his hands, and it was evident from his face that he was unwell.   And he left before his work was over, for the first time in his life.   And he ate no dinner.   Towards evening he wrapped himself up warmly, though it was quite warm weather, and sallied out to the Kovalenkos'.   Varinka was out; he found her brother, however.

" ' Pray sit down,' Kovalenko said coldly, with a frown.   His face looked sleepy; he had just had a nap after dinner, and was in a very bad humour.

" Byelikov sat in silence for ten minutes, and then began:

" ' I have come to see you to relieve my mind.   I am very, very much troubled.   Some scurrilous fellow has drawn an absurd caricature of me and another person, in whom we are both deeply interested. I regard it as a duty to assure you that I have had no hand in it. . . . I have given no sort of ground for such ridicule — on the contrary, I have always behaved in every way like a gentleman.'

" Kovalenko sat sulky and silent.   Byelikov waited a little, and went on slowly in a mournful voice:

" ' And I have something else to say to you.   I have been in the service for years, while you have only lately entered it, and I consider it my duty as an older colleague to give you a warning. You ride on a bicycle, and that pastime is utterly unsuitable for an educator of youth.'

" ' Why so? ' asked Kovalenko in his bass.

" ' Surely that needs no explanation, Mihail Savvitch — surely you can understand that? If the teacher rides a bicycle, what can you expect the pupils to do? You will have them walking on their heads next! And so long as there is no formal permission to do so, it is out of the question. I was horrified yesterday! When I saw your sister everything seemed dancing before my eyes. A lady or a young girl on a bicycle — it's awful! '

" ' What is it you want exactly? '

" ' All I want is to warn you, Mihail Savvitch. You are a young man, you have a future before you, you must be very, very careful in your behaviour, and you are so careless — oh, so careless! You go about in an embroidered shirt, are constantly seen in the street carrying books, and now the bicycle, too. The headmaster will learn that you and your sister ride the bicycle, and then it will reach the higher authorities. . . . Will that be a good thing? '

" ' It's no business of anybody else if my sister and I do bicycle! ' said Kovalenko, and he turned crimson. ' And damnation take any one who meddles in my private affairs! '

" Byelikov turned pale and got up.

" ' If you speak to me in that tone I cannot continue,' he said. ' And I beg you never to express yourself like that about our superiors in my presence; you ought to be respectful to the authorities.'

" ' Why, have I said any harm of the authorities? '
asked Kóvalenko, looking at him wrathfully.
' Please leave me alone. I am an honest man, and
do not care to talk to a gentleman like you. I
don't like sneaks ! '

" Byelikov flew into a nervous flutter, and began
hurriedly putting on his coat, with an expression of
horror on his face. It was the first time in his life
he had been spoken to so rudely.

" ' You can say what you please,' he said, as he
went out from the entry to the landing on the staircase. ' 1 ought only to warn you: possibly some one
may have overheard us, and that our conversation
may not be misunderstood and harm come of it, I
shall be compelled to inform our headmaster of our
conversation . . . in its main features. I am bound
to do so.'

" ' Inform him? You can go and make your report ! '

" Kovalenko seized him from behind by the collar
and gave him a push, and Byelikov rolled downstairs, thudding with his goloshes. The staircase
was high and steep, but he rolled to the bottom un-
hurt, got up, and touched his nose to see whether
his spectacles were all right. But just as he was
falling down the stairs Varinka came in, and with
her two ladies; they stood below staring, and to
Byelikov this was more terrible than anything. I believe he would rather have broken his neck or both
legs than have been an object of ridicule. Why,
now the whole town would hear of it; it would come
to the headmaster's ears, would reach the higher

authorities — oh, it might lead to something! There would be another caricature, and it would all end in his being asked to resign his post. . . .

" When he got up, Varinka recognized him, and, looking at his ridiculous face, his crumpled overcoat, and his goloshes, not understanding what had happened and supposing that he had slipped down by accident, could not restrain herself, and laughed loud enough to be heard by all the flats:

" ' Ha-ha-ha! '

" And this pealing, ringing ' Ha-ha-ha! ' was the last straw that put an end to everything: to the proposed match and to Byelikov's earthly existence. He did not hear what Varinka said to him; he saw nothing. On reaching home, the first thing he did was to remove her portrait from the table; then he went to bed, and he never got up again.

" Three days later Afanasy came to me and asked whether we should not send for the doctor, as there was something wrong with his master. I went in to Byelikov. He lay silent behind the curtain, covered with a quilt; if one asked him a question, he said ' Yes ' or ' No ' and not another sound. He lay there while Afanasy, gloomy and scowling, hovered about him, sighing heavily, and smelling like a pothouse.

" A month later Byelikov died. We all went to his funeral — that is, both the high-schools and the seminary. Now when he was lying in his coffin his expression was mild, agreeable, even cheerful, as though he were glad that he had at last been put into a case which he would never leave again. Yes, he had attained his ideal! And, as though in his honour, it was dull, rainy weather on the day of his funeral, and we all wore goloshes and took our umbrellas. Varinka, too, was at the funeral, and when the coffin was lowered into the grave she burst into tears. I have noticed that Little Russian women are always laughing or crying — no intermediate mood.

"One must confess that to bury people like Byelikov is a great pleasure. As we were returning from the cemetery we wore discreet Lenten faces; no one wanted to display this feeling of pleasure — a feeling like that we had experienced long, long ago as children when our elders had gone out and we ran about the garden for an hour or two, enjoying complete freedom. Ah, freedom, freedom! The merest hint, the faintest hope of its possibility gives wings to the soul, does it not?

"We returned from the cemetery in a good humour. But not more than a week had passed before life went on as in the past, as gloomy, oppressive, and senseless — a life not forbidden by government prohibition, but not fully permitted, either: it was no better. And, indeed, though we had buried Byelikov, how many such men in cases were left, how many more of them there will be!"

"That's just how it is," said Ivan Ivanovitch and he lighted his pipe.

"How many more of them there will be!" repeated Burkin.

The schoolmaster came out of the barn. He was a short, stout man, completely bald, with a black beard down to his waist. The two dogs came out with him.

"What a moon!" he said, looking upwards.

It was midnight. On the right could be seen the whole village, a long street stretching far away for four miles. All was buried in deep silent slumber; not a movement, not a sound; one could hardly believe that nature could be so still. When on a moonlight night you see a broad village street, with its cottages, haystacks, and slumbering willows, a feeling of calm comes over the soul; in this peace, wrapped away from care, toil, and sorrow in the darkness of night, it is mild, melancholy, beautiful, and it seems as though the stars look down upon it kindly and with tenderness, and as though there were no evil on earth and all were well. On the left the open country began from the end of the village; it could be seen stretching far away to the horizon, and there was no movement, no sound in that whole expanse bathed in moonlight.

"Yes, that is just how it is," repeated Ivan Ivanovitch; "and isn't our living in town, airless and crowded, our writing useless papers, our playing *vint* — isn't that all a sort of case for us? And our spending our whole lives among trivial, fussy men and silly, idle women, our talking and our listening to all sorts of nonsense — isn't that a case for us, too? If you like, I will tell you a very edifying story."

"No; it's time we were asleep," said Burkin. "Tell it tomorrow."

They went into the barn and lay down on the hay. And they were both covered up and beginning to doze when they suddenly heard light footsteps — patter, patter. . . . Some one was walking not far from the barn, walking a little and stopping, and a minute later, patter, patter again. . . . The dogs began growling.

"That's Mavra," said Burkin.

The footsteps died away.

"You see and hear that they lie," said Ivan Ivanovitch, turning over on the other side, "and they call you a fool for putting up with their lying. You endure insult and humiliation, and dare not openly say that you are on the side of the honest and the free, and you lie and smile yourself; and all that for the sake of a crust of bread, for the sake of a warm corner, for the sake of a wretched little worthless rank in the service. No, one can't go on living like this."

"Well, you are off on another tack now, Ivan Ivanovitch," said the schoolmaster. "Let us go to sleep!"

And ten minutes later Burkin was asleep. But Ivan Ivanovitch kept sighing and turning over from side to side; then he got up, went outside again, and, sitting in the doorway, lighted his pipe.

1898

GOOSEBERRIES

GOOSEBERRIES

THE whole sky had been overcast with rain-clouds from early morning; it was a still day, not hot, but heavy, as it is in grey dull weather when the clouds have been hanging over the country for a long while, when one expects rain and it does not come. Ivan Ivanovitch, the veterinary surgeon, and Burkin, the high-school teacher, were already tired from walking, and the fields seemed to them endless. Far ahead of them they could just see the windmills of the village of Mironositskoe; on the right stretched a row of hillocks which disappeared in the distance behind the village, and they both knew that this was the bank of the river, that there were meadows, green willows, homesteads there, and that if one stood on one of the hillocks one could see from it the same vast plain, telegraph-wires, and a train which in the distance looked like a crawling cater-pillar, and that in clear weather one could even see the town. Now, in still weather, when all nature seemed mild and dreamy, Ivan Ivanovitch and Bur-kin were filled with love of that countryside, and both thought how great, how beautiful a land it was.

"Last time we were in Prokofy's barn," said Burkin, "you were about to tell me a story."

"Yes; I meant to tell you about my brother."

Ivan Ivanovitch heaved a deep sigh and lighted a pipe to begin to tell his story, but just at that moment the rain began.   And five minutes later heavy rain came down, covering the sky, and it was hard to tell when it would be over.   Ivan Ivanovitch and Burkin stopped in hesitation; the dogs, already drenched, stood with their tails between their legs gazing at them feelingly.

" We must take shelter somewhere," said Burkin. " Let us go to Alehin's; it's close by."

" Come along."

They turned aside and walked through mown fields, sometimes going straight forward, sometimes turning to the right, till they came out on the road. Soon they saw poplars, a garden, then the red roofs of barns; there was a gleam of the river, and the view opened on to a broad expanse of water with a windmill and a white bath-house: this was Sofino, where Alehin lived.

The watermill was at work, drowning the sound of the rain; the dam was shaking.   Here wet horses with drooping heads were standing near their carts, and men were walking about covered with sacks. It was damp, muddy, and desolate; the water looked cold and malignant.   Ivan Ivanovitch and Burkin were already conscious of a feeling of wetness, messiness, and discomfort all over; their feet were heavy with mud, and when, crossing the dam, they went up to the barns, they were silent, as though they were angry with one another.

In one of the barns there was the sound of a winnowing machine, the door was open, and clouds of dust were coming from it. In the doorway was standing Alehin himself, a man of forty, tall and stout, with long hair, more like a professor or an artist than a landowner. He had on a white shirt that badly needed washing, a rope for a belt, drawers instead of trousers, and his boots, too, were plastered up with mud and straw. His eyes and nose were black with dust. He recognized Ivan Ivanovitch and Burkin, and was apparently much delighted to see them.

"Go into the house, gentlemen," he said, smiling; "I'll come directly, this minute."

It was a big two-storeyed house. Alehin lived in the lower storey, with arched ceilings and little windows, where the bailiffs had once lived; here everything was plain, and there was a smell of rye bread, cheap vodka, and harness. He went upstairs into the best rooms only on rare occasions, when visitors came. Ivan Ivanovitch and Burkin were met in the house by a maid-servant, a young woman so beautiful that they both stood still and looked at one another.

"You can't imagine how delighted I am to see you, my friends," said Alehin, going into the hall with them. "It is a surprise! Pelagea," he said, addressing the girl, "give our visitors something to change into. And, by the way, I will change too. Only I must first go and wash, for I almost think I have not washed since spring. Wouldn't you like to come into the bath-house? and meanwhile they will get things ready here."

Beautiful Pelagea, looking so refined and soft,

brought them towels and soap, and Alehin went to
the bath-house with his guests.

"It's a long time since I had a wash," he said,
undressing. "I have got a nice bath-house, as you
see — my father built it — but I somehow never
have time to wash."

He sat down on the steps and soaped his long hair
and his neck, and the water round him turned brown.

"Yes, I must say," said Ivan Ivanovitch mean-
ingly, looking at his head.

"It's a long time since I washed . . ." said Alehin
with embarrassment, giving himself a second soap-
ing, and the water near him turned dark blue, like
ink.

Ivan Ivanovitch went outside, plunged into the
water with a loud splash, and swam in the rain, flinging his arms out wide. He stirred the water into
waves which set the white lilies bobbing up and
down; he swam to the very middle of the millpond
and dived, and came up a minute later in another
place, and swam on, and kept on diving, trying to
touch the bottom.

"Oh, my goodness!" he repeated continually, enjoying himself thoroughly. "Oh, my goodness!"
He swam to the mill, talked to the peasants there,
then returned and lay on his back in the middle of
the pond, turning his face to the rain. Burkin and
Alehin were dressed and ready to go, but he still went
on swimming and diving. "Oh, my good-
ness! . . ." he said. "Oh, Lord, have mercy on
me! . . ."

"That's enough!" Burkin shouted to him.

They went back to the house. And only when the lamp was lighted in the big drawing-room upstairs, and Burkin and Ivan Ivanovitch, attired in silk dressing-gowns and warm slippers, were sitting in arm-chairs; and Alehin, washed and combed, in a new coat, was walking about the drawing-room, evidently enjoying the feeling of warmth, cleanliness, dry clothes, and light shoes; and when lovely Pelagea, stepping noiselessly on the carpet and smiling softly, handed tea and jam on a tray — only then Ivan Ivanovitch began on his story, and it seemed as though not only Burkin and Alehin were listening, but also the ladies, young and old, and the officers who looked down upon them sternly and calmly from their gold frames.

"There are two of us brothers," he began —"I, Ivan Ivanovitch, and my brother, Nikolay Ivanovitch, two years younger. I went in for a learned profession and became a veterinary surgeon, while Nikolay sat in a government office from the time he was nineteen. Our father, Tchimsha-Himalaisky, was a kantonist, but he rose to be an officer and left us a little estate and the rank of nobility. After his death the little estate went in debts and legal expenses; but, anyway, we had spent our childhood running wild in the country. Like peasant children, we passed our days and nights in the fields and the woods, looked after horses, stripped the bark off the trees, fished, and so on. . . . And, you know, whoever has once in his life caught perch or has seen the migrating of the thrushes in autumn, watched how they float in flocks over the village on bright, cool days, he will never be a real townsman, and will have a yearning for freedom to the day of his death. My brother was miserable in the government office. Years passed by, and he went on sitting in the same place, went on writing the same papers and thinking of one and the same thing — how to get into the country. And this yearning by degrees passed into a definite desire, into a dream of buying himself a little farm somewhere on the banks of a river or a lake.

" He was a gentle, good-natured fellow, and I was fond of him, but I never sympathized with this desire to shut himself up for the rest of his life in a little farm of his own. It's the correct thing to say that a man needs no more than six feet of earth. But six feet is what a corpse needs, not a man. And they say, too, now, that if our intellectual classes are attracted to the land and yearn for a farm, it's a good thing. But these farms are just the same as six feet of earth. To retreat from town, from the struggle, from the bustle of life, to retreat and bury oneself in one's farm — it's not life, it's egoism, laziness, it's monasticism of a sort, but monasticism without good works. A man does not need six feet of earth or a farm, but the whole globe, all nature, where he can have room to display all the qualities and peculiarities of his free spirit.

" My brother Nikolay, sitting in his government office, dreamed of how he would eat his own cabbages, which would fill the whole yard with such a savoury smell, take his meals on the green grass, sleep in the sun, sit for whole hours on the seat by the gate gazing at the fields and the forest. Gardening books and the agricultural hints in calendars were his delight, his favourite spiritual sustenance; he enjoyed reading newspapers, too, but the only things he read in them were the advertisements of so many acres of arable land and a grass meadow with farm-houses and buildings, a river, a garden, a mill and millponds, for sale. And his imagination pictured the garden-paths, flowers and fruit, starling cotes, the carp in the pond, and all that sort of thing, you know. These imaginary pictures were of different kinds according to the advertisements which he came across, but for some reason in every one of them he had always to have gooseberries. He could not imagine a homestead, he could not picture an idyllic nook, without gooseberries.

" ' Country life has its conveniences,' he would sometimes say. ' You sit on the verandah and you drink tea, while your ducks swim on the pond, there is a delicious smell everywhere, and . . . and the gooseberries are growing.'

" He used to draw a map of his property, and in every map there were the same things — (a) house for the family, (b) servants' quarters, (c) kitchen-garden, (d) gooseberry-bushes. He lived parsimoniously, was frugal in food and drink, his clothes were beyond description; he looked like a beggar, but kept on saving and putting money in the bank. He grew fearfully avaricious. I did not like to look at him, and I used to give him something and send him presents for Christmas and Easter, but he used to save that too. Once a man is absorbed by an idea there is no doing anything with him.

"Years passed: he was transferred to another province. He was over forty, and he was still reading the advertisements in the papers and saving up. Then I heard he was married. Still with the same object of buying a farm and having gooseberries, he married an elderly and ugly widow without a trace of feeling for her, simply because she had filthy lucre. He went on living frugally after marrying her, and kept her short of food, while he put her money in the bank in his name.

"Her first husband had been a postmaster, and with him she was accustomed to pies and home-made wines, while with her second husband she did not get enough black bread; she began to pine away with this sort of life, and three years later she gave up her soul to God. And I need hardly say that my brother never for one moment imagined that he was responsible for her death. Money, like vodka, makes a man queer. In our town there was a merchant who, before he died, ordered a plateful of honey and ate up all his money and lottery tickets with the honey, so that no one might get the benefit of it. While I was inspecting cattle at a railway-station, a cattle-dealer fell under an engine and had his leg cut off. We carried him into the waiting-room, the blood was flowing — it was a horrible thing — and he kept asking them to look for his leg and was very much worried about it; there were twenty roubles in the boot on the leg that had been cut off, and he was afraid they would be lost."

"That's a story from a different opera," said Burkin.

"After his wife's death," Ivan Ivanovitch went on, after thinking for half a minute, "my brother began looking out for an estate for himself. Of course, you may look about for five years and yet end by making a mistake, and buying something quite different from what you have dreamed of. My brother Nikolay bought through an agent a mortgaged estate of three hundred and thirty acres, with a house for the family, with servants' quarters, with a park, but with no orchard, no gooseberry-bushes, and no duck-pond; there was a river, but the water in it was the colour of coffee, because on one side of the estate there was a brickyard and on the other a factory for burning bones. But Nikolay Ivanovitch did not grieve much; he ordered twenty gooseberry-bushes, planted them, and began living as a country gentleman.

"Last year I went to pay him a visit. I thought I would go and see what it was like. In his letters my brother called his estate ' Tchumbaroklov Waste, alias Himalaiskoe.' I reached ' alias Himalaiskoe ' in the afternoon. It was hot. Everywhere there were ditches, fences, hedges, fir-trees planted in rows, and there was no knowing how to get to the yard, where to put one's horse. I went up to the house, and was met by a fat red dog that looked like a pig. It wanted to bark, but it was too lazy. The cook, a fat, barefooted woman, came out of the kitchen, and she, too, looked like a pig, and said that her master was resting after dinner. I went in to see my brother. He was sitting up in bed with a quilt over his legs; he had grown older, fatter, wrinkled; his cheeks, his nose, and his mouth all stuck out — he looked as though he might begin grunting into the quilt at any moment.

"We embraced each other, and shed tears of joy and of sadness at the thought that we had once been young and now were both grey-headed and near the grave. He dressed, and led me out to show me the estate.

"'Well, how are you getting on here?' I asked.

"'Oh, all right, thank God; I am getting on very well.'

"He was no more a poor timid clerk, but a real landowner, a gentleman. He was already accustomed to it, had grown used to it, and liked it. He ate a great deal, went to the bath-house, was growing stout, was already at law with the village commune and both factories, and was very much offended when the peasants did not call him 'Your Honour.' And he concerned himself with the salvation of his soul in a substantial, gentlemanly manner, and performed deeds of charity, not simply, but with an air of consequence. And what deeds of charity! He treated the peasants for every sort of disease with soda and castor oil, and on his name-day had a thanksgiving service in the middle of the village, and then treated the peasants to a gallon of vodka — he thought that was the thing to do. Oh, those horrible gallons of vodka! One day the fat landowner hauls the peasants up before the district captain for trespass, and next day, in honour of a holiday, treats them to a gallon of vodka, and they drink and shout 'Hurrah!' and when they are drunk bow down to his feet. A change of life for the better, and being well-fed and idle develop in a Russian the most insolent self-conceit. Nikolay Ivanovitch, who at one time in the government office was afraid to have any views of his own, now could say nothing that was not gospel truth, and uttered such truths in the tone of a prime minister. 'Education is essential, but for the peasants it is premature.' 'Corporal punishment is harmful as a rule, but in some cases it is necessary and there is nothing to take its place.'

"'I know the peasants and understand how to treat them,' he would say. 'The peasants like me. I need only to hold up my little finger and the peasants will do anything I like.'

"And all this, observe, was uttered with a wise, benevolent smile. He repeated twenty times over 'We noblemen,' 'I as a noble'; obviously he did not remember that our grandfather was a peasant, and our father a soldier. Even our surname Tchimsha-Himaláisky, in reality so incongruous, seemed to him now melodious, distinguished, and very agreeable.

"But the point just now is not he, but myself. I want to tell you about the change that took place in me during the brief hours I spent at his country place. In the evening, when we were drinking tea, the cook put on the table a plateful of gooseberries. They were not bought, but his own goosberries, gathered for the first time since the bushes were planted. Nikolay Ivanovitch laughed and looked for a minute in silence at the gooseberries, with tears in his eyes; he could not speak for excitement. Then he put one gooseberry in his mouth, looked at me with the triumph of a child who has at last received his favourite toy, and said:

" ' How delicious! '

" And he ate them greedily, continually repeating, ' Ah, how delicious!   Do taste them! '

" They were sour and unripe, but, as Pushkin says:

" ' Dearer to us the falsehood that exalts
   Than hosts of baser truths.'

" I saw a happy man whose cherished dream was so obviously fulfilled, who had attained his object in life, who had gained what he wanted, who was satisfied with his fate and himself.   There is always, for some reason, an element of sadness mingled with my thoughts of human happiness, and, on this occasion, at the sight of a happy man I was overcome by an oppressive feeling that was close upon despair. It was particularly oppressive at night.   A bed was made up for me in the room next to my brother's bedroom, and I could hear that he was awake, and that he kept getting up and going to the plate of gooseberries and taking one.   I reflected how many satisfied, happy people there really are!   What a suffocating force it is!   You look at life: the insolence and idleness of the strong, the ignorance and brutishness of the weak, incredible poverty all about us, overcrowding, degeneration, drunkenness, hy-

pocrisy, lying. . . . Yet all is calm and stillness in
the houses and in the streets; of the fifty thousand
living in a town, there is not one who would cry out,
who would give vent to his indignation aloud. We
see the people going to market for provisions, eating
by day, sleeping by night, talking their silly nonsense,
getting married, growing old, serenely escorting their
dead to the cemetery; but we do not see and we do
not hear those who suffer, and what is terrible in life
goes on somewhere behind the scenes. . . . Everything is quiet and peaceful, and nothing protests but
mute statistics: so many people gone out of their
minds, so many gallons of vodka drunk, so many
children dead from malnutrition. . . . And this order of things is evidently necessary; evidently the
happy man only feels at ease because the unhappy
bear their burdens in silence, and without that silence
happiness would be impossible. It's a case of general hypnotism. There ought to be behind the door
of every happy, contented man some one standing
with a hammer continually reminding him with a tap
that there are unhappy people; that however happy
he may be, life will show him her laws sooner or
later, trouble will come for him — disease, poverty,
losses, and no one will see or hear, just as now he
neither sees nor hears others. But there is no man
with a hammer; the happy man lives at his ease, and
trivial daily cares faintly agitate him like the wind in
the aspen-tree — and all goes well.

"That night I realized that I, too, was happy and
contented," Ivan Ivanovitch went on, getting up.
"I, too, at dinner and at the hunt liked to lay down

the law on life and religion, and the way to manage
the peasantry. I, too, used to say that science was
light, that culture was essential, but for the simple
people reading and writing was enough for the time.
Freedom is a blessing, I used to say; we can no more
do without it than without air, but we must wait a
little. Yes, I used to talk like that, and now I
ask, ' For what reason are we to wait? ' " asked
Ivan Ivanovitch, looking angrily at Burkin. " Why
wait, I ask you? What grounds have we for waiting? I shall be told, it can't be done all at once;
every idea takes shape in life gradually, in its due
time. But who is it says that? Where is the proof
that it's right? You will fall back upon the natural
order of things, the uniformity of phenomena; but is
there order and uniformity in the fact that I, a living,
thinking man, stand over a chasm and wait for it
to close of itself, or to fill up with mud at the very
time when perhaps I might leap over it or build a
bridge across it? And again, wait for the sake of
what? Wait till there's no strength to live? And
meanwhile one must live, and one wants to live!

" I went away from my brother's early in the
morning, and ever since then it has been unbearable
for me to be in town. I am oppressed by its peace
and quiet; I am afraid to look at the windows, for
there is no spectacle more painful to me now than
the sight of a happy family sitting round the table
drinking tea. I am old and am not fit for the struggle; I am not even capable of hatred; I can only
grieve inwardly, feel irritated and vexed; but at night

my head is hot from the rush of ideas, and I cannot
sleep. . . . Ah, if I were young! "

Ivan Ivanovitch walked backwards and forwards
in excitement, and repeated: " If I were young! "

He suddenly went up to Alehin and began pressing
first one of his hands and then the other.

" Pavel Konstantinovitch," he said in an imploring voice, " don't be calm and contented, don't let
yourself be put to sleep! While you are young,
strong, confident, be not weary in well-doing! There
is no happiness, and there ought not to be; but if
there is a meaning and an object in life, that meaning
and object is not our happiness, but something
greater and more rational.   Do good! "

And all this Ivan Ivanovitch said with a pitiful,
imploring smile, as though he were asking him a
personal favour.

Then all three sat in arm-chairs at different ends of
the drawing-room and were silent. Ivan Ivanovitch's story had not satisfied either Burkin or Alehin.
When the generals and ladies gazed down from their
gilt frames, looking in the dusk as though they were
alive, it was dreary to listen to the story of the poor
clerk who ate gooseberries. They felt inclined, for
some reason, to talk about elegant people, about
women. And their sitting in the drawing-room
where everything — the chandeliers in their covers,
the arm-chairs, and the carpet under their feet — reminded them that those very people who were now
looking down from their frames had once moved
about, sat, drunk tea in this room, and the fact that

lovely Pelagea was moving noiselessly about was bet-ter than any story.

Alehin was fearfully sleepy; he had got up early, before three o'clock in the morning, to look after his work, and now his eyes were closing; but he was afraid his visitors might tell some interesting story after he had gone, and he lingered on. He did not go into the question whether what Ivan Ivanovitch had just said was right and true. His visitors did not talk of groats, nor of hay, nor of tar, but of something that had no direct bearing on his life, and he was glad and wanted them to go on.

" It's bed-time, though," said Burkin, getting up. " Allow me to wish you good-night."

Alehin said good-night and went downstairs to his own domain, while the visitors remained upstairs. They were both taken for the night to a big room where there stood two old wooden beds decorated with carvings, and in the corner was an ivory crucifix. The big cool beds, which had been made by the lovely Pelagea, smelt agreeably of clean linen.

Ivan Ivanovitch undressed in silence and got into bed.

" Lord forgive us sinners! " he said, and put his head under the quilt.

His pipe lying on the table smelt strongly of stale tobacco, and Burkin could not sleep for a long while, and kept wondering where the oppressive smell came from.

The rain was pattering on the window-panes all night.

1898

ABOUT LOVE

ABOUT LOVE

AT lunch next day there were very nice pies, crayfish, and mutton cutlets; and while we were eating, Nikanor, the cook, came up to ask what the visitors would like for dinner. He was a man of medium height, with a puffy face and little eyes; he was close-shaven, and it looked as though his moustaches had not been shaved, but had been pulled out by the roots. Alehin told us that the beautiful Pelagea was in love with this cook. As he drank and was of a violent character, she did not want to marry him, but was willing to live with him without. He was very devout, and his religious convictions would not allow him to " live in sin "; he insisted on her marrying him, and would consent to nothing else, and when he was drunk he used to abuse her and even beat her. Whenever he got drunk she used to hide upstairs and sob, and on such occasions Alehin and the servants stayed in the house to be ready to defend her in case of necessity.

We began talking about love.

" How love is born," said Alehin, " why Pelagea does not love somebody more like herself in her spiritual and external qualities, and why she fell in love with Nikanor, that ugly snout — we all call him ' The Snout '— how far questions of personal happiness are of consequence in love — all that is unknown; one can take what view one likes of it.   So far only one incontestable truth has been uttered about love: 'This is a great mystery.'   Everything else that has been written or said about love is not a conclusion, but only a statement of questions which have remained unanswered.   The explanation which would seem to fit one case does not apply in a dozen others, and the very best thing, to my mind, would be to explain every case individually without attempting to generalize.   We ought, as the doctors say, to individualize each case."

" Perfectly true," Burkin assented.

" We Russians of the educated class have a partiality for these questions that remain unanswered. Love is usually poeticized, decorated with roses, nightingales; we Russians decorate our loves with these momentous questions, and select the most uninteresting of them, too.   In Moscow, when I was a student, I had a friend who shared my life, a charming lady, and every time I took her in my arms she was thinking what I would allow her a month for housekeeping and what was the price of beef a pound. In the same way, when we are in love we are never tired of asking ourselves questions: whether it is honourable or dishonourable, sensible or stupid, what this love is leading up to, and so on.   Whether it is a good thing or not I don't know, but that it is in the way, unsatisfactory, and irritating, I do know."

It looked as though he wanted to tell some story. People who lead a solitary existence always have something in their hearts which they are eager to talk about.   In town bachelors visit the baths and

the restaurants on purpose to talk, and sometimes tell the most interesting things to bath attendants and waiters; in the country, as a rule, they unbosom themselves to their guests. Now from the window we could see a grey sky, trees drenched in the rain; in such weather we could go nowhere, and there was nothing for us to do but to tell stories and to listen.

" I have lived at Sofino and been farming for a long time," Alehin began, " ever since I left the University. I am an idle gentleman by education, a studious person by disposition; but there was a big debt owing on the estate when I came here, and as my father was in debt partly because he had spent so much on my education, I resolved not to go away, but to work till I paid off the debt. I made up my mind to this and set to work, not, I must confess, without some repugnance. The land here does not yield much, and if one is not to farm at a loss one must employ serf labour or hired labourers, which is almost the same thing, or put it on a peasant footing — that is, work the fields oneself and with one's family. There is no middle path. But in those days I did not go into such subtleties. I did not leave a clod of earth unturned; I gathered together all the peasants, men and women, from the neighbouring villages; the work went on at a tremendous pace. I myself ploughed and sowed and reaped, and was bored doing it, and frowned with disgust, like a village cat driven by hunger to eat cucumbers in the kitchen-garden. My body ached, and I slept as I walked. At first it seemed to me that I could easily reconcile this life of toil with my cultured habits; to

do so, I thought, all that is necessary is to maintain
a certain external order in life.   I established myself
upstairs here in the best rooms, and ordered them to
bring me there coffee and liquor after lunch and
dinner, and when I went to bed I read every night
the *Vyestnik Evropi*.   But one day our priest, Father Ivan, came and drank up all my liquor at one
sitting; and the *Vyestnik Evropi* went to the priest's
daughters; as in the summer, especially at the hay-
making, I did not succeed in getting to my bed at
all, and slept in the sledge in the barn, or somewhere
in the forester's lodge, what chance was there of
reading?   Little by little I moved downstairs, began
dining in the servants' kitchen, and of my former
luxury nothing is left but the servants who were in
my father's service, and whom it would be painful
to turn away.

" In the first years I was elected here an honourary
justice of the peace.   I used to have to go to the
town and take part in the sessions of the congress
and of the circuit court, and this was a pleasant
change for me.   When you live here for two or
three months without a break, especially in the
winter, you begin at last to pine for a black coat.
And in the circuit court there were frock-coats, and
uniforms, and dress-coats, too, all lawyers, men who
have received a general education; I had some one
to talk to.   After sleeping in the sledge and dining
in the kitchen, to sit in an arm-chair in clean linen,
in thin boots, with a chain on one's waistcoat, is such
luxury!

" I received a warm welcome in the town.   I made

friends eagerly. And of all my acquaintanceships the most intimate and, to tell the truth, the most agreeable to me was my acquaintance with Luganovitch, the vice-president of the circuit court. You both know him: a most charming personality. It all happened just after a celebrated case of incendiarism; the preliminary investigation lasted two days; we were exhausted. Luganovitch looked at me and said:

" ' Look here, come round to dinner with me.'

" This was unexpected, as I knew Luganovitch very little, only officially, and I had never been to his house. I only just went to my hotel room to change and went off to dinner. And here it was my lot to meet Anna Alexyevna, Luganovitch's wife. At that time she was still very young, not more than twenty-two, and her first baby had been born just six months before. It is all a thing of the past; and now I should find it difficult to define what there was so exceptional in her, what it was in her attracted me so much; at the time, at dinner, it was all perfectly clear to me. I saw a lovely young, good, intelligent, fascinating woman, such as I had never met before; and I felt her at once some one close and already familiar, as though that face, those cordial, intelligent eyes, I had seen somewhere in my childhood, in the album which lay on my mother's chest of drawers.

" Four Jews were charged with being incendiaries, were regarded as a gang of robbers, and, to my mind, quite groundlessly. At dinner I was very much excited, I was uncomfortable, and I don't know what I said, but Anna Alexyevna kept shaking her head and saying to her husband:

" ' Dmitry, how is this? '

" Luganovitch is a good-natured man, one of those simple-hearted people who firmly maintain the opinion that once a man is charged before a court he is guilty, and to express doubt of the correctness of a sentence cannot be done except in legal form on paper, and not at dinner and in private conversation.

" ' You and I did not set fire to the place,' he said softly, ' and you see we are not condemned, and not in prison.'

" And both husband and wife tried to make me eat and drink as much as possible. From some trifling details, from the way they made the coffee together, for instance, and from the way they understood each other at half a word, I could gather that they lived in harmony and comfort, and that they were glad of a visitor. After dinner they played a duet on the piano; then it got dark, and I went home. That was at the beginning of spring.

" After that I spent the whole summer at Sofino without a break, and I had no time to think of the town, either, but the memory of the graceful fair-haired woman remained in my mind all those days; I did not think of her, but it was as though her light shadow were lying on my heart.

" In the late autumn there was a theatrical performance for some charitable object in the town. I went into the governor's box (I was invited to go there in the interval) ; I looked, and there was Anna Alexyevna sitting beside the governor's wife; and again the same irresistible, thrilling impression of beauty and sweet, caressing eyes, and again the same feeling of nearness. We sat side by side, then went to the foyer.

" ' You've grown thinner,' she said; ' have you been ill? '

" ' Yes, I've had rheumatism in my shoulder, and in rainy weather I can't sleep.'

" ' You look dispirited. In the spring, when you came to dinner, you were younger, more confident. You were full of eagerness, and talked a great deal then; you were very interesting, and I really must confess I was a little carried away by you. For some reason you often came back to my memory during the summer, and when I was getting ready for the theatre today I thought I should see you.'

" And she laughed.

" ' But you look dispirited today,' she repeated; ' it makes you seem older.'

" The next day I lunched at the Luganovitchs'. After lunch they drove out to their summer villa, in order to make arrangements there for the winter, and I went with them. I returned with them to the town, and at midnight drank tea with them in quiet domestic surroundings, while the fire glowed, and the young mother kept going to see if her baby girl was asleep. And after that, every time I went to town I never failed to visit the Luganovitchs. They grew used to me, and I grew used to them. As a rule I went in unannounced, as though I were one of the family.

" ' Who is there? ' I would hear from a faraway

room, in the drawling voice that seemed to me so lovely.

"'It is Pavel Konstantinovitch,' answered the maid or the nurse.

"Anna Alexyevna would come out to me with an anxious face, and would ask every time:

"'Why is it so long since you have been? Has anything happened?'

"Her eyes, the elegant refined hand she gave me, her indoor dress, the way she did her hair, her voice, her step, always produced the same impression on me of something new and extraordinary in my life, and very important. We talked together for hours, were silent, thinking each our own thoughts, or she played for hours to me on the piano. If there were no one at home I stayed and waited, talked to the nurse, played with the child, or lay on the sofa in the study and read; and when Anna Alexyevna came back I met her in the hall, took all her parcels from her, and for some reason I carried those parcels every time with as much love, with as much solemnity, as a boy.

"There is a proverb that if a peasant woman has no troubles she will buy a pig. The Luganovitchs had no troubles, so they made friends with me. If I did not come to the town I must be ill or something must have happened to me, and both of them were extremely anxious. They were worried that I, an educated man with a knowledge of languages, should, instead of devoting myself to science or literary work, live in the country, rush round like a squirrel in a rage, work hard with never a penny to show for it. They fancied that I was unhappy, and that I only talked, laughed, and ate to conceal my sufferings, and even at cheerful moments when I felt happy I was aware of their searching eyes fixed upon me. They were particularly touching when I really was depressed, when I was being worried by some creditor or had not money enough to pay interest on the proper day. The two of them, husband and wife, would whisper together at the window; then he would come to me and say with a grave face:

" ' If you really are in need of money at the moment, Pavel Konstantinovitch, my wife and I beg you not to hesitate to borrow from us.'

" And he would blush to his ears with emotion. And it would happen that, after whispering in the same way at the window, he would come up to me, with red ears, and say:

" ' My wife and I earnestly beg you to accept this present.'

" And he would give me studs, a cigar-case, or a lamp, and I would send them game, butter, and flowers from the country. They both, by the way, had considerable means of their own. In early days I often borrowed money, and was not very particular about it — borrowed wherever I could — but nothing in the world would have induced me to borrow from the Luganovitchs. But why talk of it?

" I was unhappy. At home, in the fields, in the barn, I thought of her; I tried to understand the mystery of a beautiful, intelligent young woman's marrying some one so uninteresting, almost an old man (her husband was over forty), and having children by him; to understand the mystery of this uninteresting, good, simple-hearted man, who argued with such wearisome good sense, at balls and evening parties kept near the more solid people, looking listless and superfluous, with a submissive, uninterested expression, as though he had been brought there for sale, who yet believed in his right to be happy, to have children by her; and I kept trying to understand why she had met him first and not me, and why such a terrible mistake in our lives need have happened.

" And when I went to the town I saw every time from her eyes that she was expecting me, and she would confess to me herself that she had had a peculiar feeling all that day and had guessed that I should come. We talked a long time, and were silent, yet we did not confess our love to each other, but timidly and jealously concealed it. We were afraid of everything that might reveal our secret to ourselves. I loved her tenderly, deeply, but I reflected and kept asking myself what our love could lead to if we had not the strength to fight against it. It seemed to be incredible that my gentle, sad love could all at once coarsely break up the even tenor of the life of her husband, her children, and all the household in which I was so loved and trusted. Would it be honourable? She would go away with me, but where? Where could I take her? It would have been a different matter if I had had a beautiful, interesting life — if, for instance, I had been struggling for the emancipation of my country, or had been a celebrated man of science, an artist

or a painter; but as it was it would mean taking her
from one everyday humdrum life to another as humdrum or perhaps more so.   And how long would
our happiness last?   What would happen to her in
case I was ill, in case I died, or if we simply grew
cold to one another?

" And she apparently reasoned in the same way.
She thought of her husband, her children, and of her
mother, who loved the husband like a son.   If she
abandoned herself to her feelings she would have to
lie, or else to tell the truth, and in her position either
would have been equally terrible and inconvenient.
And she was tormented by the question whether her
love would bring me happiness — would she not
complicate my life, which, as it was, was hard
enough and full of all sorts of trouble?   She fancied
she was not young enough for me, that she was not
industrious nor energetic enough to begin a new life,
and she often talked to her husband of the importance of my marrying a girl of intelligence and merit
who would be a capable housewife and a help to me
— and she would immediately add that it would be
difficult to find such a girl in the whole town.

" Meanwhile the years were passing.   Anna
Alexyevna already had two children.   When I arrived at the Luganovitchs' the servants smiled
cordially, the children shouted that Uncle Pavel
Konstantinovitch had come, and hung on my neck;
every one was overjoyed.   They did not understand
what was passing in my soul, and thought that I, too,
was happy.   Every one looked on me as a noble

being.　And grown-ups and children alike felt that a noble being was walking about their rooms, and that gave a peculiar charm to their manner towards me, as though in my presence their life, too, was purer and more beautiful.　Anna Alexyevna and I used to go to the theatre together, always walking there; we used to sit side by side in the stalls, our shoulders touching.　I would take the opera-glass from her hands without a word, and feel at that minute that she was near me, that she was mine, that we could not live without each other; but by some strange misunderstanding, when we came out of the theatre we always said good-bye and parted as though we were strangers.　Goodness knows what people were saying about us in the town already, but there was not a word of truth in it all!

"In the latter years Anna Alexyevna took to going away for frequent visits to her mother or to her sister; she began to suffer from low spirits, she began to recognize that her life was spoilt and unsatisfied, and at times she did not care to see her husband nor her children.　She was already being treated for neurasthenia.

"We were silent and still silent, and in the presence of outsiders she displayed a strange irritation in regard to me; whatever I talked about, she disagreed with me, and if I had an argument she sided with my opponent.　If I dropped anything, she would say coldly:

"'I congratulate you.'

"If I forgot to take the opera-glass when we were going to the theatre, she would say afterwards:

" ' I knew you would forget it.'

" Luckily or unluckily, there is nothing in our lives that does not end sooner or later. The time of parting came, as Luganovitch was appointed president in one of the western provinces. They had to sell their furniture, their horses, their summer villa. When they drove out to the villa, and afterwards looked back as they were going away, to look for the last time at the garden, at the green roof, every one was sad, and I realized that I had to say good-bye not only to the villa. It was arranged that at the end of August we should see Anna Alexyevna off to the Crimea, where the doctors were sending her, and that a little later Luganovitch and the children would set off for the western province.

" We were a great crowd to see Anna Alexyevna off. When she had said good-bye to her husband and her children and there was only a minute left before the third bell, I ran into her compartment to put a basket, which she had almost forgotten, on the rack, and I had to say good-bye. When our eyes met in the compartment our spiritual fortitude deserted us both; I took her in my arms, she pressed her face to my breast, and tears flowed from her eyes. Kissing her face, her shoulders, her hands wet with tears — oh, how unhappy we were! — I confessed my love for her, and with a burning pain in my heart I realized how unnecessary, how petty, and how deceptive all that had hindered us from loving was. I understood that when you love you must either, in your reasonings about that love, start from what is highest, from what is more important than happiness or unhappiness, sin or virtue in their accepted meaning, or you must not reason at all.

" I kissed her for the last time, pressed her hand, and parted for ever. The train had already started. I went into the next compartment — it was empty — and until I reached the next station I sat there crying. Then I walked home to Sofino. . . ."

While Alehin was telling his story, the rain left off and the sun came out. Burkin and Ivan Ivanovitch went out on the balcony, from which there was a beautiful view over the garden and the mill-pond, which was shining now in the sunshine like a mirror. They admired it, and at the same time they were sorry that this man with the kind, clever eyes, who had told them this story with such genuine feeling, should be rushing round and round this huge estate like a squirrel on a wheel instead of devoting himself to science or something else which would have made his life more pleasant; and they thought what a sorrowful face Anna Alexyevna must have had when he said good-bye to her in the railway-carriage and kissed her face and shoulders. Both of them had met her in the town, and Burkin knew her and thought her beautiful.

1898

THE LOTTERY TICKET

THE LOTTERY TICKET

IVAN DMITRITCH, a middle-class man who lived with his family on an income of twelve hundred a year and was very well satisfied with his lot, sat down on the sofa after supper and began reading the newspaper

"I forgot to look at the newspaper today," his wife said to him as she cleared the table. "Look and see whether the list of drawings is there."

"Yes, it is," said Ivan Dmitritch; "but hasn't your ticket lapsed?"

"No; I took the interest on Tuesday."

"What is the number?"

"Series 9,499, number 26."

"All right . . . we will look . . . 9,499 and 26."

Ivan Dmitritch had no faith in lottery luck, and would not, as a rule, have consented to look at the lists of winning numbers, but now, as he had nothing else to do and as the newspaper was before his eyes, he passed his finger downwards along the column of numbers. And immediately, as though in mockery of his scepticism, no further than the second line from the top, his eye was caught by the figure 9,499! Unable to believe his eyes, he hurriedly dropped the paper on his knees without looking to see the number of the ticket, and, just as though some one had given him a douche of cold water, he felt an agreeable chill in the pit of the stomach; tingling and terrible and sweet!

"Masha, 9,499 is there!" he said in a hollow voice.

His wife looked at his astonished and panic-stricken face, and realized that he was not joking.

"9,499?" she asked, turning pale and dropping the folded tablecloth on the table.

"Yes, yes . . . it really is there!"

"And the number of the ticket?"

"Oh, yes! There's the number of the ticket too. But stay . . . wait! No, I say! Anyway, the number of our series is there! Anyway, you understand. . . ."

Looking at his wife, Ivan Dmitritch gave a broad, senseless smile, like a baby when a bright object is shown it. His wife smiled too; it was as pleasant to her as to him that he only mentioned the series, and did not try to find out the number of the winning ticket. To torment and tantalize oneself with hopes of possible fortune is so sweet, so thrilling!

"It is our series," said Ivan Dmitritch, after a long silence. "So there is a probability that we have won. It's only a probability, but there it is!"

"Well, now look!"

"Wait a little. We have plenty of time to be disappointed. It's on the second line from the top, so the prize is seventy-five thousand. That's not money, but power, capital! And in a minute I shall look at the list, and there — 26! Eh? I say, what if we really have won?"

The husband and wife began laughing and staring at one another in silence. The possibility of winning bewildered them; they could not have said, could not have dreamed, what they both needed that seventy-five thousand for, what they would buy, where they would go. They thought only of the figures 9,499 and 75,000 and pictured them in their imagination, while somehow they could not think of the happiness itself which was so possible.

Ivan Dmitritch, holding the paper in his hand, walked several times from corner to corner, and only when he had recovered from the first impression began dreaming a little.

"And if we have won," he said —"why, it will be a new life, it will be a transformation! The ticket is yours, but if it were mine I should, first of all, of course, spend twenty-five thousand on real property in the shape of an estate; ten thousand on immediate expenses, new furnishing . . . travelling . . . paying debts, and so on. . . . The other forty thousand I would put in the bank and get interest on it."

"Yes, an estate, that would be nice," said his wife, sitting down and ropping her hands in her lap.

"Somewhere in the Tula or Oryol provinces. . . . In the first place we shouldn't need a summer villa, and besides, it would always bring in an income."

And pictures came crowding on his imagination, each more gracious and poetical than the last. And in all these pictures he saw himself well-fed, serene, healthy, felt warm, even hot! Here, after eating a summer soup, cold as ice, he lay on his back on the burning sand close to a stream or in the garden under a lime-tree. . . . It is hot. . . . His little boy and girl are crawling about near him, digging in the sand or catching ladybirds in the grass. He dozes sweetly, thinking of nothing, and feeling all over that he need not go to the office today, tomorrow, or the day after. Or, tired of lying still, he goes to the hayfield, or to the forest for mushrooms, or watches the peasants catching fish with a net. When the sun sets he takes a towel and soap and saunters to the bathing-shed, where he undresses at his leisure, slowly rubs his bare chest with his hands, and goes into the water. And in the water, near the opaque soapy circles, little fish flit to and fro and green water-weeds nod their heads. After bathing there is tea with cream and milk rolls. . . . In the evening a walk or *vint* with the neighbours.

"Yes, it would be nice to buy an estate," said his wife, also dreaming, and from her face it was evident that she was enchanted by her thoughts.

Ivan Dmitritch pictured to himself autumn with its rains, its cold evenings, and its St. Martin's summer. At that season he would have to take longer walks about the garden and beside the river, so as to get thoroughly chilled, and then drink a big glass of vodka and eat a salted mushroom or a soused cucumber, and then — drink another. . . . The children would come running from the kitchen-garden, bringing a carrot and a radish smelling of fresh earth. . . . And then, he would lie stretched full length on the sofa, and in leisurely fashion turn over the pages of some illustrated magazine, or, covering his face with it and unbuttoning his waistcoat, give himself up to slumber.

The St. Martin's summer is followed by cloudy, gloomy weather. It rains day and night, the bare trees weep, the wind is damp and cold. The dogs, the horses, the fowls — all are wet, depressed, downcast. There is nowhere to walk; one can't go out for days together; one has to pace up and down the room, looking despondently at the grey window. It is dreary!

Ivan Dmitritch stopped and looked at his wife.

" I should go abroad, you know, Masha," he said.

And he began thinking how nice it would be in late autumn to go abroad somewhere to the South of France . . . to Italy . . . . to India!

" I should certainly go abroad too," his wife said. " But look at the number of the ticket! "

" Wait, wait! . . ."

He walked about the room and went on thinking. It occurred to him: what if his wife really did go abroad? It is pleasant to travel alone, or in the society of light, careless women who live in the present, and not such as think and talk all the journey about nothing but their children, sigh, and tremble with dismay over every farthing. Ivan Dmitritch imagined his wife in the train with a multitude of parcels, baskets, and bags; she would be sighing over something, complaining that the train made her head ache, that she had spent so much money. . . . At the stations he would continually be having to run for boiling water, bread and butter. . . . She wouldn't have dinner because of its being too dear. . . . .

" She would begrudge me every farthing," he thought, with a glance at his wife. " The lottery ticket is hers, not mine! Besides, what is the use of her going abroad? What does she want there? She would shut herself up in the hotel, and not let me out of her sight. . . . I know! "

And for the first time in his life his mind dwelt on the fact that his wife had grown elderly and plain, and that she was saturated through and through with the smell of cooking, while he was still young, fresh, and healthy, and might well have got married again.

" Of course, all that is silly nonsense," he thought; " but . . . why should she go abroad? What would she make of it? And yet she would go, of course. . . . I can fancy . . . In reality it is all one to her, whether it is Naples or Klin. She would only be in my way. I should be dependent upon her. I can fancy how, like a regular woman, she will lock the money up as soon as she gets it. . . . She will hide it from me. . . . She will look after her relations and grudge me every farthing."

Ivan Dmitritch thought of her relations. All those wretched brothers and sisters and aunts and uncles would come crawling about as soon as they heard of the winning ticket, would begin whining like beggars, and fawning upon them with oily, hypocritical smlies. Wretched, detestable people! If they were given anything, they would ask for

more; while if they were refused, they would swear
at them, slander them, and wish them every kind of
misfortune.

Ivan Dmitritch remembered his own relations,
and their faces, at which he had looked impartially
in the past, struck him now as repulsive and hateful.

" They are such reptiles ! " he thought.

And his wife's face, too, struck him as repulsive
and hateful. Anger surged up in his heart against
her, and he thought malignantly:

" She knows nothing about money, and so she is
stingy. If she, won it she would give me a hundred
roubles, and put the rest away under lock and key."

And he looked at his wife, not with a smile now,
but with hatred. She glanced at him too, and also
with hatred and anger. She had her own daydreams, her own plans, her own reflections; she
understood perfectly well what her husband's
dreams were. She knew who would be the first to
try and grab her winnings.

" It's very nice making daydreams at other people's expense ! " is what her eyes expressed. " No,
don't you dare ! "

Her husband understood her look; hatred began
stirring again in his breast, and in order to annoy
his wife he glanced quickly, to spite her at the fourth
page on the newspaper and read out triumphantly:

" Series 9,499, number 46 ! Not 26 ! "

Hatred and hope both disappeared at once, and
it began immediately to seem to Ivan Dmitritch and
his wife that their rooms were dark and small
and low-pitched, that the supper they had been eat-

ing was not doing them good, but lying heavy on their stomachs, that the evenings were long and wearisome. . . .

"What the devil's the meaning of it?" said Ivan Dmitritch, beginning to be ill-humoured. "Wherever one steps there are bits of paper under one's feet, crumbs, husks. The rooms are never swept! One is simply forced to go out. Damnation take my soul entirely! I shall go and hang myself on the first aspen-tree!"

1887